3 Great Romances

THE HOUSE OF ROMANCE

THE HOUSE OF ROMANCE - TRIO 5
ISBN 0-88767-006-7
Published February 1977
March 1979 Second Printing

The stories in this volume were originally published
as follows:

LOVE HAS A HARD HEART
Copyright © Robert Hale & Company 1972
First Published in U.K. by Robert Hale & Co. in 1972

SPRINGTIME OF JOY
Copyright © Georgina Ferrand 1972
First Published in U.K. by Robert Hale & Co. in 1972

RUN AWAY FROM LOVE
Copyright © Grace Richmond 1974
First Published in U.K. by Robert Hale & Co. in 1974

THE HOUSE OF ROMANCE is published by
HOUSE OF ROMANCE PUBLICATIONS INC.,
a NEVASCO CORPORATION, Toronto, Canada.

Printed for PRESTIGE BOOKS INC.
New York, N.Y.

LOVE HAS A HARD HEART

KATHLEEN BARTLETT

He reached out to touch her and found no resistance. She was warm and fragrant and firm in his arms. When he found her mouth she destroyed his restraint by meeting his quiet passion with a quick, hard fire of her own.

ONE

Chaney The Poised Stilletto

THE CURLY-HEADED man lolling at the massive antique Spanish desk said, " Henry, I know what I'm doing. Buy all the shares Morrison sells . . . Yes, regardless of price . . . Henry, you talk too damned much." The curly-headed man put the telephone back upon its cradle and smiled at the greying, somewhat older and very distinguished individual standing near a drape-darkened window with a clinking highball glass in one hand.

"Everybody knows better," said the curly-headed man, good-naturedly. " There is a stockbroker, Henry Squires, who wants to save me from myself. Why is it that people without money always assume that those who have it are either stupid or naïve? It's just the other way around, Paul, eh?"

The distinguished man smiled a bit indulgently and moved with measured tread back towards the front of the desk. " You can't blame Squires; those shares have been falling for a week. He's in business to make money, if he can, and to prevent his clients from losing any more than they have to. That stuff Morrison sold is pure junk on today's market. How could Squires know you want it for something altogether different? After all, Chaney, you are a devious person. Apart from me, who understands you?"

The curly-headed man still lolled at his magnificent desk. He was lean and dark eyed, casual in appearance, and in fact quite handsome. "No one," he conceded, then he laughed, "and you only think you do, Paul."

The greying man looked into his highball glass. "Chaney, I've been your lawyer for how long, six years, seven years? I've watched you pull these deals one after another. They may all differ outwardly, but inwardly you are predictable the way you move against these people, because basically the Morrisons all make the same mistake. Actually, it didn't even require much imagination to work out your procedure, did it?"

Chaney studied his lawyer from the half-droop of eyelids. "Remember the story about Christopher Columbus and the egg no one could make stand on end, Paul? Once someone shows you how to do something, it becomes easy."

Paul nodded, and met the steady brown gaze being directed at him. He wagged a finger. "Don't get that look on your face. I'm not going to elbow my way into your racket. I'm not the type that likes living dangerously. Besides, why should I? You pay me the retainer and I let you take all the risks. That's a nice arrangement isn't it?"

Chaney smiled. "I can't think of a nicer arrangement, Paul. Unless someday you're tempted to sell me out."

The older man looked surprised. "Why would I do that?"

Chaney leaned his chair forward and toyed with a

gold pen atop the desk. " Oh, I don't know. But it's being done isn't it?"

Paul put his highball glass on the oak mantel before answering. " Maybe. But not here, not in this house nor down at my office. Your trouble is that you don't trust anyone, Chaney."

" Why should I? I deal in people, Paul. In people who have been trusted by lots of other people. In ten years I've made well over a million dollars exploiting those noble and trustworthy people. Do you know what it's taught me, in ten years?"

" Not to trust other people."

" No. Not to trust *any* people," corrected Chaney, and tossed aside the golden pen. " Not even you." Paul started to speak. Chaney held up a hand to stop him. " But I've got something a hell of a lot better than trust, Paul. For example, I pay you an annual retainer-fee of a quarter of a million dollars, and you don't even have to earn it, some years. Now tell me—who could you peddle what you know about me for even half that much money?"

Paul Carroll sat in a deep leather chair and lit a cigarette. " No one," he replied, through smoke. " But you're overlooking something, Chaney. I just don't happen to come of the kind of stock that sells out. Oh, that's no bid for your trust. I don't care whether you trust me or not, because *I* know I can be trusted, and it's one hell of a lot more important to each individual to believe in themselves than it is to need the respect of others."

Chaney smiled. He was tanned, so his teeth shone perfect and white. " I never trusted philosophers either, Paul, did you know that?"

"Did you ever trust *anyone*, Chaney?"

The handsome man leaned upon his desk. "Twice. I trusted a father who disappeared when I was twelve, and I trusted a mother who moved in with a guy who beat the hell out of me every time he saw me."

Paul Carroll flipped ashes into a fragile little Dresden dish on the table beside his chair. "Well, maybe you're right at that. Certainly for a man in your unique business, you're right. The minute you trust someone, like Squires for example, and rely on his judgement, you're going to lose your shirt, eh?"

"What are you talking about," scoffed Chaney. "I can't lose my shirt. I can't even lose a damned sleeve off it. I've got my funds in land, in commercial buildings, in bonds. I'm so diversified, Paul, even you'd need a year to ferret it all out. I can't lose much because I don't ever put out very much on these crooks like old Morrison." Chaney studied the lawyer for a moment before speaking again. "Or didn't you mean I could be cleaned by some hustling shyster?"

"I meant," said Paul Carroll, "that the law of averages work against every damned one of us, Chaney; either against our health, our lives, our wealth, our hopes and plans, or just against us our best judgements." Carroll glanced at his wrist and put out the cigarette. "Morrison is a fool," he said, and stood up to smooth his jacket in the cool, dark silence of the study.

"They're all fools," stated Chaney, also rising. He was attired in a white shirt open at the throat, white flannel trousers, and white shoes. The only visible thing that wasn't snow-white was the massive and heavy solid-gold wristwatch and chain-bracelet on his left wrist.

"I'll tell you what makes them fools, Paul. In one word, it's greed."

Carroll did not accept that. "Not Alfred Morrison. Read that financial statement I brought you. He's worth a solvent two million dollars."

Chaney didn't even glance down at the envelope on his desk, which was what had brought Paul Carroll out to Chaney's Beverly Hills mansion today. "Then explain to me, Paul, why Morrison, a man with a twenty-year reputation for integrity around all the stock exchanges in the country, forged the signatures on those shares and sold them over the board for cash? Either he's *not* worth two million and is desperate, or he's like a lot of them get—so greedy he only thinks in terms of profit. I've seen this happen a hundred times before, Paul, and take my word for it, it's greed."

Carroll straightened up. He was an inch or two taller, and much fairer, than his client. He also looked to be about ten or twelve years older, but he was an aristocratic featured man, who had a normally pleasant expression, and an affable, easy manner, as well he could afford to have, being reputedly one of the best estate and investment lawyers on the West Coast. He said, "I just plain don't know the answer about Alfred Morrison, I'm puzzled. No, I'm bewildered."

"Hang on," said Chaney, smiling again. "Read about it by the end of the week in the newspapers. He'll have his reasons."

Paul nodded and started slowly towards the doorway. He looked thoughtful as Chaney caught up and walked with him all the way through the wonderfully cool large fieldstone house to the front door. As he stepped out into the midsummer sunshine and turned to lift his hand in a casual salute to Chaney, he said, " It's also puzzling to me why someone hasn't backlashed you, Chaney, because it's pretty obvious what you do when you break these people."

" Paul, it's legal. You've told me that a hundred times."

Carroll looked steadily at his client. " Yes, I'm aware of all that. Still, when you break people, even in an orderly and more or less civilised society, Chaney, they don't always react in an orderly and civilised manner, do they?"

Chaney reached, gave his lawyer a light tap on the shoulder, stepped back inside and closed the door. He returned to the study, called Squires back, ascertained that the shares had been bought, listened to another protest and another admonition from Squires, then he said, " How much would that stock drop, if the head of the company was arrested for embezzlement, Henry?"

For a long second Squires did not reply. Finally, he said, " I don't believe it. Alfred Morrison has a reputation for honesty second to none on the West Coast, Mister—"

" How much would it drop, Henry?"

" I can't predict but I'd guess ten to twenty points. But Steel Fabricators never was a glamour stock, it's an honest kind of steady growth stock, so it's not very high anyway."

" I know, Henry," said Chaney, " that's why I liked it.

So if I lose it won't be very much." Chaney rang off, flicked an intercom on the desk and asked his cook-and-housekeeper if lunch would be ready shortly. When she said it would be, he thanked her and left the desk to go stand a moment in front of an old painting of a very beautiful woman in very old-fashioned clothing. In the dark and aged background of this exquisite oil was a distant castle. There was no name on the canvas and no little brass or silver nameplate beneath the painting on the gold-leafed baroque frame. The beautiful woman, no doubt turned to dust centuries earlier, was as unknown as the artist who had portrayed her, and that, along with her robust, clear-eyed beauty was what had prompted Chaney to buy the painting—again, against the better judgement of an art-dealer.

But the art-dealer hadn't understood; with Chaney it had been love at first sight. He smiled at her now. As always though, she was gazing coolly at something just out of sight over his left shoulder.

He returned to the desk, dialled a number and said, " Securities Commission? Alfred Morrison of Steel Fabricators forged his name to four hundred shares of company stock and sold them over the board for half a million dollars. Check it out and you'll find the name-of-record of the new owner, and the name-of-record of the legal owner."

He put the telephone down very gently and turned to wink at the beautiful girl hanging above a brass lamp that softly lighted her portrait, then he went out to the dining-room for his lunch. He was about to lose roughly a half million dollars when the newly-acquired shares plummeted as the result of the scandal to ensue. If that would have sent most men into a state of profound shock, it had a reverse effect on Chaney; it not only pleased him, it also made him hungry.

TWO

A Mild Case of Nerves

PEOPLE KNEW about Chaney. Men of his kind had been taking over governments, storming barricades, and in former times, breaching castle walls and sailing into harbours under black flags to sack cities. They had always been newsworthy. Never universally respected, but always colourful and newsworthy. In Chaney's case, he was also eligible; no parents approved of him but a lot of daughters did. He was a handsome man with flashing dark eyes, curly hair and a beautiful smile.

Women had been able to breach his armour, but only temporarily. He liked women, he liked everything that came with them, but he had never really loved one and as he'd told Paul Carroll several times at the country club, he wouldn't marry one if she brought as dowry the British crown jewels.

In fact, Chaney Lincoln was satisfied with himself, and with excellent reasons since he had come out of nowhere with nothing and no prospects, and now owned a fabulous Spanish-style Beverly Hills estate complete with housekeeper and yardman, a Cadillac and a Continental, as much money as he would ever need, and was tied to nothing, and loved life.

Alfred Morrison would be the last of his professional enterprises. He meant to retire. The Morrison deal should net him, by his best estimate, probably a million and a half dollars, which was a decent profit—a hundred and fifty per cent. It was one of the largest such deals he'd ever engineered.

How he managed his legal piracy was not very complicated. He bought names of wealthy industrialists who were in financial trouble from three banking and two loan syndicates. Because that kind of information was strictly confidential, Chaney had to pay well to get it. He also had to maintain absolute secrecy about his sources.

He then got copies of every financial statement the companies headed by these men had put out for the past five years, pin-pointed the exact time when the first defalcation occurred, and bought the stock, usually at a low point, gave the authorities the industrialist's name, and after disclosure when the stock fell drastically, he picked up enough additional shares to gain controlling interest in the complex, and, with a voting majority, put high-priced—and cold-blooded—imported executives in charge and sat back after agreeing to share profits wth his executives, and waited. When the companies had recovered, production curved upwards, sales increased as much as three, four hundred per cent, or government contracts were secured further to heighten the value of the stock, Chaney Lincoln sold out.

Sometimes it took a year, sometimes two or three years,

but as Chaney had told the beautiful girl in the painting, there was no other way that he knew of to make upwards of a half million dollars a year; sometimes twice that much.

The week following his disclosure to the Securities Commission that Alfred Morrison had embezzled shares from the company he headed, Steel Fabricators, Chaney flew to Honolulu and spent five thousand dollars dining, dancing, surfing, exploring the natural beauties of the islands, and having an iced highball before dressing for dinner each evening while reading the financial section of the mainland newspapers, waiting for the roof to fall in on Morrison and Steel Fabricators.

It didn't fall.

Chaney flew home, tanned, vibrantly healthy, and worried, at the end of that idyllic week, and the moment he walked into his house he went to his gleaming, dark study and put in a call to Henry Squires.

" What the hell's happened to Steel Fabricators?" he demanded.

Squires was bland. " Nothing, Mr. Lincoln. As I told you last week, it's growth stock, not a glamour stock."

" Where does it stand today?"

" Three points higher than when you bought in."

Chaney put down the telephone and looked at the beautiful lady. She was still gazing slightly to his left, but in the late-day shadows of the room she could have been smiling ever so slightly. It probably was Chaney's imagination.

He delved in a desk-drawer, brought out all the accumulation of files he had on Steel Fabricators and went over them again, very meticulously. Next, he telephoned a member of the Board of Directors of the bank where Morrison had his personal accounts, ascertained that he had not been granted a loan and that his accounts were still relatively exhausted, and after that Chaney telephoned to the local Securities Registry and double-checked the fact that two thousand shares of Steel Fabricators, owned by a Natalie Heatherstone, were still listed in her name. He did not bother to say that he had bought those shares because he did not want his name to appear as owner-of-record, yet; not until after the Securities Exchange people had turned up the fact that Natalie Heatherstone thought she still owned them.

He could have bypassed all this by simply talking to someone at the Commission's offices, but he deliberately neglected doing that for one very good reason : he could feed them information, but they would not give him any in return.

After dinner Paul Carroll called to ask, in his quiet way, how the holiday in Hawaii had been. Chaney was not in the mood for irony and he knew his solicitor too well to believe Paul cared a damn about his holiday, so he said, " There's no such thing as a bad vacation in Honolulu. What went wrong on the Morrison deal?"

Paul's suave voice was silky. " I didn't know anything had."

" Like hell you didn't; there hasn't been anything in the newspapers has there? And the lousy stock's picked up three points instead of hitting bottom."

Carroll let a moment pass before saying, " Chaney, what's the worst that could happen? You told me yourself that you can't get hurt very much. Maybe this time you don't make as much, but if worst came to worst and you had to dump those Steel Fabricators shares, if they've gone up a little you'd still clear a few thousand."

"Find out tomorrow why Morrison's defalcation hasn't hit the newspapers," snapped Chaney, and rang off.

He went back to studying the scattered papers atop his desk and did not hear the door-chimes, but then they were muted anyway, and had no idea someone had been out front until his housekeeper brought in a florist's box with an impassive face. A delivery-boy had just called and left the box, she said, and retired.

Chaney eyed the box. There was no florist's name on it although it was unmistakably that kind of a box.

No one had ever sent him flowers in his life. *He* had sent some, upon occasion, but this was the first time he had ever received any.

He opened the box, and there, lying in a tastefully arranged bed of baby-breath fern, was one large black dahlia. It looked positively sinister. It was fully opened and full-bodied. Each of its many curving black tendrils was firm and fresh. It was not an attractive flower at all, and lying there upon the delicate fern it looked rather like a decapitated head.

Chaney, who was an indifferent smoker and drinker, went to a carved humidor and got a cigarette which he lit before returning to the side of the desk to look again.

That ugly flower was obviously meant to convey exactly the message he got from it. Dark and powerful hostility. He threw it, box and all, into the fireplace and remained a moment or two longer standing beside the desk.

Enemies were nothing new; he'd never worried much about making them, which was fortunate, because in some circles he had made his share of them. But this kind of thing was ridiculous. It was also frustrating because he could not—and he stood there earnestly trying —imagine which among the grey and grizzled and iron-hard financiers he had made enemies of, would send him, or anyone else, one unpleasantly ugly black flower.

That was not at all the kind of thing men in his environment would even think of.

He knew better than to go ask his housekeeper what the delivery-boy had looked like; if he'd had a florist's name upon his cap, or perhaps his jacket. He also knew better than to re-examine the box.

In exasperation he flung the cigarette after the black dahlia and went off to bed. The best way to live with minor mysteries, like minor inconveniences, was to put them out of one's mind, to absolutely ignore them. Moreover, he had something infinitely more pressing to think about.

Chaney slept well under just about any circumstances. He had once been a combat-infantryman and had survived a dozen and more battles in Asia . He had learned from battle-wise comrades that when a man got a chance to sleep he should do it no matter where he was or what the circumstances were. It was one of those lessons life had taught Chaney, the hard way; those were really the only lessons he ever learned well, and remembered.

He put Morrison, and that damned flower, out of his mind during the shower, and by the time he climbed into bed and doused the light, he was ready to sleep.

The following morning sunshine coming through a side-wall window awakened him, and the splendid aroma of coffee and bacon got him out of bed. He went through his normal routine of showering again and shaving, and finally of dressing, beginning to wonder if he'd somehow, somewhere down the line, made a serious miscalculation about Alfred Morrison and Steel Fabricators. When he went out to breakfast to eat and sift through the mail, always ready and stacked neatly beside his plate in the morning, it occurred to him that perhaps a personal investigation might produce more than Paul Carroll could turn up by discreetly telephoning around town to his equally discreet and cold-blooded legal and financial acquaintances.

He took the mail to the study, along with the morning newspaper, disposed of the mail and sat at the desk to go through the paper page by page until he got to the last section, which carried all the latest stock-market quotations, and there it was : Steel Fabricators had gone up another two points.

He folded the paper very meticulously and turned to hurl it into the fireplace. The black dahlia lay exposed in its box still resting upon the baby-breath fern. It had not wilted and it still looked to Chaney Lincoln like a decapitated head. He tossed the paper so that it would land over the box and hide that damned, repulsive flower, then he went down the back of the room and out of the french doors to the patio.

Chaney's yardman was nothing short of a sheer genius. Of course, the Southern California climate helped immensely, but the trees, rose-beds, lawn, bedding-plants that bloomed riotously forming beautiful borders on all sides, were kept ablaze with colour for all but about two months out of the year.

Chaney liked flowers but only as part of the outdoors. He did not know a hibiscus from a Bougainvillaea, but he knew what fed his soul, and that was natural beauty and natural serenity. His garden was a pure luxury, and an expensive one too, but he wouldn't have parted with it, or his yardman, for anything. Chaney loved natural things, although even Paul Carroll, his friend, solicitor, and at times, his one and only confidant, did not know this was true.

The yardman was a sinewy, turkey-necked older man by the name of Angus Stewart. He was a taciturn, nut-brown, rawboned individual with unwavering, squinty light eyes and coarse, greying hair that was not brown and was not red, either, but was a rather rusty combination of both. At a guess, Angus Stewart was in his sixties, but he could just as easily have been one of those juiceless, tireless, ageless Scots who was eighty.

Chaney went out where Stewart was examining some limp leaves with the grim visage of an executioner. Angus looked up and nodded, " Good morning, sir," he said, and showed Chaney the leaves. " Blight, I think it is. It'll have to be checked or it'll spread."

Chaney looked disinterestedy at the leaves, and said, " Angus, did you ever see a black dahlia?"

Stewart nodded. " Aye. Did you have in mind making a bed of them, Mr. Lincoln?"

Chaney shook his head. " Ugliest damned flower I ever saw."

Stewart was relieved. " They are, sir, for a fact. You don't see many growing. There's something sort of,"

Angus groped for the word he wanted, and settled for second best, "sort of sinister about them. Even when they're flocked amidst prettier blooms, they detract, sir, they spoil the beauty."

"Do they have any particular significance that you've ever heard of?"

"No sir, just that black's an evil colour."

Chaney shrugged off the black dahlia and went back towards the house. The morning was cool and sunshiny and beautiful. It was March, which did not mean midday temperatures did not soar uncomfortably, but in general the worst heat was still a couple of months off.

Chaney chose his Cadillac for the drive down to the far side of Los Angeles where Steel Fabricators had its factory-complex. It was not quite as long as the Continental, and, being a two-door, handled better in traffic.

THREE

An Interesting Interlude

THE CITY was unpleasant as soon as one reached its leathery heart by way of its clotted arteries, and there were only two ways to reach the industrial area; one was like a fullback bucking the line straight through the worst heat and traffic and smog, which was the direct and shortest way, or by way of the Inglewood area which was not as congested but was roundabout and took more time. Chaney was in the mood for bucking the line so he drove directly through the heartland of the city.

Finding Steel Fabricators was no chore; most of the larger factories were concentrated in one six-mile radius. Finding a place to leave his car was much harder. And afterwards, without any real intention of doing much more than looking and listening, he went to lunch in one of those beaneries where office and blue-collar workers ate. He wanted to get the feel of Steel Fabricators, but what he got was more than that.

His nook was back-to-back to a nook where a man from Personnel Department and a very sexy-looking girl from Accounting Department, were also having lunch. The man said, " It looks as though I'll have to break the date for Friday, Flora," and when she asked why the man startled Chaney by saying, " Because the word just filtered down this morning : we got the Boeing empennage-assembly contract and will start tooling up in the plant next week, which means we'll be starting a hiring programme tomorrow or the next day—and that, sweetheart—means the mobs will start queueing up Thursday and Friday."

The girl murmured something to which the man made a softly placating reply but Chaney hardly heard. Something, somewhere, was very wrong. He paid his tab, went back to the car and headed home.

He even wondered if perhaps there hadn't been some kind of conspiracy to suck him in, but of course the bankers, the loan people, everyone including the Steel Fabricators' auditors and accountants who had got out the twice-annual shareholders statements, could hardly have got together over the past five years in anticipation of his move against Morrison.

The moment he entered the house he put in a call to Paul Carroll. He was out, his secretary said, throatily, and probably would not be back until the morning.

" Golfing," exclaimed Chaney, and slammed down the telephone.

It had been a long, sweaty drive and a dismal day all round, so he went to shower, dress in very expensive casual clothing; then he left the house and drove over to the country club.

There was a lovely golf course and some splendid tennis facilities at the club, but most of all, since it was atop a low, wide hilltop dividing the Pacific slope from the great inland valley of San Fernando, there was a magnificent view and there was also, at any rate usually, a benign breeze.

Chaney had a drink on the flagstoned veranda and read the *Wall Street Journal* seeking a clue about Steel Fabricators. The stock quotations were listed but nothing else; no mention of a large contract, no mention of any difficulties, in fact there was nothing at all.

A statuesque woman passing by stepped on an uneven flagstone and Chaney heard the heel of her shoe snap. He lowered the paper. The woman had very dark blue eyes and jet hair. Her complexion was golden rather than tan and even in the brief moment of his swift appraisal, Chaney saw no flaws.

He rose to offer his help, and his chair. She smiled but she looked in pain. As he eased her down into the chair she said she would be just fine in a moment or two, but her ankle must have taken the full impact when the heel broke.

Chaney picked up the broken heel, saw the shiny solidified glue and shook his head. " For as much as you probably paid for those shoes you would think they'd use an epoxy, or even brads." He showed her the brittle glue.

She crossed her legs and leaned to probe the sore ankle. That was when Chaney noticed her wedding ring. He put the heel upon a little table and said he'd get her a highball. As he walked away he glanced at the legs. Exquisite, like the legs of a thoroughbred, but with more muscle.

Inside at the mahogany bar he ordered a Scotch-and--soda for himself, and a pink-lady for the woman, then, on a sudden inspiration, he beckoned the white-jacketed barman over to a window and pointed. " The woman in the chair, massaging her ankle; do you recognise her?"

The barman gazed out and nodded. " Yes, Mr. Lincoln. Is that who the pink-lady is for?"

" Yeah. What does she drink?"

The barman smiled softly. " Manhattans."

" What's her name?"

"Henderson, something like that. She usually shows up with the Almedas. You know them, don't you?"

Chaney didn't but he brushed that aside and went back to perch at the bar until the drinks were put in front of him. He signed the tab and departed, without the barman even glancing up.

The exquisite woman smiled when Chaney handed her the cocktail and drew up a chair to ask how the ankle felt now. He called her Mrs. Henderson. She looked blankly at him for a moment, until he explained that he'd learned her name from the bartender, then she nodded.

"You have an advantage over me, but thanks for the drink."

Chaney said his name briskly, and asked again about the ankle. Mrs. Henderson wiggled it gingerly and said it hardly hurt at all any more. She pointed to the uneven flagstone, the only uneven one in sight. "They ought to do something about that. Fortunately, I'm not the lawsuit type."

She settled back and looked out over the cool patio where a humpbacked, dusty and bristly ridge of snake-like rims divided the city from the valley. "This is without doubt one of the most spectacular views I've ever seen."

Chaney looked too; he could admire it now because his former worries had been shelved. Her profile from forehead on down to the high, proud thrust of breasts, was perfect. Her colouring intrigued him. She had Saxon features but Latin tints. She turned and caught him studying her. At once she leaned to set the glass aside.

"Well, you've been awfully kind, Mr. Lincoln." Her eyes lifted with a faint twinkle. "No relation to Abe, I suppose?"

He'd heard it ten thousand times, at least, but this time he smiled. "Not Abe, George. George Lincoln was a foundryman and the only thing he ever emancipated was bottled whisky."

She started to rise, to test the sore ankle. Chaney came up with her to lend a hand. "Maybe," he suggested, " I'd better help you to your car then hunt up your husband."

She was concentrating on the ankle when she said, " The car is on the far side of the south terrace and I would appreciate the help . . . I am single, Mr. Lincoln."

He looked again to be sure of that ring. It was still there and it was broad and unmistakably a wedding band. Of course divorcées quite often wore their rings, sometimes as a warning to strange men, and sometimes because they still needed something to cling to. Chaney did not speculate at the time.

It was a long hike around the rambling, one-storey club building to the southside car park. He thought she should rest midway and found two chairs. He also thought there must be a doctor on the premises. He knew for a fact half the wealthy Beverly Hills practitioners belonged to the club.

She smiled at his concern but demurred. " It's only a minor sprain, Mr. Lincoln. It'll be sore for a day or two, which will keep me off it, but the last thing I need is a doctor."

He wondered if she needed another highball. She laughed that off too. " Not for my ankle, and certainly not if I'm to drive myself home."

He almost volunteered, but stopped himself; that would be too obvious.

She looked at him with fresh interest. " I haven't seen you up here before; are you a regular member?"

" For the last five years," he averred. " But I haven't come up for the past couple of months." He squinted out where dazzling sunlight lay upon the emerald golf course. " I don't care for golf, bridge, roulette, or shop-talk while leaning over bars."

She laughed. " What's left, tennis?"

He was good at tennis although of late he hadn't played. " Loafing," he said. " A change of scenery." He saw her interest. " Tennis now and then, yes. Do you play?"

She looked at her ankle and so did Chaney. It was as lean and muscular and finely-turned as any ankle he had ever seen. " Not for a while, I'm afraid," she said. " But yes, I like tennis." She leaned to rise for the last lap to her car, then she swung her very dark blue eyes and said, " You weren't challenging me by any chance, were you?"

He helped her up. " Definitely." He steered her across the shaded loggia and around to the broad stone steps leading to the parking area. " After your ankle is up to it."

She leaned more on him going down the stone steps, the ankle seemed to be troubling her more. She pointed out her car, a pale blue Jaguar with red upholstery that glistened all by itself at a far corner of the lot, and he shook his head. " Park closer after this. Even if you don't sprain an ankle every day, what's the point of walking if you don't have to?"

" Exercise, Mr. Lincoln, muscle-tone. I should have thought you'd know that. You look very fit and athletic."

" But not from walking," he replied. " I hate it. Now mountain-climbing is all right, and surfing, but walking just to get from one point to another isn't my bag."

She stopped beside her car and lay a hand upon the door to brace herself. " I see. You like strenuous things.

Well, so do I, but not to prove anything, Mr. Lincoln. I'm at heart a person who believes in nature as it is, not as something to be bested and conquered and coerced."

He helped her down into the car, and made his one male pitch of the entire interlude. " Mrs. Henderson, whatever you like, believe me, I also like."

She looked away, started the car, then looked back, smiling. " You have been very kind, Mr. Lincoln. Could I send you a case of Scotch, perhaps?"

He eased the door closed. " No thanks. Just take it easy on the ankle, and when it's fit again, remember the challenge."

She nodded and drove away. He stood a moment watching, then sauntered thoughtfully back to where he'd left the *Wall Street Journal*. Some confounded waiter or bus-boy had come along and scooped up everything, except the broken heel, including both highball glasses, the *Journal*, and even a book of matches which had been on the little table when Chaney had first sat out there.

He picked up the heel, pocketed it with some vague idea of returning it when next he saw her, and decided to go home. A boy came to say Mr. Lincoln was wanted on the telephone in the bar. He went inside at once.

It was exactly whom he thought it might be; Paul Carroll. " Got your call from the office," said the lawyer, sounding his usual suave, bland self. " I also have a little information for you on Steel Fabricators. They're angling for a multi-million dollar Boeing contract."

Chaney got sardonic. " They aren't *angling* for it, Paul, they got it. They start tooling up next week and tomorrow they'll start running employee recruitment campaigns in the newspapers."

Carroll was mildly crestfallen. "Your sources are better than mine," he said soothingly. "Well, what now?"

"I don't know, but somewhere down the line I think I've been fed some misinformation."

Carroll raised his voice just a little, as though in mild protest. "Chaney, what the hell's the difference; that stock will climb as soon as it's known they got a big contract. You'll make a very decent and legitimate profit, won't you?"

Chaney said, "Paul, would you like to explain why you used that word—legitimate?"

Carroll's soft gasp was audible, then he got apologetic. "Terribly sorry, and you know I didn't mean it *that* way."

"People never mean to say exactly what they think, do they?" shot back Lincoln. "As for the other—I have no objection at all to any profit . . . any *legitimate* profit, Paul . . . but I'm not playing pick-up-sticks, I'm playing dog-eat-dog. I don't want ten thousand, I want a million or two."

Chaney put down the telephone, nodded at the bartender who was eyeing him, and stalked out to his car to drive home. It was getting along towards dinner time. The club served superb meals, but Chaney's appetite, while it appreciated rich and elegant meals, had never kept pace with the rest of him as he'd climbed up to the heights. He still only ate when he was hungry, and only solid food at that.

FOUR

The Cave-in

STEEL FABRICATORS was in the morning paper but not as Chaney wanted it to be, and in the financial column the stock had climbed a robust five points. One of those syndicated journalists who always managed to write five hundred words about the market without ever saying anything, came out with a splendid eulogy. Steel Fabricators, he stated, was one of the more solid, substantial growth companies on the West Coast. Its dividends, not large, never failed to materialise, and its management, absolutely conservative, was composed of men like Alfred Morrison, an original founder, whose integrity no one would ever be able to question or impugn.

Chaney flung the paper aside and put in a call to the Securities Commission, which was a reckless thing for him to do, and also a pointless thing since they never gave out confidential information.

The man he spoke to was named Wheatley. He sounded like a sleek, ivy-league graduate in economics. When Chaney mentioned Alfred Morrison, Wheatley said, " Yes, as a matter of fact I recognise your voice. You're the man who called us a couple of weeks ago claiming Mr. Morrison was an embezzler. Well, let me tell you something, whoever you are, you could get into an awful lot of trouble for trying to start a rumour like that. Mr. Morrison is sound. Read any of the daily morning papers."

Chaney rang off. Something sure as hell *had* gone wrong. The worst part of it, Chaney had no idea how it had happened. Paul Carroll had known what Chaney had been up to, but despite his occasional snide comments to Paul, he knew Carroll wouldn't sell him out; wouldn't sell anyone out. Paul Carroll just wasn't that type. Also, Paul Carroll already had wealth; he certainly didn't need more money at the risk of losing his largest client, and that client's annual retainer.

Chaney sat at the Spanish desk and leaned back to gaze at the beautiful girl in the painting. He got a distinct shock. The beautiful girl's eyes were the identical shade of very dark, smokerise-blue, as were the eyes of Mrs. Henderson.

Chaney got up and went to light a cigarette. That had nothing to do with the Steel Fabricators matter. He decided to drive down to the local brokerage office first thing in the morning and see Squires. If the Commission still thought Alfred Morrison was so honest, Chaney Lincoln would disclose ownership of those two thousand shares of Steel Fabricators. Let the Commission blink its damned bureaucratic eyes when the *two* owners showed up on record as owners of the same shares.

He did that. The next morning shortly after breakfast he drove down to the Palm Drive office of Squires' establishment. Henry Squires was actually a member, not a partner but he had a growing clientele and was well on his way to becoming a partner. When Chaney walked in he rose to offer a chair and a cigar. Chaney took neither; he did not care for cigars and he didn't intend to stay long enough to get comfortable.

" Look, Henry," he exclaimed. " I want those Steel Fabricators shares made on record to me."

Squires smiled and made a notation on his desk-pad. Then he said, " You can sell them high today, Mr. Lincoln. Up until today we haven't had one call a month for those shares."

" They aren't for sale," growled Chaney, and looked long at his broker. " Is anyone selling?"

Squires gazed almost pityingly at Chaney. " No sir. We've got orders by the dozen but no sellers. I think you could probably pick up in the neighbourhood of thirty thousand dollars if you'd sell. It may not be much of a return on an invested half million, Mr. Lincoln, but if you consider the length of time—about two weeks—I'd say it's a very nice profit."

Chaney went out of the office and over to the electronically-operated Big Board simile to watch. Every change in values was flashed across the glass-beaded squares. It took him a moment to find the alphabetised segment for S, then he waited, and when Steel Fabricators flashed, it had climbed a half-point. Chaney went over to a rank of upholstered chairs to sit and wait. Henry Squires had come out of his office only a few moments before Steel Fabricators' slot showed Chaney Lincoln's pre-dated acquisition. Now let the damned Securities Commission blink into sitting up and taking notice.

Chaney left the brokerage establishment, looked for a cool, clean restaurant to have luncheon, and afterwards went back home to peruse the papers for another sick company.

He had no intention at all of starting another investigation with a view towards moving in, though, because it bothered him that he'd slipped up this time. If he had perhaps developed a blind-spot somewhere, he had better find it before he set up any more deals. Otherwise, he just might set himself up, and not someone else.

By eliminating Squires and Carroll, and by eliminating the man at the bank who had passed on the secret information about old Morrison being in bad financial shape, Chaney was left with very little. Also, if he went back to the banker he knew he'd be told the same thing again; Alfred Morrison's personal accounts were drained.

It hit Chaney like a blow!

He went out to the bar-room, mixed himself a stiff one even though it was scarcely afternoon yet, then returned to the study and picked up the telephone to call the banker who had passed him that highly confidential information. As soon as he'd exchanged brief amenities, Chaney said, "Look, I need one more piece of information on Alfred Morrison : did he clean himself all at once? I mean, did he withdraw from his checking and savings and household and emergency accounts the same day?"

The banker replied quietly and impatiently. "Yes. It was a sizeable withdrawal. We've been expecting him to drop in for a loan; he's never been this poor before in all the years he's banked with us."

Chaney smiled at the beautiful lady on the wall and tinkled the ice cubes in his glass. "Well, I'll tell you something," he said, " that damned old cuss isn't coming in for a loan. He just profiteered to hell and back."

Chaney put down the telephone, sipped his drink, swivelled the chair around and shot up to his feet. What he had done wrong—and he'd done exactly the same thing a number of times before without once having it come back to hit him in the face—was neglect to find out what Morrison had done with that money, and why he had needed it. "Morrison," he told the beautiful lady, "took the bull by the tail, and that's no pun. For a man with a conservative, flinty kind of reputation, he went 'way off the deep end. Beautiful Lady, do you know why no one's selling Steel Fabricators when anyone in his right, profit-taking mind would be dumping it all over the place? I'll tell you—because that damned old cuss nearly broke himself to buy it all himself. Do you know why, Beautiful Lady? Because the old bastard *knew his firm was getting the big Boeing contract!*"

Chaney hoisted his glass, turned his back on the painting and crossed to the fireplace where he drained the glass and set it atop the mantel. He didn't even remember the black dahlia until he stood a moment looking into the immaculate, black hole. His housekeeper had removed not only the dahlia, but the box, the fern, and even the newspaper Chaney had hurled in there to conceal the dahlia from sight.

He felt better that night, for no particular reason unless it was because he had solved his private riddle. He also felt relieved; not just because he'd found his mistake, but because, glaringly bad and hazardous as it had been, he had, with nothing but good luck, surmounted and survived it.

When he retired he lay in the soft moonlight wondering whether he ought to sell the shares or keep them, and whether he ought to begin all over again with another company. By the time he dropped off he hadn't made up his mind about either, and that too, was unusual because Chaney was a direct, dynamic, forceful type person. Or at least he always had been up to now.

The following morning a man called Garrison, representing the brokerage house of Shilling, Adams and Tomkins, called to make a good offer for the Steel Fabricators shares. Chaney's profit would be sixty-five thousand dollars.

He had to tell Garrison that he really hadn't made up his mind what to do with the stock, which was the simple truth. Garrison was very persuasive and Chaney listened almost willing to be influenced, then declined, finally, and rang off.

He laughed as he went out into the back garden to read the mail. There was a saying about it taking money to make money. It certainly was the truth. Chaney was making money when he'd wanted to lose money. While he sat out there reading his mail he was still making money. While he had been sleeping last night, he had been making money.

But he finally decided what to do; sell Steel Fabricators and to hell with it, Morrison and all the rest of it. It wasn't Morrison's fault anyway; he hadn't even known Chaney Lincoln was moving in on him. He'd just managed to be on the inside where he could capitalise better.

It had never been a personal thing with Chaney, when he went after some embezzler. Often, he only knew them by name and only saw their faces in the newspaper after the Commission had moved in to expose them.

Morrison had the inside track and had done exactly what any financier would have done. Chaney finished with the mail, decided to drive to the country club, and when he stepped back into the house his housekeeper said he was wanted on the telephone. He went on through to the study where he took most of his calls, picked up the instrument, spoke his name, and recognised Henry Squires at once.

The broker said, " Mr. Lincoln, it's slipped seven points."

Chaney's mind was blank. " Steel Fabricators?"

" Yes sir. Excuse me . . . Mr. Lincoln, I've just been handed a new quotation . . . it's down another three points. Would you like me to see if I can sell it for you now?"

Chaney ignored the question. " What the hell is going on, Henry?"

" It looks to me . . . mind you, this is just a guess, I haven't been out there on the floor . . . it looks to me as though some big shareholder is dumping, and dumping hard. Shall I sell for you?"

Chaney said, " No. I'll get back to you," and put down the telephone. He stood a full minute looking at the beautiful lady, then he turned and dropped down at the desk. " By gawd," he said aloud, " that damned Morrison profiteered. He bought and held until the news hit, then he waited until it climbed up there—and he sold out. He and I are the only big shareholders of record. Why, damn his lousy soul to hell, he just knocked me out of a small fortune."

He lunged for the telephone, looked up Steel Fabricators' number and put through the call, person-to-person for Alfred Morrison. He got a woman with a liquid-pleasant voice who reported that Mr. Morrison was not in his office but that she would have him return the call if Chaney would leave his name and number.

He didn't. He didn't even thank her, he simply put the telephone down and got up. Chaney was mad; of course there was no reason to blame Morrison. On the face of it this was precisely how profiteers operated. It wasn't the only way, but it was one way.

Morrison had been under no obligation at all to call Chaney Lincoln, introduce himself, and explain that Chaney had better sell because Morrison was going to unload. This had been done, almost invariably among associates, but it was not even common then, because the first shareholder to unload got the top price, and after all that was the name of the game. Chivalry was as dead as the dodo in the financial world.

What stung equally with the loss of something like seventy thousand dollars profit, was the bald fact that Chaney had been taken. He did not, right then, even remember that his original scheme had been to let the shares become depressed.

That was a dead issue, too; with that new contract there would be no way under the sun for Chaney Lincoln to gain majority-shareholders control of the company. Any bank in the country would advance anything Steel Fabricators needed in the way of funds.

"Squeezed out," he told the beautiful lady. "As neat and clean as can be."

But he still had two thousand shares. He decided to go up to the country club for dinner, for a change, and maybe get a little sloshed. It was always more comforting somehow, to get quietly sloshed around other people.

FIVE

Chaney and Blackbeard and Jesse James

THE COUNTRY club had dinner-dances now and then, usually to celebrate something; the first day of spring, Hallowe'en, the New Year, or perhaps just some charity drive. It sent out small engraved invitations but Chaney Lincoln, who was not much of a party-goer, usually did not even open the envelopes. Even when he did open them he never went to any of those affairs.

Not until he drove into the car-lot and saw the number of sleek vehicles on all sides, did he figure out that the latest envelope he'd flung unopened into his wastebin beside the desk had been sent to notify him that a celebration was to be held tonight. He almost turned about and drove away but a vacant parking space beside a robin's-egg-blue Jaguar appeared, and he drove into it and cut the switch.

He recognised her car at once. He also wondered if she had come alone. It was perfectly acceptable, although at dinner-dances women ordinarily had escorts. He stood beside his car looking across the bonnet at the Jaguar wondering too, if she had brought an escort, what he was like. He lit a cigarette, shrugged heavy shoulders and started forward. If he did not like it in there, if it was too crowded, there was no law that prohibited his leaving.

He wasn't quite dressed for a gala affair, but then most of these country club dinner-dances were not formal. He flipped away the cigarette and went on up the stone steps to the south loggia. Music came out into the warm night. Chaney stood a moment looking out where moonlight cast a pewter paleness over the golf course. It was quite possible to imagine oneself a thousand miles from any city. He saw a seablaze of lights south and eastward, and westerly curving up the coast where only the Pacific Ocean stopped the city's advance.

Chaney went into the dining-room and found the place packed. He glanced around, saw a number of people he knew, and was beginning to think he wasn't up to all this when a waiter named Henry, except that he spelled it with an i instead of a y, and with whom Chaney Lincoln was on excellent terms, came by, looked at Chaney, stopped and said, " What a hell of a mess." It startled Chaney; the country club's personnel were usually deferential. Henry had sounded just too exasperated to remember his place. Grinning, Chaney asked what was the trouble. The waiter, a greying man, looked out over the crowded, noisy room and shook his head. " Four waiters called in sick today and we couldn't even get the lousy union to help out with substitutes." Henry looked at Chaney and smiled. " I've got a single table over near the far windows Tonight, you can't give away tables for singles. Do you want it, Mister Lincoln?"

Chaney allowed Henry to lead him through a veritable regiment of flushed faces, mostly smiling. He nodded four or five times to acquaintances before he reached the table. Henry sat him down then said " How about a Scotch-and-soda first; that'll give me time to get a bit caught up."

Chaney was agreeable. In fact, it had been his intention to visit the bar while waiting for his dinner.

The ballroom was really a multi-purpose room; when there were banquets it was transformed into a vast dining-hall; when there were private soirées, it was again transformed; and when, as tonight, it became a ball-room, that too was handled with efficiency. For example, the band had a raised dais, the walls and ceiling had been tastefully decorated, and the cut-glass chandeliers, probably through the good auspices of a hidden reostat, gave out only just barely enough subdued, prismic light to make it seem as though the dancers were floating inches off an invisible floor.

In his full five years of membership, Chaney Lincoln had only danced in that room once. That had been the occasion when Paul Carroll's niece from New Hampshire had visited him one summer, and Paul had thrown a very expensive birthday party for her. She was married now and had two children, that's how fast time sped past.

Chaney's drink came. He ordered his dinner and sat back to study faces, always an intriguing pastime but tonight when there were so many of them, an absorbing pastime as well.

He did not see *her* though, and he looked. He saw Paul, however, with a very attractive blonde. Paul was a widower and although Chaney had never heard him spoken of as much of a swinger, his private opinion was that no one as handsomely aristocratic-looking as Carroll spent all his evenings at home with good books.

He also saw a man named Grillandus with whom he'd had dealings some years back while acquiring a company he had later sold. Grillandus was one of those wealthy, unctuous, swarthy, completely amoral and unscrupulous people who rang as false as a lead bell, and yet he was popular in both the social and business worlds, which had always mildly amazed Chaney.

The president of an immensely wea' .y holding and mortgage company Pau. knew was also present; he looked a little brighter of eye and redder of face than was customary, which w ; amusing. One of the odd things about financiers wa. that their vocational world was so damnably dull and boring that when they got a chance to shed inhibition many of them shed them too fast. It was like jumping rom hell into a hot place; from extreme to extreme. No wonder the predominant fringe-hazard in that profes on was cardiac trouble. The president of the holding c mpany looked as though he were on the verge of a heart attack right then, even though he was laughing and apparently enjoying himself immensely.

The music stopped, people began drifting back into the dining-room, and he saw her. She was smiling at something a tall, pale man was saying. The man, Chaney recognised. He was a Beverly Hills plastic surgeon, reputedly extremely wealthy and separated from the little drab who had worked seven years to help him through college, med-school and his internship.

She had her ebony hair worked into some kind of soft Grecian set, not piled high, but swept up to show her exquisite neck and shoulders. Her gown was not quite white, and that accentuated the tan-bloom of her skin. She looked breathtakingly stunning, and she was not limping.

Chaney finished his Scotch-and-soda, watched her progress to a table where a pair of older people smiled upwards as she approached, and where the older man, a large heavy-boned, wide-shouldered individual with a ruddy face and a white mane of hair, rose as she took a chair. The plastic surgeon leaned, a hand falling lightly upon her bare shoulder, to say something to them all, then he strolled away. Chaney did not bother to see where he went.

The older woman had her back to Chaney, and Mrs. Henderson was profiled to him. All he could see head-on, was the Viking-like older man, who did not interest him in the least.

Chaney's dinner arrived, Henry sighed as he served it looking more harassed than ever, and when Chaney finally lifted his face, Henry said, " They tried to get those damned wine stewards to pitch in. It's beneath their dignity, how do you like that?"

Chaney smiled and started eating. When he was alone the music started up again. It was really very good music, too. Chaney, who was a good dancer and who liked to dance, ate and listened, and finally had an idea. A few couples were drifting from the dining-room in the direction of the ballroom. He looked up, saw

Mrs. Henderson saying something to the older woman, caught a good view of her beautiful, animated face, and stared. She kept on talking, but as though by some magic Chaney's mood reached over all the intervening tables, her very dark blue eyes moved slightly, drifting slowly around until she saw him. He thought she paused an imperceptible moment in what she was saying to the older woman. He softly smiled and nodded. She did the same and Chaney made his decision. He touched his lips with a napkin, rose and started through the thronged room towards her. He knew she saw him coming by the way she seemed to straighten back in her chair as though she were bracing, or as though she were anticipating what would happen and was organising her thoughts, to be prepared.

He saw the white-headed older man shoot him a quick look and also pull perceptibly upright where he sat. Chaney smiled, passed between several tables and halted beside the older woman, who raised her face. Chaney saw what he had been unable to discern before; the older woman had that same golden coloured skin, that same jet hair although hers was shot through with silvery grey.

Chaney introduced himself to the older couple, both of whom looked almost stonily at him. It was Mrs. Henderson who smiled and said the older couple were her parents. With that past, Chaney asked if Mrs. Henderson would care to dance. She rose at once, almost as though she were anxious to leave the table. Chaney nodded gently to the older people, saw how they were looking at him, still without much animation, and decided that they had heard the tales about Chaney

Lincoln. Normally, that never bothered him. It didn't now, except that it made him a little defensive and a little uneasy. He wanted the good will of Mrs. Henderson's parents.

People looked up as Chaney escorted Mrs. Henderson towards the dining-room exit; she was easily the most stunning woman in the room. In fact, in Chaney's view, and he had been studying people since his arrival, she was the most beautiful woman in the entire clubhouse.

When it was possible to pause just inside the ballroom archway, he asked about her ankle. She smiled, held out a foot and wiggled it. " Good as new."

" I thought it had to be when I saw you dancing with Dr. Jarvis."

She did not look as though that remark required an answer, but instead glanced out where other dancers were gliding. She turned, and Chaney raised his arms as she smiled up into his face. " Have you helped any old ladies through traffic lately, Mr. Lincoln, or come to the assistance of any other twisted ankles?"

He eased forth over the polished floor and found that she was feather-light in his arms. Also, her scent was very exotic. " No old ladies and no twisted ankles, Mrs. Henderson, but an awful lot of formality." When she looked blank he laughed down at her. " My name is Chaney. Admittedly, it's a hell of a given name, but there it is. And your first name is?"

" People call me Lee."

" And that," he said, whirling her expertly to the music, " disposes of the formality. The next order of business, then, is—can your ankle stand the tennis match?"

She leaned close to gaze over his shoulder when she replied, " In a day or two."

He did not push it. Chaney had a feeling for opportunities, for specific moments, with women and with companies. It was a developed attribute. He changed the subject. " I got the impression back at the table that your parents were not overwhelmed when we met."

She stayed close with her face hidden from him. " Should they have been, Chaney? Aren't you a bit notorious?"

He tried to pull her out to see her eyes but she clung. " You too?"

" Don't be surprised," she murmured, " and I don't really believe you are surprised. The higher a man climbs the more select becomes the clique around him. It's like the gossip in small towns, isn't it?"

" And you've heard it."

She finally stepped back a few inches so he could see her face. " Of course I've heard it. So have my parents. I would imagine most of those people in the dining-room have heard it, and know you on sight. What do you expect; Captain Kidd, Jesse James, Blackbeard, were as indifferent to the popular consensus as you have been. What do you want now, Chaney, a different image?" She shook her head gently. " You'll never be able to create one."

It was quite a put-down for him; he did not know whether to be dismayed because she'd let him have both barrels, or flattered that she had obviously enquired about him and had come to this judgement of him.

He said nothing as he roughly pulled her close and went on dancing. He was acutely conscious of her, and that had never happened in exactly the same way with a woman before, even when he'd held one in his arms.

She must have interpreted his long silence as sullenness because near the end of the dance she said, " Why is it that bullies can't stand being bullied?"

He smiled at her. " I can stand it, if you mean me. As for being compared with those pirates or whatever they were—it's your opinion."

" And it's wrong?"

He continued to smile. When she was this serious she was more beautiful than ever and her eyes turned almost black. " It's right, Lee. It's dead-right. How well do you know the world of finance? Only the killer-sharks ever get to the surface. Go soft and they'll tear you to pieces."

The music stopped, she hung in his arms a moment looking up. " Why did we have to spoil a perfectly good dance arguing?" she asked, and freed herself, but clung to his hand as they headed back towards the dining-room. " I'm sorry, Chaney."

He stopped and turned. " Another dance later?"

Her eyes twinkled. " Right."

SIX

One Very Bad Error

THEY DANCED three times than night and she promised to meet him for tennis on Friday, and along towards the end she responded to the fact that he never turned defensive by teasing him, and evidently enjoying his company when he took it with good humour.

On the drive home a little shy of midnight, though, he remembered the steady, testy look of her father. The old man looked as hard as granite and as uncompromising as an avalanche. Presumably, perhaps as much as thirty years earlier, her father had been a ham-handed bear of a man.

On the other hand her mother, reserved and petite, with her French or Spanish look, had been rather sweet. Chaney had liked her mother.

There was a hall-light burning in the entry and another night-light burning in his study. He ordinarily would not have gone to the study but that little light attracted him. It was usually left on when the servants retired to let him know someone had called, some message was on the desk.

But it wasn't a message. That is, it wasn't a *written* message; it was another of those white, small florist's cartons and as he opened it he knew what was inside.

He was correct. The black dahlia was exactly as before, lying nestled atop a bed of baby-breath fern. He got a cigarette from the humidor, lit it and strolled back to lift out the sinister flower and examine it very closely. Next, he examined the fern, and finally the box. There was absolutely nothing in the way of a clue as to who had sent the thing or where it had come from. He pitched the lot into the fireplace as he'd done before, said a fierce word and went off to bed. Up until he'd returned home he'd been able to forget a lot of things. That damned black flower brought it all back with a rush. As

he showered he put Lee Henderson out of his mind and thought about Steel Fabricators; if it hadn't been much too late he'd have telephoned Henry Squires.

He would do that first thing in the morning.

Sleep evaded him for a while, until he resolutely put Steel Fabricators, the black dahlias, and everything else unpleasant, out of his mind. Then he slept.

The ensuing morning right after breakfast he went to the study to telephone Squires. He had the post and his morning newspaper in one hand. He dropped those things atop the desk as he leaned for the telephone. The newspaper flopped open. With his hand hovering above the telephone he saw a front-page item that stopped his breath for two seconds. The heading said : *Local Company Faces Contract Cancellation.* In smaller print there were more details. Steel Fabricators which had been awarded a Boeing empennage contract only a week earlier, now faced cancellation on the grounds that ultimate delivery schedules, according to management at Steel Fabricators, were unlikly to be met. There was a penalty clause in case those schedules were not met which Boeing was willing to negotiate but which Steel Fabricators said was too unrealistic on the basis of the exactness of the work required.

Chaney let his hand drop to the telephone and hang there. In simple language, all that meant was that his Steel Fabricators shares were going to drop again. He re-read as much of the article as he had read before, did not have to finish reading it, and finally lifted the telephone, which had in the interim become very heavy.

Henry Squires confirmed the worst. " They have been sliding steadily, Mr. Lincoln, since that damned newspaper report hit the street. It's a shame management felt impelled to make that announcement public."

"Where are they now?" asked Chaney.

"Two points lower than when you bought them."

In plain language Chaney Lincoln had lost half a million dollars. He did not even consider the sixty-five or seventy thousand dollars he could have picked up in the way of profit only yesterday.

Squires broke into the long silence to ask if Chaney wanted to list his shares. Chaney's answer was abrupt. "What the hell for; I can't lose any more by hanging on."

Squires was sympathetic. "Not very much more anyway. I'm awfully sorry."

"What is rock-bottom?" asked Chaney.

"Another six or eight points," said Squires. "But if a little *good* news would come out of that complex they'd have to start up again."

Chaney didn't even dignify that comment with an answer. He rang off, leaned back to gaze at the beautiful lady in the picture, and she, as always, looked slightly to one side of him.

Paul Carroll had said that the law of averages would work against him someday, and it had; today in fact. Yesterday at this time he was smiling because he'd been getting richer while he slept and read his mail. Today after a night he'd always remember, he was half a million dollars poorer.

The telephone ran. In fact, it rang three times and his housekeeper appeared in the doorway as though she hadn't thought he'd been in the study, before Chaney picked it up. The caller was Paul Carroll. He wanted to know if Chaney had seen the morning paper. Chaney's answer was rough.

" Seen it? I'm sitting here right now with it, and if you have some commiserating words of wisdom, save them."

" No," replied the lawyer in his usual urbane tone of voice. " But I think that if you haven't anything better to do today, you had better see me for lunch at the country club."

Chaney started to decline, but something in his lawyer's voice, or choice of words, made him hesitate. " You have some information?"

" Yes."

" Well, since when can't you talk over the telephone?"

Carroll was quietly dogged. " At lunch, Chaney. Make it about one o'clock. I'll be in court until eleven. See you then."

Chaney put the telephone down thoughtfully. Paul Carroll was a discriminating man. When he was dead-serious it paid others to listen.

Chaney went back to reading the newspaper. By the time he got to the financial section, where his loss was verified in print, he was feeling more frustrated than furious. As Henry Squires had said, what Steel Fabricators should do is give the press some *good* news. Chaney lit a cigarette and went out to the kitchen for a cup of black coffee which he took back to the study with him.

There was a way out; at least there was a chance to recoup *some* of his great loss. The trouble with the idea was that it required at the very least some slight stretching of ethics by the management of Steel Fabricators :

they would have to accede to Chaney Lincoln's suggestion based on Henry Squires' thought, and work up something encouraging to hand the newspapers.

Would someone with Alfred Morrison's reputation do such a thing? Probably not, and for a most excellent reason. Morrison had already profiteered; Chaney had no idea how much Morrison had made, but it had to be a sizeable amount; why should Morrison do something unethical to save a half million dollars for a man he had never seen, and whose reputation would probably make someone like Morrison think Chaney had got just exactly what he deserved.

But a negative approach never achieved a positive effect. Chaney hoisted the telephone again, dialled Steel Fabricators, asked for Mr. Morrison, gave his name to the switchboard girl, and got Mr. Morrison's executive secretary. She said Mr. Morrison was in a very serious conference and she had no idea when he would be out of it. She said she would have Mr. Morrison return Mr. Lincoln's call.

Chaney almost said ' like hell ', but just on the outside chance Morrison *might* do that, Chaney gave the club's telephone number and rang off, left the study to go change for his luncheon engagement with Paul Carroll, and an hour later, slightly past twelve o'clock, was at the bar in the clubhouse having an iced Scotch-and-soda while he ranged a totally disinterested gaze along the back wall where framed, autographed pictures of great golfers including a few club members, showed a lot of smiles, golf stances, and evenly tanned faces.

The cleaning-up after the supper-dance was still in progress in the formal dining-room and the ballroom.

Otherwise, what few members were around seemed to be out on the greens. Chaney had the bar almost entirely to himself. A couple were in a shadowy corner relaxing over chilled beer. They looked red and rumpled as though they'd just come in from golfing. The man was hulking and amiable-acting and the woman, with short, curly fair hair and a beautiful figure, looked tired but pleasantly so. Chaney guessed they were husband and wife; there was a kind of easy, comradely acceptance of each other that marked the successful marriages. He had seen it before, and had even marvelled a little at it without ever really wondering how it came about.

Otherwise, there was a wispy, older man having some kind of gin and orange-juice concoction at the far end of the bar while he read the *Wall Street Journal*. He looked like a retired broker or banker, or perhaps just another damned financial pirate. Chaney smiled icily to himself. The Scotch-and-soda was getting to him a little. He very rarely drank this early in the day. Also, he was upset, and that undoubtedly worked against him too.

The soft-speaking barman came along to smile and look into the glass. Chaney shook his head. "Another one and I'd climb the wall." The barman nodded in silence and smilingly retired. The club did not employ talkative barmen, and as a rule its waiters were equally circumspect. Henry, last night, had been the exception, and maybe he'd been justified.

Chaney heard someone crossing towards the open doorway on the flagstones and thought he knew that measured, unhurried step. He signalled the barman for a second Scotch-and-soda without bothering to explain that he hadn't changed his mind, that this also happened to be Paul Carroll's drink.

Chaney was correct; Paul poked his head in at the doorway, saw Chaney and strolled on in. He was attired in a business suit instead of casual clothes, which meant he'd come directly from his court hearing to the country club. As he nodded and straddled the upholstered bar stool beside Chaney the barman brought that second drink and placed it in front of Paul because Chaney nodded his head in Carroll's direction.

As soon as the barman had retreated Paul tasted the drink, sighed and put it aside. " How about lunch?" he said. " I'm starved."

Chaney did not budge. " Yeah. Right after you tell me what the mystery is."

Paul Carroll picked up the highball and drank again. He also lit a cigarette. Chaney's temper was warming up. Paul turned sideways on the stool to give Chaney look for look. " I don't think you're going to like this very much, Chaney. I saw you here last night at the dance."

" Why shouldn't I like that, for gawd's sake !"

Carroll remained his unflappable self. " That was a very beautiful woman you were dancing with."

Chaney drummed atop the bar. " Get to the point, Paul."

Carroll still took his time. " How well do you know that woman, Chaney?"

A cold feeling came into Chaney's stomach. He stopped drumming. " She twisted her ankle on the patio last week. That's when I met her. Last night, she was here, and we danced. That's how well I know her."

" What's her name?"

" Lee Henderson."

" Who told you that?"

" Who told me . . .? She did. No wait," Chaney looked down the bar and caught the bartender's eye. As the man came up Chaney said, " Last week when I bought a Manhattan for a woman out on the patio, I asked you her name; do you recall that?"

The barman's fixed smile began fading. Paul Carroll was also staring at him. " Yes, Mr. Lincoln, I remember that. I told you her name was Henrickson, or something like that."

" You told me," corrected Chaney, " that her name was Henderson."

The barman shrugged slightly. " Yes sir, something like that. Henrickson or Henderson . . ."

Paul Carroll said, " Thanks. Bring us a couple more Scotch-and-sodas will you?" and as soon as the barman withdrew Paul blew out a big breath and wagged his head. " Chaney, her name is Heatherstone. Natalie Heatherstone. Her friends call her Lee, but her given name is Natalie. Paul turned and winced inwardly at the expression on Chaney's face.

" That woman," said Chaney very slowly and a trifle thickly, " is Alfred Morrison's *daughter*?"

" Yes, I'm afraid so." Carroll signed the tab when their drinks came, conscious of the way Chaney was staring at him. Paul slid one of the glasses over and spoke again. " And I'll tell you something else I found out this morning : Morrison didn't forge Mrs. Heatherstone's signature to those shares. He has her Power-of-Attorney. She went in with him on a huge gamble to sell down, then re-buy, and when that Boeing contract shot the shares soaring, he sold and they both picked up two million dollars profiteering."

Chaney lifted the glass and drank deeply then put it out of reach and leaned on the bartop. "What else?" he asked.

"Just one more thing; the moment you bought those shares Morrison found out who had done that. He knew exactly who you were and what you were planning. This morning he moved to break you wide open."

Chaney nodded. "That cancellation story was deliberately leaked to the newspapers."

"Yes, I'm afraid that's about the size of it. Care for another drink?"

"No. Tell me something, Paul, did you see those people she was here with last night?"

"Yes."

"Those were her parents, she told me; was that man old Morrison?"

"Afraid so."

Chaney threw back his head and laughed. No wonder Morrison had glared, and no wonder Lee had jumped up so quickly when Chaney had asked her to dance. "Christ Almighty," he said, gasping for breath. "Do you know what I did, Paul? I set *myself* up. I set myself up for them to cut to pieces. I lost half a million dollars between yesterday and today, and so help me Gawd, I went in with both eyes open like a college boy."

SEVEN

A Special Day Called Friday

PAUL CARROLL dropped his bomb on Wednesday and that evening Chaney Lincoln got smashed alone in his own residential bar-room. Thursday he felt like there was an internal physical conspiracy at work seeking to destroy him as neatly as that Morrison-Heatherstone conspiracy had tried. He didn't get his appetite back until late in the evening. Both his housekeeper and yard-man kept well out of his way and to themselves until he began feeling, and looking, a little less murderous.

He had a late supper Thursday night and went to bed little before eleven o'clock, got almost nine hours sleep and rose to shower and shave with a golden sun flashing its warmth into his bedroom window, feeling so much better than he had felt the day before, that later, after breakfast when he asked his housekeeper where his tennis things were, he could smile at her expression; drunks usually moped around for several days.

Lee Henderson-Heatherstone had said she would meet him for tennis on Friday. This was Friday. He tossed the rackets into the car and drove deliberately up to the club in the hope that he might be able to induce one of the club professionals to play a few sets with him before Lee arrived—*if* she arrived—although he was confident that she would; she would have no way of knowing what Paul Carroll had learned, and had passed along.

He had awakened that morning with the germ of an idea. On the drive to the club he expanded it, broadened it, fleshed it out until it had solid substance. It was madness, really, because if it failed he would be broke. Not just poorer to the tune of half a million dollars, but bankrupt.

He remembered telling Paul Carroll no one could ever do this to him. He also remembered more recently telling Paul he had set himself up for Morrison and his daughter to knock over. Well, what he had in mind now was the same thing all over again, only this time he was going to liquidate, or borrow, and put the whole damned accumulation of several millions on one toss of the dice.

He parked in the sunshiny car-area and sat in his car for a full ten minutes, trying to convince himself he was a fool, an idiot, a maniac, and a cretin, to risk everything he'd been carefully building up over the years. He had always made it firm policy to re-invest the lion's share of the money he made; to gamble only with about a third of each killing. That was good, sound, common business sense. Anyone would understand and approve of that.

He got out of the car, slammed the door, picked up his tennis gear and started for the wide stone steps. Good, common business sense be damned; there was something else involved. Pride. Self-respect. Lee Heatherstone and her father had probably laughed all the way home the night of that damned dance.

They had clipped him for a half million very deftly. He smiled as he entered the tennis shop. All right; now he would given them a chance to clip him for about four times that much—only this time Chaney Lincoln would know what the name of the game was; he would establish the ground-rules.

The clerk asked if he could help Chaney. The answer he got was succinct. " Yeah, I'm rusty at tennis. I need someone to work out a little with me. Can it be arranged?"

The clerk was sure that it could be. Chaney handed over his rackets and looked around. " Where's the telephone?"

" In that little booth, Mr. Lincoln. While you're making your call, shall I find someone and ask them to meet you at the courts?"

Chaney nodded and went over to look for the telephone. He called Henry Squires first, told him to buy another two thousand shares of Steel Fabricators, and when Henry gave a little embarrassed cough, Chaney said, " On second thoughts make it four thousand shares. Will that give me a majority?"

Squires was certain that it would, but he also said, " Mr. Lincoln, it's no good. That stock won't go up for a very long time. You're just throwing good money after bad."

Chaney laughed. " We'll see."

" Do you wish to be owner-on-record?"

" You're damned right I do. And call me this evening at home as soon as you've got the shares."

Squires sighed. " Yes sir."

Chaney made one other telephone call, to the banker

from whom he had in years past borrowed large sums. He told him he wanted his complete estate appraised and he wanted to know no later than tonight how much the bank would advance against that collateral. The banker was startled, but he was also a banker; he agreed.

Then Chaney went out to play tennis.

He found out that he really wasn't rusty at all, he was just incapable of concentrating on the game. Even when the club pro tactfully pointed that out and Chaney tried to improve, he didn't do much better. Finally, he went off to sit in the shade of the loggia overlooking the courts where he could think and wait.

As the club pro smiled on his way past, back into the clubhouse, Chaney looked after the man. How the hell did anyone ever concentrate on a silly game of tennis when everything they had bit and kicked and clawed to get, as well as their guts, were on the line in a win-or-lose toss !

How would some golden boy in tennis attire know what *that* was like?

" Hello."

He looked up, saw her approaching, and came heavily to his feet. She had a white band holding her jet hair. Her blouse was loose and sleeveless and full of her. The skirt was very brief and also very feminine. Her long legs were solid and golden. He let his breath out a trifle unsteadily. There was one more question to follow in the wake of those other unanswered ones : how did a healthy man look at a woman as beautiful as this one, and ever manage to hate her enough for what she'd deliberately done to him, to want to do it right back again?

"You look like you've already played," she said, smiling.

"A warm-up," he told her, and moved in a chair so they'd be sitting close together. "I'm rusty. I don't mind you beating me, but I want you to have to earn it all the way." He kept smiling. "I wasn't sure you'd show up."

Her violet eyes were level under climbing, arched dark brows. "I told you, Friday."

"Yeah, I know, but your father didn't like me."

She settled in the chair and glanced out where a pair of teenagers were playing a savage and violent game. "Wouldn't it be wonderful to be that young again?" she said, and he had to look at her profile the same way a dying man on the desert had to keep stumbling in search of water.

"No it wouldn't, Lee. When I was their age I didn't have even the tennis racket, let alone the white shoes and the country club to play in."

She turned. "You're in a bad mood, aren't you? I saw that the moment I walked up."

He had to struggle very hard to keep up the act because she knew exactly why he would be in a bad mood, and when she mentioned it like that, so reflectively and softly, it was worse than a taunt, it was like she was secretly laughing her heart out at him.

"I lost some money," he said, and looked out at the youngsters.

"That's serious," she agreed, "but then money doesn't keep you healthy and with a good outlook, does it?"

He wished he had a cigarette. He also told himself he was going to have to stop this, or he was going to have to do much better at it; if he didn't become better at it he just might ruin things. It was the chilling thought of all he was gambling with that made him reach deep down and pull up an easier expression, a pleasanter smile, as he said, " Lunch before or afterwards?"

She smiled into his eyes. " That's better. Afterwards— do you want a cramp?"

He winked and rose to take her racket, his own, the cartons of new tennis balls, and escort her out of the cool shade towards the courts. He saw several loungers, all young men, turn very slowly and watch her all the way across the lawn. " You know," he told her, " you're going to start a riot someday, in that costume."

She looked back, saw the men, looked up and said, " Not really. Do you know how long it has been since I was in school?"

" What's that got to do with it?"

" I keep forgetting," she said, gazing at him. " You've never been married. Well, schoolgirls and grown women are as different as night from day. Have you ever been really put down by a grown woman, Chaney?"

He made an exaggerated grimace as though he were trying to recall, then he shook his head. " No, not that I can recall, anyway."

" You'd be able to recall it if you ever had," she said very sweetly, and stepped off the grass to the pavement outside one of the high-fenced empty tennis courts.

He opened a steel gate and watched her walk past. He had never for a moment considered her to be an easy score, so that sweet smile and that implied threat didn't really upset him very much. But it made his speculations about her a little more cautious.

The sun was right, it would not hit either of them

in the face. The weather was warm but fortunately one of those little ridge-top afternoon breezes was sweeping inland up the funnel-canyons from off-shore down by Santa Monica. It kept the temperature pleasant without being hot.

She was a good tennis player, but she was not very aggressive, not at first, so Chaney beat her rather steadily until she seemed to either loosen up and turn competitive or until his unyielding attack and fierce pressure got her angry; then she played against him as though more than just a game were at stake.

He beat her. She was a good loser. He had never for a moment thought she would be otherwise. They went to lunch and relaxed for a solid hour afterwards. She was very easy to be around; he liked her sense of humour, her voice, the way she never seemed to let small things annoy nor distract her. The longer he was with her the more he forgot that other thing, which was good because without tennis for an outlet, and her company, Chaney would have worked up a creditable case of high blood pressure, one of the bad things about being civilised, and at the same time being aggressively dedicated, even for a short while.

She refused a weak Manhattan when a waiter came round. She waited to see if Chaney would order a drink. He didn't. She smiled. " Why don't you have a nice chilled beer?"

He looked steadily at her as he said, " That's how Delilah destroyed Samson, isn't it; not by cutting his hair, but by softening him up?"

" That's exactly how she did it, Chaney, but what other weapons do women have?"

"What do they need weapons for, if they're honest, Lee?"

She picked up her racket and balanced it across lovely knees. "Sometimes you don't sound real, Chaney. Sometimes I don't believe a grown man can be as naïve as you act." She stood up. "Come along. Up until now I've been a proper female, subservient to the dominant male. Okay, now I'm going to be something else."

It was the truth. She beat him, not once but twice, and when it was all over she took his perspiring hand and held it a moment. "Want an explanation?"

He nodded.

"To see if you were the same when you beat me as when I beat you."

He held the rackets as they strolled back to the club-house side-by-side. "Well, does the pirate with the terrible reputation measure up?"

She stopped and looked up at him. "Are you in the mood for buying my dinner? Does that answer you?"

EIGHT

A Long Afternoon

HE SHOWERED at the clubhouse and three-quarters of an hour later met her at the bar. She still looked like a tennis player but it wasn't the same blouse nor skirt.

The bartender was a night-duty man and therefore thought nothing of seeing Chaney and the woman together; the daytime-man, though, would have thought something of it.

He felt loose and relaxed and freshly-scrubbed, which was a very pleasant way to feel. It was also very nice to have her beside him, close enough so that he could detect the fragrance of her perfume. After a while he asked her about herself and she laughed that off.

" Uninteresting, Chaney. I suppose you mean about my marriage."

He had meant that too, but she had never lied to him, not outright nor specifically, and he wanted her to do that. At least he *thought* he wanted her to do that, so actually what he wanted her to do right now was reaffirm that her name was Henderson.

She didn't do it, but she skirted close by saying, " It was a short marriage, Chaney. I met Ben the year I graduated from college. He was an activist, among other things, terribly handsome and with one of those dynamic overpowering personalities. However you looked at him, right or wrong, he most certainly was one of a kind. We were married in Reno, and he killed himself three months later."

Chaney was jolted. " Killed himself?"

She sighed and lifted her highball glass. " An overdose of heroin. Would you believe that I had no idea he used drugs? You aren't the only naïve one, are you? Yes; it was suicide. The coroner left that aspect open to interpretation on the grounds that quite often drug-users are so foggy they inject too much without meaning to kill themselves." She raised her violet eyes. " Pretty, isn't it?"

Chaney didn't really know what to say, so he fell back on a hallowed cliché. " I'm sorry. Lee."

She tasted her drink. " I got over it, eventually." She held up the hand with the wedding band on it. " But I didn't give this up; I suppose because it's the only memorial in the world to a beautiful and brilliant man." She put the glass down. " Otherwise, I live with my parents, play tennis with strangers, like men who can make themselves good company when they don't want to be, and I also eat like a horse."

He smiled, taking the hint, signed for their drinks and led the way to the dining-room. Their waiter was Henry. He seemed much more relaxed and compatible than he'd been the evening of the dinner-dance. He also seemed to approve of Chaney's companion, or perhaps it was just that everlasting masculine chemistry at work as it always seemed to be when Chaney caught men looking at her.

She said, " Well, you know about me; what about you?"

" I started life as a baby," he said, and grinned at her. " My father left and I never saw him again; my mother was not alone very long afterwards, and when the lumps became unbearable I struck out on my own. Sometimes I washed dishes, sometimes I pitched hay, sometimes I worked as a carpenter's helper or as an apprentice auto mechanic, and I saved as much money as I could while at the same time reading books at night to give myself what passed as an education. Eventually I put the money to work."

" Rags to riches," she said. " I didn't know it was still being done."

He held up a finger. " Not so fast. I lost my money the first two times. Both times it was because I trusted people. Both times they cleaned me out. So the *next* time, *I* was the one who was trusted—and I banked three thousand dollars. After that I learned what they don't write about in books nor teach in schools : that money-men are ethical outlaws."

She gazed at him thoughtfully. " And that is why you became one too."

He nodded. " There is no other way that I know of to become wealthy before you're fifty, and life being as short as it is, I had to have my money before I was too old to enjoy it. Is that a crime?"

She kept studying him. " I don't know, Chaney, whether it's a crime or not." She smiled a little. " But then, I'm not really terribly financially oriented."

He had to glance at his plate after that remark, and for a while he ate in silence. For someone who wasn't financially oriented she had picked up a cool million dollars very handily.

" Chaney?"

He raised his eyes and found her watching him with her head slightly to one side.

" When I first came up to you this afternoon it was pretty clear you were upset about something. But now I'm getting wavelenghs from you that say I'm somehow involved."

He laughed that off quickly, because he had to; what he was going to do, beginning today, depended absolutely on secrecy, particularly where she and her father were concerned.

" I think I'm falling in love with you," he said, " and

it's inexcusable. I'm not a misogynist, but neither am I a chaser nor a seeker."

She continued to gaze across at him. As she had said, she was a woman, not a girl, so she didn't drop her eyes or avert her face or blush, or act either self-conscious or embarrassed. "After two Manhattans," she said, "three dances, a couple of tennis games and a dinner?"

He put down his fork. "Is there a prescription for these things? Can't it happen like that?"

They stared at one another for a moment, then the waiter interrupted to give them a choice of desserts. Chaney was not much of a dessert-eater so he declined, but Lee had blueberry pie and another cup of coffee. As the waiter departed she bridged the awkwardness by saying, "See; I told you I ate like a horse."

He took his cue from that; the former topic was closed. "If you keep it up you'll be as large as a house."

"Not really, because I only do it when I've had a lot of exercise." She shot him a sudden look. "What about the money you lost?"

A warning buzzed in his brain. "A bad investment, nothing more. The hardest part, I suppose, was the discovery that I'm both mortal and fallible." He winked at her. "It was a leavening experience but I'll survive it." He paused, then told her a deliberate lie. "I'll write it off and forget it. I'm far from bankrupt."

Her dessert arrived, along with the second cup of coffee. She said she was embarrassed, sitting there eating in front of him like that, then she laughed to prove that wasn't quite true, and bit into the blueberry pie while he watched, and thought, and grew a little baffled about his relationship with her and his feelings for her.

He could rationalise everything he was doing, though; if she were part of the conspiracy to humble him, then he was certainly entitled to deceive her as she had deceived him. Moreover, he really was in love with her, but until he'd framed it into words in front of her it had been an embryonic sensation of blind restlessness, and no man living should neglect the opportunity to prove superiority in the masculine world. He didn't have to dominate her, didn't think about it and wouldn't want to do it, but where it counted he had to prove himself capable. If she thought much about it she would understand; a man who couldn't out-think a woman in the realm of masculine things could not possibly be a success at anything; the accumulation of wealth, the ordering of his life or destiny—or for the matter of that, he couldn't be a success at marriage either.

She finished the pie and threw him a defen~~s~~ ~~look~~.
" Did you know that a woman requires twice as n~~~~
iron as a man?"

He smiled. " Just be careful it doesn't turn to lead."

She laughed. " I like you, Chaney. By the way, I met as associate of yours last night at a gathering at the Almedas' house; Paul Carroll the lawyer."

Chaney pricked up his ears. " As smooth as a greased pig," he said. " What kind of party was it?"

" Cards, which I detest, and a sonorous discussion of politics at the state level. Mr. Carroll is quite urbane. When I mentioned you he said you two had been friends for years."

" He's my solicitor as well as a friend." Chaney thought only briefly about Paul's acting ability, then decided that if anyone could conceal what he knew about Lee and her father, and what they had deliberately done to Chaney Lincoln, it would be Paul Carroll. "If you ever need legal help, I'd recommend him."

The meal was finished so they left the dining-room and returned to the covered flagstone loggia out back where the empty tennis courts looked like huge bird-cages in the reddening late afternoon. She did not act particularly anxious to leave. When they were sitting in the same chairs they'd used much earlier, she admired the view, and so did he, but in his case *she* was the view, not the lift and fall of spiky hills and the majestic far sweep of the northward valley where it fetched up hard at the base of the Santa Susanna Mountains, heat-hazed now in the cool and delightful evening.

Out of nowhere she asked a question, "Do you think you could beat me at golf?"

He didn't think he could beat anyone at golf and said so. "No. But then I've never found anyone worse at it than I am. Are you challenging me?"

She looked over with a slight nod. "Day after to-morrow morning, just as the sun is coming up. Have you ever been up here at sunrise?"

He hadn't. "At sunrise? People who get up at sunrise are either troubled by insomnia or bad consciences."

She laughed. "*Before* sunrise, Chaney. You should be here, on the grounds, at sunrise. It's the most perfect time of day."

He felt around through his pockets for a cigarette, found none and gave it up. "I'll be here, but I doubt if they'll serve us breakfast at that ungodly hour."

"Eat before you leave home," she said. "By the way, where do you live?"

He told her, then, on the spur of the moment, he said, "Why don't you come by and we'll have breakfast together?"

She was usually so quick with her responses, and so frank, that her hesitation this time came across to him like a hard rebuff. Then she answered. "All right. Because if I don't you'll probably oversleep."

He balanced the thought of bringing up his feelings towards her again, but that intuitive judgement he'd developed told him not to, not right at this time at any rate, so he simply said, "Anything in particular you'd like?"

"Coffee, I know you won't believe this, but I never eat much breakfast."

His thought drifted a little; by his evening her father would undoubtedly have learned that Chaney Lincoln, instead of wailing to high heaven and rending hi clothing in anguish over being wiped out, had plung in like a madman to pick up all the outstand·   ...res of Steel Fabricators. Her father would undoubtedly tell her. By the day after tomorrow she probably would feel less hungry at breakfast time than she normally felt. Also, after that long an interval she just conceivably might have figured out that he knew who she was, and that ought to prove very interesting too.

He would be damned before he'd bring all that up. That was one of the ground-rules he was establishing in this game. If anyone was going to shout accusations and recriminations it wasn't going to be Chaney Lincoln —he was going to sit back and let the Morrison-Heatherstone combine do that, and while they were doing it, he was going to sit and smile at them—at her.

After all, for a half million dollars a man was entitled to smile. In fact, a half million dollar smile was something not very many people could afford; Chaney could, he never would have voluntarily done such a thing, but now that he'd been manoeuvred into it, damned if he wouldn't smile until his jaws ached, and make her like it.

She stirred, glanced at her wrist and said, sounding genuinely sorry, "It's time to go home, Chaney. I've had a wonderful afternoon. Really." She rose and he came up with her. He offered to meet her out front while she gathered up her things but she kept a locker so that wouldn't be necessary. They started slowly on around the sprawling clubhouse building with the setting sun giving a cloistered look to the stone wall on their left, to the massive overhead roof and even to the great wooden supports spaced the full length of the patio that completely encircled the building to provide an adequate dead-air space so that the interior rooms would always be cool.

Even the parking area was shadowed when they reached it, and crossed to her robin's-egg-blue car. Neither of them said anything until he opened the door for her. She smiled. "Sunrise?" she said, watching his face with a mischievous look.

He stepped back and straightened up. Without premeditation but with a powerful urge, he leaned and kissed her cheek. "At sunrise, the day after tomorrow."

She hesitated for a fraction of a second, then got into the car. "Thank you, Chaney. I'll remember it."

He looked down gravely. "The afternoon or the kiss?"

"Both. See you in a couple of days."

He watched her drive away, and turned to go to his own car. The emotional turmoil was worse than ever.

NINE

An Alignment Of Forces

HENRY SQUIRES called right after dinner to say that Chaney now owned slightly more than four thousand shares of Steel Fabricators, a one-third majority, and not more than fifteen minutes later, getting him away from the supper table, the banker called to say an inventory and loan evaluation had been made of Chaney's holdings and the bank was prepared to advance him, at low interest because he was a preferred customer, a million and a half dollars. But the bank also wanted to know what he intended doing with that much money; bank policy, was the way the banker put it.

" Control Steel Fabricators from the top," Chaney replied bluntly, and the banker paused so long the silence got embarrassing.

" Are you fully aware what's happened out there, Mr. Lincoln? They've lost that Boeing contract, the stock has hit bottom, and a shake-up of management is pending."

Chaney had a good answer. " The physical plant is worth ten times my loan, and the indebtedness on it is so low that the worst thing that could happen would be that I'd have to re-finance it to pay you off. But that's not my point."

"What is, Mr. Lincoln?"

"Control, then a re-negotiation with Boeing with a view to a re-awarding of that empennage contract."

The banker almost purred. "I see. And you have reason to believe this is re-negotiable?"

"I have," said Chaney, without any such reason at all beyond a strong hunch he was playing. The newspaper accounts had never once said the Boeing contract had been *cancelled*, they had all said the company faced the *possibility* of cancellation. If the banker did not know that this was part of the game, that was not Chaney's worry.

The banker had to have Chaney's signature on some papers therefore he would appreciate it if Chaney would stop by the bank the next day. That amused Chaney, as he replaced the telephone upon its stand. Signing the papers would be only the formal excuse for their visit. Bankers were notorious profiteers too; if this one could satisfy himself that Chaney's inside information concerning Steel Fabricators' prospects of re-securing that Boeing contract were foolproof, he would try hard to pick up some shares and ride Chaney's coat-tail.

Chaney went to bed feeling satisfied with himself in a grim way, and he awakened the following morning in the same mood. By now Morrison and every one of his executives and associates who read newspapers knew there was a new face on their private industrial horizon.

Of course, just acquiring controlling shares in a company did not automatically carry with it a seat on the Board of Directors; that had to be confirmed at a shareholders' meeting, but it *did* carry with it a great bit of leverage and power; enough, in fact, to throttle a company if the majority shareholder really wished to make that his life's work.

Morrison and his Board, as well as his executives, knew all this. As Chaney drove to the banker's office he wondered if, right about now, Alfred Morrison was holding an executive meeting. It was pleasant to think so.

The banker had everything ready for Chaney's signature. He also had the questions Chaney had anticipated ready, but he was a Beverly Hills banker, not one of that brusque Los Angeles variety; he wanted Chaney to step into the walnut-panelled directors' room and have a cup of coffee with him. Chaney obliged. It was excellent coffee, and he did pass on a little information, but he also said that he had control of Steel Fabricators, proposed jerking all the strings himself, and while he most certainly intended to profiteer, his basic reason for doing all this went a lot deeper and was a personal matter. He knew, because he'd known bankers all his life, that nothing dampened their enthusiasms as quickly as a remark that emotionalism, not coldly functional sound business judgement, was involved in any kind of a business transaction.

After leaving the banker's office he drove over to Paul Carroll's office willing to buy the lunch. Paul was in, for a change, and he was quite willing to be treated. They went out along the boulevard to a very expensive and exclusive restaurant on Wilshire Boulevard, got a private table in a quiet corner, and Chaney told Paul what he had done, in detail.

Paul lolled comfortably in his chair and smiled. " You are insane," he said affably. " I've always admired your total and efficient detachment, Chaney. Not every businessman can so consistently display it. Those who can, of course, achieve whatever eminence they seek. It's the reward, isn't it, for sacrificing feelings and desires and emotions? And now you do this thing. For me it's a terrific let-down."

Their luncheon arrived. Chaney was not hungry so he scarcely touched his food. " I've already got where I wanted to go," he told Paul Carroll, " and I did it a few years under my long-range estimate."

Paul said, " So?"

" So—here I am, rich and comfortable, secure, fixed for life, and what the hell am I supposed to do for the next forty or so years that probably remain to me—sit on my duff and drink imported sherry and watch television?"

" You wouldn't have done that anyway, Chaney. You'd have found something to keep busy at. But my point is simply that there are a dozen things that can go wrong with this deal and you know what they are as well as I do. Supposing just *one* of them *does* go wrong?"

" I'll still own control of Steel Fabricators, Paul."

Carroll touched his lips with a linen napkin. " What in the holy hell do you know about running a very complex industrial establishment? Your speciality is buying in, breaking embezzlers, kicking out borderline-bankrupts, and hiring key personnel who are thoroughly experienced."

" I can do exactly the same thing here," exclaimed

Chaney, "but the difference will be that for once, Chaney Lincoln will sit in the President's chair. After all, industrial success, Paul, is built around having the best executives money can buy."

Carroll gently shook his head. "Not quite," he said. "Maybe you've made millions taking over companies, but Chaney, I've had a little more experience than you've had in the industrial field. It's every bit as much of a damned jungle as is the financial field. The minute you bust Alfred Morrison you will inherit not only all his woes, but a whole damned mountain more that will result from your having kicked him out."

"I don't expect to kick him out," said Chaney. "I intend to use him."

Paul said, "Nope, it won't work. You can import all the skilled executives you'll need; all that's required is money and ethics of a pirate. But independent career industrialists of Morrison's calibre can't be bought and sold. By the way, don't you like the seafood lunches they serve here; you have hardly touched your luncheon?"

Chaney ignored both the question and the food before him. He sat glaring at his solicitor. "I spent the afternoon at the club yesterday, with his daughter."

Carroll nodded gently, as though this did not surprise him in the least. "You intrigue her. She was at a party I attended earlier in the week. She asked a lot of questions about you."

"And you answered them. I know, she told me she'd seen you there."

Paul finished his lunch. He sat comfortably gazing across the table, his pleasant, aristocratic features softly pensive. "It wasn't curiosity, Chaney, it was personal interest. In women, there is a vast difference between those two things. Did you know that? I doubt that you did, but women have been a hobby of mine for years. Lee Heatherstone is a very special woman. Not just beautiful, with a compatible disposition, a wonderful sense of humour, and an exquisite body. She's got a lot more."

Chaney fished out some cigarettes, lit one and flung the pack over in front of Carroll, who ignored it. Two men pacing past in earnest conversation looked over, recognised Paul and Chaney, mechanically smiled, and nodded without breaking stride. The waiter came discreetly to remove dishes and to bring an ashtray for Mr. Lincoln. When he had departed Chaney looked round the room and looked back.

" We've never mixed our personal lives in our relationship, Paul. I mention that because you sound like an old father about to impart some wisdom to a profligate son."

Carroll took the warning in stride. " I don't intend to break the rules, Chaney, only to say that I just don't quite understand how this will end. Of course you'll alienate the woman; she is very loyal. And of course you'll gain control of the company. Beyond that— what?"

" Get that Boeing contract back in good standing, to start with."

Paul Carroll was not all that naïve. " It never was actually in bad standing, was it? I mean, old Morrison did what he had to do in order to profiteer, and then to bust you. What else?"

Chaney knew exactly the reaction he was going to get when he made his next statement. " Teach the Morrisons, father *and* daughter, that I'm not the rustic they seem to think I am."

Carroll reconsidered and lit a cigarette with an expression, and a sigh, of patient resignation. " Splendid," he said with gentle sarcasm. " Look, Chaney, *they* did not start this silly business, *you* did, and it is perfectly normal, when a human being has been attacked, to attack back. I'm truly surprised that you'd go off the deep end like this . . . unless, well, unless something that has not happened with you before is happening now." Before Chaney could challenge that innuendo, Paul rose after a swift glance at his watch. " I've got a court-appearance this afternoon. Do you mind if I run out on you, now?"

Chaney didn't mind. In fact, he was a little raw along the nerves from their luncheon conversation and was glad to be left alone for a moment. Afterwards, as he was leaving the restaurant, he wondered how Lee was spending this day, and on the drive home he had misgivings about their meeting for breakfast the following morning.

It wasn't actually something he looked forward to. In fact, the closer he got to home the more he wondered how he had ever made such an awkward mess of this other aspect of the Morrison-Lincoln skirmish. He had, he thought, handled the take-over efficiently and deftly; like a surgeon's swift-sure incision, Chaney had bought in and toppled management without ever meeting so much as one member of it. But where the girl was concerned he'd lacked the finesse, the experience to do it properly. The reason was obvious; he'd wanted revenge and he'd made sure he would get it, but with the girl he was not in his element at all, so he hadn't handled things very well.

Then too, there was that statement he had made to her. It was true. He knew himself exactly that well; he didn't require some adolescent six-months' probationary period. He was in love with her, purely and simply.

Paul had said he'd alienate her. He wasn't all that simple; he hadn't expected anything else, and if she hadn't been infuriated by his massive strike at her father, and through her father at herself, he wouldn't have had much respect for her.

He got all the way home before remembering something he'd read in a psychology book one time about the relationship between love and hate. Each, or so the book had implied, was one side of the same coin.

He doubted that, though, as he left the car and walked slowly into the house. He didn't hate her at all, not by the wildest stretch of the imagination; all he had to do, because it was as mandatory with a male animal as it was inevitable, was assert, prove, and maintain supremacy in the areas where men plainly had to be supreme.

His housekeeper came to the entry-hall to say Mr. Squires wanted Mr. Lincoln to return his telephone call the moment Mr. Lincoln got home.

Chaney strolled on through to the study, dropped down behind the desk and began dialling. Henry Squires answered on the second ring, which indicated that he'd been sitting right there at his desk .

Chaney said his name. Squires responded with a sound of relief. " I was just getting ready to start an office-to-office search, Mr. Lincoln."

" What's gone wrong?"

" Well," said Squires, being judicious in his selection of words, " nothing has gone wrong, exactly, but there has been one hell of a furore. Alfred Morrison turned up the fact that I'm your broker. He called me wanting to set up an immediate meeting with him. He said he would come here if you could not go down to his factory."

Chaney smiled at the Beautiful Lady. " Was he angry?"

Squires laughed stonily. " That is an understatement, Mr. Lincoln. He was furious and loud and rather abusive."

" Okay, Henry; when he calls back don't give him my unlisted telephone number. Just tell him that when he calms down, I'll meet with him anywhere he'd like."

" Mr. Lincoln; there is something else : no more Steel Fabricators shares are showing up either for sale or in demand, and three newsmen have dropped by to ask me what's going on."

" What did you tell them, Henry?"

" Nothing."

" That's exactly what you should have told them," said Chaney, and rang off. As he rose he felt better than he'd felt all day. He usually did feel better, more relaxed and sure of himself, when the skirmishing began.

TEN

The Damndest Golf Game

CHANEY WAS up and shaving before daylight the next
morning. When he was dressed he went out into the
front of the house to stand a moment gazing out over
the misty, pre-dawn-lighted back garden. The last time
he'd got up this early there had been star-shells over in
the east and a grizzled sergeant telling everyone to shake
a leg and get to the field-kitchen because they'd be
moving out on patrol within fifteen minutes.

He was reminiscing about that when he heard the car
drive up out front, turned and started for the entry-hall.
He had no idea how she would greet him, but it could
only be one of two ways : either quietly and gently as
she always had up until now—which he wondered if
she'd be capable of now, after all the fireworks of the
day before—or else she would come through the front
door like a Sherman tank and roll right over him.

He adjusted his jacket, opened the door, and as she
moved in closer to the brick steps from her car, he saw
her lovely face solemnly lifted towards him. He smiled.
" You must be the only woman in the city who doesn't
have to get up this early, who is doing it this morning."

She paused at the top step, gazed steadily at him a

moment, as though taking her cue from him, and making whatever adjustments were necessary to match the mood, then she trooped on over and passed him as she entered the house.

"I thought you might have forgotten, Chaney. But then perhaps you didn't sleep well last night."

He took her by the arm to guide her on through to the dining-room, and from there through the large pantry to the kitchen. "I slept like a baby," he said, holding a door for her. "That's one thing I learned long ago; sleep when you get the chance." He waited for her next statement, sure she would follow up that earlier innuendo with something more pointed.

She didn't, she glanced around the large, spotless kitchen, saw the perking coffee pot, the two saucers on the sideboard, and turned in that direction as she said, "You didn't make anyone get up, did you?"

He hadn't. He hadn't mentioned to his housekeeper that he'd have breakfast before sunrise, with a woman. "You said you weren't a breakfast-eater."

"I'm not."

"Well, there is coffee. If you'd like, I'll fry some eggs, some bacon, scare up orange juice and make toast."

She poured two cups of coffee. "For yourself, not for me."

He didn't feel very hungry, but he moved closer to her for one of the cups of coffee. She put the pot back and took her cup and saucer to the kitchen table. As she sat, she raised her violet eyes. "Golf, still?" she asked.

He remained over where he was. "That was the whole idea, wasn't it?"

She looked down. "Yes." She sweetened the coffee

and swished it once or twice with a spoon before raising her eyes again. " This has been quite a charade, hasn't it, Chaney?"

He nodded. He also thought *here it comes*, and sipped coffee while waiting for her to fire off the first round.

She failed to do it, again, " My golf things are in the car." She drank her coffee and got up. " I'll drive on up and that way you won't have to bring me back. Okay?"

He said, " Okay," and put his own cup aside. This was her initiative all the way. He'd made his mind up to that the last day they had been together. He followed her on through the house to the front door, and outside. She stepped down into the Jaguar, nodded without smiling or waving, roared the engine and eased out the clutch.

Chaney went briskly to the garage, got into his Cadillac and fumbled with the ignition switch while trying to figure out what she had in mind. Twice she'd led him to the threshold, and twice she'd turned aside as though she had nothing in mind but their golf game.

On the drive eastward with the gloomy, hushed and crumpled pre-dawn hills on their left, he felt slightly uncomfortable, and definitely unsure. She acted, or at least he *thought* she acted, as though she didn't want to bring up the disaster he had caused. But at the same time he had her figured out as the kind of person who had quiet courage, so he didn't think she was fearful of the argument that would surely follow if she did bring up what he'd done.

That didn't leave much leeway. He had to settle for

the conclusion that she meant to bring the disaster up on her own grounds and at her own time.

As he followed her smaller, lower car up the slight, paved incline towards the dark clubhouse, he had a feeling that he hadn't really made such an accurate assessment of her after all. That kind of thinking contributed to his uncertainty.

She parked, got out and hefted her golf bag as though it were almost weightless. When he did the same, and came across to take her bag, she smiled at him. " It's not heavy. Besides, I'm used to lugging it." She started towards the wide stone steps. " Look, some lights in the rear. Maybe we can get a golf-cart after all."

He nodded and plodded along at her side. They did not approach the front, dark side of the building, but went the long way around and down that flagstoned loggia that extended for the full distance of the rear of the building.

The tennis courts were more than ever like huge cages in the watery chill of pre-dawn. As for the fairway and as much of the greens as were visible, shadows and darkness lingered even though there was a thin, long ribbon of very pale pink over the farthest rims to show that sunrise was close.

The man who managed the golf shop was readying his tills and his counters for the day's business. He looked only a little surprised when Chaney and Lee entered. He agreed to get a cart ready at once. He also offered to light the mercury floodlamps but Lee declined with thanks on the grounds that the sun would be up within the next fifteen minutes.

She was right. They were at the tee-off site when the

brightness arrived; not gently and by degrees as it was supposed to, but, because this was summer in the south-land, actually a desert before man had transformed it, when summer's sun came it jumped up like a great orange-yellow ball and the entire world awakened in an instant.

Lee said, "Did you ever see anything as spectacular, Chaney? Listen, now the birds will awaken."

He leaned on his driver and looked at her. "Do you always get this carried away when the sun comes up?"

"Invariably. It means so much. If you'll stand per-fectly still you'll hear a life being renewed, and even the things that can't make a sound, show with a freshness they lacked ˚sterday."

"You ought ˋ˅ a poet," he said, looking around. The world *did* look u.˙erent. Everything was dew-washed and crisp, even the lowly grass underfoot. The air had a perfume it never had again throughout the entire ensuing twenty-four hours. But he had seen it all before; had, in fact, noticed most of it before, too. But he was a man, and all the rest of this was nature. It was enduring and ageless, and what the hell did any of it have to do with success and achievement? Nothing. It was there, and it was totally separate. He saw her looking at him and made a creditable small smile.

"Tee off."

She didn't. She said, "I didn't have any idea you would be as you are. No idea at all."

He straightened up off his driver and cast a final look around at the hushed, brilliant dawn-world. "Just answer one question for me : about the heel on that shoe . . ."

" On purpose," she confessed.

" Yeah. Well, I wondered when I looked at the thing after I got home. The glue was shiny-dry, but there had been a nail down through it from above. It wasn't there, and the glue probably wouldn't have held the heel on without it. So—the idea was to do what?"

" Meet you. See if you'd tell me what you were doing?"

" Sorry I disappointed you."

" You didn't," she said. " You told me day before yesterday that you'd lost a lot of money."

" I did, didn't I?" he replied. " I could also have told you I knew your name wasn't Henderson, and that you were in with your father to break me."

" Not break you, Chaney. We had a financial statement on you. A half million dollar loss wouldn't break you."

" It wasn't supposed to anger me either, was it? Most people who get out-manoeuvred, even by their own stupidity, are supposed to dissolve with anguish. Isn'. that it?"

She didn't answer until she'd moved over to tee-off. It was a perfect, long drive. While they watched, he knew she was going to beat him. She turned and said, " Most people, perhaps, but I doubted that you would."

He set up his tee, balanced the ball atop it and straightened back to sight down the fairway. " Did you tell your father that?"

" Yes."

Chaney stepped up into position and loosened his arms and shoulders. " But he didn't believe you. He thought anyone who preyed off fools and thieves had to be as cowardly as they were." He swung, hard, and to his astonishment the ball sailed arrow-straight and lofting-high, then came to earth well ahead of her ball, and very near the second hole.

She ignored the near-perfect drive and as they started forward she said, " I told my father that I didn't want my money used in a battle against you."

He stopped and turned. " Your money?"

" My husband left a lot of insurance, Chaney. At my father's suggestion I went in with him on his profiteering scheme. I gambled every dime I had. And I came out with a million and three-quarter dollars profit. He came out with an even two million. He told me last night when he was over his first fury at finding that you had out-smarted him and now held controlling interest, that he was going to fight you down to his last red cent. That's when I said I was through; that I wouldn't join in and I didn't want any of my money used that way."

He turned, dropped his head a little and paced forward. As they got into the cart, which was electric and operated without a sound, Chaney pursed his lips in bleak thought.

" I think it was because of that damned broken heel trick, and the wrong name, that I got fired up, Lee."

" I didn't give you that name, Chaney."

" Yeah. That was my own blunder. It was a beauty too. But it amounted to the same thing. You were setting me up and you know it. Well, what the hell did you expect, if not exactly what happened?"

" Nothing very different," she murmured. " I've already told you, Chaney : I knew you wouldn't crumple and crawl off to lick your wounds."

He halted the cart and got out. Then he turned and

looked across the width of the cart at her. He hadn't expected their difference to come out like this; he had anticipated icy coldness, even furious antagonism and violent hostility. Also, he'd planned on making her defend herself.

What was happening was quite different. She wasn't defending herself, she was quietly stating facts and being frank in a way that almost had him on the defensive. He lit a cigarette, tossed his driver into the bag and pulled out the next club. She did the same, but she was as calm, as totally poised and in control of herself as she had always seemed to be when they were together.

He leaned on the cart. "Okay, your father wants a meeting. I'll see him."

She looked on the verge of a soft smile when she commented about that. "He knew you'd meet him. So did I. The difference is that I was supposed to figure you out and pass it along, which I did very obediently. But he did not like my appraisal at all, so when you t. meet it's going to be a thorough waste of time. You see, Chaney, I know you both."

She hefted the cub in her hands and turned to consider the length of her putt. "I'll be one under par," she said, as though the golf game were important. "I think you're going to make par. Chaney, you told me you weren't a good golfer."

He dropped the cigarette, ground it underfoot and walked slowly around the cart to watch her move ahead for the putt. "I'm not. I'm a lousy golfer. I'm also a lousy judge of women. I'm going to be honest as hell with you, Lee : I can't for the life of me make you out."

She looked up. "How are you at praying? There is

no such thing as a successful putt for this distance, Chaney, without Divine intercession. Mind doing the honours while I'm getting ready?"

He gauged the distance, watched her body bend, saw the slightly pursed set of her lovely mouth, and burst out laughing.

She raised her head gravely, then stepped back and straightened up. He said, "I'm sorry. I couldn't help it. This is the most insane golf game I've ever even heard of. Lee, I reach and close my hands, and when I open them you're a long way out of reach. I give up about you."

She stepped in and set her feet, grasped the club and without a word or another glance his way, got into position again.

ELEVEN

A Bombshell For Chaney

THAT FIRST near-perfect drive of his was also his last near-perfect drive. In fact, it was his last drive of the day that deserved anything better than an apology. She beat him handily all the way to the eighth hole, and by mutual consent they'd decided to play only nine holes.

There was no little breeze as usual. It was

hot on the fairways. Her nose got shiny and he left his
sweater in the golf cart. While each waited for the other
they stood in tree-shade. There was a lot of that, which
was a blessing, and just beyond midway, at the ninth
hole, there was a large pond. She wandered off before
he'd made his last putt—three over par—to stand in a
screen of expertly contrived underbush and trees to
watch a pair of mallard ducks. When he came through
to where she was standing in dappled shade, an enterprising mosquito made its late breakfast, or its early
lunch, off the lobe of his ear. He slapped the thing and
looked when Lee pointed to the pair of ducks. Both birds
were putting on a great act of feeding. They would up-
end and re-surface, then they would cock tawny eyes
at the two-legged interlopers as though to ascertain that
their imitations were being accepted at face value. The
hen suddenly was nowhere in sight. Lee laughed quietly
about that.

" Clever, wasn't she?"

Chaney shrugged. He saw nothing especially astute
about a wild duck diving and swimming underwater
until she was lost to view.

" See those tall tules halfway round the pond?" asked
Lee. " That's where she'll be by now. If we had binocu-
lars we could see the fronds move. They have a nest
over there. What they've been doing was try to convince
us they are just transients feeding before flying on again."

Chaney placed a gloved hand upon a tree-trunk above
Lee's head and behind her. " A poet, and now a bird-
watcher. I don't believe a damned duck could possibly
have all that much devious sense."

Lee kept watching the drake, a much handsomer

bird than the dowdy little hen had been. " They have."
She turned and looked upwards. " Did you tally the
cards?"

He grinned flintily. " I buried them," he said, being
ironically facetious. " Yours, just below the surface,
mine, four feet straight down. We didn't make a wager,
did we?"

She ducked under his arm and started back upon the
little path to where they had left the golf cart. " No
wager. Don't you remember; we've been parrying and
slashing since the first hole."

He caught her at the last edge of fragrant shade.
" What is it you want from me, Lee?"

She freed her arm. " Nothing, Chaney. Not a single
thing." She turned and resumed her way to the cart.

He stood watching her move out into the brassy sunshine. Paul had been right, but her alienation ran a lot
deeper than Paul had implied that it might, and it had
shown no overt hostility at all. He swore under his
breath and followed after her.

As they climbed into the cart he said, " I don't think
I'll meet your father after all."

She gazed at him. " Why not?"

" You said it would be a waste of time. I'll take your
judgement on it then."

" Chaney, I said it would be a waste of time, but what
I didn't say was that if neither of you will make the
effort, it's always going to be a waste of time."

He swung the cart, heading back. " And you think
I should defer to him."

" I think one of you is going to *have* to defer. Otherwise, as sure as we're side-by-side, Chaney, Steel Fabri-

cators is going to break both of you. My father wasn't making idle talk when he said he'd fight you to his last red cent. I don't think you did what you did to gain control because you just wanted to rule an industrial complex. Do you follow me, Chaney?"

"Yeah." He said no more until the clubhouse was in sight, then he slackened off their rate of speed, which was not fast at best, and said, "What have I done to you, Lee?"

"I told you," she replied. "I'm out of it. I told my father last night I'd have no more to do with it. I'll tell you the same thing now. I think I'll go down to Acapulco for a month."

He groped around for some way past her coolness and did not find it. They left the golf cart and he took both their bags down to their cars while she went ahead into the dining-room to order for them both. After he'd deposited the bags he lit a cigarette and leaned in the shade of the south-side loggia. He had been smoking more the past few days than he'd smoked in years.

Now, he was on the defensive. He knew it, but it did not anger him, it simply left him feeling slightly more frustrated. He had never in all his life known a woman whose poise, and whose invulnerability, was so thoroughly unassailable, before. Acquiring Steel Fabricators had been child's play compared to what he was thinking now : how to get around her invisible armour.

"Good afternoon, Chaney."

He turned, exhaling smoke. "Hello, Paul. I suppose you've already seen her in the dining-room."

Carroll nodded his sleek head. "It's amazing how a woman can play nine holes of golf on a scorcher like this day is, and still make you think of a cool mountain lake when you look at her."

"Another gawddamned poet," Chaney grumbled. "And it's not a mountain lake, it's a lousy iceberg."

Paul Carroll hoisted an eyebrow. "She never struck me as the type. Well, I'm on my way home. It's too hot for golf, I'm not in the mood for locker-room poker, it's too damned early for drinking, so what's left? By the way, her father buttonholed me at my office a couple of hours ago."

"He wants to set up a meeting."

"Correct," purred the lawyer. "I told him I'd take it up with you. Any comments?"

"Yeah. One. Tell him to go to hell. When I want a meeting I'll let him know," Chaney straightened up to move off.

"Hold it," said Carroll. "There's something else. Another complex is moving in on that Boeing contract why he says this meeting has to be held within the next day or two. If Steel Fabricators really loses that contract you're going to have to pump in a lot more money than you've put up so far just to keep your factory doors open."

Chaney stared. He didn't have to say what he thought; he could read the answer in Paul Carroll's face. What had been said at luncheon two days earlier about the industrial element being just as much a jungle as the financial element was, shone coldly out of Paul's clear, patrician eyes.

Chaney muttered a question. "Any suggestions?"

"Yes," replied the unperturbed solicitor. "See him. Do it today. Do it this afternoon in fact, and listen to him, Chaney. Take what he hurls at you, overlook it, and make him get down to specifics about how to salvage that damned contract. Because, old friend, your future is riding on that as surely as God made green grass." Paul smiled and gave Chaney a light tap, then turned and skipped down the stone steps to hasten across through the hot sunlight to his air-conditioned car.

Chaney went thoughtfully back to the dining-room. Lee was waiting, nursing a tall, iced glass of lemonade. When he pulled out the chair to sit opposite her she studied his face. " What's wrong now?"

He didn't explain completely. " Where is your father this afternoon?"

" Why, at his office I suppose."

Chaney glanced at his wrist. " It's two o'clock. Will he be home by five?"

" He usually is," she replied, and put the lemonade glass down. " You want to see him, this afternoon?"

" Yeah. The sooner the better. Some other outfit is moving in on that damned Boeing contract."

She looked coolly across the table. " Chaney, you were born five hundred years too late. Did you know that? You're not really a pirate, you're a knight in dull armour who doesn't want to be king, just a warrior."

That went right over his head, but he was obliged to say something back so he looked at his luncheon, picked up a fork and growled at her, " When you write your book of poetry, someday, send me a copy so I can try and figure you out, Lee."

She smiled, reached unexpectedly and laid a cool hand over his unoccupied hand atop the table. " There is no real complication, Chaney. You just aren't concentrating on me—on us—today; you haven't been since you met me at the front door."

He looked from her hand up to her face. "It's true, I haven't been."

"Why do you suppose my father and I argued last night; why did I refuse to use my money in this fight any further; why didn't I slap you this morning when you opened the door; why have I been trying all morning to show you both sides of all this?" She patted his hand, withdrew her own hand and picked up the lemonade glass again, finally, not meeting his stormy and puzzled gaze. "Well, if I had a clasp-knife and an appropriate tree, Chaney, I'd carve it out for you. Chaney loves Lee . . . Lee loves Chaney."

She drank from the glass while he sat across the table without moving or blinking. When she put the glass down, she finally met his stare. "Am I blushing?"

He didn't know. "You're serious?"

She nodded, and when the waiter came to ask about preferences in dessert, he withdrew without putting the question to them; neither of them had touched their luncheon.

Chaney breathed outward as he said "I'll be damned."

Lee laughed at him. "Keep it up like you have in the past, and you probably will be. Shall we drive over to my place and wait for my father?"

"Yes," he agreed. Then he said : "No. Let's sit out back in the shade for a while first."

She was entirely willing. They left the dining-room, under the slightly baffled, slightly disgusted, stare of the waiter, who did not approve of people wasting food, and reached the long, cloistered loggia where only a few other people sat, and saw the perspiring youngsters out by the sunglared tennis courts acting as though the heat did not bother them in the least, which it didn't.

For Chaney, fitting all the jagged little pieces of all they had said back and forth since sunrise into a workable mosaic was not hard; he knew exactly how to do that. In fact, that had always been part of his take-over strategy. It all fitted perfectly, but when he turned and looked at her, his heart lugged a time or two.

Paul Carroll wouldn't have this kind of trouble at all. He would know exactly what to say and how to say it, and what kind of a look to give her along with it. He might even take her fingers and kiss them. Chaney reached, found her hand, which she gave freely, and she squeezed his fingers. He was quite content just to sit like that without making any attempt to do the other. That went with Paul's kind of a person, but it definitely did *not* go with the kind of a man Chaney was.

He finally did make a frank statement, though. " I'm damned near overwhelmed."

She looked at him. "I could have told you the day before yesterday, when you kissed me in the parking area. I almost grabbed you and kissed you back."

" Well, but what about Acapulco?"

" That depended upon you, Chaney. If you'd set your jaw and gone to war with my father, what else could I have done? You know—I spent a terrible night last night. Him on one side, you on the other side. Going somewhere a long way off seemed the only way out for me. Normally, I'm not that kind of a coward . . . but I've loved a man once before, and I couldn't go through it again—losing." She tightened her hold on his hand;

she had surprising strength for a woman. "Everybody becomes a coward at least once, don't they?"

He stripped through all this to the core of their situation, and there he stood at the centre, not a very nice effigy of a man brutalising the feelings of a wonderful woman just to strike back because his self-esteem had been dented.

"Acapulco later," he told her. "I'm ashamed of myself. I really am."

"No, it was natural, Chaney. You're a man and this is your environment. You know all the rules, and you know what happens to men who are soft or weak—or too susceptible. Actually, even before I'd met you or had heard of you, I told my father that for me to jump into the financial-industrial environment was about as foreign as for him to walk in our rose garden on a full-moon night feeling all the beauty that people can sense and feel, but can never see."

He watched the youngsters at tennis, glanced at his watch, finally, and freed his fingers. Without a word she rose to head on around to their cars at his side.

TWELVE

Sparks In The Garden

THE MORRISONS lived atop a Brentwood knoll which was north and west of Beverly Hills, and the road dead-ended in a circular cul-de-sac at their front gate and driveway. When Chaney followed the blue Jaguar up the slightly steep driveway through an almost jungle-profusion of flowering shrubs to where the mansion stood, he could see sage and chaparral, rabbit-runs and trees on all sides of the knoll, stretching downward and around for about five or six acres. Evidently when Alfred Morrison built his residence he had also purchased enough surrounding land so that no neighbour could get any closer than he wanted a neighbour to be. Chaney approved of that.

He climbed from the car and strolled on over where Lee was waiting. Behind her, stood the Tudor-style residence with late-day sunsmash glaring along the front and northwest side. The place looked as though it hadn't been built, so much as it had grown like natural stone and wood, out of its own appropriate earth and environment.

" Beautiful," said Chaney, and meant it.

Lee turned. " I've always thought so. But on rainy stormy nights when you drive up from the cul-de-sac, it gives you the impression that Count Dracula will meet you at the door." She started ahead but he detained her with an outflung hand. The three-car garage door was open and there was an empty place.

" He's not here yet, is he?"

Lee shook her head. " No, but he'll be along." She pulled at his hand. " I want to show you my pride and joy."

He was mystified but willing. She led him down through the covered walkway with its climbing roses towards the rear grounds. It was shady and fragrant on the east side of the house. Out back where the top of the knoll had been evenly sliced off to make room for development, all topsoil had been pushed far back and down the far slope, but evidently there had been quite a bit of earth to be moved because gradually several of the little arroyos had filled up, all the way to the top, and now the rear garden looked to be about two acres in size, and perfectly flat. It also happened to have benefited from that topsoil, as well as from excellent subsequent care, because just about everything that had been planted back there, had flourished.

That was what she'd wanted to show him. Here she stopped, beaming her pride, hands behind her back while she waited. Chaney took his time gazing at the massive trees, the flowerbeds that seemed to have silently exploded into riotous colour, the little shady places where ferns stood protected by hardier plants, and a delightful little collection of white-barked young birch trees. It was a wonderful garden, which he told her. It complemented the view from up there; it formed an oasis of colour in all the dull and dusty drabness of the sage.

He could see how she radiated pleasure over his praise. He recalled something she'd said about sensing and feeling beauty on a moonlit night out here, and understood that she had an inherent need for beauty, for the kind of tranquillity a person might find in this spot, on a moonlit night. He was beginning to understand her.

She took him out to the far edge of the garden where rooftops, some red, some blue-green, some tawny brown, ran downward and outward until they became orderly little block-tops stretching all the way to the sea. It was hazy beyond Santa Monica so, as she explained, the ocean was not visible.

"But sometimes it is. On special days you can . . ."

He reached, turned her gently and said, "If I could have known you first, there never would have been any scars, Lee."

She smiled. "Possibly, but in those days, Chaney, I wasn't ready for a man like you. In those days I was still more girl than woman."

She hadn't been surprised at either this abrupt switch in conversation, or his touch; in fact, she seemed almost to have anticipated it, to have been expecting it as soon as they were distant from the house and entirely alone.

"I don't suppose that makes much sense to you, does it?" She went on. "But a girl is an idealist; what she seeks is fragile, although she doesn't know it at the time. It never lasts. It *can't* last, because people just aren't made that beautiful and that good. Do you suppose that's why there are so many divorces, after a few years? But you see, Chaney, real men—someone like you for instance who knew what life was and knew how to face it—would have frightened me in those days."

"But not now?"

She leaned a little so they touched, and shook her head. "Not now, Chaney. Now, I too know what life is like. Now, I couldn't possible settle for anything less than a mature man."

He tilted her face, watched her eyes close, and kissed her gently. A lot of things rattled loose inside him; things he'd only barely known had existed, then he released her and she leaned against him with her cheek to his chest.

After a while she said, "Odd, this is supposed to happen *before* people say they love each other, not *after*."

He smiled down at all those little bunched-up rooftops. "Before or after—the important thing is that it happened."

"Chaney, do you like flowers?"

"Love 'em!"

"And fresh air, and mountains, and still lakes, and —what else?"

"And you," he said, thinking that he was becoming as adroit at this kind of thing as Paul Carroll would be, which made him smile. "Strange how this mood makes the sky bluer and the roses redder and the air more fragrant."

She leaned back and shot a look upwards. "Care to collaborate with me on that book of poetry?"

They laughed together, then turned at the sound of heavy footfalls crunching over the gravel of a small nearby path. Chaney had not heard the car arrive out front. He probably wouldn't have heard it anyway, with so much distance, and that big house, between them, but it was just as probably that a platoon of infantry could have marched past while he was kissing her and he'd not have heard them either.

Alfred Morrison loomed large and authoritative even with the mansion dwarfing him as a background. Chaney remembered everything about the older man's face; the tough eyes, the strong, wide mouth, the predatory, slightly beaked nose, and that mane of pale hair. This was the first time he'd ever seen Morrison in motion, but he moved about as Chaney would have

" You're condemning yourself," the older man said, and narrowed his eyes expecting some kind of trap.

" Not condemning," corrected Chaney, " just seeing it as it is. You're not a saint, but I'm less of one. And now that we've whittled me down, let me put a question to you : if I defer to management at Steel Fabricators, can you keep the Boeing contract?"

" You're using blackmail," exclaimed the older man, and for the first time Lee spoke up.

" He is doing no such a thing, Dad, he simply asked you a perfectly legitimate question ! Do you want to fight him so badly that you'll ruin everything, including the factory !"

Morrison blinked at his daughter. His voice had dropped slightly when he spoke again, looking at Chaney. " It's largely a matter of that damned penalty clause in their contract. We can lose all the profit if they don't revise that delivery schedule upwards—or eliminate the penalty clause. There's no sense in working a plant just to be working it, Mr. Lincoln; the idea is to produce a good product and make a decent profit for doing it."

" Will they drop the penalty clause?"

" No, they will not. I was on the telephone most of the morning. That's out."

" Will they negotiate the delivery schedules?"

Morrison rubbed a leathery jaw and kept studying Chaney. " Perhaps," he conceded.

"And what is it in the factory that might prevent you from meeting the schedules?"

" A lot of things. Tooling for example, acquiring the right kind of new personnel, and of course you always have to assume there will be work-stoppages; they can be caused by breakdowns on the line, or by union difficulties. You see, Mr. Lincoln, all I'm asking from the Boeing people is recognition of the uncertainties, and some allowance for them."

"They won't yield?"

Morrison stopped rubbing his jaw, looked down into his daughter's lovely face, then shoved big hands deep into his trouser pockets. "I don't say they *won't* yield; I'll simply say that unless they do we'd be insane to start production." Morrison swung like a harassed bear and glowered at Chaney. "Tell me something, now that I've answered your questions : if you didn't acquire controlling shares to kick me out and break the company, why *did* you acquire them?"

Chaney dropped the cigarette and stepped upon it. He had to be careful in his choice of words now. "Because, Mr. Morrison, you did your best to teach me a lesson. You made me lose half a million dollars."

"You learned, didn't you?" murmured Morrison, and smiled for the first time. "I despise financial maggots above all else, Mr. Lincoln. When I found out who had picked up those shares my daughter had owned, I knew exactly what you were up to, and why. I've never been called a dishonest man in my life and I had no intention of seeing you do it, either. You looked as if you needed a lesson. So I gave you one."

Chaney's temper strained at the leash. Paul Carroll's wise admonition came back. *Take what he hurls at you, overlook it, and make him get down to specifics about how to salvage that damned contract.*

Lee moved slightly, turning to look up at Chaney.

He smiled at her, then addressed her father again. "All right, Mr. Morrison, you taught me a lesson. That's about the only kind a man ever really remembers, I suppose. Now let's get back to that damned contract."

Lee broke it up. "We're not going to stand out here like bristling bulldogs for all this. Dad, where are your manners. Invite Mr. Lincoln into the house for a highball!"

Morrison considered his daughter. Chaney saw the slight, very slight, twinkle of affection. Then it was gone and Alfred Morrison said, "Would you care for a drink at the bar, Mr. Lincoln?"

Chaney felt Lee's elbow. He nodded. "Thank you, Mr. Morrison, I'd like that very much."

THIRTEEN

Thunder Amid The Sunshine

LEE MIXED their drinks, two Scotches-and-sodas and one Manhattan, then she left the dark-panelled barroom to look for her mother. The moment she was out of earshot her father said, "What's the point in us discussing something you're not familiar with, Lincoln? Tooling up for that empennage assembly could cost more that Boeing is willing to advance. In the old days, on government contracts, a factory very often got as much as thirty per cent in advance, but this is a civilian economy now. It's tougher."

Chaney hunched on his bar stool and gave the older man his first back-talk thus far. "Who says a man has to know how to tool-up an assembly line to establish the day-to-day quotas so that they co-ordinate with schedules?"

Morrison turned. "Did you ever work in a factory?"

"No. And I've never been to sea either, but I know from books that it's always been the landlubbers who've made seamanship progressive. What the hell has working in a factory got to do with negotiating a successful contract?"

"You'd at least have some inkling of what I'm talking about," growled Alfred Morrison.

"Don't delude yourself," said Chaney. "I know exactly what you're talking about. You're afraid your plant can't meet schedules and you'll lose the profit. If I'm treading where angels fear to, just overlook it long enough to correct me if I'm wrong about one thing. If you've met schedules before, and I happen to know that's your reputation, then what's worrying you now probably has less to do with tooling up than it has to do with something else. Am I right?"

Morrison said, "Oh hell," and downed his drink and slammed the empty glass on the bartop as he set it down. He left his stool to go behind the bar and start mixing two more Scotches-and-sodas. Chaney watched his hard, tough face and when Morrison put the second drink before Chaney, the younger man eased it to one side.

Morrison saw that, and gazed a moment at his guest

before leaning on the bartop, great shoulders hunched. "You're right. But it wouldn't do a damned bit of good to explain it to you. Even if I wanted to." He straightened up. "We're alone, so I don't have to watch my manners. I'm a blunt man, Lincoln. If I offend you, that's just too damned bad. All right?"

Chaney returned the hard stare with one just as hard. "I can take it, Mr. Morrison. Be sure that you can take it too. Fire away."

"It's getting past me, Lincoln."

"What is, Morrison?"

The older man lifted his glass, swallowed, made a face and put the glass down. "It's not like it used to be. A quarter of a century ago when I started Steel Fabricators, there were only a few large sharks in the sea. Now there are thousands of large ones and damned well millions of small ones, and they're all hungry for these fat contracts. They stoop to anything. As far as the Boeing deal is concerned, you coming in low and fast like you did, was only one more pitfall for me." Morrison finished his drink; if the liquor affected him he did not permit it to show.

"The Board of Directors hit the ceiling when I went after you. They said my chief concern should be the complex and that fat contract." Morrison looked hard at Chaney. "You started out as a thorn in my side."

Chaney returned the stare. "And now?" he said, but he thought he knew.

Morrison's voice dropped. "My daughter, Lincoln."

Chaney's guess had been correct. He could go beyond just guessing, he could anticipate and understand. "She has nothing to do with what I did, Morrison, although

I'll tell you frankly that she sure as hell was part of why I did it. I don't like being used." Chaney balanced the rest of this statement a moment, then decided to let him hear that too. "And if you don't like maggots, I've got a pet peeve too—men who use their women as bait."

Morrison didn't move for a long time. Eventually he straightened up off the bar and reached into a drawer for a cigar, which he lit. All that took as much time as he apparently needed to recover.

Chaney offered no apology. As he'd said earlier, if Morrison expected him to be able to take it, then Morrison should be sure that he could do the same. Evidently the older man was remembering that as he lowered the cigar and said, "You're a long way from being there yet, Lincoln, but I'm going to tell you something. Someday, some particular year, you'll notice that it's harder to understand a lot of things than it was the year before, and all the years before that."

Chaney nodded appreciation but not sympathy. "If you mean—what she can possibly see in me, I'll say that I'm equally as baffled, and age has nothing to do with it."

Morrison leaned down again. "Stay for dinner. Maybe if I'm around you long enough, I'll be able to figure this thing out. I mean, about you and my daughter."

Chaney smiled but not with a whole lot of warmth. "Thanks, I'd like to stay for dinner. Do we move our skirmish line to the dinner-table, or do we finish the skirmishing in here?"

"You know, Lincoln, twenty-five years ago I'd have cracked your skull and stepped over you to go on to whatever came next."

"Twenty-five years ago," retorted Chaney, "you could have done that very easily. I was a kid washing dishes in cheap cafés and reading history books at night. Also, when I'd figured out how men got rich, that long ago, I met a couple of sharks like you, Morrison, and they cleaned me out down to my socks. I started over again. That was my first lesson. I didn't forget it. I won't forget my most recent lesson either. But as for the rest of it—cracking heads—forget it. You couldn't do it today, but if you don't hang tight and *make* Steel Fabricators meet those schedules, *I'll crack yours*." Chaney got off the bar stool and did what Alfred Morrison obviously did not expect at all, he shoved out his hand.

"You're management, Morrison, I'm majority shareholder. You know what's got to be done, and I know how to keep your back protected."

Morrison drew up off the bar, grasped Chaney's hand and pumped it twice, then dropped it. "Should I trust you?" he asked.

"Suit yourself, but you can—all the way."

Morrison picked up his cigar and bit down on it. At that moment Lee came to the doorway and looked at both of them a moment before announcing that dinner would be ready in a few minutes. Then she asked Chaney to stay and her father grumbled that he had already extended that invitation. She smiled at them. "I wasn't sure whether I'd ought to just barge in here, or send in a white flag ahead of me."

She held forth a hand to Chaney and took him out into the large sitting-room. Beyond the glassed-in west wall the night was down all around, shot through with countless scores of tiny lights, some moving but mostly stationary. There were stars over the distant ocean, and more stars inland over the highest humps in the Coast Range of mountains. She squeezed his hand. " My mother said I shouldn't leave you two in the bar room without a referee. I asked her to keep her fingers crossed, like I was doing."

He turned. She was more exquisite than the night. He hadn't noticed in the bar room, but she'd changed. Now, she wore a creamy dress with embroidery at the throat and part way down the front. The sleeves were full, with matching embroidered cuffs. The narrow dark belt accentuated the perfection of her figure, but it was her face, the eyes and lips, and the ebony hair, that captivated him.

" Your father said something I had to agree with : what could a woman like you see in a man like me?"

Her smile congealed a little at a time. Her violet eyes darkened. " Did he really say that?"

Chaney caught her arm. " Hold it. There's nothing wrong with what he said. It's the truth. Maybe we belong to different eras, but a straight-talking man earns my respect every time."

" He had no right . . ."

" He had every right! If I had a daughter like you I'd be ten times worse. I've never seen a woman like you before. I'm sure I'll never see another one like you. For fifteen years I've said God never made a female who could twist me around her finger." Chaney laughed at himself. " Well, what are you waiting for—twist!"

She smiled, and reached to push a heavy coil of hair off his broad forehead. " He's terrible, isn't he?"

Chaney returned her soft smile. "He's tough and he's honest. Also, he's damned tired."

She was surprised. "I didn't know men saw those things in other men. Mother's been saying that if he doesn't slow down he's heading for serious trouble. He won't listen to her."

Chaney had a simmering idea but this was neither the time nor the place, and usually he kept his private secrets to himself. That was something else he'd learned in the shark-eat-shark world. "After dinner let's walk out in the garden again."

She nodded.

Natalie's mother entered the room and came towards Chaney as though he were an old friend. Her dark eyes, of a different hue than her daughter's eyes, were also appraising. That, too, Chaney could understand. He'd been relying a lot on intuition lately; it was helping him to learn something he'd always known, but only superficially : that people are complicated even when they seem to be simple, and that basically, they are all defensive, either in their desire to protect themselves, or something they love and cherish like a beautiful, widowed daughter, or perhaps just a huge, rambling industrial empire that was on the verge of swallowing them.

Chaney politely recalled meeting Mrs. Morrison at the country club. He also recalled wondering whether she was of French descent, or perhaps Italian, or maybe even of Spanish descent. But whatever it was, she was patrician in looks, in behaviour, in conversation and even in her humour.

She had an ability Chaney envied; without touching

upon any subject that might grate, she could keep a lively conversation going. Her husband certainly lacked this attribute and so did Chaney. Even Natalie was only passably good at it, but then Natalie's life hadn't been built around the kind of security her mother's had obviously been built around. Natalie had lost; her mother, probably married thirty or thirty-five years, had only gained as the decades had passed.

Chaney liked Mrs. Morrison. He did not often like people easily nor so soon. In fact, Chaney was a sceptic where people were concerned. He had grown up in the kind of an environment where that became habit very early and very easily.

She showed him her sterling collection in the huge formal dining-room. Not to impress him, she wasn't that type at all. She was almost child-like in the way she clucked with disapproval of what some of the pieces had cost, and o. ~ older pair of small, very plain sterling candle-hoiuc.. ... confided in a lowered voice, with a twinkle, that she had got with trading stamps. They had been the start of her collection.

She also showed him the solarium, built off the rear of the house. There, she raised orchids, and laughingly said that her husband said they were not pretty, they were a nuisance, and they took too much of her time.

Chaney found himself defending her, and the damned orchids. He liked flowers, but building an expensive glasshouse for them *was* a bit off the deep end, but he wouldn't have admitted it now if wild horses had tried to tear it out of him.

Finally, when Lee's mother excused herself to go see that Natalie's father was getting dressed properly for dinner, Natalie laughed at him. "She conquered you with all that."

He smiled. "She did. And she could do it again right now. She's wonderful."

"Well yes, but we talked about you while you and dad were in the bar. She really is afraid of you."

"I don't believe it!"

"You'd better. She'd been hearing dad snarl and snap your name for two weeks almost every night at dinner. She also heard me argue with him about you a couple of times . . . I told her that I was in love with you, a while ago. She almost cried."

A servant came to say dinner was ready. Chaney sighed. "I don't know whether to march in there like a Caesar, or sneak in like a—maggot."

She offered him her arm. "How about just strolling in there with me, like you belonged here—not here, in this house, here at my side."

He leaned, kissed her swiftly, then did as she had said, strolled on towards the dining-room as though he belonged at her side.

FOURTEEN

Chaney's Decision

WITH A man like Alfred Morrison it was never possible to be altogether certain; for instance, although he looked like an aged football player, or an aged wrestler, and because one assumed those types were forthright and not devious, looking at Morrison and even listening to him left a person convinced they faced a blunt diamond-in-the-rough.

But Alfred Morrison knew all the nuances and all the subterfuges. At dinner Chaney noticed how he led a person along in the talk until he knew exactly what they had in mind, then took over their idea to dissect and analyse, until he'd either tested its validity and approved, or had found its flaw and disapproved. If it were the latter, old Morrison would rip the idea to shreds in a few sentences.

For Chaney, who was somewhat of an analyst himself, it was a revelation, being at the same table with Morrison. It did not occur to him until near the end of the meal that Natalie and her mother were on tenterhooks. He would have noticed sooner if he and Morrison hadn't been so absorbed in discussing the factory, schedules, and of course contracts. When he finally did notice, he eased the conversation around to bring both women into it.

Morrison showed an easy adaptability; he made the transition without much more than a glance at Chaney. After that, he told an amusing anecdote or two and everyone relaxed.

The difficulty arising from that kind of dinner was that afterwards, when Chaney and Lee went out back into the moonlit, fragrant garden, he couldn't remember what the food had been.

Not that it really mattered. She didn't ask him; but then she probably couldn't have remembered either; but for a different reason. Her preoccupation hadn't been her father or all that he'd had to say.

They went over by a mountain ash, and beside it, much younger but equally as sturdy, was another tree, this latter one rather unkempt. She said it was a mulberry tree. She also said no one had ever got berries from it because the birds were too smart; they arrived the day the berries were first edible, and they came at dawn. By noon the berries they hadn't eaten they'd pecked apart.

He told her about a cherry tree that grew on a farm where he had once worked. The birds did exactly the same thing, so one night he had taken his blankets out to sleep at the base of the tree. He laughed. " You can guess the rest of the story; when I awakened about ten o'clock, the birds had been there and had gone."

Moonlight, while not very bright, was nonetheless adequate to lend a certain sooty perspective to the lighted world below the knoll and outwards in all directions. It was a pleasant night without a breeze and pleasantly warm.

They strolled out where they had been standing earlier when her father had walked up. She pointed out several distant expressways where tiny lights moved outward from the city as well as inward, towards the city. She also showed him ships plying their off-shore sea-lanes, but although he was politely attentive he was very aware of her nearness, and of the fact that they were alone out there. When she turned to speak, he saw her eyes widen slightly at him. He made no attempt to conceal his thoughts; they showed in his expression even in that weak kind of light.

He reached out to touch her and found no resistance. She was warm and fragrant and firm in his arms. When he found her mouth she destroyed his restraint by meeting his quiet passion with a quick, hard fire of her own. Afterwards she breathed audibly in the silence of that secluded place and he heard how ragged her breath was.

There *was* a difference between a girl and a full woman. In most ways he decided it was greater than the difference between boys and men.

" You were going to tell me something," she reminded him, and pressed close to him the full length.

He smiled at the distant night over her head. " It's rather hard to remember, right now."

She drew away quickly and looked up, teasing him with her eyes and lips. " Excuse me."

He pulled her roughly to him again. " Right now I don't care a damn about that idea, or about anything else including my lost half million dollars."

He knew she was ready to laugh from the lilt of her voice when she said, " Chaney, you're a strong, self-sufficient entrepreneur. Remember that."

" I am also a vulnerable male." He hugged her until she made a tiny gasp, then he loosened his hold. " Did you ever read the *Divine Comedy*?"

" Required in most sophomore English Lit. classes, lover. What about it?"

" Well," he said drolly, " it occurred to me just now that if Dante had ever held Beatrice the way I'm holding you right now, he never would have written it."

They laughed together, which eased the way he felt somewhat, and she, being a woman, could relax a lot easier. She freed herself and turned to look at the view again. "About your idea," she prompted him.

"It's probably lousy, but I'll use you as a sounding-board," he replied, holding her hand and standing close enough so that they touched at hip and shoulder. "Your father needs more than that Boeing contract."

"Yes; that's true."

"And I—well—I need something. I mean besides you."

She looked at him. "That's also true."

"Well, it occurred to me that since I have the time, and since I've got an awful lot of money invested . . . maybe I could browbeat him into taking me on at the complex as an aide."

She smiled. "I like that idea very much." Her violet eyes held a hint of what could have been soft irony. He got suspicious. "And I suppose this comes as no surprise."

She reached to straighten his collar, then to say, "This afternoon, when we were sitting upon the loggia at the clubhouse . . ."

"You thought of it too," he finished for her.

She raised her eyes. "Of course it's your idea though, Chaney. I mean, unless you'd thought of it you wouldn't do it, would you?"

He saw disaster either way he answered that question. so he chose the best way out, he didn't answer it at all. "It's not fair for a woman to be intelligent and beautiful, both. It's not fair to other women, I mean."

She clung to his lapels, raised up and planted a firm kiss on his mouth, then dropped swiftly down as his arms raised. "He will roar when you make the suggestion, Chaney. Not that he hasn't had aides before—bright young college boys who usually are as sleek as well-fed cats and as unscrupulous and unethical as snakes. He never liked them."

"Sweetheart, I did not finish the seventh grade in school, and of all the things I've been called, sleek sure as hell isn't one of them. As for the rest," Chaney shrugged, remembering how her father had hung-fire over trusting him. "He'll just have to find out for himself, won't he? You can't just *tell* a man like your father you are not going to stick a knife in his back. He wouldn't believe you. So he'll just have to find out all by himself. As for roaring," Chaney lifted her face so soft moonlight fell across it. "He can roar to hell and back—I'm still majority shareholder." He bent, brushed her full lips, straightened back and said, "Then too, he's got this big damned lever over me."

She smiled. She understood exactly what that meant. "I think not, Mr. Lincoln. My father doesn't own me. How you and he work out your differences is your business. *My* business is . . . something else again."

Chaney did not believe that. "Paul Carroll told me you were a very loyal person. He warned me that if I busted your father you'd hate me. He was stating a fact. Maybe your *heart* is independent but your brain sure as hell isn't."

"You've read me that thoroughly, have you, Chaney?"

"No. With you I operate by intuition, by feeling, by the worst of all human attributes—emotion."

She smiled. "That is the prerogative of women, lover, not men, and especially not financial sharks who just happen to also be men." She raised both palms to his chest and raised up to seek his lips. " I don't care, operate any way that you wish to, just include me in your life, and *all* your love."

A dog barked far off, some soaring night-bird scudded past on soundless wings. Chaney heard the dog but missed seeing the winged predator altogether. He also missed seeing the distant but brilliantly lit outline of an excursion ship passing like an eerie ghost northward towards San Francisco, probably from down at San Pedro, or Los Angeles, harbour.

She was firm to hold and solid to feel. All the world, past and present, was embodied in how he felt about her. That empty place in his life that he'd managed to live with up until now, was no longer empty. If she was a full woman, Chaney Lincoln was learning how to be a full man, someone whose needs would be fulfilled and whose centre of existence would never have to be himself again, which was something no strong man ever wanted.

She pushed him back and sounded a little wavery when she spoke. " This could get to be a habit, Chaney, and regardless of what you think, I'm just not that strong a person."

He leaned, pecked her lightly then said, " Yield, my proud beauty, yield."

She made a little face up at him. " It's no joke. I could."

He calmly lit a cigarette and blew smoke into the warm night. "Marry me, Natalie. Marry me tonight, or tomorrow, or any time at all, just as long as it's before next Sunday. I have a date to go surf-fishing with some guys I've been fishing with for years. I don't like to carry over unfinished business from one week to the next. It's sloppy planning, don't you think?"

She laughed. "You are so different from what I first thought, Chaney."

He knew the answer to that, because he'd heard the same thing said about him before. "Baby, all that proves is that you've listened to bitter people and have made a very common mistake—you've pre-judged me." He looked gravely down into her lifted face. "Never let others make your appraisals for you; the chances are very good that their ability to judge is even worse than yours is. Okay?"

She lowered her eyes in mock humility. "Yes, oh worldly-wise—and beautiful—lord and master." Her black lashes swept upwards to show the twinkle. "I love you, Chaney. You're really wise. But you also happen to have a wonderful blend of humour and sense. I've never found it quite like that before in any other man. Do you suppose we really could be married tonight?"

He said, "That's crazy. Anyway, it's not fair to your parents. Especially your mother."

Natalie cocked her head a little, which was something she unconsciously did from time to time. "Not really. She knows."

"Knows what?" demanded Chaney, feeling that the liquid-soft look he was getting was somehow as old as time itself.

"Knows I'm going to marry you. We didn't discuss the exact date, but I told her before dinner I would marry you the moment you asked me to." Lee's teeth flashed in moonlight. "This is the moment, isn't it?

Anyway, I don't want a church wedding. I want this to be as natural as falling in love with you has been; as though it is part of my life, of my awareness. Like reaching out at a certain time in my life to something that has to be exactly where I see it, at exactly the right period." She smiled. " Make any sense to you?"

It did, and it didn't, but one thing made sense; he was on the verge of a consummation towards which everything in life was oriented, and *that* certainly made sense. He stepped on the cigarette. " I'll speak to your father."

" No."

He stood looking squarely at her. " Yes. That would be a hell of a thing to do to a man—just elope with his daughter like it was some spur-of-the-moment thing. Natalie, I wouldn't want a man to treat me like that, if I had a daughter."

She seemed torn by turmoil, not over having Chaney contradict her; she had no illusions about how often that might happen in the years ahead because she knew exactly the kind of strong man she was getting. She said, " He'll explode, Chaney."

" Maybe. I'll tell you something, sweetheart; if he and I are going to be associated—because of that damned factory or because of you—for the next generation or so, we could spend all that time sniping back and forth, or we could have one hell of a battle, and get it all out in the open right at the outset. Just one thing is certain— that is the choice. Tonight, I get to make the decision. Come along. You tell your mother while I'm telling *him*."

FIFTEEN

How to make war without really trying

ALFRED MORRISON was reading a newspaper in the sitting-room, entirely alone. There was a cup of black coffee upon a saucer at his elbow, near the end-table-lamp. He put down the paper as soon as Chaney entered the room and motioned his guest to be seated.

Chaney remained on his feet.

Morrison rummaged inside his coat and brought forth two cigars, one of which he offered Chaney. " Cuban," he said. " I know—there's an embargo on Cuban imports and it's as un-American as all hell to buy their stuff." Morrison unwrapped his cigar and gazed fondly at it. " As a matter of fact these come from Mexico." He lit up, and Chaney had to admit the aroma was excellent. He'd admired the smell in the bar-room prior to dinner.

Morrison said, " You want to marry Natalie."

Chaney stood in his tracks.

" Did you think there was a communications gap in this house, Lincoln? There isn't. There never has been." Morrison blew more smoke. " Her mother told me."

Finally, Chaney accepted the offer of a chair. Morrison knocking the props from under him with what he'd said didn't really make it a whole lot easier to discuss it, but it *had* got round the first, stiff hurdle. "This evening," he murmured, and watched fragrant smoke drift upwards around Alfred Morrison's head. "Well, she doesn't want either a large wedding, or a long engagement, so—"

"And you don't either, of course," said Morrison drily.

Chaney thought he detected an undertone, but chose to ignore it. "I want you to understand," he said, a bit lamely. He had almost said 'your permission', but that would have implied something he did not much believe in—the superiority of an older generation over a younger one based entirely upon age and nothing else.

"I understand," said Morrison, gazing through narrowed lids at Chaney. "First my factory, then my daughter." He puffed. "Or was it the other way around?"

Chaney's blood-pressure rose a couple of notches. He'd expected the explosion Natalie had forecast. Instead, he was facing the cold, analytical imperviousness that he thought was probably Morrison's normal attitude towards his factory people.

But Chaney was still a very long way from his own wrath-level, so he said, "Natalie first, Mr. Morrison. I have something else in mind for the factory. Me—as your alter ego."

"My what?"

"Aide, associate, whatever the hell you want to call it."

Several furious little puffs of smoke rose. Morrison removed the cigar and held it to one side as though it impeded his view and he didn't want anything like that, at the moment. "In the bar-room," he said, speaking as slowly as any man would, who was holding himself in with an effort, "you said you would not interfere. Now just what in the hell do you call this suggestion? Wait . . . did Lee put that idea in your head?"

"*I* mentioned it to *her*," said Chaney, without enlarging on that. "Look Morrison, I'm not going to force myself down your damned throat. It is just an idea. Call it a suggestion if you like."

"I'll call it what I like, indeed," growled the hulking older man. "You learn it all, because you're a bright young man—and because you're also majority shareholder—and when you think you've got it all down pat . . ." Morrison raised a stiff forefinger and made a slow, slashing motion in front of his own throat. "I told you I didn't trust you, Lincoln."

Chaney's wrath bubbled just below the surface, but he held it down. He took the time to light a cigarette, and afterwards to find an ashtray and return to his chair with it. Movement, even that inconsequential kind of movement, was always good for an angry person. Morrison never once let Chaney out of his sight. He was smoking the fragrant Cuban cigar again. Someone like Natalie, or his wife, would have been able to read the steely gleam in Morrison's eyes much more readily, and more correctly, than Chaney read it when he resumed his seat with the ashtray.

"You can trust me, Morrison," said Chaney quietly. "You also heard me tell you that. But I really am beginning to feel as though it doesn't make a hell of a lot of difference to me whether you trust me or not."

"You're now saying you're going to force yourself upon me. Is that it?"

"No, damn it, that is *not* it!" Chaney inhaled, exhaled, and stubbed out the cigarette he had only just lighted. "In the bar-room you complained about the way things were, nowadays. There was something else, too, but you didn't mention it. You're tired."

Morrison snorted, but sat listening, and watching.

"For my part, Morrison, I need something like this," went on Chaney. "I've got money, but that's not enough, is it? What else does a man need?"

"A wife?"

Chaney made a death's-head smile. "Very clever." He paused, then said, "You know, you're a disagreeable old—"

"Careful," purred old Morrison, his eyes narrowing still more. "Careful, Lincoln. That's one luxury a man at the top cannot afford. Temper."

"I'm not at the top, Morrison, so I can afford it. And there's something else that goes with that : people at the top don't have to work so hard at being bullies."

"Meaning me?"

This time Chaney's small smile was genuine, "I didn't say it, you did." He rose. "I'll look you up at the factory tomorrow. Now about—"

"Go ahead," said Morrison, getting upright. "She's not a child. Whatever I think of her judgement—and it's usually good enough—she's a grown woman." Morrison put the cigar aside as the sound of footfalls became increasingly audible beyond the sitting-room entrance. "But I'm still a parent, and in my case an old and somewhat sceptical and disillusioned one. I'd give an awful lot of money to prevent her from being hurt. But I can't do that, can I?"

Chaney felt sympathy for Alfred Morrison for the first time. " I guess not, Mr. Morrison." He was groping for other words, appropriate to the older man's mood, but Natalie was in the doorway, and beside her, smaller and looking forcefully cheerful, was her mother, who came across to Chaney, said nothing and raised up to kiss his cheek. He saw the brimful look and patted her hand. It was worse, trying to think of what to say to the mother than to the father.

Natalie rescued him. She had her mother's tact, along with her father's tough common sense. With a combination of both she managed to get him out of there before someone wept, or swore, or did something awkward.

He was a little reluctant to go like this. At the doorless wide exit from the room he smiled at the older woman, then lifted his dark eyes and met old Morrison's steely look. He smiled, which was all he knew to do since words weren't actually adequate at the moment, then Natalie pulled him away and led him out to the entry-hall where she let go of his hand. Three small powder-blue valises were standing side-by-side, at the door. She said, " Give me one more minute," and ran back to the sitting-room. Chaney didn't want to overhear anything so he scooped up the valises and took them out to his car.

The night felt cooler, fresher, less roiled, than the atmosphere had been back there in the house. He stolidly stowed her luggage, looked at his watch, looked at the silently moving moon, and wondered if he was dreaming.

What he had come over here for, that afternoon or

early evening, had been to discuss something with Alfred Morrison. He hadn't even thought of staying for dinner; it hadn't occurred to him that he would be invited to do that. But most of all, he hadn't expected the other thing to happen. Not tonight at any rate.

He raised his face to the high sky, saw tiny lights blinking up there, one emerald, one ruby, where an aircraft ploughed the night making a straight furrow aloft. Paul Carroll was going to be stunned. So were a lot of other people. In fact, lowering his head to glance towards the door through which Natalie would shortly come out to him, he was slightly stunned, himself.

She came slowly from the house. He waited until she was out of the shadows to see her face. She smiled at him. " It's all right, Chaney."

He nodded and opened the door for her. She had been crying; this was a time when women cried, he knew that intuitively. He leaned, closed the door, and kissed her, then went round to his side. As they drove forward, slowly, down the inclined, curving driveway towards the cul-de-sac, he felt inside his jacket to reassure himself that his wallet was there. He always carried plenty of money; that was one thing that had helped his confidence over the years, knowing he had all the money he'd need no matter what happened, when he was in the company of other wealthy people. Perhaps it was childish, perhaps it was indicative of some deeper need, he had never denied either supposition, but he still always carried plenty of cash, and tonight he was very glad that he'd acquired that custom.

When they passed down towards the city he said, " I don't know any ministers, do you?"

She scooted over close to him. " Shame on you. What do you do on Sunday mornings?"

He knew what she meant but he answered as though he didn't. He also happened to answer very truthfully. " Well, sometimes I get up early and go fishing, but usually I lie in bed reading the Sunday papers and drinking coffee."

She pointed. " Turn right. I happen to know an Episcopal minister."

He followed her directions, and such was his innocence that he did not realise they were by law required to have both a licence to get married, and a blood-test beforehand. If he'd thought much about it he would have guessed it just wasn't all this simple, but he let her have the entire initiative.

A salt-scented seabreeze came in over the palisades down along the beach. By the time it reached up where they drove through the indifferent traffic of the residential areas, it had lost most of its strength as well as most of its strong scent.

Chaney detected the sea-scent at once. He also noticed that lights were brighter, stars closer, night-shades and shadows were distinct, and that time did not seem to be moving at all.

Natalie curled both legs under her on the seat and leaned her head upon his shoulder. " Just like teenagers," she murmured, " except that you aren't driving eighty miles an hour."

" I'm not sure my foot is even on the accelerator," he replied, and corrected that. " In fact, I'm not even sure I *have* a foot. Would you care to share my second confidence of the night?"

She wiggled closer still. " I would care to."

" I'm scairt stiff, Natalie."

She lifted her head, craned round to look at him head-on, and settled back again. " You look it. That's natural though."

" Are you?" he asked, and got an answer that baffled him for years to come.

In her calmest voice Natalie said, " Not in the least, sweetheart, but then I'm a woman."

She didn't add anything to that, so he was left to try and puzzle it out by himself. He never did puzzle it out, then or later, but it seemed to make perfect sense to her.

SIXTEEN

A Surprise

HE DID not arrive at the factory until shortly before noon the following day, which might have had an adverse affect except that it also gave Natalie's father more than enough time to reach a decision about Chaney Lincoln, and because Alfred Morrison was the kind of man life had made him, Chaney had barely reached the executive suite to tell the receptionist who he was, than he was directed to go at once to the Department of Production Planning. There , with very few preliminaries he was taken in tow by two shirt-sleeved men, one named

Benedict, the other named Harrison. He was shown diagrams, plans, production charts, and a complete layout in miniature of the assembly line as though Benedict and Harrison expected him to know how to put a finger on the areas needing improvement, and those faulty places that required sophisticated expertise in order to facilitate production.

At first he wanted to protest, to explain to Benedict and Harrison, that he knew nothing of industrial complexes, but gradually he recognised Morrison's subterfuge and bewilderment became indignation. Finally, and irritably, he dismissed Benedict and Harrison, shed his coat and went on a tour of Steel Fabricators alone.

Two things impressed him at the outset. One was the noise, the other was the number of people working on the line and in the corollary departments.

By two o'clock in the afternoon, when he was paged to the telephone to take a call from Natalie, he had a fairly comprehensive idea of how an assembly line functioned, and what the purpose of all those other departments were, such as Tooling, Maintenance, Engineering, and Inspection.

Natalie asked what the noise was in the background and he confessed that he had taken her call down in the plant-proper. She said it sounded like a huge battle was in progress; then she told him she'd made an appointment for them to have proper blood-tests the next morning, and to get the proper marriage licence after that. She also said she and his housekeeper were preparing a very special dinner and if he arrived home later than six o'clock she would be very aggravated.

He would have talked longer but it was impossible. Not only was the noise intolerable, but Benedict and Harrison were back, hovering like solicitous mother-hens. He rang off and turned with a scowl. Harrison said Mr. Morrison would like to see Mr. Lincoln in his office upstairs—now!

Chaney went as far as their own department, where he'd left his coat, put it on, lit a cigarette and sat at a draughtsman's tilt-table to ask why, specifically, an assembly line that was as efficient as the one downstairs, and which had met all schedules up to now, couldn't handle the Boeing contract.

Harrison looked pointedly at his watch, a reminder that Mr. Morrison was waiting. Chaney knew he was waiting and reiterated his question. Benedict, a pipe-smoker, fired-up, puffed a moment then said, " Our line is one of the most efficient in the country. It can meet the schedule."

" Then what's the hang-up?" asked Chaney.

Benedict studied Chaney, then looked at Harrison as though it were Harrison's turn to comment. But however that might have been, evidently Harrison was not going to involve himself, so Benedict said, " There is no hang-up. Not in the way I think you mean it—a bottleneck, or a fouled-up procedure, something like that."

Chaney persisted. " But there is something, or people wouldn't be making such a big show of this particular contract. What is it?"

Harrison shot Benedict a look that Chaney thought was a warning to speak carefully or not to speak at all. Benedict, though, ignored that look : " Mr. Morrison," said the pipe-smoker, between puffs. "He's never balked at a standard penalty clause before, but this time he's turned so cautious we're about to lose out. None of us are management-analysts or psychologists, Mr. Lincoln. All we know is that he gave the Contract Department instructions to insist on an easier penalty clause if it couldn't be negotiated out altogether."

Lincoln held up a hand. "Correct me if I'm wrong, but isn't this damned Boeing contract already signed?"

For the first time Harrison spoke out. "Something like two weeks ago."

"And has the tooling gone ahead?" asked Chaney.

Harrison nodded. "Yes; fact the line will be ready to roll come next Monday. We've got key plant personnel in orientation classes, with several supervisors visiting the Boeing plant up north. Everything is geared to a switch-over the first of the week."

Chaney stood up. "Then what in the hell is all the fuss about?"

The telephone rang and as Benedict turned to reach for it he said, "I believe the answer to your question is on the other end of this line." He lifted the instrument, spoke his name, listened a moment then said, "Yes sir. Right away," and put the telephone down. "Mr. Lincoln, that was Mr. Morrison again. He's waiting."

Chaney left Production Planning, passed through a heavy, fireproof door into the long, carpeted corridor of the soundproofed executive section, and paced along, hands in pockets, until he entered Alfred Morrison's elegant outer office where a greying, handsome woman waved him on past as though in her anxiety he might not move fast enough to prevent Mr. Morrison from coming forth roaring with wrath.

Chaney opened the door to Morrison's large, airy office and nodded at the man standing with his back to the room gazing out a window made of glass louvres, who looked around at the sound of the opening door. Morrison had one of his cigars clamped between his teeth. He looked harder, tougher than ever when Chaney crossed to a chair and stood, waiting to be asked to sit.

Morrison went back to his desk before extending that offer, so that they both sat down at about the same time. Then Morrison placed the cigar in a huge, blue-glass ashtray and settled back in his leather-upholstered executive chair.

" Well, you saw, Lincoln, what did you think?"

" That it's a highly efficient plant," Chaney replied, watching the older man's craggy face. " That there isn't a single damned reason why you can't keep a schedule that your planners are sure the line can handle. Unless you just don't want the Boeing contract, and since it's already signed, I'd hazard an ignorant man's guess that you'll be laying yourself wide open to a lawsuit for breach of contract if you default now. A judgement in Boeing's favour could cost you one hell of a lot more than the penalty clauses might cost you."

Morrison's eyes drew out narrow. " Have you read a copy of that contract?"

Chaney hadn't. It was, of course, the crucial aspect of this entire affair, but Chaney felt positive what he had just said remained valid, contract or not. " I haven't read it," he replied, " and even if I had, I doubt that the contract is really the issue."

"I see," purred the older man. "And what *is* the issue?"

"I don't know, Mr. Morrison." Chaney got comfortable and waited. Whether Benedict and Harrison had put their fingers on the basic difficulty or not Chaney had no way of knowing, beyond his own personal appraisal of Natalie's father, but he held this kind of judgement in abeyance. He may have known next to nothing about industrial facilities, but at Morrison's level that was never the essential experience one needed. At that level almost without exception, a person dealt in personalities, in character, in whatever the men of power and authority were—or were not—and Chaney's position was very unique; he was majority shareholder, which gave him the power to force things if he wanted to make a battle of it, but he was also the new husband of the daughter of the man at the top, and that quite obviously precluded a battle.

Morrison did not say anything until he'd retrieved his cigar and had puffed it to life again, but his narrow-eyed study of Chaney Lincoln did not slack off. Ultimately, he said, "Suppose we begin production next Monday on schedule, and suppose that I relegate full authority for seeing to it that every aspect of that production is kept on schedule, to you; do you believe, that having no experience at all, just lots of brass and confidence, you could make certain the delivery dates would not be in default?"

Chaney hadn't really expected anything like this. He and Natalie had discussed the probabilities of his slow advancement under her father's tutelage; *reluctant* tutelage, in fact, with a possibility that Chaney might, in a couple of years, be able to make an occasional independent decision. They had never even considered the likelihood of her father, after one night of specu- lation, dropping anything like the entire empennage contract into Chaney's lap.

He sat and met the older man's narrowed, tough gaze, doing some rapid thinking. Chaney was not an organisation-man but he understood the basics of that aspect of life because he'd bought and sold enough industrial facilities to realise that the key to industrial success was having the right men in the key positions.

But there was a whole lot more to becoming a man- agement executive than just making sure he got the right subordinates; there also happened to be the matter of becoming completely involved with the industrial com- plex, and that meant having very little time at home with Natalie.

Even before Natalie, Chaney Lincoln had cherished his independence, but as he'd told her, and as he'd implied to her father, he'd won a big slice of life, and now he needed more.

All these things ran through his head. He understood the hard look he was getting from old Morrison too : let this man who had made a profession of profiteering see what it was like on the other side of the fence; let him sweat and worry and strain to make an industrial complex function properly. And there was more in the older man's face : let Chaney, who had made a fortune and who had now also tasted love, learn something about discipline.

Morrison sat and smoked and acted in no hurry at all. When the telephone rang he turned, ignoring

Chaney altogether, spoke quietly to one of his key-men, then rang off and put the cigar from him before swivelling around.

"Well," he said, "do we sit here all afternoon like a pair of chess players, Lincoln?"

Chaney, driven to an immediate decision, smiled because the older man had taught him one more lesson. Never go anywhere to face anything, without having considered every possibility, no matter how far-fetched and be ready to act according to the best possible judgement. Chaney said, "I leave this damned factory every night at five o'clock."

Morrison laughed for the first time, rose and went back to the window to stand looking down over the metal rooftops of his establishment. "That's the first thing you've said that proves you don't have a clear concept of what it's like in the executive department." He turned. "Everybody leaves at five o'clock *but* you and me. Everybody closes the factory out of their minds as they drive home to their family—but you and me." Morrison kept smiling. "But you're luckier than most, at that; you have a wife who knows what it's like." Morrison stood wide-legged like a captain on his bridge in a rough sea. "You're my son-in-law, Lincoln. I didn't choose you and a lot of people aren't going to like you. It also happens that you're majority shareholder—so among your duties will be presiding at the half-year shareholders' meetings. You've got three months to brush up on that, so you're lucky again. Now tell me straight out—are you man enough or aren't you?"

Chaney lit a cigarette. "I'm man enough."

Morrison continued to stand where he was for a

moment or two, no longer smiling. "There is one rule among people on this level. You'd better hear it from me first, then you'd better order your life by it. No excuses." Morrison gestured with a balled fist. "I don't care a damn what goes wrong, whose fault it may be, or what steps have to be taken to rectify it; I simply expect all those things to have been corrected before I even hear anything, because the minute someone tells me part of the assembly line is down because of a broken machine, I'll telephone you—not to hear some damned explanation, but to hear you say that everything is repaired and operational again. Clear?"

Chaney rose and went to put out the cigarette he had hardly tasted. "Clear. But tomorrow I'll be out all day, so I hope nothing breaks down until the day after tomorrow." Chaney straightened back and looked across at the older man. "And I want a free hand to pirate any man I need from any department at any time. Clear?"

Morrison's narrowed eyes shone. "Clear," he replied.

Chaney nodded, turned, and walked out of the office out past the handsome, greying woman, who watched him with interest, and went all the way out to his car before he let out a string of heartfelt profanity. It didn't alleviate any of the commitment he was now involved with, but as he got into the car and headed for home, it made him feel a lot better.

SEVENTEEN

Chaney's New World

NATALIE WAS aghast. She wanted to rush right to the telephone and upbraid her father, but Chaney shook his head.

"He's tough and uncompromising, and I'm positive we're going to lock horns plenty of times, Lee, but your father is doing what he thinks is right."

Natalie shot back her indignant comment on that almost breathlessly. "But, you don't know anything about production or those other things, Chaney."

"He knows that, sweetheart. His objective is to make me or break me. His opinion of me isn't very high, but I got the feeling he wants me to succeed. Not because of *me*, Lee, because of *you*. And that's exactly the reason why I'm going to succeed."

"Chaney, darling, he should have given you some seasoned, practical factory-men to—"

"I'll choose those myself," explained Chaney. "I've already got one in mind. A man named Benedict."

They were sitting on the patio behind his house overlooking the garden in the soft glow of pre-dusk. Natalie had met him at the door with a kiss, and after making him go out back had gone to the pantry to mix two drinks. It was partly his highball, partly his recollection of the flint-on-steel meeting with her father, that made Chaney smile slightly as they talked.

" I think," he told her, " that your father isn't just being arbitrary, Lee. I think he probably got his start pretty much the way he's breaking me in." At her indignant expression, Chaney laughed aloud. " It's all right, baby. The point is—can I hack it or can't I? And I'm not some college kid who's learned a lot of theory from some academic fool who learned his subject from books. I'm a grown man who has already made my pile. Your father knows all those things. And there is more : he wants me to have to sweat a little; learn to be tough."

Natalie finally smiled, but it was a more understanding smile than an amused one. " You'll be tough enough," she said. " You'll succeed. It's just that I don't approve of his methods."

Chaney looked over tolerantly. " I won't approve of them either, if I fall flat on my face. But if I make the grade, I'll swear they're the best of all methods." He finished the drink. " About that surprise you had, for dinner . . ." He arose, still holding the highball glass. Dusk was fast settling. He leaned to help her up and at the same time placed his empty glass upon a little redwood table. " I told him I wouldn't be in tomorrow."

" Did he ask about me?" she wanted to know.

" No, except by innuendo." Chaney took her in his arms. " Old ironsides. I think that's what I'll call him. Ironsides Morrison." He kissed her tilted face. " I've never ducked a challenge in my life—but you *and* him

—well—that ought to be enough challenge to last a lifetime."

She snuggled close in his arms. "It had better be, Mr. Lincoln. Now would you care to stay out here making love to me, or go inside and have the special dinner your housekeeper and I prepared?"

"*Our* housekeeper," he corrected her. "As for the rest of that—what a foolish thing to ask a man."

They returned to the house, and while Chaney went to shower and change Natalie went out to put the finishing touches on dinner. She and his housekeeper had created a gourmet's supper complete with silver candlesticks and muted music from the stereo.

When Chaney came back, dressed casually and acting hungry, they served him, and he had to admit that, for a man to whom food had never meant very much, he was delighted. He may have felt part of that delight because across the table was the most beautiful woman he had ever known, her golden flesh-tones more subtle than ever by candlelight.

After dinner they returned to the patio, but she took him exploring with her. She had, she told him, spent the day getting acquainted with her new home. Her mother had called on the telephone but had wisely and discreetly not driven over.

Lee said her mother had wanted to know where they would be going on their honeymoon, and Chaney winced, because he remembered whispering of exotic places to her before their marriage. He said, "What did you tell her?"

Natalie leaned to smell a rose. "I told her that we might stay right here."

He watched her, waiting for her to straighten up and look at him, but she stepped over to another rose instead. He reached and pulled her back. "Why would you tell her that?"

"Chaney, I had a feeling something like this was going to happen as soon as you and my father sat down in his office. Anyway, why does a honeymoon have to be done right now, as though it were some kind of ecstatic penance?"

"Your father said you'd understand what it's like being married to someone who is, in turn, married to a damned factory."

She nodded. "That's true. After all, I grew up knowing what it's like."

"But you resented it, or didn't approve of it."

She smiled. "No, not really, sweetheart. I grew up understanding that life didn't just drop a big cheque in the post-box once a month." She paused, then said, "I wasn't so sure I'd ever marry a man who would be that involved in his work—but I did, didn't I?"

"I'll chuck it," he said, dropping both hands from her shoulders. "You'll be a full-time occupation with me, anyway."

She cocked her head. "You won't chuck it, and even if you wanted to, I wouldn't let you. If my father thinks he can browbeat you, I'm right here beside you to help prove how wrong he is."

Chaney laughed, and wagged his head. "What's worse than one bull-headed Morrison; I'll tell you— *two* bull-headed Morrisons."

The housekeeper came to say that Mr. Carroll was in the living-room. Chaney nodded and made a wry face as he took his wife's fingers to pull her along beside him. " Too bad everyone isn't as discreet as your mother," he grumbled, as they went through the silvery shadows to the house.

The solicitor looked as casually urbane as always, and offered his profuse congratulations at the same time that he said he'd been contacted three times by newspaper reporters who had picked up the rumour that the majority shareholder of Steel Fabricators had married the daughter of the president of the company.

Carroll smiled. " I told them you two would be more of an authority on that, than I would be."

Chaney offered Paul Carroll a drink, and when Carroll accepted Natalie said she'd get it and left the room. For a moment both men watched her depart, then Carroll turned and said, " Well; did Morrison offer to shoot you?"

Chaney smiled. " Not exactly. He did something almost as bad though. He dropped the entire Boeing contract in my lap."

Paul did not act very surprised, but he gazed at Chaney with a degree of mild doubt that did not escape Lincoln. " Do you think you can do it?" he asked, and dropped his bombshell in the same suave voice. " Because that's why I drove over tonight. There's an outfit headed by a man named Grover Smith that is very actively going after that contract."

Chaney shrugged. " Let him. The contract is signed, Paul. It's Steel Fabricators' property."

Carroll got mildly thoughtful. " Well, but you see, Chaney, the Boeing negotiators aren't all that satisfied. They have a cancellation clause, as I'm sure you know if you've seen the contract. It would enable them to stop production even if Steel Fabricators were already turning in acceptable work."

Chaney stared, then he swore and strode to the nearest telephone, dialled Alfred Morrison, and the moment he had the older man on the line he said, "I want a copy of that Boeing contract sent over here tonight."

Old Morrison laughed with a sound of stones falling. "Lincoln, it's past eight o'clock."

"Mr. Morrison, I don't give a damn if it's three in the morning. I've got to see a copy of that contract tonight."

Morrison's tone changed slightly. "Why? What's wrong?"

Chaney did not explain he simply asked if Morrison knew someone named Grover Smith. Morrison growled a bleak reply. "Know him? I fired him two years ago for trying to sell us out. He went with a new company called Metal Components. What about him?"

"He's hot after the Boeing contract," said Chaney. "That's what about him. And tell me one more thing : how sound is the cancellation clause in that Boeing contract?"

"Standard," replied Morrison. "Are you suggesting that Smith is trying to get Boeing to cancel us out?"

Chaney looked at Paul Carroll rather flintily as he replied to the question. "Something like that."

Morrison's reply was forceful. Chaney cut through it to reiterate his demand for a copy of the contract within the next hour or two, and put down the telephone shortly before Natalie returned with a tray holding three highballs. Paul Carroll, accepting his drink with a quiet compliment for Natalie gave Chaney time enough to get over his angry frustration. He went over to take the drink Natalie offered, and to kiss her cheek with all the solemn and grim resolve of a man who was not going to allow bad news to ruin what his wife thought was probably just a pleasant social call on Carroll's part. But she fooled him, as she would continually do in the years ahead, by guessing at once that something was wrong.

They told her. She said she knew Grover Smith; had in fact gone dancing with him a couple of times about three and a half years ago. He was an aggressive, ambitious man who had divorced his wife shortly after going to work for Natalie's father.

" If anyone can make real trouble," she told Paul and Chaney, " I'd say it's Grover. Also, I think he'd do anything he could to strike back at my father for firing him."

Paul sipped his drink, sat comfortably on a sofa and seemed even more relaxed and unruffled than usual. " Of course," he said, " you can get an injunction prohibiting this Grover Smith from interfering, Chaney, but the trouble with doing something like that is simply that he can counter-sue, and before you know it the contract will be lost in the dust of a lot of suits and countersuits."

Chaney hadn't even considered anything like that. He was not a lawyer and his mind did not work the same way. " How busy are you right now?" he asked, and when Paul shrugged, Chaney said, " Good. From now on consider yourself part of my staff at Steel Fabricators."

Paul winked at Natalie and smiled at Chaney. "I'm flattered. Being connected with one of the oldest and largest and most respected industrial—"

"Fly north tomorrow," exclaimed Chaney, firing the words at Carroll, "to the Boeing administrative offices, Paul, and take anyone to dinner that you have to, but get it firmly across to Boeing that Steel Fabricators will be in production by next Monday, and will meet each delivery schedule. Make it so clear they won't even listen to anyone like this Grover Smith." Chaney smiled wolfishly. "You could also hint, if it seems that this might help, that as a lawyer who is retained by Steel Fabricators' majority shareholder, you are certain any attempt at cancellation will land Boeing in court the very next day."

Carroll sipped his highball gazed at Chaney and after a moment gently inclined his head. "I always wanted to be one of those lawyers who jet around the world negotiating contracts for huge industrial empires." He swung his attention to Natalie. "You're good for him, you know. I've worried about him this past year; he kept getting more restless and irritable. He needed something. Not just a wife, although he certainly needed that too, but he needed some kind of tough challenge, and I think that, through you, he's finally got it." Paul put his partially consumed drink aside and arose with a gentle smile.

Chaney laughed. "You *think* I got a tough challenge," he exclaimed. "Paul, you don't know *how* tough a challenge."

The three of them went out to Carroll's car and as the lawyer drove away, another car turned in down at the kerbing. Natalie sighed aloud. " Father and mother," she said, and squeezed Chaney's hand. " Well, at least we had a little time together this evening."

He looked quickly at her, but she met his concerned expression easily. " That's how it goes, lover; I've seen it happen all my life." She raised up to peck his cheek before the oncoming car was close, then she said, " I'll take mother through the house, show her the patio and the garden, and you are supposed to take my father into the bar-room or the study, and foul the air with tobacco smoke while you plan strategy." She winked up at him. " What was it the solicitor said—you needed a challenge? Lover, today you most certainly accepted one."

EIGHTEEN

Morrison's Final Challenge

NATALIE WAS correct on both counts, Chaney had certainly accepted a challenge when he'd decided to go with Steel Fabricators, and when his in-laws entered the house, right after he had greeted Mrs. Morrison, Natalie's father muttered some kind of brusque greeting, then brought out a thick envelope from a jacket pocket and asked if they could go to the study.

Chaney saw Natalie's look, and smiled ruefully at her. He took Morrison down the short corridor to the room with the Beautiful Lady on the wall, and offered him a drink which Morrison refused as he grunted down into a large chair and handed the thick envelope to Chaney as he spoke.

"That's my personal copy of the contract. The original is down at the factory. What is it you specifically wish to know; the details of the penalty clause?"

Chaney tossed the envelope upon the desk. "The details of the cancellation clause," he said.

Morrison nodded, not at all surprised. "It's a typical failure-to-perform clause. Boeing can cancel the contract if Steel Fabricators does not abide by Boeing's quality-control standards, fails to abide by the delivery schedules, and so forth."

"And suppose Boeing decided before any deliveries were due that someone else—this Grover Smith for example—might be able to do the job better?"

Morrrison smiled. "Not much chance of that. In the first place Boeing is not a gyppo outfit. In the second place we've done quite a bit of work for Boeing in the past and have always had excellent relations. In the third place, Grover has a reputation for being a good hustler and a damned poor deliverer." Morrison fished out one of his cigars and lit it, stretched his legs out and leaned back comfortably in the chair. He was different under these circumstances than he'd been in his office at the complex. He acted almost patronising, but amiably so. "Now you know what I meant when I mentioned the sharks, big ones and little ones, but all swimming around waiting for an opening to tear you to shreds."

"The homilies I don't particularly need," said

Chaney. "I just don't know very much about this business yet so I'm perhaps making issues where none actually exist. On the other hand I have no intention of making any serious mistakes."

Morrison nodded and said nothing. He seemed in agreement with Chaney's statement. He studied the delicate white ash on his cigar, then turned and slowly gazed round the study, letting his eyes rest upon the oil painting of the beautiful girl. That arrested his attention for quite a while. When Chaney spoke again, Morrison pulled his gaze from the Beautiful Lady and became quietly attentive.

"I sent my lawyer to the Boeing administrative offices. He's to fly out tomorrow."

Morrison's brows settled lower. "What the hell for?"

"To ascertain just what this Grover Smith can do, and what he might do. He, and all the others like him. And to also assure Boeing that we will meet all schedules."

Morrison thought about that for a moment before commenting. "I think, after this, before you do anything like that, you should consult me. Boeing doesn't need to be threatened nor interrogated. We have the contract. All we have to do is meet its requirements. That's all. Starting on Monday we go into production. Can you call your lawyer and cancel that visit?"

"Yes."

"Do it," said Morrison. "When we're going full-blast and you can get away for a few days, fly to the head office yourself, you and Lee. Meet their executives; cultivate a few of them, then, later on when you have a problem, just pick up the telephone in your office. Incidentally, I've had the office next to mine put in shape for you."

Morrison smiled, but his hard old eyes were still steely. He puffed on his cigar and kept studying Chaney, which was an uncomfortable sensation for Chaney, but he weathered it easily enough.

"I've assigned a bright young man from Engineering as your aide. His name's Horton."

"Benedict," said Chaney, "from Production Planning."

Morrison puffed a moment, then gently inclined his head. "Yes, of course, I should have known. I've been on the verge of having him fired for the past couple of months. I should have known you'd like him. He's contentious, tireless in his criticisms, and, as far as I'm concerned, a thorn in the flesh."

"I want a few thorns," said Chaney.

Morrison kept up his pitiless study. "Crawl before you walk. No one ever changed a factory or the world overnight. Be sceptical of everything Benedict or anyone else tells you. Remember, Lincoln, you are the only one who can make you fail. Every judgement will be strictly yours, as far as I'm concerned."

Chaney said, "Save the lecture. That one in your office this afternoon got the idea across very well."

Morrison put aside his half-smoked cigar. "There is a man named Sanderson in our Contract Department; whenever you need information about people like Grover Smith, talk to Sanderson. He's known them all, has competed with most of them, and can give you a thorough break-down."

Chaney tucked away that name for future reference.

Morrison made a slow, slow smile. His hard gaze turned saturnine. He said, " Natalie's mother and I are going to Bermuda for two or three weeks, Chaney. We'll be leaving day after tomorrow."

The blow was so sudden that Chaney quite missed being called by his given name for the first time. He leaned upon the front of his desk looking at the older man. It was on the tip of his tongue to protest, to perhaps swear a little in outrage at being abandoned like this before he'd even got the feel of the factory, and his new position. The reason he curbed the desire to upbraid the older man was because of that slow, slow smile.

Morrison was doing this on purpose; he had been tough on Chaney right from the start. He was going to be tougher. There was not going to be any probationary period at all. Chaney was on his own, and that was exactly how old Morrison had probably planned it right from the start.

As though Chaney's expression did not reflect his indignation, and still smiling, Morrison said, " That's where Lee's mother and I went on our honeymoon a long time ago. Of course it'll be all changed, but still, she wants to go back and so do I. You know, there's nothing as refreshing as walking barefoot down a clean beach with white sails on a blue sea right beside you."

Morrison got heavily up to his feet, considered his smouldering cigar, decided against retrieving it, and gazed again at the oil painting. While doing this he said, " You know, Chaney, I never did believe in babying people; the only ones who make it in this life are the ones who don't need anyone. That doesn't mean people may not *want* other people around. It means that if they had to do it alone, they could." He kept studying the painting. " That's a beautiful oil. She's got the same colour eyes as Natalie. You wouldn't care to sell it would you?"

Chaney said the painting was not for sale and old Morrison shook his head. He professed to know nothing about art beyond the ability to appreciate something that pleased him, which of course was all basic art appreciation was, for anyone.

Chaney wondered if he shouldn't ask for some instructions. He decided not to for two reasons : one, Morrison had probably already told his other executives what was to be done in his absence, and that majority-shareholder Chaney Lincoln would be chief while Morrison was gone, and the second reason Chaney did not ask was because he thought Morrison was standing there admiring his oil painting waiting for Chaney to do just exactly that; he'd be damned to the nethermost hell before he'd give the old devil that much satisfaction.

Morrison turned from the painting and watched Chaney light a cigarette. His gaze was hard, unrelenting, and faintly, sardonically amused. His expression said very plainly that since Chaney Lincoln had committed himself, as far as Morrison was concerned, he was going to have everything thrown at him that could be thrown.

Chaney blew smoke, met the older man's gaze, and decided that from tonight on he would develop the knack of anticipating things as old Morrison had advised him to do at the office; he would be prepared for every contingency, starting right now. He smiled and said, "Have a good trip, and if a couple of weeks isn't enough, stay down there for a month."

Morrison's sardonic amusement faded. He did not lower his eyes and they got a faintly suspicious look as he pushed both hands into trouser pockets and said, "You'll have plenty of experienced help. The department heads have been briefed."

"When?"

"This afternoon."

"Why wasn't I notified that there would be an executive meeting?"

Morrison's last vestiges of humour blinked out and his face reddened slightly. Chaney did not give him the opportunity to be brusque.

"Look, Mr. Morrison, hereafter whenever there's any kind of executive conference I want to be notified. I don't give a damn if its purpose is only to discuss the new shade of paint to be used in the rest-rooms, I want to sit in."

Morrison stood like a stone image, his red face showing anger, but he kept control rather admirably for a man who had not had to practise much self-restraint with subordinates. "You will get a memo from my secretary every time," he conceded. "Now about my absence . . ."

"Just have a nice holiday," said Chaney, and pushed up off the desk and strode past to the doorway. "I think we ought to join the ladies now." He stood aside politely waiting for old Morrison to precede him out of the room. "You haven't forgotten I won't be in tomorrow, have you?"

Morrison turned to follow Chaney with his eyes but

he still did not move out of his tracks, and he did not reply to Chaney's last question. "If you get cocky, or think you can buy yourself out of any mistakes you make," he said a bit grimly, "forget it. I'll be back in three weeks at the most."

"Yeah," exclaimed Chaney, "and the day you return you'll call in all your department heads for a confidential report on the progress of Chaney Lincoln. Remember what I said : I am notified of *any* executive meetings. That means *all* of them. As for getting cocky, don't worry about it. You want to throw obstacles at me, fine, I'll accept them, but you'd better adjust to the idea that I'm going to be down there making damned certain schedules are met. Now, let's go and join the ladies."

Morrison moved, finally, but he still looked red and upset. He said no more, though, until just before they left the hallway heading in the direction of the sitting-room, then he halted just short of the far exit and said, "About Natalie; I suppose she told you about her first husband."

Chaney nodded, watching Morrison struggle with himself because he was not a man who gave confidences very readily.

"Well; he was a very handsome man, Chaney, and as weak and worthless as most dreamers are." Morrison was not looking at Chaney, and he was also scowling slightly as he spoke. "You are probably as near to being his opposite as a man could be."

"So?"

"Well, I don't exactly know what I'm trying to say, except that she isn't very hard, and that she can be hurt easily." Morrison finally peered upwards from beneath bushy brows. "This other thing—it isn't going to be easy for you, and maybe I'm doing everything all wrong, because if I make you crack or if I make you bring it all home each night and you take it out on her . . ."

Chaney said, "Look, you knocked me out to the tune of half a million dollars; did I rush down there and take it out on you, or did I take it out on her because she initially went along with you?" Chaney stepped past and turned. "They're in the sitting-room, I can hear them. We'd better join them."

This time it was Morrison on the defensive, Chaney on the offensive; neither of them accepted the difference as indicative of anything; men like them never did. Like professional soldiers, they were the kind of men who understood that victory never remained permanently with anyone, any more than defeat did, but that each skirmish was something independent of all other skirmishes, and what really mattered was never the battles but end result of the entire campaign.

They strode along side-by-side heading towards the liquid-soft sounds of female voices, and as far as Chaney was concerned, he was already beginning to accept the enormous responsibility that had been dumped in his lap.

NINETEEN

One Day Together

It was past ten o'clock before the Morrisons left, and Chaney went at once to telephone Paul and cancel his instructions about Carroll's flight east.

Natalie stood in the study doorway listening. When Chaney put down the telephone she asked if her father had mentioned holidaying in Bermuda. Chaney laughed at his wife's expression. "Cheer up," he said, "it's not all that bad."

Lee was not placated. "It was a terrible thing to do to you. Mother and I both agreed that it was. But she didn't want it brought up when all four of us were together."

Chaney could appreciate that. "Not when it's the first time we sat down as family," he said, rising from behind the carved desk. "They deserve a holiday don't they, lover?"

"Well, of course, but not right at this point, Chaney."

He went over to her, smiling. "Look, you are going to undermine my confidence always talking as though your father ought to be right behind me in case I sag a little."

"It's a whole lot more than just sagging a little," she

retorted with spirit, "and anyway, he's being unnecessarily rough with you."

"Would you believe me, Lee, if I said I prefer it this way?"

She looked at him with a small frown. "No one likes being figuratively stood up against a wall, Chaney."

He laughed and took her hand. "You're making it a lot worse than it is. Come along; let's go out in the garden for a bit."

The house was warm. It was also redolent of tobacco-scent, but beyond the french doors, on the patio, night-air as clean as though Smog-City was not only about twenty miles south-easterly, was cool and fragrant. There was a thicker moon than there had been the previous few nights. There were also more stars in view, or at least it seemed so to Chaney as he stood with her admiring the night, the tree-shadows, and the dull colour of the blooms his yardman managed to always have on display.

She leaned close to him and sighed. "Why does life always have to be a matrix of light and dark?"

He turned, her face was lifted towards the far stars. He remembered her father's one weak moment before they had entered the sitting-room; that comment about how easily Natalie could be hurt, and he kissed her cheek before answering.

"What would it be like if life was always sweet and serene? People's moods aren't always conducive to those things."

She smiled at him. "Usually orphans—well, *near-*orphans then—never quite come to grips with life, but you've done it."

"Not very commendably," he said truthfully. "I lashed out too, but my idea was to lash out and make it pay—in cash."

"And now?"

He matched her soft smile. "That's something else about life; it's a process of constant change, isn't it? Well, I'm poised for the leap, but frankly, trusting people has never been my strongest virtue." His eyes brightened. "I don't really have any strong virtues, only a few meagre and weak ones. But I'm going to make that leap anyway because that's required for this phase of change in my life. Like marriage, like falling in love, like laying down the law to your father when he did the same to me." He paused. "I'm not so sure that's really coming to grips with life though."

"No? Then what would you call it, Chaney?"

He didn't know. Maybe it *was* coming to grips; maybe she was correct, but for the time being he wasn't going to get bogged down in any rose-garden philosophy. He said, "Later, after the moon has gone down," and leered until she said, "Men!" and walked out into the night towards a spiky border of conifer-hedge.

When he came close again he gestured. "See; no dahlia plants." She turned and without any coyness or subterfuge laughed at him.

"They're sinister aren't they, lover?"

He nodded. "And it showed on the stems where you had cut them."

"You noticed?"

"Sure; as soon as you said you wanted to show me your garden I decided to look for dahlia plants. There they were, black and, as you say, sinister, with the clipped stems. Tell me something : was it a threat or a warning?"

She thought, then said, " Both. Shall I send one to Grover Smith?"

" No. I think you ought to reserve this unique distinction only for very special villains. If he's no more dangerous than your father seems to think, it would demean the black dahlias."

They went out where the largest trees stood, and watched a military aircraft soar overhead—it's lights did not blink on and off like the lights of civilian aircraft. He told her of his army service in Asia, and when she asked, he told her of some of the tales of his boyhood and maturing years. He chose only amusing or interesting little vignettes; he would tell her of the bitterness the pain and resentment later, because she would want to know, but not tonight.

She, in turn, told him a little about her first husband, about her life as a young girl, and finally how she had worked out a philosophy that made a lot of the things that had happened, and which she could not understand, easier to bear and live with.

She was not a fatalist; she wasn't mentally lazy so fatalism wouldn't have appealed to her. But she *was* capable of accepting the things she could not change, and that was very much in her favour.

They remained in the garden until past midnight. He would have been perfectly content to stay even longer because she was with him, and also because it was a beautiful, warm night, but she said he needed his rest, that aside from the things they had to do the next day, have blood-tests and get their licence to marry—

belatedly, but still, the law insisted that it be bought and paid for—she wanted to have dinner up along the coast somewhere because tomorrow was a special day.

He didn't really resist at all. By the time she was through with all that explaining he had lit a cigarette and was regarding her in the soft gloom with fond tolerance. She saw his expression and said, " Am I being domineering?"

That tickled him. "Well, maybe a little bossy, but not really domineering."

She went into his arms, he dropped the cigarette in the dewy grass and for a moment the only sound was made by the cigarette's cherry-red tip as it succumbed hissingly to moisture.

She stirred after a moment to say the telephone was ringing. He hadn't heard it, and he wasn't particularly interested anyway, not even to the extent of being curious as to who might be calling so late. They let it ring itself into silence, but moments later, Natalie freed herself and pulled him along towards the patio.

No question about it, it was late.

For Chaney it had been a somewhat traumatic day and evening, but his resiliency was equal to all he'd gone through. He was so sure of that he passed up Lee's offer of hot chocolate before they retired; he had always been able to adjust to the exigencies of the immediate moment, while at the same time being prepared for the next one.

But he fooled himself by barely getting into bed before going off to sleep. Lee leaned to kiss him and he stirred, but that was all. She wanted to laugh but didn't.

The following morning she was already up, showered

and dressed before he stirred, and even after opening his eyes to the deplorable world of a celibate bridegroom, he did not move very fast. Evidently there really was a limit to the amount of nervous strain he could take.

She and the housekeeper were laughing in the kitchen by the time Chaney got out there for breakfast. When the housekeeper's back was turned, and kept turned for some time, she kissed him, clung to him, and afterwards made a little giggle that only he and she understood— at least they *thought* they were the only ones, but the housekeeper, although now a widow, had been married many years too, and regardless of how old a person got, memories never aged at all.

After breakfast they took her car for the drive down to the licensing bureau. It seemed foolish he said, and she agreed, that the red-tape had to be complied with. With an almost Latin shrug she said, " That's life, lover."

Getting blood-tests was quicker, and also slightly more uncomfortable, but the fee was the same in both instances. It was slightly past noon when all the requirements had been complied with, so they went to a Wilshire Boulevard restaurant for luncheon where the food was supposedly unsurpassed anywhere on the West Coast. Chaney had eaten there before. His opinion was that the only unsurpassed attribute of the establishment was the amount of the tab.

Here, Natalie met some friends and introduced them to her husband. They hadn't heard the rumours, evidently, because they were mildly stunned, but full of seemingly genuine congratulations. As soon as they walked out to her car she told him she had always suspected the wife of that duo she had introduced him to, picked up her pin-money by selling gossip to the newspaper rumour-mills.

"This will be a perfect way to find out, won't it?" she said, "and what will all the other shareholders say?"

He didn't know what they'd say and he didn't give a very big damn, either.

Her blue car purred its way out towards Santa Monica and the sea, from Beverly Hills. There shouldn't have been as much traffic as there was, not in the early afternoon when presumably most people were at their desks somewhere, but as a matter of fact there was only slightly less traffic than there was on any summertime Sunday.

Neither Lee nor Chaney liked traffic, but neither did they particularly dislike it. When she mentioned it today, he said it was simply one of those small discomforts she'd referred to when they'd been discussing the redundant requirements the law imposed on lovers back at the licensing bureau.

"That's life, lover," he said, quoting her and smiling as he did so. "Where, in particular, did you want to have dinner?"

Without batting an eye as she tooled the Jaguar onto the Coast Highway ramp, heading northward, she said, "Santa Barbara."

He looked, but she wasn't being facetious. "That's a hundred miles from here," he said.

Her answer was typically feminine. "Well, lover, you won't be hungry before then, anyway, will you?"

He wouldn't be, but then if they'd only gone half that distance it would have suited him just as well.

As soon as they had got beyond the smell and sound of the city though, he loosened and actually began to enjoy himself. The sea was as smooth as green glass, all the close-in beaches were crowded with people, and the sun, for a change was warm without being as hot as it usually was. He settled comfortably at her side, and without having any such intention at all, fell asleep. She was careful not to get into any positions where she'd have to use her brakes suddenly, and slowed a little as well.

The sun got round to where it would have been squarely in her eyes but for the tinted windscreen and the little visors she could lower and adjust. Otherwise, it was a very pleasant drive. Even the traffic eventually thinned out, or perhaps that wasn't quite true, perhaps it was just that the farther one drove away from Los Angeles and its environs upon the majestic new high - ways, which were so enormously wide and sleek, that the traffic was simply less congested and noticeable.

She gauged her speed against the time of day, thought they would probably arrive in Santa Barbara about six or six-thirty in the late afternoon, and did not increase speed to get up there any sooner.

After a while Chaney opened his eyes, sat perfectly relaxed for a few moments remembering where he was and what he was doing there, then he straightened a bit and yawned.

Natalie laughed at him. "Enjoy it while you can, lover, because I think that starting tomorrow, you're going to wish you'd be able to get away once in a while and rest."

He was a bit derisive about that. "You don't know

your husband very well. I'll come bouncing home every night ready for new worlds to conquer."

She could have reminded him that as a conqueror he hadn't accomplished very much the night before, but she simply reached over to hold his hand as she drove towards the discernible outskirts of the yonder city, and said nothing at all. Wise women didn't about as often as they did, and that was what made them wise women.

TWENTY

The Day of Grace

THEY HAD dinner at a secluded restaurant with a good bit of Spanish, or Moorish, wrought-iron metal work on the tiled patio where their table stood. A nearby giant catalpa tree had pale blooms almost as large as cabbages. Natalie said she loved this restaurant; the food wasn't anything to write home about although it was good enough, but the atmosphere, she told Chaney with soft-bright eyes, reminded her of some peaceful, quiet part of old Spain.

The city was all around them, but it was different from most California cities; originally created as a retirement area for wealthy people, Santa Barbara had not been allowed to grow and expand and go industrial until very recently, and even now there were still enough powerful, influential residents to hold the lines of restrictive activity.

Chaney had been up there often but he had never seen this particular restaurant before. Over a pale Napa Valley wine he said he hadn't been able to arrive at what kind of a wedding present to buy her yet. "How about this restaurant? Then we could drive up here and have dinner every now at then."

She showed how much she appreciated his gesture with a sultry, grateful look, but she also said if he wasn't just teasing her, if he were serious, he should see a psychiatrist, then they both laughed.

There were birds in the ancient catalpa tree that evidently were accustomed to people and lights down below. They didn't scold but every now and then one of them, quite hidden in very dark green foliage, would make a little drowsy sound as though perhaps reassuring himself that his mate was close by on the same limb.

The music that was piped from inside the restaurant where most conventional diners chose to have dinner, was like the settling dusk; warm and vibrant, and perfectly appropriate to the mood of the lovers at their private table out on the patio.

Natalie asked if Chaney really liked to dance, or if he'd danced with her that night at the country club just because he'd wanted to know her.

"That particular night was special," he admitted. "I wanted to learn all about you. If you'd suggested going out fully clothed and diving into the pool, I'd have thought that was quite all right too. But yes, I like to dance." He finished his wine and considered his dinner. "Except that you've spoilt me for ever dancing with other women."

She re-filled his wine glass with a look of gentle concentration. "I'm not a good dancer but I love dancing. Especially Latin American dancing."

She was a very good dancer and he insisted on this point. She lifted her face and said, "Is this like that adage about beauty being in the eye of the beholder; are you saying that because you—?"

"I'm saying it because it's true. And beauty isn't just in the eye of the beholder. Do you remember the afternoon we played tennis? Every man we walked past turned and looked, and looked some more. There's simply no one like you, that's all; it's not just my opinion."

She looked very close to being genuinely embarrassed as she laughingly said, "As long as you believe that, Chaney, no one else on earth has to look at all."

A waiter came to offer dessert and to clear away their plates. He also poured wine into their glasses. Chaney watched this with some doubt and after the man had departed he said, "It looks mild and it tastes delicious, but another glass or two and I won't be fit for the drive back."

Natalie raised large, smokerise-coloured eyes. "Lover, we're not going back tonight."

He looked blankly at her.

"Didn't I mention it? I'm so terribly sorry if I forgot. I phoned up early this morning and made reservations for us at one of the beautiful little country-club cottages overlooking the sea. " She kept her face expressionless as long as possible, but the dumbshow expression he retained finally shattered her control and she leaned over to laugh. " Don't you like surprises?" she asked, when the laughter ended.

He picked up the wine glass and made a high dip with it as though saluting her. " *This* kind of a surprise I most certainly do like." He drank and put the glass aside. " Are you ready to go?"

She looked up where the moon was becoming visible above their catalpa tree. " I'm finished with dinner, if that's what you mean, lover, but we're not going to the cottage right away."

He watched her put aside the napkin and rise. " We're not?"

" No, sweetheart," she said in her most tender voice. " First, we're going to hold our shoes in our hands and walk along the beach, through the surf."

He got up, sighed and dropped two large notes atop the silver salver where their waiter had discreetly left the tab. " I can't even walk across a tiled floor in my bare feet," he said, resignedly, but when she took his arm he did not hesitate.

She knew the area very well, and when he asked about that she said that as a child she'd visited an aunt who had lived in Santa Barbara. As soon as school was over with for the summer, she would come up here for a few weeks with her aunt.

While she explained about this, she was driving down to the seashore, and instead of turning northward up the moonlit rolling shoreline, she turned southward where the same high, mustard-coloured barrancas stood guard against the surf. Chaney was an observer. Of course he had been up there before, many times in fact, but he was nowhere nearly as familiar with the area as she obviously was.

Finally, where a rather steep incline led downward off the highway, the Jaguar dipped its nose towards a long, pale silver of beach. Natalie made a wide turn at the base of the hill, parked, cut the switch and jumped out with a laugh at Chaney's dubious expression.

There was a fire northward on the beach, close to the sea, where people were evidently enjoying themselves, but otherwise the beach was empty. She led him down to where the sand began, then sat on a small bench to remove her shoes and stockings. He did the same but without the same abandon. He also removed his tie and jacket.

There was always the possibility of encountering broken beer bottles or sharp bits of discarded metal in the sand, on almost any beach, anywhere, but when he mentioned this she took his hand to lead him along, and thought that he was being needlessly inhibited.

The sand was warm, the air smelled of sea-salt, the sky was wonderfully clear, and off on their right as they strolled along, was the restless surf.

A low sea was running. On their right was the unchangeable world of sea and kelp. Where the moon touched, making pewter paths over shiny dark water, nothing had changed in a million years, while on their left, simply by looking up, they could see twin headlamps busily passing back and forth over the expressway, and beyond, where men had been altering the land and terracing the slopes for centuries, until there was very little left of the world that had been, on the land side.

Natalie turned with a soft smile of encouragement. "When I was a little girl I loved to do this—walk on the empty beaches barefoot in the moonlight. Isn't it fun, Chaney?"

He was beginning to enjoy it, actually. Having encountered nothing hazardous, at least yet anyway, he could appreciate why she had liked it. There was some kind of primitive pleasure in walking along next to the rolling surf and feeling soft damp, sand underfoot. It was, he thought, very close to being a kind of therapy.

He slid an arm round her waist as he agreed that it was pleasant. Once, when he turned to look back, that bonfire seemed no more than a match-flare. He wondered how far they were from the car. As though she thought this meant he might suggest they turn back, Natalie kept him going until they were in sight of a low, serrated yellowish cliff on the land-side, where many years earlier people had planted coarse shrubs to stabilise the loose soil against winter's sea-assaults. There too, was a kind of cement pavilion but without a roof, and carved into the base of the sloping old yellow barranca was a little grotto where a very old brass figurine of some nameless saint stood with both feet firmly set in a massive stone.

The place was quiet and pleasant when she led him up to it. There were stone benches facing the sea. She explained that the metal saint was someone the fishermen who had once lived hereabouts taking their living from the sea, had venerated. It had originally sat atop the barranca but a group of citizens, wishing to preserve what it had stood for, had rescued it from the weeds and had created this little secluded niche for it.

He sat on a stone bench, wiggled his toes to free them of clinging sand, and watched a sea-going vessel not more than a mile off-shore, ploughing northward like a phantom.

Natalie came to sit next to him. She beamed a lovely smile and sought his hand. "It's wonderful here, isn't it? Sometimes when it gets too hot people come down here and bring blankets. The surf lulls you to sleep."

He could believe that. He also knew from experience that while the surf lulled a person to sleep, sand-fleas prevented them from getting too much sleep. Perhaps not up here on the large cement slab beside the grotto, but down there a few yards on the sand.

He watched how the moonbeams rode each breaker, shimmering silver against the strong turbulence of dark water. Sitting here like that, watching, totally relaxed and comfortable, he allowed the sea to work its hypnotic magic. He turned and said if he sat much longer he was going to fall asleep.

"Not tonight you won't," she answered, putting her head on his shoulder. "Should we start back?"

He nodded and continued to sit watching the running of the tide. Tomorrow was a million miles away; even when he thought of it, the greater thing in his life so filled him there was no room for tomorrow. He didn't even wonder what time he would get to the factory, nor did he feel guilt over what he was doing tonight, more than a hundred miles from where he would have to be tomorrow morning.

It was improbable that they could return to Los Angeles in time for him to reach the factory when the executives were supposed to check in, unless of course they rose very early tomorrow morning and drove back before daylight; it didn't worry him. Nothing worried him right at the moment.

Finally, Natalie stood up and held both hands out to him. He smiled, rose, held one hand as they crossed to the edge of the pavilion and started back the way they had come, but closer to the surf this time, so that they left temporary footprints in the glistening sand to be washed away with each surge of the riffles.

She was thoughtful on the walk back. When he offered a penny for her thoughts she said it really wasn't like her father to do what he was doing, just go off and leave his factory to run itself, unless he felt confident that Chaney could handle whatever might come up, and even then she couldn't quite equate this kind of even temporary abandonment with her father, as she knew him.

Chaney had no trouble with that kind of speculation because, as he told her, the executives ran the factory anyway, they were all experienced, knowledgeable men. All her father had done was make major decisions, and with new production starting, the decisions to be made would be technical. There would really be no need for any policy decisions to be made. What Chaney did *not* mention was that for the two or three weeks her parents would be gone, *he* was the one who would be walking the razor's edge. He kept this to himself because he was fairly confident, and also because he didn't want to dredge up her earlier anxieties about this. Not tonight.

By the time they reached the car her mood had changed. As they sat brushing sand off their feet and legs she laughed and teased him. " You did famously," she exclaimed. " You didn't step on a rusty tin or a piece of glass, and it was good for you to take that walk."

He smiled at her as she leaned to put on her shoes. " But I'd never make a beachcomber."

They entered the car and she turned it, heading back up the incline towards the highway that would take them back towards the city. He had never seen the country club at Santa Barbara but he could imagine that it would be very attractive. He could even visualise the cottage she had reserved. It would sit atop a barranca facing the sea and be surrounded by lush vegetation and seclusion. He leaned back in the car, watched her profile as she drove unerringly towards their cottage, and felt entirely at peace with the world. He had never before had quite this same feeling of total resignation and total willingness. It was as though he had somehow managed to slip through a slot in Time, and had come to rest in a place where he would never have to brood or struggle again. Of course that was an illusion, but he liked it very much and for the time being he lived every second of it.

TWENTY-ONE

One More Shocker

HIS REFLECTIONS of the night before respecting his ultimate arrival at the factory back down in Los Angeles were correct. He did not enter the air-conditioned lobby of the executive building until almost high noon, and it was clear from the smile of the receptionist and everyone else he encountered on his way to the office old Morrison had had prepared for him, that everyone knew who he was, what his position would be during Alfred Morrison's absence, and perhaps even that he was also majority shareholder—and was married to Natalie Morrison.

There was no way to underestimate the capacity of factory people to find things out, because they showed what they knew in their smiles and little deferential salutes as Chaney progressed down the carpeted corridor to his new office. Also, Morrison's private secretary was already in place in Chaney's outer office when he walked in, and greeted him with pleasant warmth and no surprise at all; he knew that the receptionist was a fast hand at the telephone.

The greying and handsome secretary, whose name was Eva Heath, said that Derek Benedict was waiting to see Mr. Lincoln. Chaney nodded thoughtfully about that. " Did you send for him, or was this Mr. Morrison's work?" he asked.

" Mr. Morrison's," said the secretary. " He telephoned me quite late last night."

Chaney went on through to his new office. It was large and airy and beautifully furnished, and although it was up where the eaves were visible out either picture-window, it had two ornate grilles high in two walls that piped in temperature-controlled cool air.

There was a small bar built into one panelled wall, and near the south window, that overlooked most of the plant and the extensive grounds, there was a little marble-topped table holding the means for serving coffee. Chaney had just finished his inspection when Benedict walked in and the executive secretary closed the door after him, very softly.

Benedict's pipe protruded from an upper jacket pocket. He regarded Chaney with a wary expression, and did not move out of his tracks until Chaney offered coffee and said, " I've asked to have you assigned to me as my personal assistant. I don't know what your title will be, because I don't even know what my title is." Chaney leaned to figure out which setting would produce best results on the electric percolator and Benedict came over to stand a little closer as Chaney went on speaking. " You won't get any raise in pay, and you'll probably have to put in some overtime until I'm firmly in the saddle." Chaney set the timer on the percolator, set the dial for the kind of coffee he wanted, and straightened up to smile at Derek Benedict. " Well, give that thing ten minutes and I'll know whether my first independent achievement at Steel Fabricators has been a success or not."

They laughed together, and Derek Benedict loosened up. " I was told I'd probably be fired for what I said to you the other day, Mr. Lincoln."

Chaney motioned for Benedict to be seated and refrained from mentioning that, in fact, there had been some kind of termination-sentiment in the air. " If you work out," he said, " you'll stay as long as I do. If you don't work out, you'll leave damned soon." Chaney didn't sit behind the massive desk but took one of the other chairs around the room. He lit a cigarette, offered the pack, and discovered that Benedict only used a pipe.

"Your baby will be the Boeing contract—all aspects of it, day and night, like it was your wife, Derek; if you only *think* something might go wrong you come directly to me. Don't wait until there's a breakdown; anticipate it. Don't pay a damned bit of attention what other people say, including Mr. Morrison. You will be responsible only to me. You enter this office any time you feel you have to. Don't knock. I'll pass instructions to the receptionist about this. Now then tell me just one thing. Can you do what I want; do you feel capable of doing it, and are you willing to do it without any reservations?"

Derek Benedict's eyes were twinkling in a tough way as he fished out his pipe and went rummaging for his pouch. "I can do it, Mr. Lincoln."

"Chaney. Chaney Lincoln. To hell with this executive demeanour crap. I have to produce results and you also have to produce them, so we'll start out as though this is a partnership and not a question of who's boss and who's the subordinate." Chaney blew smoke and watched Benedict fire up his pipe. "There is one more thing, Derek : you will sink or swim with me. If you like your job, if you want more money, which I'll see that you get as soon as I'm satisfied you're worth it, then you'd better bear one thing above all others in mind— you have to keep me in my job in order for me to keep you in your job."

Benedict still had that tough twinkle in his eyes. "I understand exactly—Chaney. If I can't handle it I'll let you know in plenty of time for both of us to bail out before the ship goes down." Benedict puffed a moment while he studied Chaney. Then he apparently came to some private decision because he removed the pipe and stopped smiling as he said, " We can handle the empennage contract; I don't have any serious doubts about that. And we'll deliver on schedule. As your assistant, or expeditor, or trouble-shooter, or go-to-hell-man, whatever it's called, I'll make certain of the line and the production—but what do we do about Mr. Morrison?"

Chaney leaned to punch out his cigarette. " What do you mean—what will we do about him? He's the president."

Derek Benedict's voice dropped a little as though he thought the walls might have ears. " I mean about his heart."

Chaney stared at the other man, with a slow premonition building up. " What about his heart?"

" I was out in the plant with him a couple of weeks ago, when he ran out of breath and had to sit down. Afterwards, I drove him home in mid-afternoon."

Chaney didn't really believe what he said, but that didn't prevent his saying it. The premonition got stronger by the second. " Well, he just got short-winded, Derek. It happens to everyone some time or other."

Benedict shook his head. " I described the symptoms to my father at dinner. He's a doctor. Without an examination and just guessing, he said it was heart trouble."

Chaney settled deeper in his chair feeling as though he'd just been struck from behind. Then he remembered what Morrison had said about always planning ahead, always anticipating events; that helped him to rally somewhat but the blow had been a hard one. Ultimately he rose and walked to the west-wall picture window where louvred blinds kept direct sunlight out. "Well, Derek, to start with we'll keep this strictly to ourselves. He didn't mention anything about any physical trouble to me, but then I don't visualise him doing that with anyone." Chaney turned, thinking of what Natalie's father had said about wanting to go back where he and his wife had spent their honeymoon. Chaney had no more than three weeks to prove himself capable, and this too had evidently been in Morrison's mind. Chaney rallied. "Okay, we'll star out by calling an executive meeting within the hour. After that, you pick the place where you'll want your office, and I'll see that it's arranged for. After that, drop by for coffee every damned morning, and the rest of the time don't let up on the assembly line and production for a minute." Chaney stood studying the pipe-puffing man across the room. "I hope to hell you work out," he said, and sounded almost as though that were a prayer.

Benedict stood up, and smiled. "*I* know I can do it," he assured Chaney. "For you, I guess, it'll just be a matter of waiting and seeing. Now, if that's all, I'll shove off."

Chaney smiled. He too was confident Derek Benedict could do the job. "Tell Mrs. . . . what's her name?"

"Eva Heath. Mrs. Heath."

"Tell Mrs. Heath she's to let you know every time there's an executive conference. Okay, now I'll start the wheels turning for the first one."

Benedict nodded, smiled at Chaney, and left the office with a springy step. Chaney remained over by the big window for perhaps ten minutes, before rousing himself from the grim speculations that had come out of the blue to cause him his worst moment thus far, and finally went out to tell the executive secretary to arrange for an executive meeting right at two o'clock.

"No excuses," he said. "Every executive department head is to be there."

Mrs. Heath turned briskly to her inter-plant telephone directory and Chaney returned to his private office to have another cup of coffee, and to think.

A lot of small things fell into place, finally. Old Morrison had probably been rough right from the start for exactly the reasons Chaney thought, but now it also appeared that he'd been that way for another, over-riding reason; he was neither a fool nor a man who cherished delusions. He had undoubtedly made his own judgement of that bad moment he'd had too. He might even have verified it through some private physician, and being a tough individual of the variety who scoffed at any kind of personal and physical immortality, he had decided that instead of leading Chaney by the h.. .. until Chaney could take over and Morrison could step down, it would be better for Chaney to start in by grabbing the bull by the horns. In fact, and Chaney had to smile about this, old Morrison was exactly right; in his position Chaney would have done the same thing.

He went over to the desk and telephoned Natalie for no particular reason except that he wanted to hear her voice, and perhaps her liquid laughter. He did not mention what he had inadvertently found out. That would be better told her by her father who was the only one, so far at any rate, who could speak authoritatively about it.

After he rang off, feeling much better, and Mrs. Heath

buzzed him on the intercom to announce that the conference had been set up with all executives attending,
Chaney leaned back and relaxed while he made the
biggest decision of them all : did he really want to devote
whatever remained of his life to Steel Fabricators, for
that was what it all boiled down to.

He decided that, at least for the time being, he would
act as though he did want to. But this was only his first
day. Smiling to himself and employing Morrison's tactic
of anticipating the future, he told himself he'd hold that
final decision in abeyance. Then he rose, glanced at his
wrist, and went along to the executive conference room.

They were all there, as was Derek Benedict and Mrs.
Heath, who had been keeping the minutes of these
meetings for over ten years, and if the well-groomed,
solemn department-heads Chaney was introduced to
felt a little uncertain, Chaney put them all at ease by
announcing that he felt twice as uneasy, which brought
a few smiles and a general loosening around the Board
Room table.

Chaney pulled no punches. He did not refer to Alfred
Morrison's probable physical condition at all, but he
did tell the executives that as majority-shareholder, and
also as Morrison's son-in-law, he intended to see that
every policy and practice Morrison had put into effect
would be continued. He stressed team-effort on the empennage contract, his own accessibility at any time of
the day or night, and one other thing, which he didn't
really have to mention but which he brought up anyway, simply because he was Chaney Lincoln.

" Any private rivalries or inter-factory politicking that
gets beyond the personal level will result in someone

going packing. I doubt if Alfred Morrison stood for that, and I can promise you that I won't stand for it either. . . . That's about all I have to say, gentlemen. Any questions?"

An older man who wore heavy, black-rimmed glasses and looked tweedy, said, "In my department, Mr. Lincoln, which is Accounting, we have a fund that everyone pitches into for the full year, and at the end of that time we have a golf match with low-scorer taking the kitty. Do you, by any chance, play golf?"

The look on Chaney's face brought loud laughter. He made it even louder by asking the tweedy individual if he might not have his wife substitute for him, because he'd never won at golf in his life.

It was a good way to break up the initial conference and afterwards as Chaney walked back to his office with Derek Benedict, the younger man's wry smile lent substance to what he said.

"You came out of that smelling of roses. They know you mean business, but they also saw you laugh a little at your own expense. Men usually like a man who can do that."

Chaney was pleased, but he adopted a page from Alfred Morrison's book by saying, "I'm not here to win any popularity contests." He paused at the door to his receptionist's office. "Is the line functioning on the new contract?"

Benedict nodded, and regarded Chaney with approval. "I'll bring you up the first completed component. It's traditional."

Chaney grinned. "Am I supposed to bless it or something?"

Benedict's grin crept up. "No, not necessarily, but that's not a bad idea."

They parted in good humour.

TWENTY-TWO

Loving And Living

IT ALL took time, many days of it, but by the time the Morrisons were due back from Bermuda Chaney told Natalie he had most of the kinks worked out and that the empennage production was actually a day and a half ahead of schedule.

She had something to tell him, as well. Her mother had telephoned from Kingston; she and Natalie's father were having such a wonderful time down there that they thought they might stay another week or two.

Chaney thought about that, and smiled in spite of himself. Obviously, old Morrison had talked to someone at the complex and had been told that Chaney Lincoln was turning in a bang-up performance. He supposed that he really ought to find out who that spy was, and sack him, but after all, Morrison was still president. Perhaps, too, whoever had turned in the report about Chaney was justified in his loyalty. If Chaney could inspire a similar dedication in his executives, then there really wouldn't be any contract Steel Fabricators could not handle.

Natalie wanted him to go out to the patio with her, which he did willingly. They had already eaten, the day was quite ended, and she said the best way for a busy man to unwind was to relax in the warmth of a lovely summertime night where he could see stars and smell flowers, and sit quietly without being interrupted.

He could have added something to that : to have the profile of a beautiful woman to look at.

She asked if he wished by now that he had never got involved at the complex. He had come to a final conclusion only the previous day, but it hadn't been definitive nor unilateral. " It's up to you," he told her. " I'm perfectly willing. It's a challenge. Every morning you walk through those front doors you know you'll be called upon to say something in the course of the day that will test every bit of sense and judgement you possess. I can understand now, finally, why your father was so fanatical when he found out a profiteer was moving in on him. But it's up to you, Lee. You certainly know much more than I'll probably ever know about what the wife of a chief executive has to put up with, has to adjust to, has to live with. You saw it with your parents, and if you don't want to go through it too, we'll make other plans."

He kept his figurative fingers crossed. He didn't really believe she'd be negative, but on the off-chance that she might, he was beathing shallowly while awaiting her reply. If she decided against Steel Fabricators, he was going to have to tell her about her father's heart condition, which he most certainly did not want to do.

She smiled over at him. " You're hooked, lover. I've

heard the wives of executives say it dozens of times, my own mother included. Once a man has a taste of what it's like in the Executive Suite, he becomes an addict. In less than a month you're even beginning to look the part."

He raised arched brows. " Look it?"

She reached for his hand and squeezed. "Oh, the expression when you walk in each night, the attitude of judgement when someone tells you something. Even the way you make love to me—as though you have to put a lot of other things aside first, so that you can concentrate on what you're doing."

He mulled that over and decided she had to be correct, because when he came home at night she was the one best qualified to see him as he really was at the close of day.

" It might get worse," he mused aloud. " I know the type you've described. Usually, they turn into humour-less men with a cold stare and a bear-trap mouth, who exist exclusively for some damned silly factory." He swung to his feet, and twisted to offer a hand as she too rose from a chair. " That's the last kind of a caricature of a human being I want to be." He watched her stand. When she moved over closer to him and he caught the perfume-scent, he grinned downward. "Not much danger, lover. I've found something I like so much better here's just no comparison." He slid his arms around her. He could feel the high hardness of her breasts against him, and the supple roundness of her strong legs. "In-cidentally, I think I volunteered you in my place for a factory golf tournament at the end of the year."

For a moment she clung to him, but then she pushed

And thanks for filling me in on the other matter, but frankly, I'm not worried about the empennage timetable and deliveries. We'll make it all right. Goodnight, Paul."

Natalie was sitting with her head slightly to one side when Chaney looked over. " It is the custom," she said, " for a husband to *first* clear all social dates with his wife." She smiled. " You look extremely handsome and executivish standing like that—beside the carved desk with one hand on the telephone and with all those shelves of books behind you. I think you'd make a perfect study for one of those ads in the magazines. The caption should be : ' Only the captains of industry drink Doer's whisky '."

He eased over and perched upon the edge of the desk, smiling. " Why just a captain of industry? Why not a conqueror like Hannibal or Wellington? Today Steel Fabricators, tomorrow the moon."

They laughed and she rose to cross the room to him. " You really are very handsome, you know, Chaney. When I sat with you that first time, I'd look, then I'd wonder what the flaw was; truly handsome men aren't still single when they pass twenty-five unless there's something wrong with them."

" Or," he added to that, " unless they are on guard with every female they take to supper."

" You didn't impress me as a man on guard, lover."

With her he hadn't been; had never felt the need for a guard. It had been the other way around, he'd wanted to get past *her* guard. " I wasn't," he conceded. " That first time I had a hell of a time to keep from staring. Then I also wondered—until I saw the wedding ring.

I can tell you very frankly if you'd turned in your chair that first time and said let's get married, I'd have taken you directly to a minister."

"And after you found out who I was? Incidentally, who told you?"

"Paul Carroll. And yes, I think I'd still have done it after I found out. But that was one hell of a shock; I'd always prided myself on being so thorough. I almost slipped up twice, seriously, when I tangled with the Morrisons. The first mistake—well—I'm still out a half million dollars, but that ought to come back by the end of the year if everything works out properly at the factory. As for the second blunder—you, and my acceptance of the wrong name because I was too blinded by you to be as sceptical as I usually am, that was the luckiest day of my life."

She put her hands on his knees and leaned against the desk to be kissed. He obliged. Afterwards, looking upwards, she said, "Care to know a secret? If you'd asked me, that same day on the patio, I think I'd have said yes. I'd been looking for a long time; the difficulty was that I only knew boys. Even if they were old enough, they were still boys. After you helped me out to the car and I drove away, I had to pull to the curb down by the boulevard and pull myself together. There you were, a man in every way, and there I was, committed to fighting you. Now do you understand why my father wasn't surprised when you told him we were going to be married?"

Chaney got off the desk and, holding her by one hand, started out of the study. "I understand a hell of a lot of things now I couldn't begin to understand two weeks ago," he said. "It's bedtime; remember, I'm a working man with a schedule."

She trooped along with him, and when they reached the master bedroom she went over to slide back the wall-to-ceiling glass doors so that sweet night air could enter the suite. She then turned off the bright overhead chandelier he'd thoughtlessly flicked on when they'd entered, and switched on the pair of softly glowing reading-lamps on the reading stands that sat at each side of the wide bed.

He sat a moment watching all this, but watching her particularly. She was as graceful, as supple and perfectly co-ordinated as a woman could be. Golf, tennis, all the participation-sports she had taken up over the years, had given her a variety of muscular poise he couldn't remember ever having seen in another woman. Then, of course, there were the smokerise eyes, the ebony hair, the golden skin-tone. She was flawless, as far as he could see. He wondered if he really deserved this kind of luck. He hadn't been any model of ethical virtue for most of his life. True, he had only gone after men who were already stealing and cheating, but did that give him the right to punish them by capitalising on their dishonesty?

He bent over to untie a shoe. No, it didn't give him the right, and from now on he wouldn't be able to do any more of that kind of endeavour even if he wanted to; from now on he was going to have to fight like hell just to get a few weeks off each year so he and Lee could have a decent holiday.

He tossed the shoe aside and crossed his leg to remove the other shoe. She was at the dressing-table combing and brushing her thick black hair. He watched, and saw her looking at him over her shoulder in the mirror. "How long does this kind of a feeling last?" he asked.

She half-turned when she answered. "How long do you want it to last?"

He laughed. "That's easy; forever. Maybe for a couple of years beyond that."

She kept her heavy dark lashes only half raised. "Then that's how long it will last, if you're willing to do more than just wish it. I am; I'm willing to work very hard to make it permanent."

"Chaney . . .?"

"I haven't asked you before . . . how do you feel about children?"

He felt the brief, hard lugging of his heart in its dark place. "That is probably the only thing I didn't like about bachelorhood. One time I talked to Paul about adopting a couple of them; one boy and one girl. He said they didn't give kids to single people."

"You wouldn't have to adopt any, if you didn't want to, Chaney," she murmured, and turned back facing the mirror while she continued to brush her shiny hair. "Not if you didn't want to."

He sat there with one shoe on his hand, scarcely moving. "Do you like kids, Lee?"

"I adore them. But I always had some idea that I'd have four or five of them." She smiled tenderly at him in the mirror. "Maybe enough for a polo team."

He remembered the shoe he was holding, looked at it, then tossed it aside and rose to walk over where she sat and leant down to kiss her ear, her neck, her throat, and finally, her lips.

SPRING TIME OF JOY

GEORGINA FERRAND

CHAPTER ONE

CAREEN heard the front door open, a gust of wind whistle through the narrow hall and then a bang as it slammed shut. She gave one more puzzled glance at the photograph in her hand before pushing it quickly into her pocket.

"Are you there, Careen love?" she heard a familiar voice say.

"Upstairs, Aunt Rose." She sank dejectedly on to the bed next to the neat pile of clothes and heard the rustle of a plastic raincoat as her aunt took it off and then her heavy tread as she lumbered up the stairs.

She came into the bedroom and saw her niece looking small, pale and incredibly young as she glanced around the room, smiling kindly. "Now, what are you doing?"

Careen brushed a weary hand through her unruly bronze curls. "Oh, I thought I'd sort some of mother's clothes ready for the church bazaar. It has to be done and there's no point in being sentimental—she wouldn't want it—not when her belongings can be doing some good."

"It's not a job you should be doing, love; you should let me do it."

Careen flashed her a grateful smile. "I can manage, thanks, Aunt Rose. It's just that I can't get used to the idea she's gone. It's so final." She felt the hot tears start up again and fought them.

"I know—it's hard to take. But you've got us now, Uncle Harry, me and our Joyce. We're your family now."

"You're very kind to me," Careen sniffed. She was fond of Aunt Rose and Uncle Harry, but she knew they were no substitute for her parents. Joyce was always her best friend as well as her cousin, but now she was married, and Kenneth, her husband, was her entire world at the moment.

"Have you had breakfast yet, Careen?" Her aunt's voice became brisk.

"Yes."

"A cup of tea will do us both good. I'll go down and put the kettle on."

"I'll come down in a few minutes. Oh, by the way," she added, just as Aunt Rose was going out of the room, "if you'd like to choose something to keep, you're quite welcome."

"Well, there was a little pearl-and-turquoise brooch I always admired. . . ."

Careen crossed the room and, opening a drawer in the dressing-table, brought out a small box. After a second or two she picked out a brooch and handed it to her aunt.

Rose Hardaker turned it over in her hand. "Are you sure you don't want it?"

"There are other things I can keep. You take it; she was fond of you."

"Thanks, Careen. I did think a lot of your mother and I'd like a keepsake. Well, I'll go and get that kettle on."

The door closed softly behind her and Careen crossed the room and stared out of the window across the drab, grey rooftops to the bleak moors. This is my world, she thought; this is all I have known for twenty years. Witterton, the little village balancing precariously on the edge of the Yorkshire moors, forgotten in winter and only accidentally discovered by day-trippers in the summer. Surely, she thought, in twenty years I should have seen more than this and the occasional shopping trips to Leeds or Bradford and two weeks in Scarborough each July. She sighed disconsolately; Mother had been content; she had never wanted anything more.

But there must be more to life than this. Now there is nothing to keep me, I can go anywhere.

"Careen, the tea's ready!"

Her hand closed over the crinkled paper in her pocket as she turned and went out, down the stairs. Aunt Rose was standing by the table, one hand on her plump hip, pouring the hot, strong tea into the cups.

"This will do you good," she said as she pushed the cup across the table. "I need it myself. The weather's foul—the wind fair blew me along the street. I suppose it's having one last fling before spring." She glanced out of the kitchen window. "This time next week we'll probably find winter's gone."

"I hope so; I hate this weather." Careen put two hands round her cup and sipped the tea appreciatively. "How is Joyce? She didn't look too well yesterday."

Aunt Rose pu... u a chair out and sank down gratefully. "To tell you the truth, she's not; she's expecting."

"Oh, I am glad, Aunt Rose. It will be nice to have a baby in the family."

"Well, it's not until the autumn and she doesn't want it known just yet, so don't mention it, will you, love? You know how news spreads in this place."

"Of course, but tell her I am pleased."

"I will." Her aunt bit into a digestive biscuit and poured out second cups. "What are you going to do with yourself now, Careen?"

"I'm not sure," she frowned.

"This house is too big for you alone. Why don't you sell it? Now Joyce is married there's plenty of room at the farm and we'd love to have you."

"I appreciate your asking me, Aunt Rose. I think I will sell the house and I'll have enough money to keep myself while I take a secretarial course and perhaps get a job somewhere. There's no real prospects here."

"That's a very good idea, Careen." She paused for a

moment. "Talking of prospects, is there anything between you and that Needham boy?"

Careen laughed. "Mike won't qualify for at least two years and then he's got a long way to go before he'll earn enough to support a wife—supposing he wants one, that is."

Her aunt looked at her shrewdly. "And how do you feel about that?"

"We like each other very much. I've known him all my life, but there should be more than that when one is considering marriage." She fumbled in her pocket and brought out a piece of paper, looking across at her aunt as she passed it over the table. "I got this letter this morning; a most peculiar letter."

Aunt Rose looked at it apprehensively. "The best thing is to take it to Constable Hardy. He'll know what to do about it."

Careen smiled indulgently. "It's not *that* kind of letter. Read it."

Rose Hardaker picked it up and, holding it at arm's length, she squinted at it for a moment or two before reading. "It's from a firm of solicitors—Messrs Hart and Hart . . . a London address . . . sounds respectable enough." "Dear Miss Lacey," she read, "We have been instructed to write to you b, our client Mr Joseph Steele, Pierce End, Stokeley, Sussex. He wishes us to convey his sincere regret at the passing of your mother, Mrs Helen Lacey, *née* Forbridge."

"Mr Steele was acquainted with Mrs Lacey many years ago and expresses the wish to meet you. He is, unfortunately, a sick man and cannot travel. Therefore, should you agree to meet him it will be necessary for you to travel to his home."

"If you are agreeable to this we should be obliged if you would write to us so that the necessary arrangements can be made. Mr Steele will be responsible, of course, for all expenses incurred."

Aunt Rose looked at the letter and then at Careen. "It is strange, isn't it?"

"Don't you know him?"

Aunt Rose shook her head and refolded the letter. "Never heard of him."

"Neither have I, but then, mother never spoke about her life before she came here. What do you know about it, Aunt Rose?"

"Not much more than you, I expect." She collected up the cups and took them to the sink.

Careen followed her. "Tell me what you do know."

Aunt Rose turned on the tap and the hot water gushed into the sink. She drew back her hand quickly. "Your father met her towards the end of the war. He'd been injured during the Normandy landing and was shipped back home. Helen was a volunteer helper in the hospital—she actually worked in a munitions factory, but in her spare time she helped out at the hospital. She once told me she'd wanted to join one of the Forces at the beginning of the war, but she wasn't strong enough." She sighed, wiping her hands on a tea towel and turning to face Careen. "By the time he was discharged the war was over, so he brought her up here and they were married. Your grandma ran the post office and when your dad came home she handed it over to him. I was already married then."

Careen put the dried cups back into the cupboard. "But she must have mentioned relatives. . . ."

"Not to me; she only said her parents had died before the war and your dad once told me she came from somewhere in Sussex."

"I knew that much. I found this when I was sorting out her things. Do you recognise him?" She handed over the photograph.

Aunt Rose studied it carefully and shook her head. "Handsome, isn't he? Must have been about thirty when it was taken. Maybe it's her father."

"No, it can't be. I thought that at first, but look carefully at his clothes; he must have been about her own age, or a little older. If he's alive now he'll be about sixty, I should think."

"Perhaps she had a brother who died."

Careen took it back and drew a deep sigh. "We'll never know now."

Aunt Rose frowned. "How did those solicitors know about her and your address?"

"That was my fault," Careen admitted. "It was a sudden impulse; I put an obituary in the local Sussex paper."

Her aunt looked wide-eyed. "Why on earth did you do that?"

"I thought perhaps there were some relatives who might like to know. She must have come from this place . . ." she peered at the letter, "Stokeley. I wonder who this Joseph Steele is."

"If you accept his invitation you'll find out."

"Accept his invitation? Aunt Rose, do you really think I should?"

"Why not? You've been asked."

"There's no point. After all, he must have known her more than thirty years ago and, if he'd been a close friend, wouldn't she have mentioned him or kept in touch? I shall write, thank Mr Steele for his kind regrets and politely decline."

Aunt Rose gazed at her earnestly. "Don't be so hasty, love."

The girl looked back in amazement. "You're not really suggesting I go?"

"You have nothing to lose." Careen started to say something but her aunt heedlessly continued. "No, listen, love, listen to what I have to say. You've had it rough over the past few years, what with your dad passing on and then having to look after your ma; it's been no life for a young girl. When was the last holiday you had?"

"Five years ago," she answered in a small voice.

"There, you see? You were fifteen years old; a school-girl. You need a break, Careen. You can go and meet this Mr Steele; he'll pay your rail fare. You could spend a couple of days in London or Brighton on the way back and then you'll be fresh to start your secretarial course." She put her arms around her niece's shoulders. "You're a good girl, Careen; Uncle Harry and I think about you a lot and you've been a good daughter. Going away for a few days will do you good, and when you come back there'll be a room waiting for you at our house for as long as you want it."

Careen looked up at her and smiled. "I'll think about it."

*   *   *

It was exactly a week later when Careen stepped from the train on to Platform Five at King's Cross Station. She hesitated for a moment, overawed by the dirt, the deafening noise and the number of people hurrying down the platform in a seemingly solid wave.

She gripped her new handbag tightly in one hand and her suitcase in the other and allowed herself to be drawn along with the crowd. At the barrier she handed in her ticket and then she realised with a little quiver of fear that she was alone and had to find her way across London to the hotel.

Sitting down on a bench between a fat woman with two large cases and an elegant-looking man reading a newspaper, she tucked her case underneath her legs and drew the letter out of her handbag.

Careen had decided that she may as well accept Mr Steele's invitation. Her aunt had been right—it would do her good to get away for a few days; but more than that she realised there was always a chance of finding out about her mother's life before she came to Witterton at the end of the war. The thought that she might have a whole host of relatives she had never seen excited her. Almost immediately she had written to the solicitors expressing her willingness to meet Mr Steele and a reply was received by return of post, including precise instructions, a railway ticket to London and a cheque to cover her expenses during the journey. Aunt Rose was almost ecstatic when she read the letter.

"On your arrival at King's Cross Station you are to take a taxi to the Regina Hotel, Park Lane, where a reservation has been made in your name." "Park Lane! The very best hotels are on Park Lane, Careen! Mr Steele must be very rich."

"There must be some smaller hotels too, Aunt Rose. Not all the hotels on the front at Scarborough are large and luxurious."

"Well, you've to take a taxi and they've sent enough money to cover the cost." She began to read again. "Mr Steele wishes you to spend the night at the hotel and the following morning also. At two-thirty precisely a car will collect you from your hotel to take you to Pierce End."

Aunt Rose peered at her niece from over her spectacles. "They're certainly going to look after you. They've thought of everything."

"So it seems," Careen replied with a smile.

"You'll have a day in London after all, and at their expense. I wonder how long you'll be staying at Pierce End? They didn't say."

"Probably overnight."

"Yes, I expect that'll be it." She looked at Careen critically. "You'll have to get some new clothes; you've nothing suitable for staying at a big house."

"We don't know it's a big house and I've enough clothes for three days, which is about as long as I'll be away."

"It must be a big house, love; Pierce End sounds big. There's no street number. It's about time you had some new clothes. If you haven't enough money I'm sure Uncle Harry would. . . ."

"I do have enough," Careen told her. "When shall we go shopping?"

In the end Careen settled on a spring-weight tweed suit and bought a pair of leather court shoes and a handbag in the latest style. She also allowed her aunt to talk her into two fine wool dresses, one with long sleeves and one with short. She had to admit she felt more confident in her new clothes and was glad Aunt Rose had persuaded her to buy them. She didn't want Mr Steele to think she was only a simple country girl—even if that was how she felt.

At the station Aunt Rose and Uncle Harry excitedly waved her off as if she were going away for good. "I'll be back on Friday at the latest," she protested, with a laugh as Aunt Rose pressed a bag of fruit on to her and Uncle Harry piled magazines into her lap.

As the whistle blew Aunt Rose gave her a bear hug and, as they were about to leave the carriage, Uncle Harry pressed a five-pound note into her hand. "Have a good time, lass," he said gruffly.

For a minute or two she was so touched that she could not speak, but just as the train jolted and began to move out of the station she ran into the corridor and, opening the window, she waved to them until they were no more than specks on the horizon.

She sat on the bench staring at the letter and, suddenly realising she would have to leave the station sooner or later, she began to refold it and put it back into her handbag. The man next to her began to fold his newspaper and she leaned over impulsively.

"Excuse me, but could you tell me where I can get a taxi?"

He glanced round vaguely and pointed to a long

queue a little way away. "Those people are waiting for a taxi," he explained. "You'll have to join the queue."

Careen tried to hide her dismay as she followed his arm with her eyes. Another illusion went bang and with it the vision of herself imperiously summoning a taxi, as she had seen sophisticated people do in countless films. She gave a little sigh of resignation and, picking up her suitcase, she walked over to the queue. At least this would be more dignified than her arrival at the station in Uncle Harry's rackety truck; the smell of pigs still persisted despite Aunt Rose's insistence that it had been cleaned out in honour of her trip.

Once installed in the taxi, she peered out of the window absorbing everything she saw and was amazed at the enormity of it all. Her studies at school had prepared her for a large city, but she had never expected it to be this big.

The taxi swung round from Oxford Street and into Park Lane; a minute later it halted in front of the Regina Hotel. A doorman resplendent in a scarlet uniform and shiny black top hat sprang forward to open the door. Hesitantly she looked from him to the taxi driver. "I wanted the Regina Hotel, Park Lane."

"This is it, lady."

"Are you sure? I expected a much smaller hotel." She looked doubtfully towards its magnificent exterior.

"This is the only Regina in Park Lane," he replied with bored indifference. "There are no small hotels along here. Forty-two pence on the clock, lady."

She fumbled in her purse for the money and handed it to him. She was about to pick up her case when the doorman took it from her.

"I'll take care of this, madam. Have you a reservation?"

"Yes . . . I think so."

"Go through to the reception, madam."

He held the door open for her and she found herself

ankle deep in carpet; feeling just like Alice through the looking glass, projected into an entirely different world. To her left and right were large marble pillars flanked by deep luxurious armchairs and overhead sparkled one of the most beautiful crystal chandeliers she had ever seen. A mink-coated matron stared at her curiously as she hovered indecisively near the door, trying to take in the scene before her.

Taking a deep breath, she started across the hall towards the reception desk at the far side, convinced that a terrible mistake had been made and the solicitors had given her the name of the wrong hotel, unless there was a more modest Regina somewhere nearby.

The tall, slim young man behind the reception desk smiled superciliously as she approached. "May I help you, madam?"

"I believe I have a reservation for tonight. . . ."

"Yes, madam, and your name . . . ?"

"Lacey. Miss Careen Lacey."

He ran an elegantly manicured finger down a list and Careen waited patiently, almost hoping that her name was not down.

"Ah, yes, here it is—Suite 347. If you'd just fill in this form, I'll have someone take you up."

Dazedly she filled in the form and pushed it back across the desk. The young man snapped his fingers and from nowhere a page appeared; the man handed him a key. "Suite 347," he said abruptly.

Careen was about to follow the page when she suddenly turned back. "But my suitcase. . . ."

The young man smiled again. "It will be sent up, madam."

Careen followed the page and was whisked up to the third floor in the lift and led along a thickly carpeted corridor. When he unlocked the door to Suite 347 she found herself in an elegant sitting-room which was unlike anything she had ever seen outside the cinema.

She walked dazedly into the centre of the room, which seemed overfull of gilt reproduction chairs which looked too delicate to carry her weight, marble-topped tables, and even a writing desk.

The page crossed the floor and opened a door. "The bedroom is through here," and then he opened another door, "and this is the bathroom."

She gazed around at the splendour before her.

"Will there be anything else, madam?" she heard him say.

Careen was startled out of her reverie. "Oh, no. No thank you." She found some coins in her purse and handed them to him, fervently hoping it was enough. But it must have been because he smiled, saluting smartly before going out.

She walked over to the window and stared down at the never-ending line of crawling traffic, realising with wonder that there was almost no noise from outside. Slipping off her suit jacket, she went into the bedroom. It was as sumptuously equipped as the rest of the hotel and she especially admired the enormous bed with its filmy pink drapes. With an impish grin she skipped into the bathroom and then back into the sitting-room. She was still dancing round joyously when there was a muted knock at the door. Smoothing down her skirt, she went over and opened it.

"Your suitcase, madam," the porter informed her, pushing the door open further. She almost attempted to take it from him, but remembered, just in time, where she was. She watched him carry it into the bedroom and then as he went back out. After he had gone Careen remembered the small desk near the window and, impulsively, sat down to scribble an excited note to Aunt Rose and Uncle Harry on the hotel's own heavily embossed paper.

When it was done, she decided to have a bath to wash away the grime of the journey which she felt must be ingrained into her skin. It was while she was soaking that she suddenly remembered the man who was making all this possible—Joseph Steele. Who was he? she wondered. Why did her mother know someone so rich and never mention him? Careen consoled herself that by this time tomorrow she would probably know.

She had only just dressed when the telephone rang. Gingerly she lifted the receiver, wondering who could be ringing her here.

"Is everything satisfactory, madam?" She recognised the voice of the thin young man at the reception desk.

"Yes, thank you," she replied in a level voice. "Very satisfactory."

"Mr Steele has given instructions that you are to order anything you wish."

Was there a note of disapproval in his voice? Probably not, she decided. "Thank you," she repeated and replaced the receiver.

She was beginning to feel the first pangs of hunger, but the thought of eating on her own in the large restaurant downstairs daunted her. After a moment's hesitation she lifted the telephone receiver. "Is it possible to have a meal served in my room?" she asked.

"Certainly, madam. What would you like?"

She thought for a second or two and then ordered her favourite meal; what she always had on her occasional outings with Mike Needham—avocado pear with prawns, roast duckling and peach melba—then sat back to wait.

Whatever the outcome of her meeting with Joseph Steele, it would be worth the journey just for this one night of luxurious living. She realised that although the Regina had already spoiled her for the more mundane hotels, this experience would have to last for the rest of her life.

*   *   *

Careen awoke late the next morning and for a moment or two she could not remember where she was. Then the realisation that this was the day she was to meet Joseph Steele dawned on her; she jumped out of bed and, after ordering breakfast, dressed swiftly. There was no doubt about how she would spend this morning; recklessly she had decided to spend Uncle Harry's five pounds on hiring a taxi to take her on a whirlwind sight-seeing tour.

The previous evening had still been young when she had finished her dinner and, after slipping on her coat which Aunt Rose insisted she take, she went out of the hotel to savour a little of London's after-dark atmosphere. She remembered her journey from the station and knew she was not far from the main shopping area. A few minutes' walk brought her to Oxford Street and for what seemed like hours she wandered along peering in at the brightly-lit windows filled with the most wonderful array of goods she had ever seen. When she found her way back to the hotel it was late, but in her excited state she found that sleep was a long time in claiming her.

After a hearty breakfast she re-packed her suitcase and went downstairs to inform them at reception that it was ready for collection. With that done, she went out into the early spring sunshine, swinging her bag happily. She stepped into the taxi the doorman had hailed for her with all the aplomb of one who had done it all her life.

She expected the driver to be surprised at her request, but he simply said, "Anywhere particular, Miss?"

"No. Buckingham Palace, Westminster Abbey and all the usual places." She glanced at her watch. "But I must be back at the hotel for two-thirty."

"We'll do it easy by then," he replied, and she settled back to enjoy herself.

The driver was right, she saw all the places she had

asked for and a few that she had not. It was still early so she asked to be let off in Oxford Street, and after another session of window shopping she had a quick lunch at a cafeteria. There was still some time in hand when she arrived back at the Regina, so she bought a newspaper and settled herself down in one of the plush, oversized armchairs near the door.

For the first time Careen realised she had no idea who was coming for her, or, indeed, if anyone at all. The letter simply stated that a car would call for her and she had automatically assumed that Mr Steele would come himself. Now she admitted to herself that the letter could have meant just that—a car would call for her.

Again she found herself wondering about Joseph Steele. Why hadn't he written direct instead of using a solicitor? Involuntarily she shuddered; what if this were an elaborate trap of some kind? Someone who wanted an orphan for some diabolical plan?

She smiled at her own silly thoughts; she was being ridiculous. A person of that type would not have used a solicitor nor would would he spend money putting her in such an expensive hotel. Nevertheless, she wished she knew more about him. How old was he? He could not be too young, she reasoned, if he knew her mother, who had lived in Witterton for twenty-five years. She pictured him first as a crusty old bachelor living amid a houseful of cats, then as a jolly middle-aged man surrounded by a horde of children.

She concentrated on reading the newspaper and tried to put all thoughts of Joseph Steele out of her mind; she would find out soon enough.

She was deeply engrossed in the newspaper when a dark shadow fell across the page. She looked up sharply and gasped when she found herself staring, a little incredulously, at the face in the photograph.

CHAPTER TWO

BUT that was impossible! The man in the photograph was at least thirty years old and that must have been more than thirty years ago, judging by the condition of the photograph and the style of the clothes; this man was not much more than that now. But he was very like him. He gave the illusion of great height, but she realised, foolishly, that it was because she was sitting down and looking up at him. Nevertheless, he *was* tall and dark—very dark. His almost black eyes seemed to bore into her from beneath a pair of bushy eyebrows.

"Miss Lacey?" His voice was what she would have expected from him; deep, rich and educated.

She realised then how stupid she must look, gaping foolishly at him. "Yes." She wished she could think of something clever or witty to say.

"I'm Jonathan Steele. My uncle asked me to call for you."

She sprang to her feet. "I am ready." In her haste she dropped her handbag and before she could retrieve it he had stooped and, scooping it up, he handed it back to her.

"Thank you, Mr Steele; that was very clumsy of me."

She smiled at him, but he was unmoved, and to her embarrassment she realised he was studying her very carefully; his gaze seemed to burn through her skin.

Abruptly he said, "Shall we go." It was not a question; more a command.

"I don't have my suitcase although I did ask them to bring it down this morning."

"It's in the car." His voice held a hint of impatience.

He began to move away, leaving her where she was standing, and after a moment she hurried after him. A black limousine stood at the kerb and Jonathan Steele opened the door for her to get in. He stood stiffly to attention without looking at her, staring across the road as if something very important was happening over there, and once she was seated he slammed the door shut. She watched him curiously as he slid behind the wheel of the car, trying to fathom what he was thinking. His attitude so far was far from friendly and it puzzled her.

"I'm so excited," she told him in an attempt to draw him into conversation as the car glided away from the kerb and into the stream of traffic. "This is my first visit to London."

He did not reply.

"Have we far to go?" she ventured again.

"It will take us about an hour and a half. We have to cross London and the traffic is quite bad."

"You don't like me, do you?" she said suddenly, with her usual forthrightness.

To her surprise he smiled, although it far from reassured her. "Is there anything in that letter from my uncle's solicitors to say I should?"

For a moment she was completely at a loss for words and then she recovered. "No, of course not, but it's not usual to hate on sight. I don't know what you expected, but if I'm a disappointment to you I'm sorry. I haven't come all this way to please you, Mr Steele, I'm here at your uncle's invitation."

The smile curled his lips again. "That's perfectly true, Miss Lacey, and I'm not disappointed I assure you. You are almost what I expected, more . . . prettier than I imagined and certainly more spirited."

Careen was far from flattered at such a description and she turned indignantly in her seat. He really was the most peculiar man. "Well, I certainly asked for that.

You're being very objectionable I must say, and in the ten minutes or so we've known each other I can't confess to any great liking for you, but I'm sure I don't know why I warrant such cavalier treatment. All I do know is your uncle wanted to meet me and that is why I'm here. I can't find anything terrible in that."

"Let's just say I dislike fortune hunters in general." He stared ahead, his face expressionless.

Her green eyes opened wide and her skin turned a shade paler. "What did you say?" She almost choked.

He did not reply, just kept on staring ahead in a way which only served to infuriate her more.

"What did you mean by 'fortune hunter'?" she insisted.

"Miss Lacey," he said with an air of tired patience, "the traffic is particularly bad around here and I'm not used to driving this car. My uncle insisted on my using it for you instead of the smaller car I prefer. Since his illness last year he doesn't leave the house, so we dispensed with the chauffeur. I'd be grateful if you would spare me the innocence."

She choked back an angry retort, knowing that it would be useless. This man had already presumed to judge her for some reason and come to his own conclusion, although it was obviously the wrong one. The way he spoke—his words carefully chosen and specifically delivered—indicated his disagreeable nature. He was cold, she thought, and unfeeling; he would never resort to anger, but she knew he could be a formidable enemy.

Now why did that word come into my mind? she thought. His dark good looks were menacing enough in his present mood, but that was no excuse for dramatics. She began to wonder about the rest of the Steele family. Did Jonathan have a wife? Men of his age usually do.

The factories and houses soon gave way to fields and farms, and as they passed through several villages and small towns she longed to ask him a dozen questions that had been plaguing her since that first letter from Hart and Hart, but she knew he had brought down a curtain between them and she would not be allowed through.

The countryside flashed past and it was only when the car slowed down and they passed through the little village of Stokeley that Careen realised her destination was near. Her palms felt damp and she rubbed them on her handkerchief, fervently hoping Jonathan Steele did not notice her nervousness.

A little way past the village the car swung sharply into a narrow side road and a mile farther on swept through a pair of tall iron gates and up a curving drive lined with tall majestic poplars. She could not see the house because of the curve of the drive until they were almost up to it, but when she did she gave a loud gasp.

"It's lovely," she exclaimed; she couldn't help herself.

The big black car stopped in front of the house, behind a smaller but nonetheless luxurious car. Careen gazed admiringly from the car window at the perfectly proportioned Queen Anne house. "Just like a doll's house," she breathed.

She realised then that Jonathan Steele had already collected her suitcase from the back of the car and had come round to open the door. She was still staring at the house as she stepped down and almost stumbled, and although he stood stiffly by her side he made no move to help her. When she went towards the front door, which was flanked at either side by white tubs filled with azaleas, he followed silently behind.

There was no need for him to knock at the door—it opened as they approached and Careen felt herself being carefully examined for the second time that day. Instinct told her that the woman standing just inside the hall was not hostile, merely curious. She was a middle-aged woman dressed completely in black, with no air of distinction.

Jonathan Steele put her suitcase on the floor, which was brightly polished and smelt as if it had been freshly waxed. Careen gazed around her. She knew this was not a large house, but it was certainly the largest she had ever been into. At the far side of the hall there was a curving staircase leading to a balcony upstairs and lining the wall going up were a row of sombre-looking portraits, which somehow looked out of place in the bright and sunny hall.

"Is Mrs Steele in?" Jonathan asked briskly.

So he does have a wife, Careen thought, and gave a silent prayer that she would be more welcoming than her husband.

The woman dragged her gaze away from Careen. "Yes, she's in the sitting-room, waiting for you."

He nodded curtly as he took off his dark overcoat and handed it to the woman. "This way, Miss Lacey," he said as he took her arm. It was the first physical contact they'd had and she resisted the urge to pull away; she was very conscious of his hand on her arm.

Careen found herself automatically holding her breath as he pushed open the door, but he appeared not to notice; in fact he managed to convey the impression that he was hardly aware of her presence at all.

Reluctantly she allowed him to guide her into the sitting-room and she was immediately aware of shades of apricot and green, gleaming woodwork and chintz-covered furniture. A warm room, she decided, but still managing to retain a comfortable elegance. The sweet, cloying perfume of hyacinths emanated from several pots dotted around the room and mixed incongruously with the smell of *Cuir de Russie* worn by the woman who was studying her carefully.

She stood up the moment they entered. She was tall, slim and there was no sign of grey in her sleek black hair. Careen was at first surprised when she realised this woman must be Jonathan's aunt—or mother.

She extended one elegant hand. "How do you do, Miss Lacey. I'm Joseph Steele's sister-in-law, Jonathan's mother."

"I'm very pleased to meet you, Mrs Steele," Careen managed to stammer. Her hope that the woman of the house would be more welcoming was dashed in the face of such a cold manner.

"I notice Dr Mandley is here, Mother," he spoke for the first time. "If you'll excuse me I'll go and see him."

Strangely enough, Careen was sorry to see him go; unfriendly as he was he had made no secret of it and his presence had been like a shield. Now she was alone with his mother who was as hostile, but in a well-bred way was trying to hide it behind a polite exterior. Careen had the distinct impression that everything she would say had been well planned in advance.

"Please sit down." Louise Steele indicated the chintz-covered sofa in front of a coal fire.

"I hope Mr Steele isn't ill," she ventured.

Louise Steele gave her a stiff smile. "My brother-in-law had a serious stroke almost a year ago. He'll never fully recover, unfortunately. Dr Mandley makes a routine call twice a week."

The sitting-room overlooked the garden and Careen, for the want of something other to do, stared out at the colourful show of daffodils and tulips. Suddenly she turned to the older woman, who was examining her hands with more concentration than was really necessary.

"Mrs Steele, just why am I here?"

Louise transferred her interest to Careen. "I imagine it's because Joseph asked you to come."

"Yes, I know that, but why did he ask me?"

Louise smiled in a derogatory way. "Now, Miss Lacey, I think you know that better than anyone."

She turned anxiously. "But I don't."

For the first time Louise Steele did not seem to be in command of herself. She looked at Careen with a puzzled frown. "Your mother must have told you about Joseph."

Careen looked her levelly in the eyes. "I never heard of him before I received the letter from his solicitors. I think my mother had a photograph of him—he looked like your son—but I didn't find it until after her death and even then I didn't know who he was."

Louise stood up and walked slowly over to the fire. "Do you honestly mean to tell me your mother never mentioned Joseph Steele?"

"Never."

She turned to face her, her eyes glittering malevolently. "I find that particularly hard to believe."

"Well, it's true. Mrs Steele, please tell me, am I related to your brother-in-law?"

A contemptuous smile curved her lips which made her look, for the instant, remarkably like her son. "Certainly not. Do you really want to know?"

Careen was a little afraid; she bit her lip. "Yes," she whispered.

"Your mother worked here as a maid."

Careen shook her head in disbelief. "That's impossible."

The other woman smiled again. "I don't know what airs and graces she gave herself after she left here, but I assure you she was a maid at this house just before the war."

Careen stared unseeingly into the flames. She had hardly dared to imagine what connection her mother had with the Steeles, but this certainly was a surprise she hadn't bargained for. She brushed a hand through her carefully combed hair. "Perhaps there was another Helen Forbridge. . . ."

"My dear," Louise said, a little more kindly, "you told me a moment ago that you recognised Jonathan from Joseph's photograph; the moment I saw you I knew you were Helen's daughter—you look exactly like she did when she lived here. There's no disgrace in being a maid, especially in those days; there just weren't the opportunities for young girls without an education."

"I find it hard to believe," she said at last, "but it must be so. She never spoke of her childhood or youth, so I suppose I shouldn't be too surprised. What is bothering me now is why Mr Steele wants to see me— the daughter of a maid who left over thirty years ago."

She looked up expectantly into the older woman's face. Louise Steele averted her gaze and stooped to poke the coals.

"Mrs Steele, your son called me a fortune hunter." Her voice was unusually hard. "I want to know why."

She dropped the poker and looked directly at Careen, her blue eyes glittering brightly, but Careen did not waver. "Very well," she said, "you want to know and I will tell you, although Joseph will be annoyed." She walked over to the window and stared out. "I married Arthur Steele, Joseph's younger brother. When my father-in-law died we were left quite well off, but Joseph inherited most of the money and this house. I knew your mother in those days and I liked her until we found out that Joseph and Helen were having an *affaire*."

"Oh, no," Careen protested.

Louise turned to face her. "Don't be naïve, girl. Men and women do fall in love and they often have *affaires*. Your mother was no saint and she was tempted; Joseph was very handsome and what is more he is rich."

"That wouldn't influence my mother," Careen insisted stubbornly.

Louise ignored her protest. "My mother-in-law was alive then and when she found out she insisted it end. I don't know what happened then; we all presumed Helen had been paid well to go. Anyway, we never heard from her or about her until now."

Careen took a deep breath. "And now you think I've come to get more money from your family."

"It isn't an unreasonable conclusion, is it?"

"It is if you knew my mother at all."

The door opened and Jonathan Steele came back in, followed by a short, slightly plump and rosy-cheeked man. He smiled benevolently at Careen, who found herself feeling relieved at his lack of malice. Involuntarily she had tensed herself for more disapproval.

At the sight of him Louise Steele's manner changed drastically; her smile was completely open and charming as she came forward. "Dr Mandley, how is Joseph today?"

"No worse, Louise, and for that we must be thankful." He cast an enquiring eye over Careen. "This must be the young lady I've been hearing about." He extended a plump hand to her. "I'm pleased to meet you, my dear."

Louise broke in before Careen could respond. "Tell Miss Lacey, Dr Mandley, that the excitement will be too much for Joseph. I don't think she should see him."

"Yes, perhaps you're right," Careen agreed quickly and started to get up. She looked at Jonathan, who was standing in front of the fire, his hands clasped behind his back. "If you'd be good enough to drive me back to London, Mr Steele. . . ."

Jonathan and his mother exchanged surprised glances and then he stared at Careen again. She found she could not meet his eyes—those dark, bottomless pools.

"It's a pleasure, Miss Lacey," he said with his usual economy of words.

"Now just a minute," the doctor interrupted. "I haven't given my opinion and even you, Louise, must agree that I'm the one to give it." He looked from one to the other, obviously enjoying himself. Careen watched him with interest. "Joseph told me about this young lady on my last visit. He is looking forward to her visit enormously and to deny him the undoubted pleasure," his eyes rested on her and she blushed, "could do more harm than good."

The look of icy reserve was back on Louise's face, but what was more startling was the hatred she could see in Jonathan's eyes.

"We can't very well argue with that, can we?" Louise said coolly. "Jonathan, you'd better take Miss Lacey up to Joseph's suite."

He held the door open for her and she passed through; a vague feeling of guilt was gnawing away at her. Why should the events of more than thirty years ago concern her? And why did Joseph Steele want to see her now when he'd allowed her mother to be sent away?

Not for a moment did Careen believe her mother had had an *affaire* with the master of the house, but anger was beginning to smoulder inside her at these people who had judged and dismissed her mother just as they already had judged her. No wonder her mother had refused to talk about her past.

As she followed Jonathan Steele up the curving staircase she glanced behind her and was able to admire the full magnificence of the hall. He led her along a corridor and stopped outside one of the doors. Before he knocked he gave her a long appraising look. Now that Louise Steele had told her about her mother she understood his assumption that she was a fortune hunter; she realised her sudden appearance must make it look very much that way.

She started as the door opened—she had expected to see Joseph Steele himself. The man who stood there was dressed correctly as a manservant—the kind of old retainer she didn't believe existed these days. Later she learnt his name was Lawson and he had been Joseph Steele's personal valet and devoted friend for more than twenty years.

"Miss Lacey? Mr Steele is waiting for you."

His gaze flickered over Jonathan and back to Careen.

She drew her head up proudly. As soon as this interview was over she must go back to London; she would have to get away from this peculiar and alien household as soon as possible.

She followed the manservant into a sunny sitting-room, which she realised must be over the sitting-room downstairs. The door closed behind her; she turned and was dismayed when she realised Jonathan had stayed outside. Once more she felt unreasonably deprived of his company.

"This way, Miss," Lawson showed the way.

There were two deep wing chairs arranged round a blazing coal fire. Joseph Steele was sitting with his back towards her, hidden by the tall back of the chair. She walked around the chair and finally faced the man she had come to see.

His once thick black hair was sparse and white and his dark eyes, so like his nephew's, were shielded behind a pair of thick-lensed spectacles. He had once been powerfully built, but now he seemed to have shrunk and his flesh hung loosely across his bones.

He lifted his eyes to her face and the pupils seemed frighteningly large behind the lenses. He half-lifted one scrawny hand. "You came," he said softly. Lawson seemed to melt away into the background.

It was difficult for Careen to imagine the sick old man as a passionate lover who must have looked very much like Jonathan did today, and she found she was no longer angry with him. Her mother must have loved him once, or she would never have kept his photograph.

"Come closer, child, so I can see you better." He let out a long sigh. "Yes, you're Helen's child all right. You're very much like her," he smiled. "Not as beauti-ful, of course, but you'll pass."

"Thank you," she said stiffly.

He waved his hand towards the other chair. "Sit down, sit down, child."

Careen moved backwards and eased herself into the chair. She could do nothing but obey; Joseph Steele had such an authoritative air.

He leaned forward a little. "Was everything at the hotel satisfactory? They sent you enough money?"

"Oh, yes, Mr Steele. Thank you. The hotel was far too luxurious; you should have booked me into a smaller one."

"Nonsense, child." He chuckled. "The more I spend, the less there is to leave to them."

"You mean your family?" she ventured timidly.

He nodded.

"Don't you like them?"

He chuckled again. "As much as one can like one's family."

She was satisfied that Joseph Steele liked his relations no more than she did, but none the less, considered it a peculiar state of affairs.

"How old are you, child?"

"Twenty. Twenty-one in April."

He breathed deeply. "Your mother was older than that when I . . . when I knew her. But in those days girls weren't as advanced as they are today."

"Why did you ask me here?" she asked bluntly.

He looked down at his hands, which were gripping the arms of the chair. After a few minutes' silence he said, "I was in love with your mother."

"I know that, but why do you want to meet me now she is dead?"

"Did she ever mention me?" His eyes behind the spectacles were pleading.

Careen shook her head. "No."

"Then how did you know about me?"

"Mrs Steele told me, just before I came up here."

He nodded again. "She didn't waste much time," he said almost to himself, and then to Careen, "I'm surprised you stayed long enough to speak to me."

"I felt bound to, Mr Steele. You spent a lot of money in bringing me here; the least I could do was see you."

"I can imagine what my sister-in-law must have told you and I'm sure she distorted the truth, as always. She's an ambitious woman. She married Arthur knowing he was a wealthy man, but it didn't stop her wishing he was the heir to my father's entire fortune so she could be the mistress of this house. When my brother was killed in action during the war, she turned her ambition towards her son. As it happens she will be rewarded; Jonathan is my heir and it is very likely he will marry a woman whom his mother regards as suitable."

His description of Louise Steele matched Careen's own hasty conclusion about her. "I don't see what that has to do with me," she said aloud.

"Nothing—it has nothing to do with you, but I wish you would let me tell you my story—the true one."

"I can hardly refuse. . . ."

"Just having you sit there brings back so many happy memories—and a few sad ones. Ah, but that was so many years ago now. Helen was a maid here in those days. She had lived in Stokeley for most of her life. We fell in love—deeply in love—and I was determined to marry her. Helen didn't want any trouble. She was a very gentle person."

Careen nodded.

"But, as I say, I was determined to make her my wife and I was a very stubborn young man."

Careen could believe it.

"When I told my mother my intentions she was furious. She had a very Victorian outlook which forbade us to socialise with 'the servants' and she also had a 'suitable' young lady lined up for me. I told her in no uncertain terms I would have no one but Helen. After our confrontation I slammed out of the house and stayed away for most of the day.

"When I came back Helen had gone. My mother, in

her wisdom, had quite calmly informed her of the depri-
vations I should suffer if I married her. Helen, bless
her, not wanting to cause trouble in the family, packed
her things and left."

"And you let her go?" Careen whispered.

"For six months I had a firm of private enquiry
agents search every corner of the country, but it was
useless. It was the last few months before the war and
the whole country was in a turmoil; a person wanting
to disappear could do so quite easily." His head drooped
and his voice faltered.

Careen's heart swelled with sympathy and tears began
to well up in her eyes. "She kept a photograph of you.
I found it only after she died. I didn't know it was you
until I came here."

"Is that really so?" He became animated and
drummed his bony fingers on the arm of the chair. "She
never forgot," he said almost to himself, and Careen
knew he was in a far-off time. "I always kept one of
her," he said suddenly after he had been staring into
space. He put one hand into his jacket pocket and drew
out a small photograph. With a slightly shaking hand
he proudly handed it to her.

Careen looked at it reluctantly; she did not want to
see how her mother had looked thirty years ago. It was
like taking an intimate look at a stranger. When at last
she forced herself to look at it she recognised the general
appearance of Helen Lacey. It was a faded photograph;
an amateur had taken it and Helen had not known
whether to smile or not. Her clothes were laughably old
fashioned and the background appeared to be a beach.
Careen was filled with compassion for this lonely old
man who had lived only for the memory of the love
he lost.

"She was beautiful," the old man said with a sad
smile, and held out his hand for it as if afraid she would
keep it and so sever his last link with his lost love. "She

bye now, Mr Steele. Your nephew promised to drive me back to town and I don't want to leave too late."

Joseph Steele levered himself up and stood unsteadily in front of her, taking her hand in his. "No, you mustn't go just yet. Stay a while longer. Please, promise me you'll stay."

Careen shot an anxious glance at the doctor.

"I think it would be wise if you agreed, Miss Lacey."

"All right, I'll stay a little longer, Mr Steele."

"Overnight," he insisted.

She looked at the doctor and he nodded. "Yes, I'll stay overnight."

CHAPTER THREE

CAREEN followed Dr Mandley along the corridor, already regretting her impulsive agreement to stay. "Dr Mandley," she asked timidly, "is Mr Steele so ill that he has to stay in his room?"

The doctor smiled and stopped. He considered her carefully for a while. "He had rather a serious stroke just under a year ago," he said at last. "He has to take things easy; he understood this and resigned most of his directorships and handed his other business to Jonathan, but to answer your question—no, he doesn't *have* to stay up there; he chooses to."

"I just wondered. . . ."

"You don't know this family, Miss Lacey. They're an odd mixture. For some reason Joseph has taken a dislike to his sister-in-law and nephew. I've been his physician for the past fifteen years and as he's grown older he has become more and more of a recluse. In fact I really believe he welcomed his illness as an excuse to retire altogether. Knowing Joseph as I do, I would put the blame on his side—he's a very difficult man to please."

She looked at him thoughtfully for a moment. "Why are you telling me all this?" she asked at last.

They stood in the hall looking at each other. Dr Mandley, after nearly forty years in the medical profession, considered himself a good judge of character. He had taken a particular liking to this young woman whose *naïveté* in this modern world had impressed him, and the general air of sincerity she exuded. Her appearance did not impress him less, and even in her modest clothes and wearing only a trace of lipstick on her face, she was a very pretty girl, and the fact that she seemed not to be aware of it heightened her attraction. For a moment he let himself imagine how stunning she would look in expensive and well-chosen clothes, with the right kind of make-up expertly applied to enhance those trusting green eyes and her pale, flawless skin. The vision almost took his breath away.

He snapped himself out of his daydream. "I don't really know, Miss Lacey, and I don't know why you're here; what is more I don't want to know. But since Joseph heard you were coming he's been almost a different person. He'll never improve healthwise, but in spirits, well, I have never seen him so well. One doesn't have to be a doctor to see it. I also know you're not entirely welcomed by the rest of the family, which seems to be very unreasonable. You're the kind of young lady who should be welcomed anywhere."

She looked down at her shoes. "You flatter me, Dr Mandley." But despite her embarrassment she was pleased that at least one person did not look upon her with disdain.

"Shall we go in for tea?" he suggested. "Louise will wonder where we are."

As they entered, Jonathan Steele rose from his chair. He was holding a delicate china teacup and saucer which looked somehow incongruous in his large hand. His mother was in the act of pouring out another cup and her glance travelled over them.

"Do sit down, Miss Lacey, and have some tea. Milk and sugar?"

"Please," Careen managed to say as she perched on the sofa as far from Louise Steele as she could manage.

She handed the cup to Careen, who was aware that both Jonathan and his mother were watching her carefully. Perhaps, she thought with amusement, they are waiting for me to drink it out of the saucer.

Louise turned her attention to the doctor. "Milk and plenty of sugar for you, Doctor."

"As always," he beamed, apparently unaware that he was participating in anything other than a very pleasant gathering.

Careen watched her as she dispensed the tea from a silver teapot and had to admit that despite her age she was a remarkably handsome woman. It was probable she had never been beautiful or even pretty, but it was certain that in these latter years she had mellowed into a very striking-looking person. She fitted in well, too, she thought, as lady of the house, even though she had been denied the honour of ever being the actual mistress of Pierce End.

"Have a scone," she invited pleasantly. "Our cook does all the baking herself and we have to admit she is first class at her job, especially scones."

Careen accepted one, realising that Louise's façade of pleasantness was a result of expecting her to leave after tea, and she dreaded having to announce that she was, after all, staying.

"Did you find my uncle well, Miss Lacey?" Jonathan broke his silence and his clipped tones, devoid of emotion or concern, made her jump.

"Very well, I think," she answered non-committally, knowing that he had probably had a full report from Dr Mandley already.

"Another cup of tea, Miss Lacey?" Louise lifted the teapot. "It will refresh you before your journey."

Careen flashed a startled glance across to the doctor, whom she felt was her only ally, but he simply smiled reassuringly. "Mr Steele has asked me to stay here to-night and I have accepted his invitation," she replied firmly, looking directly at Louise.

The teapot clattered back on to the tray and the smile seemed to freeze on her face. Jonathan had not appeared to have moved a muscle, but Careen knew he was alert and as anxious as his mother.

"Well, I think he could have consulted me first . . ." Louise began, but Dr Mandley interrupted to Careen's relief.

"To be fair, Louise, Miss Lacey was most reluctant to agree, but I suggested she did. Joseph was getting rather agitated at the thought of her returning tonight."

The malicious look Louise gave him was enough to make most men quail, but Godfrey Mandley ignored it.

"I see," she said coolly, and looked to her son for further comment. He simply got up from his chair, placed his cup back on the tray, and said, "You'd better tell Cook there will be one more for dinner."

Careen could have laughed out loud, but managed to control herself. They seemed to be living a fairy-tale life, still imagining themselves to be feudal overlords.

"Will you join us?" Louise asked the doctor, more out of her well-bred politeness than a desire to have him stay.

He eased his rotund body out of the chair and shook his head. "Love to, but I'm afraid I must get back to town. My wife is expecting me home and I've stayed far too long already. Where is Rodney this afternoon? I thought things were a little quiet round here."

Louise smiled, a little indulgently, but it was a natural smile. "It was such a pleasant day, he went off this morning with his easel to find a suitable landscape to paint."

"Has he sold many lately?"

"A few. He doesn't get much for them, but it keeps him in pocket money."

Careen wondered who Rodney was. An artist? Perhaps he was Louise's younger son. But no, he couldn't be; somewhere she had heard Jonathan referred to as an only child, and she couldn't imagine anyone remotely like Jonathan being something as sensitive as an artist.

Dr Mandley came over to Careen and shook her hand. "It's been a pleasure meeting you, young lady."

"I hope we'll meet again some day," she said truthfully, and watched him go.

Jonathan nodded curtly before following him out of the room, and Careen was unwillingly left alone in an uneasy atmosphere with Louise Steele. After a moment she too rose from the sofa. "You'll have to excuse me too, I'm afraid. I must see Cook and arrange for the guest-room to be prepared." She began to walk away and suddenly she turned. "I hope you're quite satisfied with the way you've inveigled your way into this household."

For a full minute Careen was too startled by this surprise attack to say anything, and then she heard herself reply, "I'm as anxious to leave here as you are to have me go, Mrs Steele. What Dr Mandley said was perfectly true; I only agreed to stay because Mr Steele was becoming agitated. I believe he is the owner of this house and entitled to ask me." Once she had started to speak she was unable to stop and the words gushed out regardless. "And I must admit to a very ordinary upbringing, my mother being no more than a common housemaid and I can't confess to have blue blood in my veins, but I was taught good manners. The home I lived in all my life would fit into your hall, but whoever came into it was treated with a courtesy you seem to be completely unaware of. . . ."

Careen stopped and held her breath, already regretting her hasty outburst as she had regretted the one in the car. How she wished she could be more sure of herself and in command of her temper, as were Louise Steele and her son.

Louise stood stiffly erect and white faced before turning sharply on her heel and marching out of the room. Glad to be alone at last, Careen relaxed against the back of the sofa. It was hard to believe that only this morn-

ing, a mere few hours ago, she had delightedly toured
the tourist spots of London; it seemed like years ago.

She was suddenly exhausted and emotionally drained;
she doubted if this visit was going to prove therapeuti-
cally restful, as she had hoped. She must have dozed off
for a few minutes because suddenly she sat bolt upright,
her senses telling her that she was being watched. She
shivered from the draught round her feet and then she
noticed the door opening slowly.

Involuntarily she stiffened, expecting Louise Steele to
return, but the wizened little face which peered round
the door was nothing like Louise and Careen was
curious. The old woman made an exaggerated show of
looking behind her before tip-toeing in and closing the
door.

"You must be Helen's girl," she said in a loud
whisper.

"Yes, I am. Who are you?"

"I'm Hetty. I look after the babies in this house."

Careen stared at her curiously. "Are there any babies
here?"

"Not now, but I'm looking forward to Miss Julia's
babies." She tip-toed over to the settee and sat down
next to Careen.

"Who is Miss Julia?" she asked in a bemused voice,
wondering if she were still asleep and dreaming.

"Miss Julia's going to marry Jonathan. She's the
squire's daughter. He's not a real squire, but they live
in the Old Manor at the other side of the village. She's
a flighty little baggage," Hetty confided, "but the
Steeles were always fools for a pretty face."

She squinted shrewdly at Careen, who found herself
completely at a loss for words. "You've got them worried," the old woman cackled. "Her ladyship thinks the
old man'll marry you and cut Jonathan out of his will."
She cackled again and Careen noticed how few teeth she
had left.

"Then they must be mad," she retorted indignantly. "Mr Steele is old enough to be my grandfather."

The old woman became serious and put an arthritic hand on Careen's arm, and it was all she could do to stop herself snatching it away.

"I'm glad," the old woman said hoarsely, "Jonathan's like a son to me and I want him to get what's his. I was there at his birth and a real scene her ladyship made; screaming and squealing. I looked after him till they took him off to school. Yes, he's more my son than hers."

Careen felt herself backing away from Hetty. The door opened and Louise returned; Careen for once was glad to see her.

"Hetty, what are you doing here?" she said irritably.

"I came to see our visitor," she said slyly, "to tell her how welcome she is."

"Well, get along now, Hetty; you should be changing for dinner."

"We can talk some more another time," Hetty said to Careen as she was going out. Careen sincerely hoped not.

"You'll have to excuse poor Hetty," Louise said, "she's getting old and her mind tends to wander. Don't take any notice of what she says."

"Thank you, I won't. Is she a relative?"

"She was my son's nanny. In her bemused mind she thinks he's still a child. I had your suitcase put into the guest-room," she said more briskly. "I expect you would like to wash and change before dinner; I'll take you up."

Careen hastily picked up her handbag and suit jacket and followed Louise Steele into the hall and up the curving staircase she admired so much.

"You have a beautiful home, Mrs Steele," Careen said in an attempt at placation. She could not rid her mind of Hetty's words; but it was best to heed Louise's advice and disregard everything she said. But something had set Louise and Jonathan against her before she even arrived and, ludicrous as the idea seemed to her, she could understand their worry.

"Thank you," Louise replied stiffly, "but I am as much a guest here as you are."

"Oh, I'm sure Mr Steele considers you very necessary," Careen replied hurriedly, hoping she had not unwittingly antagonised this proud woman whom she was beginning to admire.

"My dear girl," she said with a patient smile, "my brother-in-law employs a cook, a housekeeper, a maid, a daily cleaning woman and a gardener, all of whom are first class at their work. My son, who incidentally is a qualified solicitor, deals with all his business matters. The only reason I have remained buried out here for the past twenty-five years is because I am determined that my son shall get what is his." She opened a door and ushered Careen into a spacious and bright bedroom. "If there is anything you need, ring this bell, it's connected to the kitchen."

Careen stared out of the window, down on to the drive. The limousine stood where it had been left on her arrival. She twisted her hands together and turned suddenly. "I'm sorry I was rude to you before, Mrs Steele. I understand how you feel, but I assure you I didn't come here with designs on your brother-in-law's money." Careen did not miss the surprise on Louise's face and somehow she found the courage to continue. "As soon as I've seen him tomorrow I shall leave this house and I promise you won't ever see or hear of me again." She moved across to her suitcase and, snapping it open, began to lay her clothes across the bed.

For a moment Louise stood rigidly silent and then said, "Dinner is at eight o'clock prompt. We assemble in the sitting-room at seven forty-five."

With that she turned on her heel and went out of the room, leaving Careen staring at the closed door.

* * *

In her anxiety not to be late, Careen was downstairs at seven-thirty. The sitting-room was deserted and she sat down, glad of the opportunity of composing herself before the others came down.

Because of the excellent heating in the house, she had decided to wear the short-sleeved dress, and she was glad Aunt Rose had insisted she buy it; the shade of green suited her and for once she felt smart and, more important, confident.

The door burst open and she looked up sharply. A tall young man with a mop of long fair hair rushed in and only stopped when he was halfway across the room. They stared at each other in wide-eyed surprise until the young man suddenly smiled. It was a warm, generous smile, revealing a row of slightly uneven teeth which gave him an impish appearance.

"You must be Careen Lacey," he said in an excited voice.

"And I bet you're Rodney," she replied, happy to see such a friendly face.

He looked surprised. "Now how would you know that?"

"It's easy," she explained. "Dr Mandley asked Mrs Steele about you this afternoon. There can't be anyone else I haven't met, can there?"

"I don't know who you have met, but I should think not." He crossed the room to the sideboard in two lanky strides. "Will you have a sherry?"

"No thank you, I rarely drink."

He gazed at her in frank admiration. "Curiouser and curiouser. I always come down earlier so I can have a double whisky." He poured one out and, filling the glass with soda, held it up. "Cheers. The others don't approve of whisky before dinner; it has to be sherry or nothing." He pulled a face which made her laugh.

He suddenly became serious. "Have things been grim since you came?"

She toyed with the strap of her handbag. "I don't blame them. If I'd have known how things were here I would never have come."

He finished his drink. "Oh, don't bother about them. Jon's a bit stiff-necked at times, especially if he senses danger to the family security, but he's all right really; just a bit spoiled and pampered by his fond mama and that old witch Hetty."

It amused Careen to have the correct upright Jonathan referred to as a spoilt child, and she checked the impulse to laugh. "You don't resent my being here, do you?"

"Why should I? It's marvellous to have someone as charming and decorative as you in the house."

She managed not to blush and looked directly into his face. "Don't you see me as a threat to your security?"

He gave an explosive laugh. "No! You don't threaten my security one bit; I don't have any." He saw her puzzled frown. "Perhaps I'd better explain," he said, flinging one arm round the back of the sofa. "I'm not related to the Steeles, just to Aunt Louise. She was my mother's sister. My parents died within months of each other and she gave me a home here when I left college —with Joseph's permission, of course. How did you find the old man, by the way?"

"I liked him."

The door opened again and Rodney moved smartly away from her and over to the fire. His aunt smiled fondly when she saw him and he clasped her hands and kissed her lightly on the cheek.

"You look ravishing, Aunt Louise. You spoil me for other women."

She smiled indulgently but Careen could tell that she was pleased. Jonathan followed his mother into the sitting-room. For a moment, which seemed like a lifetime to Careen, his dark eyes bored into her and then he turned to smile at his cousin. Careen realised with something of a shock that it was the first time she had seen him smile and it transformed his face; he looked years younger and very attractive, she thought unwillingly.

"Did you find something to paint?" he asked.

"A beaut., Jon. I had to go all the way to the coast, but it was worth it. I found a deserted cove and with all that sunshine—magnificent. I managed to sketch most of the scene and the next good day I'll go back and start painting." As if suddenly aware that Careen was deliberately excluded from the conversation, he turned to her. "Are you interested in painting, Careen?"

"I haven't had much chance, but I used to be quite good at sketching when I was at school."

"I could lend you a pad if you'd like to do some while you're here."

She smiled gratefully. "Thank you, but I won't be here long enough."

Just then the maid came in to announce dinner and Careen and Rodney followed Louise and Jonathan into the high-ceilinged dining-room. Hetty was already seated at the well-polished mahogany table. Careen found herself sitting opposite Jonathan and she was aware that on several occasions during the meal he was eyeing her gravely. Most of the meal was eaten in silence, but when she did speak it was usually to Rodney, and she was grateful for his presence; it was cheering to know someone in the house liked her. Hetty was hard to understand; she spoke only rarely, but Careen had the impression that she missed very little. On the occasions when she looked at the old woman she was smiling gently to herself as if she were enjoying a private joke.

As they came out of the dining-room, Careen turned to Rodney. "Who are those people in the paintings?" She looked up towards the wall where the paintings were neatly lined.

He took her arm. "Come on and I'll show you."

As they stood on the stairs Careen could see that they were very old, much older than the house in fact.

"These," Rodney explained, "are the Steeles of days gone by—Jon's ancestors. I told you the family were very important to him."

"I'm not surprised; it's wonderful to have such a heritage." She looked at a man in one of the photographs. He was dressed in a top hat and Victorian costume and he stared back with Jonathan's penetrating eyes. "And this house, too," she breathed.

"This house is quite a recent addition to the Steele family—Queen Anne. That gentleman you're looking at is Jonathan's grandfather."

He led her up another couple of steps and she found herself looking at a bewhiskered gentleman, dressed in a splendid military uniform.

"Rupert Forster Steele fought under Sir Francis Drake against the Spanish Armada," he explained. "The Queen rewarded him with this land and he built a magnificent house, took a bride and started the distinguished line of Steeles. That's his portrait over there. The Steeles have an illustrious fighting history, practically every male member distinguishing himself in whatever war was going on at the time. Jonathan's father was killed at the end of this one; he received the Military Cross posthumously."

Careen looked with interest. "What happened to the original house?"

"Mad Rupert put an end to that."

She was amused. "Mad Rupert, who on earth was he?"

"The great-grandson of the first Rupert. He killed his

bride for her dowry and later on, when his madness became really apparent, he set fire to the house and perished in the flames. Some enterprising chap saved the family portraits, but not his; he started the fire with it."

"You must be joking," she said with a laugh.

"No, I assure you it's true. He smothered his wife with a pillow."

Careen shuddered. "How terrible."

"Well, it was a few hundred years ago and there was another Steele to carry on the family name, and, after all, that is the important thing."

She laughed then.

"Let's go in for coffee," he suggested.

"I'm glad you told me about the family history. It helps me to understand Jonathan a little better."

"Do you want to know him any better?" he asked with an arched smile.

For some reason the question annoyed her. "After tomorrow I hope I shall never see him again," she said vehemently.

CHAPTER FOUR

THE next morning proved to be as sunny and warm as its predecessor. Careen awoke early and lay in the bed reflecting on everything that had happened in the past twenty-four hours. It was incredible to imagine that such a short time ago she knew nothing of the Steeles and their fascinating history. She could well sympathise with her mother's desire to escape from becoming an unwelcome bride; it was a position which would require much strength of character and Careen was under no illusions about her mother's shy nature.

After washing and dressing she repacked her suitcase in readiness to leave as soon as possible and, when she judged the time was right, she went downstairs. The housekeeper, Mrs Gilshaw, was waiting in the hall, hovering around and looking slightly uncomfortable. She started towards Careen when she saw her. "Mr Steele 'ud like to see you as soon as you've finished breakfast," she told her.

"Mr Joseph Steele?"

The housekeeper nodded and Careen was aware of an absurd feeling of disappointment. Somewhere in the recesses of her mind she was harbouring the hope that Jonathan would apologise for his surly behaviour and offer her friendship. She realised then it was useless to hope; Jonathan Steele would not yield once his mind was made up.

Careen smiled at the woman who was looking at her once more with intense interest. "Thank you, Mrs Gilshaw. I'll go immediately after breakfast." She started to move away, but the housekeeper put a restraining hand on her arm.

"I'm glad you're here, dear," she said in a low whisper, and Careen looked at her curiously. "I was a maid in this house with your mother, when the old lady was alive. They made her very unhappy and she was a good soul. She'd have made a good wife for Mr Joseph, but they wouldn't let her."

"I remember the day she left; she was heartbroken. I tried to stop her going but she was determined. She had nowhere to go, but she said she didn't want to cause trouble for *him*. It was a pity to see him; beside himself he was with grief. Seemed to age overnight. He's never been the same since."

"She was the only person he really cared for, except the old lady, and after that he never cared for her. You've as much right to be here as any of them. . . ."

"Good morning, Miss Lacey—Mrs Gilshaw."

They both looked to where Louise was standing at the top of the stairs.

"Good morning," they both chorused.

Louise walked elegantly down the stairs. Before Mrs Gilshaw scuttled in the direction of the kitchen, Careen gave her a reassuring smile and waited for Louise to join her.

"Have you had breakfast yet?" she asked politely.

"I was just on my way," Careen replied, wondering how much she had heard.

"We can go in together. My son is out on business at the moment, but he asked me to tell you he will be back later this morning—in time to drive you back to London."

*   *   *

As soon as she could make her escape from the dining-room, Careen went up to Joseph's room. Breakfasting alone with Louise Steele and Hetty had been almost too much of an ordeal. Rodney had already gone out to finish his sketch of the lonely cove.

She knocked gently at the door, to have it opened by Lawson. He smiled, bowed stiffly and ushered her in. Joseph was sitting in the same chair as on the previous day. His face broke into a broad smile when he saw her.

"Well, my dear, did you sleep well?"

"Very well, thank you," she lied, and sat down opposite him.

"What do you think of my house now that you've had time to look at it properly?"

"It's very beautiful and comfortable," she replied truthfully.

He raised one eyebrow. "A bit different to the one you live in, eh?"

Careen couldn't resist a smile. "It certainly is." She paused for a moment and then continued. "Mr Steele, may I ask you a question?"

"Certainly, Careen—you don't mind my calling you that? It's a very pretty name."

"Of course you may."

"Good. What is your question?"

"The main reason I put the obituary in the local paper and why I accepted your invitation was because I was hoping to discover some relatives of my mother. I discovered I was not related to the Steeles, but perhaps there is someone in the village who is part of the family."

"I'm sorry your visit has been fruitless in this respect, my dear. Your mother had two elder brothers. Her parents died just before she came to work here and the eldest brother and his wife tenanted one of my farms not far from here. He was considerably older than Helen and he and his wife spent most of their spare time and money on drink. A great deal of the farm work was left to Helen and the other brother; that was why I had her come here to work—it was no life where she was."

"What happened to them?"

"When the war came the younger of the two brothers joined the army. He never came back. Whether he was killed or used the war as an excuse to cut loose I don't know, but no one around here has heard of him since. The elder brother and his wife died in an influenza epidemic several years after your mother left."

"Well, that is certainly that," Careen sighed. She looked at him carefully for a moment or two and then said, "I don't know whether I should ask you this, but. . . ."

"Go ahead, Careen. What is it you want to know?"

She twisted her hands in her lap. "Please don't think I'm being morbid or anything and don't think it matters to me after all these years, but. . . ."

"Out with it, child. I'm old and my skin is quite thick now." He smiled gently.

"Your sister-in-law said that you and my mother were lovers."

He nodded his head slowly. "I see." Then he sat forward a little. "The answer is no, Careen. I loved your mother very much and although I had sown some wild oats in my time—you wouldn't believe it now, would you?—I wasn't going to reduce our relationship to something they could sneer at."

Careen looked down at her hands and then back to the old man. "I'm glad I know."

"Have they been treating you right?"

"Yes, they've been very kind." She didn't want to be accused of telling tales as well as fortune hunting.

"That is very unchactertistic of them."

Careen suddenly became angry. "How do you expect them to act? They actually believe that you're going to ask me to marry you!"

Joseph Steele leaned his head back on the chair and laughed. He brought a large spotted handkerchief out of his pocket, took off his spectacles and mopped his eyes. "Let me assure you," he said at last, "I have no such intention."

Careen looked at him warily. "I'm happy to hear it and I must say one other thing, Mr Steele: if you leave me so much as a penny in your will I will sign it over to your nephew." She sat back and waited for his reaction. She knew she had no right to speak to him in that way, but she did want her position to be clear.

He looked mildly surprised. "You're certainly more spirited than Helen ever was. You'd fight for what you wanted, wouldn't you?" She did not reply. "Of course you would. You wouldn't run away."

He brought out an old-fashioned pocket watch and flicked it open. "You'll have to leave me now, my dear. I have a visitor coming to see me any time now."

She rose, trying to hide her relief at the end of the interview.

"I want to see you again after my visitor has left," he told her.

"But your nephew is going to take me back to town . . ." she protested.

He waved away her protests. "Jonathan will wait until I am ready."

Careen hoped she would not be the one who had to tell Jonathan, but if she had known then what was to come, she would not have worried about so trivial a task.

She hovered uncertainly in the corridor, wondering whether to go downstairs or simply return to her room and wait for Mr Steele to call her again. It would be simpler still if the house was in a more inhabited area and she could just walk out. As it was, she was unfamiliar with the district and was not even sure where the house was exactly situated.

Slowly she walked towards the stairs and down the first couple. The doorbell rang and she stopped where she was, hoping that it was not Jonathan. At that precise moment she was unwilling to face his open hostility.

Mrs Gilshaw went to open the door and Careen was relieved that it was not Jonathan who entered. The man was short and thickset; what remained of his sparse hair was brushed across his shiny scalp. This must be Joseph's visitor, she thought.

He put his briefcase on to the floor and allowed Mrs Gilshaw to help him out of his coat. Just then the sitting-room door opened and when Louise came out and saw him her eyes opened wide with something like horror or fear, and the colour completely drained from her face.

Her hands flapped helplessly. "Why, Mr Baldwin, what are you doing here?"

Careen sensed the tension in the atmosphere and she had a strange foreboding of trouble.

"Mr Steele—Mr Joseph Steele—sent for me, dear lady," he said. "He should have told you."

Louise recovered herself then. "It doesn't matter. Perhaps you'll take coffee with me before you go up?"

"You know what a stickler for punctuality he is; I'd better go straight up."

The man named Baldwin followed Mrs Gilshaw up the stairs and Careen started down again. As they passed the man nodded pleasantly and the housekeeper looked particularly smug. Careen could not help but wonder who he was to raise such animation in Louise Steele.

When she reached the bottom Louise was staring after the man and followed him with her eyes until he disappeared down the corridor; then she turned to Careen with the same fury, this time distorting her face and making it quite ugly.

"I hope you're satisfied," she said in a choked voice.

Before Careen had a chance to question that statement the front door opened again and this time it was Jonathan who entered. His face wore a half-smile and

Careen wondered what he had been doing to make him look so satisfied. When he saw his mother his smile faded and Careen recognised his usual fierce expression. He glanced at Careen and then back to his mother.

"What is it, Mother? What has happened?"

"Baldwin is here," she said.

He banged his fist against his open palm. "I knew it!" He gazed fiercely at Careen, who shook her head helplessly.

"Will someone please tell me what is going on! Why are you looking at me as if I've done something diabolical? Who is that man?"

"Mr Baldwin is a member of Hart and Hart, a firm of solicitors," Jonathan told her in a level voice. "They drew up my uncle's will," he added softly.

Careen covered her face with trembling hands. "I told him I didn't want anything," she gasped.

Louise looked at her dispassionately. "Very clever," she said, and with that she slammed back into the sitting-room.

Careen turned desperately to Jonathan. "You don't believe it, do you? I swear I don't want a penny."

He looked at her wearily, without malice or real interest. "There's no point in worrying about that now." And then he followed his mother into the sitting-room and closed the door, leaving Careen to calm herself as best she could.

*   *   *

Louise was standing in front of the window staring out into the distance when he entered. "There was no need to say that to her, Mother," he said as he closed the door.

She did not turn. "Why not? Her scheming may have paid off but there's no need for us to *like* it."

"Nevertheless, she is a guest in Uncle Joseph's house."

He went over to the fireplace and absently began to examine a small china shepherdess. "Anyway, we may be misjudging her. I don't really think she's as mercenary as we first thought."

Louise reeled round on him. "Don't tell me she's taken you in, too. Oh, what fools men become when they see a pretty face! She must have rolled those big green eyes at you and you believed her!" She turned her back on him again.

Jonathan carefully replaced the shepherdess on the mantelpiece. "She did nothing of the kind," he replied with quiet exasperation, "and I think I am as rational a judge of character as anyone. I don't doubt she hopes for something, but that's only human." He walked over to where his mother was standing and put two hands on her shoulders, his expression softening a little. "And what does it matter if he gives her a couple of thousand or even ten thousand pounds? It's nothing compared to the rest of the estate. We can afford to be generous, Mother."

Louise laughed mirthlessly. "You silly boy. I don't care if he does give her ten thousand pounds, but I know your uncle; he hasn't brought her here simply to give her that." She was silent for a moment. "He's got something more in mind, you'll see. He's not so old and he's not as ill as he pretends to be. How would you like to call her aunt?"

"Now that is ridiculous," he said in an amused voice.

"Is it? They can be married long enough to produce an heir and then it will be you who gets the ten thousand pounds, and after all the work you've put into this place and the money you've made for him."

"Would that be so terrible?" he asked in a gentle voice. "We still have the money father left and I can earn my own living. We could move to London; you can enjoy the shops and the theatres—everything you've missed. You might even marry some lucky man. But somehow I don't think it will come to that. Whatever else he is, Uncle Joseph is not a fool."

Louise put her hand on his and smiled. "You're probably right. Why don't you ask Julia to marry you now, Jonathan; it would please Joseph."

"When I ask someone to marry me, Mother, it will be because I want to and not because I want to safeguard my inheritance."

"It would be a good match, but I know it's useless pushing too hard. You're very much like Joseph and you'd resist all the more." She gave a sigh. "All the same, I wish I knew what was going on up there."

* * *

Meanwhile Careen had found herself shaking like a leaf after that emotional scene and in an attempt to calm herself she sat on the stairs and hugged herself until it stopped.

She blamed everyone in turn for her predicament. Firstly Aunt Rose for persuading her to come, then Jonathan and his mother for making such an issue of her visit, Joseph himself for disregarding her wishes, and finally herself for being so naïve as to believe this would be a simple visit with no strings attached.

She was relieved that Joseph had denied that he was going to ask her to marry him; she had thought he was too sensible to even consider it, but she had been afraid all the same. The idea that he was going to leave her some money in his will could not be discounted so easily, knowing how deep his love for her mother had been and how he blamed his family for her disappearance. He would do it out of spite for his family. Yes, it was obvious that this autocratic old man had completely ignored her wish not to be left money and was going ahead with arrangements to alter his will.

Cupping her chin in her hands, she stared ahead. She

knew he was a wealthy man, but how much money did
one need to be wealthy? She had no idea. All she knew
was that she didn't want his money; she just wanted to
be able to earn her own.

As she stared unseeingly ahead she realised that the
doorbell had been ringing for some time. Slowly she got
to her feet and looked around; there was no sign of the
young maid and Mrs Gilshaw had still not come down.
Careen walked slowly to the door and opened it.

The girl who was standing on the step started forward
until she saw Careen and then she stopped abruptly.
They eyed each other curiously. Careen considered the
other girl, who was about the same age as herself; she
was very pretty—almost angelic—with fluffy blonde
hair and wide blue eyes. She wore a pair of tight black
slacks, a deep-pink sweater and a matching bandeau
around her hair. She dangled a car key between her
fingers as she appraised Careen.

"Aren't you going to let me in?" Her eyes sparkled
mischievously.

Careen hastily flung open the door. "I'm sorry. I
don't work here you see, but the maid seems to have
disappeared."

The girl sauntered into the hall and then turned back
to Careen. "I'm Julia Cresswell."

Careen shook her limp hand and returned her smile.
"I'm Careen Lacey."

Julia laughed delightedly. "I know."

There was nothing else to say. Careen felt awkward
in the presence of such an attractive and self-confident
girl. She could not help thinking what an unlikely bride
she would make Jonathan, but conceded that perhaps
her bright ebullience was exactly what he did need.

"You are Mr Steele's fiancée, aren't you?" she ventured, in an attempt to make conversation.

"If you mean Jon—he hasn't asked me yet."

"Oh—I'm sorry if I. . . ."

Julia laughed again. "Don't be embarrassed, it's just that Jonathan and I haven't. . . ."

Just at that moment Jonathan came out of the sitting-room. He grinned when he saw Julia and she gave him a dazzling smile.

"Julia, how nice to see you!"

She looked at him coyly from beneath her thick eye-lashes. "If only I could be sure about that."

Careen watched them with interest. How utterly cap-tivating she is, she thought, and how wonderful it must be to have a man look at you the way Jonathan is looking at her. Steady on, she warned herself, thoughts like that could be dangerous.

"I've just been acquainting myself with Miss Lacey. You didn't tell me she was so pretty, Jon—shame on you."

Jonathan took her arm and his glance passed over Careen with only a flicker of interest. "Didn't I? Well, now you've seen for yourself. Come along to the sitting-room, Julia, Mother will be pleased to see you." He glanced across at Careen again. "Won't you join us, Miss Lacey? Are you staying for lunch, Julia?"

"No, I can't. Mummy and Daddy want you, Louise and Rodney to come for dinner tomorrow night and they sent me along to issue the invitation."

Careen hung back, feeling very much the outsider. She would have stayed in the hall only Jonathan and Julia waited for her before they went in, and reluctantly she joined them. Louise made an exclamation of delight when she saw Julia, who repeated the invitation as they embraced.

Louise flashed some kind of message with her eyes to her son. "I don't know, Julia," he said.

She waved her hands airily. "If you're thinking of Miss Lacey, of course she is invited too."

"Thank you, Miss Cresswell," Careen found her voice at last, "but I don't think I'll be here."

"Oh—what a pity. Well, if you are, you're welcome to come."

"May I let you know, Julia?" Jonathan interrupted quickly.

"Naturally, there's no hurry—as long as we have half an hour's notice! It was only an excuse to come over anyway, but I suppose you've already guessed that." She looked coyly at Jonathan again.

"I hope you don't need one," Louise said lightly.

Julia walked round the room, exhibiting herself, no doubt for Jonathan's benefit, Careen thought. "Where is Rodney today?" she asked nonchalantly.

"He's at the coast, sketching a deserted cove on to his canvas, I believe," Jonathan told her.

Her pretty pink lips pouted an "Oh" and her pink-tipped nails danced across the back of the sofa.

"How are your parents?" Louise asked in an effort to support the flagging conversation.

"They're fine." She tilted her head. "I hope I'm not treading on anyone's toes, but," she paused and glanced around, "do I detect a strained atmosphere?"

Louise opened her mouth to deny it, but Jonathan laughed—a deep, rich laugh. "You're the most tactless young lady I have ever met," he chided gently.

"I can see I've come at the wrong time," Julia said carefully, and made a dash for the door before anyone could stop her. "I'll see you all tomorrow night, and see that you bring Rodney along." She paused to pass Careen. "And I hope to see you, too, Miss Lacey. There aren't many women near my age in the village and I'm starved of girl talk. I hope we can remedy that."

Careen smiled gratefully. "Goodbye, Miss Cresswell."

"Julia," she whispered, and was gone.

Jonathan rushed after her, leaving the door wide open. As Louise and Careen watched her go they also saw Mr Baldwin coming down the stairs. Louise caught her breath and went out to meet him.

Careen went further into the room so that she could not see the three of them talking. She was sure Julia would bring sunshine into the house; she was bound to make Jonathan happy and for some reason Careen was glad. Suddenly she was aware of someone watching her and, turning, saw Jonathan standing in the doorway.

His eyes were hard as he stared at her and her heart raced madly. "My uncle wishes to see us in his room."

She stood rooted to the spot.

"He doesn't like to be kept waiting." He put his hand on her arm and led her into the hall and up the stairs. Numbly she allowed him to lead her. Louise had disappeared and Careen was relieved not to have her accusing eyes follow her.

CHAPTER FIVE

As JONATHAN was about to knock on the door Careen pulled his hand back sharply. He looked at her with surprise. "You have to believe me, Mr Steele—someone has to or I shall go mad. I told your uncle this morning that if he left me money I will make it over to you immediately; I don't want it and I have no use for it."

He smiled contemptuously and there seemed to be sparks in his smouldering eyes. "Everyone needs money, Miss Lacey—especially those who don't have any."

"That's precisely why I don't want it," she said fiercely. "Compared to people like you I'm poor, but there's always been enough money for the things we need and for little luxuries too. For twenty years I've been satisfied with that and I want to go on being satisfied."

His bushy eyebrows rose slightly.

"When I was a little girl, a woman who lived in the village had a small win on the football pools. She went to London and bought a whole wardrobe-full of expensive clothes and a big new car; but gradually her friends stopped calling round—they felt shabby next to her and they were frightened they would dirty her new carpets."

To her surprise he smiled and scratched the side of his face thoughtfully. "I'm not sure I understand the moral of that story, but I must tell you that if my uncle has decided to remember you in his will, I wouldn't dream of allowing you to sign it over."

"I shall give it to charity then," she said with a toss of her head.

He turned away from her to knock on the door, but

before he did she was sure he was smiling. "You must do as you wish," he said in a muffled voice.

The faithful Lawson opened the door and for the second time that morning Careen was shown into Joseph Steele's room. He smiled when he saw them, but Careen was too angry to smile back.

"Good morning, Jonathan."

"Good morning, Uncle Joseph. How are you today?"

"Very well. Very well indeed. Sit down both of you."

Dumbly Careen obeyed, but Jonathan elected to stand in front of the fire in a characteristic pose, his hands clasped behind his back.

Joseph looked up at his nephew. "No doubt you saw Baldwin while he was here?"

"Yes, Uncle," Jonathan stared ahead woodenly.

"Mr Steele," Careen began, "I told you this morning. . . ."

Joseph imperiously held up one bony hand. "I have no intention of leaving you any money."

Careen relaxed a little and looked at Jonathan, but he still stared ahead.

"However," the old man continued, "I have altered my will a little." He looked at the two young people in turn, obviously enjoying himself. "In the terms of the new will you, Jonathan, will receive everything as before, except for the usual bequests. . . ."

Careen drew a sigh of relief.

"But there is one condition. . . ."

Jonathan looked at his uncle then. "Condition?"

"Yes," Joseph smiled at them both again. "On condition that you marry Careen."

She jumped up out of the chair. "What!"

Jonathan looked at his uncle, his expression one of frozen horror, but he said nothing.

"But that is ridiculous!" she exclaimed, and managed a nervous laugh. She was aware that her face had taken on an unbecoming rosy glow, but she was past caring.

"You don't really mean this, Uncle," Jonathan managed to say after the first shock had worn off.

"He can't," echoed Careen.

The old man was still smiling and seemed completely unperturbed by the reaction to his announcement. "Sit down, my dear," he urged.

Her legs were feeling rather shaky and she was happy to comply. She sank down and buried her head in her hand.

"I think you'd better explain what you mean, Uncle Joseph," Jonathan said icily.

"I have already told you. Unless you marry Careen, on my death this house will go to an organisation which cares for elderly people and the bulk of my fortune will be put in trust for the running expenses."

Careen jumped to her feet once more. "I'm going to get my suitcase; I'm leaving this madhouse now!"

"Don't be so hasty," Joseph said silkily. "This has been a shock to you both; you must consider all the implications. I think, Jonathan, it will be worth your while to persuade Miss Lacey to stay."

So far Jonathan had not looked at her, but now he did. "Supposing I did marry her, what is there to stop us being divorced once I had benefited under your will?"

The old man chuckled. "I'm not so foolish not to have foreseen that possibility and it has been covered. If you are divorced or the marriage is annulled at any time, the house then goes to the organisation I mentioned before."

"And if we marry and stay married—what then?"

"You can do as you please. Everything will be yours absolutely and I presume the house and estate will eventually pass on to your heirs."

Careen could bear it no longer, she threw herself on to her knees in front of him. "Please don't do this, I beg you! A marriage between us is impossible. I know what you're up to—you're trying to re-live your own life through us, but it's monstrous. He doesn't even like me."

Joseph was unperturbed and looked enquiringly at his nephew. "Is that true? Don't you like her?"

"What difference does that make," he replied impatiently.

"None at all," he uncle said blandly and, with one hand under her chin, he raised her face. "Allow me to know what is best for you."

Enraged, she struggled to her feet. "I don't know what to say to make an impression on you. You're both acting as if a proposed marriage between two virtual strangers is a normal occurrence in this house!" She looked appealingly at Jonathan, who seemed unmoved by his uncle's absurd condition. "Can't you do anything?"

He seemed deep in thought and then he looked at Careen. "Perhaps we should discuss this in private."

"There is nothing to discuss!" she insisted with mounting agitation.

"I think that is a very sensible idea," Joseph agreed. "It's up to you to convince her, Jonathan; you know how much is at stake. There's no immediate rush, as long as it's done before I die."

Jonathan seemed to jerk out of his thoughts and his manner became brisk once more. "Come along, Miss Lacey. We have a lot of talking to do."

Careen looked at him in amazement. He was treating the whole affair in such a businesslike way; as if it were the sort of thing which happened every day. "How can you be so calm?" she indignantly asked as he guided her out of the room.

"Because there's no point in getting rattled."

As he closed the door behind them they heard Joseph's deep chuckle. "What a wicked old man!" she exclaimed as soon as they were in the corridor.

"I don't think he's wicked, Miss Lacey. Believe it or

not, he thinks he's doing it for our benefit."

"What benefit could there be in such a marriage? Joseph Steele of all men should know the value of love in marriage. It's revenge, that's *all* it is—revenge because of my mother." She looked up at him and was surprised to see that he was laughing at her, but she was too angry to appreciate, this time, how wonderful he looked when he laughed.

"Well, the kitten has claws," he said, and then more seriously, "Call it revenge or blackmail—it doesn't matter—it won't change the situation. We can talk in my study. No one ever goes in there besides me, except to clean, so we shan't be disturbed. This way, Miss Lacey."

She followed him along the corridor. "I don't understand you," she said angrily, hurrying to keep up with him. "You positively hated me when you thought I might get a few thousand pounds, but now when your whole inheritance is in the balance you're treating it as some huge joke."

He held open the door for her and she passed inside, almost brushing against him as she did so; she shivered once more at his closeness. The room he used as a study was not large. It was very masculine, as she imagined it would be. The floor was shiny parquet. There was a desk, a large bookcase filled with legal volumes, a Persian rug and two comfortable chairs.

He pulled one up to the desk for her and reluctantly she sat down. He walked slowly round to the other side of the desk and sat down while Careen riveted her attention on to a painting on the wall behind the desk. It was a conventional landscape showing some cows, a farmhouse, trees and part of a field. She had seen many similar paintings but this one did have a certain charm. Jonathan noticed that she was staring at it. "It's one of Rodney's," he explained.

"But he's quite good!"

"Yes, he is. That's one of the reasons we have him here. If he were simply fooling around my mother wouldn't allow him to stay." He gave her a small smile. "He has to justify his existence." He put his hands firmly palm down on the desk. "Now, down to business."

Her anger rose again. "Oh, how can you treat it like some piffling legal problem. You lawyers are all the same!"

"There's no need to be insulting, Miss Lacey, and besides, as you so perceptively said, it is my home and inheritance that is in danger, not yours, so if anyone should be angry it is I."

Suddenly she felt deflated. "What are you going to do?"

"That's what we have to discuss."

"What exactly is involved?" she asked suddenly, realising that she had no idea what Jonathan would be losing.

"This house, a great deal of money in securities, stocks and shares, two thousand acres of land around this area with the income from it and some property in London." He paused, looking at her shrewdly. "You must think me very mercenary, but I do handle my uncle's business affairs and I'm very conversant with the relevant facts."

"No, of course I don't; it just sounds like a great deal of wealth and you are entitled to it. Surely your uncle can't give it all away."

"He'll leave me something—more than enough, I should say—but the important thing is the ownership of this house and the surrounding land. Even if he did cut me out of the will completely I should still be a relatively wealthy man; my father had his inheritance, too. The Steeles made their fortune at a time when it was easily done."

"Can't you contest the will? Surely no court would uphold such conditions."

"I wouldn't like to take a chance on that. My uncle is not insane and courts are very reluctant to give judgement against the terms of a will. Apart from that such action is costly and well publicised—it would look very sordid in print."

"But it would be sinful to allow this lovely old house to become an old people's home, especially since it's belonged to your family for generations. Its history would simply get swallowed up; in ten years no one would ever remember who lived here originally."

He pushed his chair back and stood up. "It is lovely, isn't it? I was born here and so was my father and my grandfather and so on. I know every inch of it." He looked at her and smiled wearily as she realised for the first time that this had really been a bad shock to him.

"He knows you really care about Pierce End; that's why he's trying this absurd bluff," she whispered.

"Yes, he knows, but it's no bluff."

"I'm *sure* your uncle will change his mind. He must see how unreasonable his demand really is," she said without much conviction.

Jonathan began to pace up and down behind the desk, his hands behind his back and his eyes riveted to the floor. "No, he won't."

"But he must."

"I know him and he means what he says. He has no son to inherit, and I don't think he really cares what happens to the house when he dies."

"Then what are you going to do?"

He stopped pacing. "We could get married," he said abruptly.

"Married? But what about Miss Cresswell?"

"Well, what about her?" he barked, so fiercely that she jumped.

"I understand you're engaged to her, or about to be."

"There's nothing between Julia and myself which would affect a marriage between you and I."

He had put it in such an ambiguous lawyer-like way that she almost smiled. "But there is nothing between us except mutual dislike."

He sat down again and stared at her in that disturbing way of his. "Speak for yourself, Miss Lacey. However, if you feel that way, there's nothing more to be said. If you'd like to collect your things together I'll drive you back to London."

She stared at him as he cupped his face in his hands and closed his eyes. That was that, she thought. She was free. She could go. She could forget the Steeles ever existed. But how could she go now and leave him in this terrible predicament that she had unwittingly caused? She remembered how lovingly he had spoken of the house and grounds and how hard he must work making sure everything is in order. His love for his home must surely be greater than his love for Julia Cresswell.

"Would you really marry me?" she asked in a small voice.

"Yes, if you were willing." He raised his head and looked at her hopefully.

"But your mother. . . ."

He thumped his fist on the table. "Damn my mother! I'm thirty-two years old and I don't have to ask her permission!"

It was the first time she had seen him in a temper, but it didn't surprise her; she knew it was there somewhere, but always carefully controlled. Somehow now that he had unleashed it he seemed more human. "I'm willing," she said softly.

He looked up sharply. "Are you sure?"

She met his eyes. "Yes, very sure. If I hadn't come here in the first place none of this would have happened. Marrying you and assuring you get what is rightly yours is the least I can do."

"Are you sure you realise what it entails?"

"Yes," she said softly, fumbling with the hem of her skirt.

"Well, you'd better be. You heard my uncle—there's no way out and if you decide you've made a mistake I'll lose Pierce End anyway. Rather than have that happen I'd lose it now."

She glanced up at him quickly. "Don't worry, I won't go back on anything."

"Perhaps there's some young man you're attached to at home?" he asked and watched her with narrowed eyes.

"No one special. I'm not in love with anyone if that is what you mean."

He nodded. "You're very young to be tied down in marriage."

She stared at him defiantly. "Many of my school friends are already married and have families."

"Yes, but forgive me for mentioning it—they haven't spent the past four years caring for an invalid; they've probably worked among a number of people and been able to pick and choose before they married."

"How did you know about that?"

"I made it my business to know."

She stiffened. "In that case I make a better candidate. I won't expect you to wine and dine me every night and I won't flirt with the butler. My tastes are simple because of the reasons you've just mentioned."

He smiled wryly, ignoring her sarcasm. "You have all the answers."

She tried to return his smile, but her lips were stiff. It was like being interviewed for a job, she thought.

"Have you ever been in love?" he asked suddenly.

The abruptness of the question startled her. "No—no I don't think so."

"Have you considered what might happen if you did—after we are married?"

"I don't understand you."

"Everyone falls in love at least once in their lives. Your mother, for instance, fell in love twice. You're bound to meet someone sooner or later; what will you do then?"

"Who would I fall in love with?" She tried to hide her bewilderment at the strange questions he was asking.

"My dear Miss Lacey—anyone; the butcher, the milkman—anyone."

Her face took on a stony look. "You must have a very poor opinion of me."

"Opinion has nothing to do with it; I just want you to be aware of the facts."

"I've managed to exist without male adoration for the past twenty years and I think I can manage the next fifty or so without it too." She bit off a retort that she was unlike Julia Cresswell in that respect, but instead she added, "The same could be said of you."

"But I am of an age when I know my own mind and I appreciate what I'm getting into." He smiled and she wasn't sure whether he was laughing at her or not. Suddenly he stood up again and, walking over to the window, he stared out across the fields.

"The land, as far as the eye can see from any window in this house, belongs to my uncle," he said quietly after a while. "I love this place for its own sake. I've read every history book ever written which mentions my family. You probably think it's foolish to be proud of people who have been dead for hundreds of years and who weren't very good people when they were alive."

"No, I don't," she answered softly. "I wish I knew something about my ancestors," she laughed a little, "apart from the fact I had a drunkard for an uncle."

He did not appear to hear her. "I'm the last of the line so far and I want an heir."

There were a few moments of silence as she looked at him, expecting him to turn and look at her, but he kept staring out of the window. "Naturally," she replied. "I understand that."

He turned briskly. "Good, shall we get down to discussing details?" He came across to the desk. "We may as well marry as soon as possible. How long do you think you'll need?"

"I don't need any time."

"You'll want clothes," he said as he scribbled on a pad.

"I can get those on one shopping trip."

"Have you any preferences as to church or register office?"

"Not really, but I always intended to get married in church."

"Then church it is. The Steeles have always married in the village church. We'll have to wait for the banns to be called, but it will give you and Mother time to prepare. Now, you own a house I believe; will you want to sell it?"

As he fired questions she answered, until her head reeled. She felt as though she were concluding a business deal—but, of course, that's all it was.

Finally he put his pen down and glanced at his watch. "It's almost lunchtime. We had better tell Uncle Joseph our decision and then we'll go down and tell Mother."

She stood up dazedly, trying to suppress a desire to laugh hysterically. She was sure she would wake up soon and find it all a crazy dream.

"Just a minute," he said as they were about to leave, "there is one thing I forgot." Jonathan went back to the desk and, unlocking one of the drawers, he drew out a large box which unlocked with a smaller key. As he picked up yet another box he called her over and flicked it open.

The box contained a dazzling square-cut emerald, and as it flashed and winked in the light Careen gasped at its beauty. She watched him take it out of the box and slip it on to her finger. "It should fit. The last person who wore it was my grandmother and she was small too.

She was small, but she had plenty of backbone—even my grandfather was afraid of her. It's said that she was the real head of the family."

Her hand stayed suspended in mid-air and then she began to pull it off. "I can't wear it—I have no right."

He pushed it back on. "Of course you have a right. And it is perfect for you—it matches your eyes. Emeralds are your stones."

She laughed then. "I've never owned one before."

He took another box out, this time an oblong one. He opened it to reveal an emerald necklace. "This will technically be yours on our wedding day, but personally I think it's hideous. Much too heavy and clumsy for today's fashion and for someone as young as you."

She stared at it in fascination. It was ugly; the emeralds were set in heavy gold and she was glad he did not expect her to wear them. "Of course," he added, "if you want to you can."

"Oh, no," she said hurriedly, "I agree with you and I'm not overfond of jewellery anyway."

He was standing very close and suddenly she was embarrassed by his critical examination. She turned to go, but he pulled her back towards him.

"Don't you think our engagement warrants a kiss?"

"Well, I . . . yes, if you like," she stammered, feeling more than a little foolish.

She closed her eyes and allowed herself to be drawn towards him. It was like being suffocated, she thought, as his lips almost bruised hers. After a minute he let her go and she opened her eyes to see that his lips were curled into the now familiar contemptuous smile.

"It's not going to be so easy, is it?" he said.

They went first to Joseph to tell him and he greeted the news of their engagement with the confident air of one who expected absolute obedience. Careen stood stonily by Jonathan's side, still smarting with humiliation at the rough kiss he had inflicted on her. Well, that was something else she would have to get used to.

Their interview with Joseph was soon over and Careen prepared herself to face Louise. They did not have long to wait; she was in the hall when they came down the stairs, and it looked as though she had been waiting for a long time.

"Well," she said when she saw them, "what happened? I must say you've been long enough up there."

"We'd better go into the sitting-room," Jonathan told her.

Hetty was already there and when Louise asked her to leave Jonathan interrupted. "No, let her stay. She's as much a part of this family as anyone and she has a right to hear this."

Hetty looked at him, her shrewd button eyes glittering as she licked her thin lips. Slowly and unemotionally Jonathan told them about the condition and the decision he and Careen had made.

Whilst he explained Careen stood stiffly to attention near the door and unconsciously her right hand covered the left and the ring it wore. Her eyes never left Louise's face as the colour slowly drained from it. She opened her mouth to speak but no words came and one bloodless hand gripped the arm of the chair as she swayed sideways. Jonathan rushed forward, but with her eyes still closed Louise put her other hand out to stop him.

"Don't touch me! I'm all right. How could he do such a thing!"

"Miss Lacey kindly agreed to marry me, Mother."

Her eyes opened wide then and she flashed a venomous look at Careen. "Of course she would. She would jump at the chance."

"Please, Mother," he said patiently, "she is going to be my wife and there's nothing more to be said about it. It isn't easy for her either, to give up her friends and her life up in Yorkshire."

"What is she giving up?" Louise spat contemptuously. "A life of luxury here in exchange for a pitiful existence in a remote village."

"I was happy there," Careen said with quiet dignity.

Suddenly the tension was broken by Hetty's hysterical laughter and Louise became oblivious to everything for a time in an effort to stop her. "She'll be mistress here after all," Hetty cackled, and the high-pitched tone of her voice jarred on Careen's already tired nerves.

Jonathan looked steadily at his mother. "As far as anyone outside this room is aware, we fell in love at first sight. An engagement notice will go in *The Times* this week and we can announce it to our friends as soon as possible; the Cresswells will be informed tomorrow when we go for dinner."

"Oh, if only you'd married Julia when she first came home from finishing school this would never have happened," Louise wailed.

"Mother!"

"No one will believe that love-at-first-sight business and no couple become engaged after only a day's acquaintance," she argued.

Careen quailed at the thought of facing Julia. What would this do to that sweet and friendly girl who expected to become Mrs Jonathan Steele? How could Careen sit at the same table as these two who were in love and could never now marry?

"Nonsense," Jonathan replied. "People are incurable romantics; they'll love it."

"I see you have it all arranged between you," she said coldly. "Very well, Jonathan, you have my co-operation in this farce, but please don't ask for my blessing. Come along, Hetty, let's go in to lunch." She brushed past Careen as if she were not even there.

"Just a minute, Mother. I think we'd better dispense with all formality. We'll use first names from now on." His eyes sparkled mischievously. "Perhaps Careen should call you Louise. Mother-in-law doesn't suit you at all."

Louise drew a sharp breath and continued out of the room. During lunch Careen pushed her food around the plate, feeling sure she would choke if she attempted to eat. Likewise Louise picked at her food as she listened in silence to Jonathan's plans. Only he and Hetty seemed unaffected.

After lunch Jonathan went to attend to the business he had missed in the morning and Careen excused herself and went out for a long walk across the fields. She was unfamiliar with the area, but she needed the fresh air to clear her head and she was reluctant to spend the afternoon in Louise's company.

A feeling of complete unreality hovered over her. She still could not believe she was to become the wife of this tall, dark stranger whom she could not pretend to understand. If he had become more hostile towards her she would have understood, and although his treatment now was far from affectionate, it certainly was not as bad as it had been the previous day.

Pulling her hand out of her coat pocket, she stared at the emerald; as it gleamed in the sun it seemed to be mocking her. Again her thoughts turned to Julia, poor Julia, how heartbroken she would be. It was no consolation that she was pretty enough and rich enough to find another suitor before long.

Like every young woman, Careen had often thought about love and marriage; there had always been some shadowy being at the back of her mind who, one day, would materialise and become *the* man. That would never happen now. She was engaged, but she felt none of the rapture of the newly betrothed. It was a mockery of love. Their marriage would be one big lie. She would live with Jonathan, eventually run his home, bear his children and never ever know the ecstasy of true love.

Tears pricked beneath her eyelids as she turned back towards the house, fighting the fear which was now invading her heart. She determined not to let it show through; she would prove herself a good and dutiful wife—it was the only way to make up for the trouble her coming had caused.

On his return that evening Rodney was told of their engagement and his reaction was at first open disbelief which quickly turned to ridicule. In his more customary abrupt way Jonathan acquainted him with the facts and the absolute necessity for secrecy. Careen believed she was the only one who heard him say under his breath as he stared into his glass, "Poor Julia," but she warmed to him when he turned and, pecking her lightly on the cheek, said in front of Louise's disapproving eye, "Welcome, Cousin."

CHAPTER SIX

CAREEN spent most of the next morning carefully wording a letter to Aunt Rose. Finally, with a dozen sheets of paper screwed up and discarded, she was satisfied with what she had penned. As Jonathan and Rodney were out she was once again reluctant to spend the afternoon with Louise and Hetty, so immediately after lunch she took her letter and walked the long way across the fields to the village.

It was a small village and almost picturesque in the sunshine which glinted off the eaves of the cottages sitting around the small village green. Careen guessed that life had changed very little since the time Rupert Steele had first taken up residence at Stokeley. How different it was to Witterton, with its steep cobbled streets and grey stone houses, the grimness of which was not even relieved by the brightness of the sun.

After being served her stamps by a curious postmistress, she asked the direction of the church where she would very shortly be married to Jonathan. She soon found it, up one of the side streets off the main square.

She pulled open the heavy oak door and stepped inside. The dimness was blinding after the bright sunshine and the atmosphere was dank and chill after the warmth of the sun. At first she could see nothing but dim shapes, but after her eyes grew accustomed she began to walk slowly down the aisle, imagining what it would be like filled with people and flowers on her wedding day.

When she reached the altar she turned and went out of the door at the side. She found herself in the graveyard, where she knew she had unconsciously intended to visit all the time. Slowly she walked along the rows of stones until she saw what she was seeking. She crouched down and read the inscription on the stone—Eveline and Ezra Forbridge. The date of their death was twenty-sixth November Nineteen Forty-seven. As she walked along the rows she discovered several more Forbridges before she finally came upon the Steele family vault. The sombre surroundings, together with the knowledge that all her relatives on her mother's side were dead, depressed her.

She stared at the imposing vault which housed generations of dead Steeles. One day she would join them—because her name was Steele—but she would never be one of them. How could she be?

There was a small wooden bench nearby; a metal plaque fixed to the back informed her that it was donated by Albert Steele in Nineteen Twenty-one. She sat down wearily and suddenly the grey old gravestones blurred before her eyes and she buried her head in her hands, allowing the tears to trickle through her fingers.

But there was still time to back out of this awful engagement, she realised with an upsurge of hope in her heart; the engagement had not yet been publicly announced. Every nerve in her body urged her to run, right now, without waiting to collect her clothes. There must be transport from the village. I can be in London before I'm missed, she thought, and I can be back in Witterton before the day is out.

Back to the place where sanity and common sense prevailed; back among her own kind who were only concerned whether it was going to be a good summer or a bad winter and where the very idea that a mere house was of any real importance except to keep out the wet and keep in the warmth, would be met with disdain and ridicule. So what if the Steeles were proud of their history? Weren't the living more important? Careen considered her own life important and here was she planning to throw it away on a man who did not even pretend to feel anything but contempt for her.

She lost track of how long she had sat there. Somewhere nearby she heard footsteps, but she did not look up, even when the footsteps stopped.

"May I help?" a gentle voice asked.

Careen looked up then and saw the vicar standing over her. He was a slim, slightly stooped man with a shock of pure white hair, and his grey eyes smiled kindly.

"I don't think so, thank you," she gulped and fished in her pocket for her handkerchief.

"May I sit with you?"

"Of course." She wiped her eyes and stared ahead into the distance.

"Most people come here when they need help," he said.

"I didn't."

"Why did you come? You're not one of my regular parishioners and I know most people in this area, even those who don't come to church."

"I don't know why I came. To be alone, I suppose."

"We are never alone, my dear, always remember that." He paused, but she did not reply. "I don't remember ever seeing you before, but you do look familiar. Do you live around here?"

"No, I'm just visiting. If you were here thirty years ago you might have known my mother—Helen Forbridge."

The vicar thought carefully for a moment. "Ah, yes, I do remember. I had only been here a short while when she left the village, but she was a regular attender until then. How is your mother?"

"She died three weeks ago."

"I'm sorry. Now I understand your unhappiness, but you must not. . . ."

"I've already accepted it. I wasn't crying because of that."

"You realise there is no one left of the family."

"Yes."

"Who are you staying with while you are here?"

She looked at him then, wondering how much he knew of her mother's flight. "The Steeles."

His eyes seemed to flicker for a moment. "There is something troubling you and I'd like to help if I can. After all, that is why I am here."

"No one can help me."

"Let me try. Are you in trouble? Have you done something wrong?"

She looked at him again. "It's something I'm about to do and I don't know if it is very wrong or very right."

"You must weigh the considerations very carefully before you decide. If there are other people involved you must decide what is also the best for them. Happiness is never gained at the cost of others."

Careen stood up to go. He stood up also and she smiled as they shook hands. "Thank you. I know what to do now; I knew it all the time, but you have helped."

"My name is Fothergill and I would like you to look on me as your friend, Miss . . .?"

"Careen Lacey and, thank you, I will, Mr Fothergill."

On her walk back to Pierce End she allowed the cool breeze to blow away her depression. She knew, of course, now she must go ahead with this marriage. The only person who could be hurt by it was herself and that seemed unimportant compared to keeping Pierce End in the Steele family. And her life here could be no worse and no more lonely than life in a bed-sitter in some city. She would have to find some way of becoming accustomed to Jonathan's indifference and Louise's hatred; and the leisurely life she would have to lead.

When she arrived back at the house she was grateful

to reach her room without meeting anyone. She had not forgotten their dinner engagement although she was dreading it as much as ever. She would have to try and forget about Julia; if Jonathan was willing to give her up, she would not worry about it.

Despite her nervous anticipation of the way the news of their engagement would be received she made a special effort with her appearance; come what may, she wanted to be a credit to her future husband, and when she was finally dressed she was pleased with her appearance in the mirror.

They set off promptly in Jonathan's car—Rodney sitting beside Jonathan, who was driving, and Careen and Louise at the back. Careen's future mother-in-law sat straight-backed with her hands folded in her lap and her lips firmly closed in a thin line. Louise had hardly spoken to her since the previous day and Careen fervently wished she could find some words which would break through the barrier which Louise had erected between them.

Careen did not blame her for being bitter and she could not find it in her heart to dislike her. A woman who loved her son so devotedly and was so obviously fond of her nephew must have some affection to give the only daughter-in-law she would ever have. If only, Careen thought, I could make her like me a little.

Jonathan peered ahead and Careen watched him in fascination. His thick, dark hair curled into the nape of his neck and his eyes were thickly fringed. In time his hair would turn white like Joseph's, she thought. She tried to imagine what life would be like then and involuntarily she shivered.

"I had a word with old Fothergill this morning," he said brightly as they passed through the village. "I thought April Twenty-ninth would be a good day. Naturally he wants to see us together before then."

If he noticed the frozen silence from the back of the

car he made no sign, but continued to inform them about the progress he had made in arranging the wedding. Careen was numb, she hardly heard him, her mind was reeling. When she had spoken to the vicar he had already known about the wedding; and there was she, acting far from the happy bride.

"You might as well get busy issuing the invitations, Mother," Jonathan continued, undaunted by the silence he was encountering. "You and Careen can get together and decide who you are going to invite."

"There's only my aunt and uncle," Careen said in a mechanical voice which hardly seemed to belong to her. "My cousin and all my friends won't be able to come at such short notice and I've already written to Aunt Rose to prepare her."

"Can you imagine how hideous I shall look in a top hat?" Rodney quipped in an effort to lighten the atmosphere.

Careen smiled. "You'll look very handsome."

"A newly engaged lady, such as yourself, shouldn't be saying such things." He caught Jonathan's eye and sank back into his seat.

Just at that moment the car swept through the gates of the Cresswells' home. Careen's first glimpse of the Old Manor House was in the dusk. Butterflies flew around inside her as she accepted Jonathan's hand out of the car. They followed closely behind Louise and Rodney.

The butler opened the door to let them in. At a glance it was obvious that the Old Manor House was far larger than Pierce End, which surprised Careen, and even to her unaccustomed eye it was much older. Perhaps, she mused, this was how the original Pierce End looked—half-timbered, rambling with its low gables and mullioned windows.

The hall they were ushered into was large and oak panelled with low beams which seemed to sweep down from the ceiling. A bright log fire burned in the grate to take the chill off the still-cool evenings.

As Careen stared round interestedly, Jonathan solicitously helped her off with her coat, which the butler carefully laid over his arm as if it were precious mink instead of her three-year-old tweed.

Julia rushed to greet them and behind her came a woman who was unmistakably her mother; she was an older version of Julia—blonde, fluffy and pleasant. She kissed Louise's cheek and then was introduced to Careen by Jonathan.

"You're the young lady Julia told me about. We're very happy to meet you, Careen—I may call you that?"

"Of course. What a lovely old house you have here," she said, glancing round the beamed hall once again.

"It's not so old," she laughed modestly, "and we don't know anything of its history—unlike the Steeles. It's had several previous owners and we don't even know the name of the original family."

"Bellamy," Jonathan prompted.

Mrs Cresswell fluttered. "Yes, of course. Jonathan is always delving into the history books. Well, it doesn't matter now, it belongs to the Cresswells." She laughed loudly.

"Haven't you lived here long?" Careen asked.

"Only since Nineteen Forty-six."

To Careen it was a long time, before she was even born, but compared to the history of Pierce End, of course, it was not long.

"My husband is in the library. Come and meet him and our son and daughter-in-law."

Julia, she noticed, walked confidently beside Jonathan. He was looking down at her with an indulgent smile on his lips and she was chattering excitedly. At least Careen was grateful to Jonathan for not letting the unhappiness he must be feeling be apparent.

The room they were shown into had three walls lined

with books, some of which looked very old. Careen was instantly reminded of Jonathan's study, but in comparison this room had an air of artificiality and none of the character of Jonathan's. She braced herself for the second wave of introductions as she shook hands with Colonel Cresswell, his son Anthony, who was taller than Julia but just as fair, and his pale-faced wife, who could hardly contain her curiosity. She began to ask questions immediately, but was put off, to Careen's relief, by the Colonel.

"Later, Jenny. Just now we'll have some drinks. Now, Careen, what will you have? I have the prescription for the others." He laughed at his own joke and Careen felt a warm glow at how easily she had been accepted. Of course, they didn't know of her engagement—yet.

"Sherry, please."

"And the same for Jonathan and Louise. Usual for you, Rodney?"

"Please." He looked at Careen then and winked reassuringly. She smiled back, realising how apprehensive she must have looked.

The Colonel dispensed the drinks while his daughter handed them round. The red dress Julia was wearing accentuated her fragile fairness, Careen noticed, and made her look particularly lovely.

"Yesterday you weren't sure you would still be here, Careen," Julia said as she handed her the sherry. "What changed your mind?"

Careen swallowed hard. "Well, I. . . ."

"I asked her to stay," Jonathan said, coming across and standing by her side. "In fact, we can have something of a celebration tonight."

Everyone in the room turned to stare at them and as Jonathan put his hand on her shoulder she fixed her eyes on one of the books on the shelf. It was a large leather volume with bold gold lettering on the spine and Careen knew she would always remember that book very clearly as long as she lived. Somehow she resisted the over-whelming and childish impulse to throw herself into the protection of his arms as he began to speak.

"Careen and I," he announced, "are to be married."

There was a ghastly silence which seemed to last for ever before it was shattered by the crash of a glass as it hit the floor. It had slipped from Julia's frozen fingers. Suddenly everyone was talking at once and rushing to clear up the debris.

Careen stood dazedly by Jonathan's side and accepted Mrs Cresswell's bewildered good wishes, the Colonel's over-hearty handshake, Anthony's hostile glare and Jenny's perfunctory kiss.

"What a surprise!" Julia said in a choked voice. "Excuse me while I go and get a cloth; I've spilled some sherry on my dress." She fled from the room followed by her mother, who echoed her excuses.

Careen stood her ground and doubted if anyone realised how she was longing to run out too. Jonathan perhaps did for he exerted a gentle pressure on her arm. She moved away from him and sat down, sipping her drink; not because she wanted it, but because it gave her something to do.

Julia and her mother returned. She was outwardly composed, but Careen, watching for the signs, noticed how brightly her eyes shone and how flushed was her usually pale face. All attention now, mercifully, swung to Louise, who graciously accepted their congratulations with all the aplomb of a consummate actress. Even Jonathan's eyes shone with admiration.

Jenny turned her shrewd eyes on Careen. "You haven't known each other long have you?" she asked with a concentrated casualness.

"It was love at first sight," Jonathan gaily replied for her.

Careen flashed her eyes angrily. Don't lay it on so thick! they pleaded.

"How romantic," Jenny said with a harsh and, Careen thought, unbelieving laugh.

"Well," said the Colonel, rubbing his hands together, "it will be nice to have another pretty face around here."

During the dinner Careen hardly tasted her food, and from the look of Julia, neither did she. Everyone talked about weddings and brides until Careen felt she could scream. One thing which did surprise her was the attention Rodney showered on Julia throughout the evening. At first she thought it was kindness, but with dawning amazement she realised it was because he really wanted to. But Julia sat glum-faced throughout the meal and Careen did not miss the heartbreakingly appealing way she glanced at Jonathan from time to time, although he pretended not to notice.

Occasionally Careen intercepted a questioning look which Julia flashed across the table. Careen longed to tell her the truth; that Jonathan had not stopped loving her, but she was suddenly aware that his eyes were on her and, almost as if he were reading her thoughts, he smiled and shook his head. That small but very intimate gesture made her feel ridiculously weak and she looked away quickly. When she glanced at him again a moment later he was talking to his hostess, leaving Careen to wonder if she had imagined it after all.

At the first suitable moment Louise suggested that they leave and no one, except perhaps Rodney, was sorry to see the end of the evening. In the midst of the effusive farewells Careen noticed that Julia had managed to take Jonathan to one side. Despite her overpowering pride Careen was anxious to hear what was being said, so she moved a little closer.

"You don't mean to marry her, Jon," Julia said sharply, "you can't."

"I thought my intentions are very obvious, Julia," he replied as he slipped into his overcoat.

Careen kept her face averted and simulated interest in

something Mrs Cresswell was telling Louise, but she could picture the bitter expression on Julia's face as she said, "I thought they *were* obvious, Jon."

"Let us remain friends, Julia; I'm sure you won't notice the loss of one man from your army of admirers."

Careen recognised his bantering tone, which she realised he must use when he wished to cover up his true feelings.

Julia's voice took on a softer tone. "Oh, Jon, have you done this because you're jealous? Because if you have, I didn't mean to make you jealous. There's no one but you I really care for."

"Don't torture yourself, my dear. Careen and I will be married before the month is out and it certainly isn't because I'm jealous."

"We're ready when you are," Rodney shouted across, and any reply Julia might have made was left unsaid. But overhearing this little snippet of conversation was enough to plunge Careen into an ever deeper despair.

When at last they were in the car and on their way back to Pierce End, Careen laid her head back on the seat and closed her eyes wearily. Will everything always be such an ordeal? she asked herself.

Rodney half-turned in his seat. "Well, that didn't go off too badly," he said in an over-hearty way.

"It was frightful," Louise contradicted in a stiff voice.

"It was a shock to them, that's all," Jonathan said softly, and then he gave an uncharacteristic chuckle. "It was a shock for us too."

*   *   *

The next three weeks flew by in a continuous rush of activity, but to Careen it had a dream-like quality and everything she said or did was at the will of some unseen puppeteer.

After their evening at the Cresswells' Jonathan reverted to his cool, but courteous treatment of her and she realised with a heavy heart that their marriage was going to hurt him more than he would ever admit.

Louise also treated her with an icy politeness, speaking to her only when it was necessary. Even Rodney's customary cheerfulness seemed a little blighted, and only Hetty went about in her usual way. At one point Careen muttered irritably, "You'd think we were going to a funeral instead of a wedding," and no one bothered to contradict her.

During this period Careen visited Joseph each morning to keep him up to date with all that was happening. He listened happily to all she had to say, begged her to stay a little longer when it was time for her to go, but refused to listen on the occasions when she asked him to reconsider his decision.

Of Jonathan she saw little, for which she was grateful. He always consulted her on matters which were relevant, but apart from that she was uneasy in his presence and found general conversation with him tense and trite. To her intense annoyance she found herself trembling on the occasions when he did seek her out and very often her heart beat too quickly for comfort and she could not understand why. Finally she blamed this strange phenomenon on the coming nuptuals.

The family attended church on the three Sundays before the wedding. Careen stood self-consciously between Jonathan and his mother, aware of the speculative stares she was receiving from most members of the congregation. Outside the church she was introduced to a bewildering number of people and it was here that she began to realise that the Steele family owned a great deal of property in the village. There were quite a few of the older people who remembered her mother and it amused Careen to speculate on how they would react to the real reason for her engagement to Jonathan—if they ever found out. Of course she knew they must never find out, or else Jonathan and his family would become a laughing stock.

Careen was bound to see, too, Julia and her family at the church. They were outwardly pleasant, but Careen sensed the reserve in their manner towards them. On these occasions she noticed once more the adoring looks Rodney gave Julia, who seemed unaware of his worship. Careen could only hope that in time she would turn to him.

After the first Sunday at church Louise unexpectedly approached Careen about her trousseau. "Is this the only one you have?" she asked, indicating Careen's tweed suit.

"I have another at home, but it is rather old."

"You'll have to have another. Jonathan's bride cannot be seen in church each week in the same suit."

"Why on earth not?" She hid her laughter behind her hand, a gesture which made her look like an ingenuous schoolgirl.

Jonathan, who had been reading the newspaper in one of his rare moments of relaxation, stared at her. She never failed to amaze him—one moment she behaved in a completely sensible and mature way which belied her years and the next she seemed nothing more than a child.

"The villagers look to us and the Cresswells and people like us to dress well, live well and to drive large cars; they enjoy seeing it," he told her. "Perhaps you and Mother could go up to London to buy some new clothes—you'll both need outfits for the big day and, anyway, Careen will need some clothes for Venice."

Careen looked at him incredulously. "Venice?" she echoed.

"I booked our air tickets today. I hope you like Venice."

"I've never been." Her eyes were large and luminous at the thought, half fear and half pleasure.

"That's better still. How about that shopping trip, Mother?"

"Yes, we'll go tomorrow."

The following day Careen and Louise were driven to London by Jonathan. Careen was taken to a dozen shops and by the late afternoon she was exhausted and a little afraid of the amount of money that had been spent.

Louise had only waved aside her objections to some of the prices. "You must have these clothes, Careen," she said, not too unkindly. "As Jonathan's wife you have a position to maintain, and I promise you we can well afford what's been spent today. Jonathan gave me full instructions to outfit you from head to toe, so let's say no more about it."

Careen had to admit to herself that her old chain-store underwear was nowhere near as beautiful as the silk lingerie contained in the parcels she and Louise carried out of the shop which specialised in such goods. Her only regret was the momentary embarrassment she felt at having her future mother-in-law help her choose it.

Louise also insisted that she attend a famous London salon for a face mask and instruction in the art of make-up. "You have a lovely complexion," she had said, eyeing her critically, and Careen knew that from her this was praise indeed, "and your eyes could be magnificent if you used the right kind of make-up; not a lot— that would be fatal with such delicate skin—but just enough."

That evening when she received the admiring exclamations of not only Rodney, but Jonathan too, she admitted to herself that Louise was right. It was strange, though, that while she now took Rodney's friendliness and compliments for granted, it was Jonathan's admiration which gave her the warm glow.

As the wedding drew nearer so their spirits rose a

little and the atmosphere became lighter. The pace was beginning to quicken and there seemed to be so much to do that Careen hardly had time to think let alone brood on her coming fate.

She awoke one morning to find two large envelopes in the mail addressed to her. She recognised Aunt Rose's handwriting on one and on the other she was sure she recognised Joyce's. Curiously she tore them open and gasped when she saw the birthday cards they contained, and it was only then she realised that it was her twenty-first birthday. She had completely forgotten!

Slipping the cards and the book tokens enclosed into her handbag, she decided not to mention it to the others who were already at breakfast when she went in. Strangely enough it was the first time they had all been at breakfast together since she came to Pierce End. As she sat down at the only available place, a card and a small parcel appeared in each hand and simultaneously they rendered a chorus of "Happy birthday"—Louise included. Careen looked from one to the other, pink cheeked and embarrassed, hardly knowing what to say.

"Aren't you going to open them?" Jonathan asked.

With shaking hands she opened each parcel, exclaiming delightedly as she stripped off the paper. There was a silver powder compact from Rodney. "It's beautiful. Oh, thank you!" She gasped at the tiny pearl ear-rings from Louise and was completely at a loss for words.

"Well, you need some jewellery," Louise said shortly.

Even Hetty had remembered, and she admired the beautiful embroidery on her present of dressing-table mats.

Finally she opened Jonathan's and stared in unbeliev-ing wonder at the gold and diamond bracelet sparkling on its satin bed. If she could have found the courage she would have jumped up and embraced them each in turn, but her shyness inhibited her and she simply stammered, her eyes full of tears, "I didn't think anyone knew. You're all so kind and I'll always, always treasure these gifts."

"You forget—your date of birth has to be on our marriage lines," Jonathan reminded her, "and there's another present for you." He drew an envelope out of his pocket. "From Uncle Joseph."

Careen drew the cheque out of the envelope; the amount staggered her. "This can go towards the cost of all those clothes," she told Jonathan, but before he could say anything his mother interrupted.

"That money is to be spent on something for yourself—something entirely personal, do you hear?"

Careen bowed to the authoritative note in her voice and on their final trip into London she chose a set of brushes and hand mirror for the dressing-table, which Louise agreed was a necessity.

In the short time that remained before the wedding Careen kept remembering that it must have been Jonathan who was responsible for everyone knowing about her birthday, and the knowledge made her absurdly happy.

The last week flew by even more quickly than the other two. The house was invaded by an army of strangers—florists, caterers, even decorators, although Careen could not see where *they* were working. The postman was hardly off the doorstep, delivering presents and replies to the invitations.

Two days before the wedding the weather turned really warm and it was forecasted that it had settled for the time being, so the big day itself promised to be idyllic—weather-wise. One thing which did cast a shadow over the last hectic days was a letter from Aunt Rose, telling her that their head farmhand had been rushed into hospital with appendicitis and they could not, after all, be present at the wedding.

This news so close to the wedding sent Careen into a fit of depression, until, to everyone's surprise, Joseph announced his intention of giving the bride away and would not be deterred from the task.

"Can't you forbid it?" Louise cried to Dr Mandley, who was immediately summoned.

"Dear lady, I can only advise against it. Short of locking him in his room—and you can well imagine the effect that will have—there's nothing I can do."

So Joseph, on the great day, walked Careen down the aisle. She had chosen a white lace dress and coat and a small matching hat with a veil, in preference to a more traditional gown—which she would have worn on a more traditional occasion. In view of its cost she decided it would serve as a going-away outfit too, and nothing Louise could say would dissuade her.

Most of the events of that day passed as if in a dream; only afterwards did she begin to remember little snippets of it. She recalled Jonathan, impeccably dressed and stiff, waiting for her at the end of the aisle, and Rodney, standing beside him, not trying to hide his admiration at her appearance.

Jonathan said his responses firmly and Careen said hers with an uncharacteristic loudness. The plain gold band was slipped on to her finger and suddenly it was over; there was no going back. For a moment she stood paralysed at the enormity of it and then Jonathan gently turned her face to him and, lifting her veil, gave her a light kiss on the lips for the benefit of their audience before kissing her again, less gently this time, and forgetting the dozens of pairs of eyes which were upon them she threw her arms around his neck until the amused titter amongst the congregation brought her back to her senses and she pulled away.

"There's no need to overdo it," he whispered, and for a long moment they stared at each other. Careen's heart was beating a loud tattoo and she flushed slightly at the thought of what she had done in front of all these people; after all, Jonathan had done it only for appearances, but she could still feel the pressure of his lips on hers. The organ gave out a long blast and with unsteady legs she walked back down the aisle and out into the sunshine at her husband's side.

The church had been packed with people and it seemed that every inhabitant of the village had turned out to watch. Mrs Gilshaw had been there, moist-eyed and wearing a hideous hat which must have seen every christening, wedding and funeral for the last twenty years. Hetty also wore an outfit that probably hadn't seen daylight for many a year. Louise, wearing royal-blue, looked coldly elegant, but as always her true feelings were well hidden beneath a mountain of reserve.

But the one face which Careen felt would haunt her for ever was Julia's. She stood throughout the ceremony, pale and stony-faced, and only her eyes betrayed the suffering she must be feeling. How humiliated she must feel, Careen thought as she walked past her. The entire village must know she's been jilted.

Back at the house a magnificent buffet had been laid out and a never-ending river of champagne flowed freely into the bottomless glasses. Careen did not want to eat but had she been hungry she would have been far too busy shaking hands and receiving kisses from all those who wanted to make her acquaintance. She had her full share of approving glances and whispers of "So pretty. I wonder if she's related to the Nottinghamshire Laceys."

Finally, when she was cornered by a garrulous woman wearing a floral two-piece, who wanted to know her life history and Careen felt her head could stand no more, Jonathan came to her rescue. "It's time we left for the airport," he whispered.

"So soon?"

"We must give ourselves plenty of time, in case of traffic hold-ups. I'll go and put the cases into the car."

She watched him as he weaved his way through the crowds—she would be alone with him in a strange country for three weeks! Her legs became so weak that she had to sit down. The frivolous little hat suddenly became too heavy to bear and she pulled it off. She could not remember how long she sat alone in that corner trying to conquer the unreasonable but overwhelming fear which seemed to paralyse every sense. It seemed only minutes later when Jonathan returned; he had changed into a lounge suit. His face wore a worried frown. "Are you all right, Careen?"

She looked up at him and a great wave of relief washed over her—here was no monster, she thought, just an ordinary man. Perhaps he was afraid too.

She gave him a wan smile. "It's the first time I've sat down all afternoon."

He took her arm and pulled her gently to her feet. "It has been rather an ordeal, hasn't it? But we'll have lots of time to rest in the next three weeks."

After all the goodbyes had been said and all the confetti and rice had been showered on them, they were finally alone and on their way to the airport. Even Louise had tears in her eyes when she waved them off, Careen recalled as she watched the trees flash by. Since she came to Pierce End the countryside had burst into full bloom and was incredibly green and lush.

"I won't eat you, you know."

She looked at him sharply and was relieved to see he was smiling. Up until then she had not realised that unconsciously she had pressed herself into the corner, as far away from him as possible. "If you did," she answered with a smile, "it wouldn't help you."

"No, I'm sure Uncle Joseph will have that eventuality covered in his will."

They both laughed and were much more at ease with each other.

"Phew, I'm glad that's over." He stole a glance at her. "You must have been disappointed not to have your aunt and uncle here."

"Yes, I was. They're the only relatives I have and I would have liked them to be there." She was silent for a moment or two while she studied his stern profile. "I want to thank you, Jonathan," she said at last.

"Thank me? For what?"

"You've been very nice to me since Uncle Joseph dropped his bombshell." She struggled for a moment to find the right words, but finally she simply said, "It's more than I deserve."

"That's the first time I've been thanked for behaving in a normal way to anyone. My behaviour for that first day was not normal for me—as I hope you'll find out in time. Anyway, it was just as hard on you."

"No, it wasn't. I've had very little to give up." She paused. "Only the hope of love," she added in a whisper and she was not sure if he heard.

"We may as well make it as pleasant as we can, if we're going to live under the same roof. As for mother— well, you'll have to give her time to get used to you. She will eventually."

"I hope so," Careen said truthfully. "I admire her very much."

"She's a very admirable woman. If you knew about her you'd understand even more. Her father was a wealthy man and she was brought up in absolute luxury —until the early thirties, when her father lost his money. Up until then she knew nothing but good times; that is why my inheritance means so much to her."

Careen smiled at him warmly.

"Ah, we're coming up to the airport now," he said.

Careen forgot everything else; she just relaxed and prepared to enjoy the double novelty of an aeroplane trip and a visit abroad.

CHAPTER SEVEN

THEIR homecoming, viewed by Louise, Hetty and Mrs Gilshaw, was in complete contrast to the scene three weeks before when they were waved off by half the village. Careen, certainly, was not disappointed; the long journey in addition to her apprehension at returning to Pierce End as its future mistress had almost exhausted her.

They were ushered straight into the sitting-room, where the couple were glad to drink their fill of the first real tea they'd tasted since leaving England. Hetty, to Careen's amusement, fussed endlessly over Jonathan, continually expressing the fear that he must have caught some terrible foreign disease.

"How was Venice?" Louise asked in an attempt to cut her off.

"Rather cold," Jonathan replied, biting into a digestive biscuit, "but it was marvellous without the tourists. We managed to get about quite a bit."

"And how did you like it?" she asked Careen.

For a moment she was startled at being asked a direct question by her mother-in-law. "It was . . . beautiful. There was so much to see."

Jonathan finished his tea and stood up. "I'd better go and see Uncle Joseph before he starts shouting for me. Is he awake?"

Louise stared into her empty cup. "Yes, but you might as well be prepared, Jonathan. . . ." She looked up at him. "He's not very well."

"Since when?"

"Since the wedding."

"But he enjoyed it so much," Careen protested.

"Of course he did, but, as Dr Mandley pointed out to me, he may just as well have gone on a ten-mile hike. Apart from that, after you'd left, Rodney had the bright idea of playing some records and the younger people started to dance. Well, your uncle decided to join in."

Careen stifled a giggle because, amusing as it sounded, she knew it was very serious.

"He did the Viennese waltz with Julia," she added. "He said he was going to teach the young ones what real dancing was about *and* with the prettiest girl in the room."

"The old fool," Jonathan muttered, "and I thought Julia would have had more sense than to let him."

"Oh, she thought it a great giggle; said it would do him good. Well, see for yourself what good it did." Louise ended with a great sigh.

"I'll go along and see him now. Perhaps you'd show Careen to our room and I'll be along later."

After he had left Louise stood up to signal she was ready. "You'll want to have a wash and unpack your things," she said with some vestige of warmth in her voice.

Louise showed her into a large room Careen had never seen before. "This is the main bedroom—it hasn't been used for years; not since my mother-in-law was alive. The bathrom is over here."

Careen walked slowly round the room. The bed was between two large windows overlooking the garden. One wall was taken up by floor-to-ceiling cupboards and another by a large, luxurious dressing-table, at that moment impersonally devoid of ornaments; but Careen made a mental note to alter that. Vases of flowers seemed to fill the room with a delicate perfume.

"It's lovely," she said at last, knowing the words to be inadequate. "It doesn't seem to have the air of a room that has been unoccupied for so long. It seems so fresh."

"It's been redecorated while you were away."

Careen remembered the decorators who had arrived the week before the wedding and once inside the house seemed to disappear. "What a nice thought. Who chose the scheme? Even the curtains are new." She examined the delicate floral print so right for a bedroom over-looking such a colourful garden.

"I did. I hope you like it. Jonathan wanted it to be a surprise."

Careen was moved at his kindness and Louise's too, for co-operating with him in a task which, to say the least, must have been painful to her. "I love it! You have very good taste. It's just perfect!"

Louise smiled at the compliment and walked over to the door. "I'll leave you to your unpacking."

After she had gone Careen walked over to the window and stared down into the garden. In the distance Sam, the gardener, tended the roses which were just beginning to bud. During their honeymoon Jonathan had, once more, surprised her. His attitude towards her had never been effusive, but at least he had been consistently solicitous in a way which she would have believed impossible on her first day at Pierce End; but Julia's stricken face was constantly between them and always would be. Louise seemed to have thawed a little and for that she was grateful; if she could become a friend of her mother-in-law it would go a long way to making life easier.

The door opened and Jonathan came in. "Do you like it?"

She smiled. "Very much. It was very good of you to have it redecorated for me; Louise has done a marvellous job, but I'm sure it wasn't necessary to go to all this trouble and expense."

He came across the room and took both her hands in his. "You wouldn't think it unnecessary if you'd seen it before." He looked at her for a moment. "No one at the hotel would have guessed we didn't have a real love match, would they?"

She shook her head. "No, they wouldn't, and I did enjoy it. You made everything we saw so interesting that I think I saw it with enchanted eyes."

"I hope you always see things through enchanted eyes," he said with a smile.

"How was Uncle Joseph?"

He let her hands drop and his smile disappeared. "He doesn't look very well, although he won't admit it. But," he added with a sigh, "he's as tough as old boots—we all are. He'll survive.

"I have a load of work piled up; I'll have to attend to some of it straight away. I can always unpack later."

"Would you like me to do it for you?"

He flashed her a grateful smile. "I'd appreciate it."

He was gone and she sank down on to the silk coverlet on the bed, hugging herself tightly. I'm being stupid, she chided herself, there's nothing to be afraid of now. Nothing to be afraid of. . . . But of course there was; she was afraid of herself; of the way her emotions were leading her.

The realisation was slow in dawning, but now it was on her like a bolt of lightning—she was in love! It was ridiculous but it was true, she knew that without a doubt. She had probably fallen in love with him the first instant she laid eyes upon him at the Regina Hotel and she'd been a fool to ignore the signs. She was sure that if she had recognised the signs immediately she would have left Pierce End like a bird taking to the wing.

She lay full length on the bed staring up at the ornate ceiling. No woman could want more than to be married to the man she loved; but she did want more—she wanted him to love her in return. Well, she rationalised, that was out of the question. He would never knowingly show his love for Julia, but it would always be there, like a wound which could never heal. Strangely, Julia must be envying her being married to him, but here was she, Careen, envying Julia for possessing his love—one without the other was nothing.

There was a gentle knock at the door. Careen swung her legs off the bed. "Come in."

The door opened and Lawson peered round. "Mr Steele would like to see you, madam. Mr Joseph Steele that is."

"Tell him I'll be along in fifteen minutes."

After he had gone she began to unpack their cases, first taking out Jonathan's clothes and carefully hanging them in one of the roomy wardrobes; then she unpacked her own clothes—all the beautiful and expensive things she had bought in London and quite a few which Jonathan had insisted on buying in Venice.

"You mustn't deprive me of the pleasure of buying my wife's clothes," he had said, and she had remembered the warm glow she had experienced at being called "his wife", even though her heart told her she had no right to the title.

She picked up a leather wallet from a pile of gifts on the bed and went along the corridor. Despite what Louise had said and what Jonathan had told her, she was not prepared for what she saw. Joseph seemed to have aged considerably since she last saw his joyous face on her wedding day. His eyes were almost sunk into their sockets and his skin was an unhealthy grey. Even his clothes seemed to hang from him.

He showed a spark of animation when he saw her and exclaimed over his present. "It's good to have you back, child. You look a truly radiant bride."

Careen sat down, but not before giving him a disparaging look. "I'm not and you know it."

"But you do look radiant—I wasn't teasing. Marriage has done you good—I can tell."

"It was a shameful thing you did, Uncle Joseph. Do you really appreciate the people who have suffered, not even counting me? There's Louise, who is very disappointed, and you must have known that Jonathan and Julia were in love."

"Tcha. Louise would have been disappointed whoever he married, and as for Julia, she's just a young flighty baggage! She has as many lovers as there are days in the week. Jonathan is thirty-two; if he'd wanted to marry her he'd have done it before now and if he had I wouldn't consider him half the man he ought to be."

Careen raised her eyebrows a fraction. "And what kind of man is it who marries a strange girl he doesn't care for just because his uncle threatens to cut him out of his will?"

Joseph looked at her and smiled kindly. "Now don't you go worrying about Julia. She's not eating her heart out I can assure you."

"How do you know how she feels?" Careen was beginning to feel irritated, mainly, she knew, because Uncle Joseph had been astute in noticing her carefree appearance.

"Because she's been gadding about with young Rodney ever since you went away, that's why."

Careen shook her head in amusement. "You're a rogue, Uncle Joseph, you really are!"

The fact that he was confined to his room did not stop him being well acquainted with all that went on in and around the house. They would all probably be startled, she thought, if they realised how much he did know. And he was a shrewd old man too; she knew he had guessed she was in love with Jonathan.

"I may be a rogue," he replied with a chuckle, "but you'll thank me for it one day."

She gave him a wry smile. "I hope you're right."

*   *   *

May slipped into June and Careen settled into a pleasant routine. She had feared that after living such an active life before, she would be bored with life at Pierce End, but it was proving to be quite the opposite. Every morning after breakfast she spent a half-hour with Uncle Joseph and their conversations were very lively, although he seemed to grow more frail each day. She also learned that it was the custom for Louise to visit people in the area who were elderly, sick or had just had babies, and this occupied several afternoons in the week. Soon after she had returned from her honeymoon Louise surprised Careen by asking her to join her on these visits. After her initial shyness had worn off she began to enjoy these little trips and looked forward to seeing the eager faces which greeted them.

One such visit in early June was to a Mrs Johnson, who had recently given birth to a baby girl and whose husband tenanted one of the local farms. It was their fourth child, but Careen could not stifle the pang of envy she felt when she saw the tiny scrap in its well-worn crib and the radiant face of her mother, so happy in the love and security of her family.

At one point when the child began to cry Careen peered over the crib, amazed that such a tiny thing could make such a loud noise. "May I pick her up?" she asked impetuously.

"Yes, of course you can," the mother replied. "Don't be afraid of her, hold her firmly . . . that's right. It suits you," she added with a laugh, and Careen turned away so that Louise could not see her crimson face. Mrs Johnson quickly added, "It was a lovely wedding, Mrs Steele, and you had a lovely day, not like mine, they nearly had to get a snow plough to clear the way to the church. I was determined to come to yours though, even if I did take up room enough for two in the pew!"

Careen and Louise laughed as she handed the baby, who was now crying louder than ever, to its mother.

"What are you going to call her?" she asked.

"We haven't decided, but I like your name, if you don't mind my saying so. It's very unusual."

"My name?"

"It is unusual," Louise agreed. "Were you named after someone?"

Careen looked abashed. "In a way, but it's rather a silly story."

"Do tell us," Louise insisted.

"Yes, please do," added Mrs Johnson, who had quite miraculously managed to quieten the infant.

"I was born prematurely and my parents hadn't decided on a name. My mother was very ill for weeks afterwards and of course everyone was too concerned about her to worry about a name for me. My aunt looked after me for the first few weeks and one day she asked my cousin Joyce—she was only three years old at the time—what name she would choose. Well, she had this little friend called Catherine, but she couldn't say it—so I was stuck with Careen."

"Well, it's very pretty," Mrs Johnson said, "and with your permission I shall call her Careen."

"I don't know what to say, Mrs Johnson. I'm truly flattered."

That evening Louise, to Careen's acute embarrassment, recounted the whole incident over dinner. Jonathan, she was happy to see, was delighted. After dinner Rodney hastily excused himself and a few minutes after he had gone Jonathan, who had been staring out of the window, turned to Careen and said:

"Shall we go out for a while? This weather is too good to be indoors."

She flushed with pleasure at this unexpected invitation and jumped to her feet immediately. "I'd love to."

"You'd better get a cardigan to put over that thin dress," Louise said over her coffee cup. "It can turn quite chilly, even after such a hot day."

Careen knew she did not need a cardigan, but not wanting to dismiss Louise's well-meant advice, she ran upstairs to fetch one, and when she came down he was waiting for her in the hall. Outside she took a lungful of sweet air and followed him into the car. They drove towards the village, through it and into the open countryside. Careen stared ahead, resisting the longing she had to look at him, but she rarely did when he would be aware of it. Surely, she thought, now is the time to tell him how I feel. But again sheer cowardice prevented her from speaking.

Trees, houses, fields, flashed by. She did not know where he was taking her and what was more she did not even care; she was by his side and that was all that mattered. With a little start of dismay she realised that in something like three months she was not homesick for Aunt Rose or any of her friends at Witterton; even the long cosy chats over endless cups of tea had not been missed.

The car slowed down as they came into a village she had not seen before; it was larger than Stokeley. Jonathan stopped the car in front of an old inn, half-timbered and looking precariously unstable.

"I thought you might like a change of scenery, if you can call it that," he said with a smile as he handed her out of the car. "This place was here before my family came to the area. The story goes that Rupert Steele spent a night here before he went on to Stokeley and fell in love with the area. When the Queen decided to reward him with some land he asked for it to be here. Of course it was also handy for the sea; unfortunately the love of the sea was not handed down to his descendants—we've been strictly landlubbers for generations."

Careen passed through the low doorway and noticed with amusement that Jonathan had to duck his head as he entered. They were in a hot, crowded and very smoky bar. Several heads turned as they came in and many of them waved a greeting which Jonathan acknowledged as he guided her through the crowds into another room which served as a cocktail bar and, with the exception of one other couple, it was empty.

Jonathan settled her down at a table near an open window. "It's better in here. That crowd in there are hardened to it, but we'd slowly suffocate. What will you have to drink? A sherry?"

"A lemonade I think this evening—ice-cold."

He left her and while she waited for him to return she sat happily staring out of the window, hugging her arms. The chink of the glasses on the table heralded his return and she looked up contentedly. She found herself smiling directly into his eyes and for a moment she thought her heart had stopped.

He sat down at the other side of the little oak table. "Quaint, isn't it?" he said as he sipped at the ice-cold drink.

"It is rather. A bit like the Old Manor House, but I prefer Pierce End."

"So do I," he said with a laugh. "Mad Rupert did us quite a favour when he burnt the old place down. From the old plans it looked about twice the size of the Old Manor."

Careen gurgled as she drank before slapping the glass back on to the table. "Just think of all those dusty corners. I'm much too down to earth to be fond of antiques; to me they're all dust traps."

They laughed together and then suddenly he was serious. He put his hands on hers where it rested on the table. "You are happy at Pierce End, aren't you, Careen?"

"Oh, yes, I am," she replied with a contented sigh. She covered his hand with her other one.

"I'm very proud of the way you've adapted to our way of life. I know it hasn't been the easiest thing to do."

"It was easy though. Everyone's been so kind to me."

He looked at her for a long moment. "We didn't get off to a very good start, but that doesn't mean. . . ."

Suddenly he stopped, staring out into the public bar. She turned and followed his gaze. Rodney and Julia were coming through, their hands tightly clasped and oblivious to everyone except each other. Careen held her breath, hoping they would not come in and Jonathan would continue with what he was about to say; something which she sensed could be very important to her happiness. Her heart sank as they approached. She glanced at Jonathan but his face was now an inscrutable mask.

"Hi, you two!" Rodney cried when he saw them.

Careen snatched her hand from under Jonathan's and forced a smile of greeting on to her face, but her disappointment was like a physical pain.

Rodney pulled two chairs up. "If I'd known you were coming we could have arranged to come together."

Julia watched him lovingly as he went off to fetch their drinks and Careen was relieved to see that she was no longer grieving over Jonathan, although his mind was like a closed book.

The summer progressed on its lazy way and each evening Careen looked forward to the time she spent alone with Jonathan. She saw little of him through the day, but on those occasions when she did see him for a short while, or caught a glimpse of him, she was deliriously happy. She always gave him an account of her day's activities and although he said nothing more about it she knew he was pleased with the way she had settled into the routine.

He treated her at all times with a detached kind of warmth which on occasions almost became affectionate, and it was on these occasions that she was again tempted to tell him how much she loved him. She loved him more than she ever thought it was possible for her to love, and each day it seemed to grow deeper.

But she knew she could never tell him how she felt; it was a miracle that he was as warm towards her as he was. To tell him now could only spoil what little of his regard she had and she would never risk that. Often she wondered how he felt about Julia—she rarely came to the house these days. Jonathan, she guessed, was like Joseph in one respect—he could love only one woman in his life and Julia was the one. To give him credit, in no way did he ever betray his feelings, but the same could be said for Careen—and that did not mean she loved less.

There were times when she resented her love for him— times when she knew she could be content with the life she was leading if she could look upon Jonathan in the same way he regarded her.

As her love for Jonathan grew, so did her respect for his mother. Her attitude did not drastically alter, but she sensed a thawing in the ice and hoped perhaps one day it would melt away completely.

Whenever Careen was in the house Hetty fussed around her continually as she did with Jonathan, and she wondered if perhaps she too was regarded as one of Hetty's babies. One morning Careen was dawdling on the stairs, studying the portraits of Jonathan's ancestors, when she noticed one whom she did not recognise. All the paintings fascinated her and she often spent a few minutes, as she passed, looking at them and speculating on the kind of life they led in those far-off days. She imagined it would be little different to how life was being lived now.

"That's Mad Rupert's brother," a high-pitched voice cackled behind her. The shock of the surprise almost made her overbalance and she only prevented herself from falling by catching hold of the rail.

"Oh, Hetty," she gasped, "you shouldn't creep up like that." Careen had noticed that she had the annoy-

ing habit of creeping around almost silently and pop-
ping up where she was least expected. But since neither
Jonathan nor Louise complained, she couldn't very well
say anything.

"Did I frighten you, dear? I'm so sorry. I didn't
mean to. You looked so interested. His brother smothered
his wife with a pillow to get her inheritance."

"Yes, I know," Careen replied hastily.

"Well, it's one way of getting rid of an unwanted
wife." She started to laugh in that high-pitched way of
hers and Careen left her standing there.

It wasn't until later that night, as she lay beside
Jonathan listening to his steady breathing, that she recalled Hetty's words—and the memory chilled her.

Rodney had almost become a stranger and she guessed
that when he wasn't painting he was seeing Julia. She
had an unexpected chance to ask him when she found
him, in the sitting-room, one evening before dinner.
When she came in he was hungrily swallowing his first
whisky and about to pour a second.

"Hello, stranger," she said with a smile.

"Hello, Careen." His face shone with real pleasure.

"It's unusual for you to honour us with your presence
at dinner these days."

His face fell.

"No Julia?"

"She has another date tonight."

"Oh, Rodney," she said, putting her hand on his
unsteady one, "you do love her, don't you?"

Almost imperceptibly he nodded.

"How does she feel about you?" she asked gently.

"I'm not sure. She says she loves me. . . ."

"But that's wonderful! You have nothing to worry
about then."

"It isn't wonderful, Careen. How can I ask her to
marry me? I've no money—not even enough to support
an ordinary wife, let alone one who's used to luxury."

"But that wouldn't influence Julia. I don't know her very well, but I'm sure she isn't mercenary."

He sank down on to the sofa and Careen followed him. He stared morosely at his feet. "She isn't, but her father is—or rather he's exercising his parental right in trying to find a rich husband for his only daughter. That's why she's out with Graeme Northcliffe tonight; he's stinking rich. If she insisted on seeing no one but me there'd be no end of a row."

"I'm sorry—I don't know how I can help you, Rodney. I wish I could."

He smiled sadly at his feet. "You don't have to help. No one can."

"If you love each other that's all that really matters; everything else will work out. Just think how terrible it would be for you if you loved her and she didn't love you. It would be almost unbearable—I know."

He looked up sharply, the realisation dawning on his face. "Jonathan?"

She nodded.

"He doesn't realise what he's missing."

She laughed. "You're sweet. I'll learn to live with it no doubt."

"You won't, you know. I nearly went crazy when I thought Julia loved Jonathan. But it was her father who was egging her on, that's all. When Uncle Joseph made you two get married it was like an answer to my prayer—I would get my chance with Julia. It was selfish, I know, and if I'd realised how unhappy it was going to make you I wouldn't have been so overjoyed."

"Don't let it bother you. I'm not unhappy and I don't think Jonathan is."

"I hope not. God, I'm hot! I've never known it so hot."

He went over and opened a window. "There's not a breath of air."

"It said in this morning's newspaper that this was the

hottest June for fifty years," Careen told him, glad of the change of subject.

"I can believe it. Let's hope we have a storm soon or we'll all die of heatstroke."

Careen hardly heard him; she was thinking about Jonathan and his reaction to the news that Julia had never really loved him—as he was bound to discover very shortly. For Careen Rodney's revelation lightened her own burden of guilt considerably, but knowing how heart-breaking it was to love in vain she longed to comfort Jonathan—to tell him she knew how he felt—but she knew she would not.

With a sudden surge of optimism it occurred to her that Jonathan might never have loved Julia either, and if this were true there might be hope for her. She wished she was able to judge Jonathan's attitude towards Julia, but they had seen so little of the Cresswells since the wedding that it was impossible.

Strangely enough, on the following day Julia did come to Pierce End, and it was then that Careen's hopes were finally dashed.

*   *   *

The day was to prove as hot and oppressive as its predecessor. After breakfast Julia decided to walk over to Pierce End—it was high time she got to know Jonathan's pretty wife and she knew that Careen's natural reserve would prevent her from making the first move, and there was always the chance she might just bump into Rodney.

Try as she would to persuade him, he would not believe she really loved him and his lack of fortune did not matter to her—after all, she had enough for the both of them. She knew, of course, that he would never marry her on those terms; he was too proud to take a wife until he could support her. Well, that was one of the reasons she loved him, wasn't it? A frown crossed her pretty face as she remembered their last parting, when he stormed out of the house because she felt she could not keep refusing Graeme Northcliffe's invitations. And after all that the evening had turned out dull and disappointing and they had returned home before ten o'clock. She would tell Rodney that when she saw him. It was strange how she could only now enjoy herself fully when she was in Rodney's company.

She walked slowly towards Pierce End, fanning herself with an old fashion magazine as she walked. A man was coming towards her across the field; he was too tall to be Rodney and as he came nearer, head bowed and apparently deep in thought, she recognised Jonathan and began to wave the magazine wildly above her head. "Hi, Jon! Over here!"

He looked up, saw her, waved back and began to quicken his pace. "It's good to see you, Julia," he said as he approached. "You've become ... a stranger."

Her eyes sparkled with mischief. "I shouldn't have thought that honeymooners welcomed visitors."

A shadow passed across his face as if he had felt a sudden pain. "You haven't stayed away because of Careen have you, Julia?"

She began to laugh. "Of course not. Rodney has occupied a lot of my time lately, or haven't you guessed? And besides, I like Careen very much. She's far more suited to you than I was and I don't blame you for falling in love with her—I know how wonderful it is. Rod and I are very well matched. You would never have taken me out as much as Rodney does and will once we're married. Neither of us are stay-at-homes, like you two."

His face cleared and he took both her hands in his. "Careen is rather marvellous and I'm very pleased about you and Rodney. For a time I thought. . . ."

"I know what everyone thought," she broke in

quickly, "but they are wrong. At first I was stunned, naturally, but when you were away I didn't miss you at all; I guess my pride was hurt, that's all, and I am a spoilt brat, you know. I've no doubt you were quite convinced of it that evening you announced your engagement; I behaved like a real bitch." She gave a contented sigh and they began to walk together. "I never imagined love could be this wonderful; I really feel as though I'm walking on clouds."

"I hope you always will," he said, a little dejectedly.

They stopped outside the house. "So do I, but something will have to be done soon. Father is getting a little impatient with me."

"Doesn't he like Rod?"

"Oh, he likes him well enough, but an artist doesn't have substantial or even regular income and father won't even hear of our getting engaged; he doesn't realise I'm serious about Rodney." And she added quietly, "I don't think he's forgiven you, either, for marrying Careen."

"That's no obstacle, Julia. I can make Rodney financially independent; enough to satisfy the Colonel."

She shook her head and with a sad smile she took his hand. "You're so kind, Jon, and I'll always love you just a little, but Rodney would never allow that. He's confident he can make enough money from his paintings, given enough time. But time is so precious and I want to share his life now. I know he's a good painter but it may take years for him to make the grade—if ever."

Tears sparkled in her blue eyes and impetuously Jonathan put his hand in her hair and kissed her gently on the forehead. "Your father will weaken. He adores you and I've never known him refuse you anything that's in his power to give you. When he sees you're unhappy he'll agree to your marriage. Just have a little patience."

She blinked back her tears and smiled. "He probably

will, but Rodney is so proud he won't live on my money either."

"Wait and see how it works out, Julia. I suppose you've come to see Rodney, too, this morning?"

"I won't deny it, although my prime reason was this long overdue call on your wife; but, if I see Rodney I certainly won't object."

*   *   *

Careen had slept late and awoke with a blinding headache. All she could manage to eat was a boiled egg, and after laying in bed for a while, her mind full of Jonathan and Julia, she decided to get up and go for a walk in an effort to clear her head.

She dressed quickly and slipped out of the house without meeting anyone. The garden at this time of the year was ablaze with colour and, because her parents' home in Witterton boasted only a patch of coarse lawn, Careen revelled in the size and quality of this one; she spent hours discussing gardening techniques with Sam, who was thoroughly expert, and she marvelled at the amount of knowledge she had acquired in such a short time. She wandered contentedly along the paths, examining the blooms and occasionally bending to sniff at a particularly fragrant one. Despite the prolonged dry spell, the lawns were green and fragrant—thanks to Sam's loving attention.

After wandering about for half an hour her head seemed to clear and she walked around to the front of the house in the hope of seeing Jonathan, who had promised to be back for lunch. As she turned the corner she stopped dead at the unexpected sight of him standing by the front door with Julia. There was no reason why she should not walk straight up to them in the normal way, but she did not. Perhaps it was the pleading look on Julia's face which made her hesitate, or perhaps it was the one of tender concern on Jonathan's, but she stood there, hidden in the shadow of the wall. When he stooped and gently kissed her forehead it was like a nightmare coming true. Even in the heat of the mid-morning Careen was cold, and with tears streaming down her face she turned and ran blindly round to the back of the house.

Once back in her own room, she threw herself on to the bed, sobbing out her heartbreak until at last she fell into an exhausted sleep. As it turned out she had little time to brood for that same night Uncle Joseph died peacefully in his sleep. Once more the church was filled and the same people who celebrated the wedding such a short time before, came to pay their last respects to Joseph Steele.

On the day of the funeral the weather broke at last and as they huddled beneath large umbrellas in the churchyard with the rain beating down on them, Careen looked at her husband's pinched face and wondered if he was thinking the same as she; if her own mother had lived a few months longer or if Joseph had died a few months earlier, she would never have come to Pierce End and they would never have been forced to marry. Julia would not have discovered she loved Rodney and Jonathan would have been happy.

The tears rolled down her face and fused with the raindrops and no one in that churchyard guessed she wasn't crying for old Joseph, or even herself—she was crying for Jonathan.

CHAPTER EIGHT

CAREEN half-hoped that when the will was read it would contain a codicil allowing their marriage to be dissolved, but Uncle Joseph had altered nothing. She had carefully watched Jonathan's grim face as it had been read and she guessed he, too, was hoping for a reprieve. To Careen it was something of a relief when it did not come—she could not now imagine life without Jonathan.

The days began to shorten and, as if to make up for the fierce heat of the summer, autumn came early. Rodney seemed to wear a long face continuously, but he, at least, found solace in his painting. As for Careen, her heart grew heavier daily—the image of Jonathan's concerned face as he gazed at Julia continually flashed in front of her eyes and the fact that Julia was now a frequent visitor to Pierce End did not help her forget.

Careen found herself slipping into the habit of going for long walks. She tramped for miles across the fields, not even knowing or even caring where she went. The cool wind whipping through her hair and stinging her eyes brought her strange comfort.

It was one late September morning and Jonathan had risen early and gone out. Careen had pretended to be asleep, but as soon as he had gone she, too, slipped out of bed. It seemed that lately they'd had little to say to each other and Jonathan's mind seemed far distant; Careen put it down to his brooding over Julia and her unhappiness intensified.

Pulling on a warm sweater and thick tweed skirt, she let herself out of the house. The air was unexpectedly damp and a fine mist was creeping in from the sea. She began to walk through the gardens, now looking depressingly desolate, then the park, towards the open fields. When she was only a hundred yards from the house she turned to see it almost completely shrouded in mist and it looked so ghostly and deserted—quite unlike the warm, sunny place she had come to love—that she shivered. Leaves crunched loudly beneath her feet as she passed through the apple orchard; already the house had been completely enveloped by the mist and she felt alone, as if she were on some alien planet devoid of life. The trees, looking more like ghostly giants, stood to attention as she passed, her head bowed and her hands thrust deep into her coat pockets.

Unconsciously she made her way towards a copse where she had often sat for hours when the weather had been warm and where she felt she could be completely alone. She had almost reached it when a strange noise pierced the quiet of the early morning and she stopped to listen. The sound of shrieking and birds' wings beating the air filled the sky. Some extra sense told her there was danger before she was actually aware of it and then she heard the sound again—the crack of a rifle shot—and it was nearer.

Careen was rooted to the ground, not knowing which way to turn for safety. Another shot! This time the bullet whistled past her ear. The ground tilted away at a silly angle and the sky turned black.

As if through a misty curtain she was aware of being swept up by two strong arms like some weightless thing and carried along. She tried to peer through the curtain to see her rescuer, but the mist turned into a dense fog and she saw nothing more.

"She's all right. She's coming round," a familiar voice said.

"Thank God!"

Careen shook her head and tried to open her eyes. Hetty's face floated in front of her. "What's Hetty doing here?" she whispered.

"You're at home," Louise answered softly.

Careen opened her eyes again. This time she saw Louise sitting on the edge of the sofa. "Feeling better?" she asked.

"Does she want more smelling salts?" Hetty asked from somewhere in the room.

"She'll be all right now, thank you, Hetty," Louise answered.

"What happened?" Careen managed to ask.

"You fainted." It was Jonathan who spoke now for the first time.

Careen jerked her head round to look at him. It had been his voice which had said "Thank God!" He came closer and she wondered why he was wearing such old clothes. She tried to sit up. "Someone tried to kill me!"

"What!" Louise looked incredulous.

Careen gripped hold of her wrist as she tried to get up. "It's true! I was out walking near the copse when I heard shooting. Then a bullet went past my ear—a fraction nearer and I would be dead!"

Louise stared aghast at her son, whose colour slowly drained away. He sank down into a chair and buried his head in his hands. "I'm sorry, Careen," he said in a choked voice, "it's all my fault; I should have told you. I was going out shooting rabbits this morning, but you were asleep when I left and I didn't want to disturb you. I had no idea you would go out on such a morning. And to think I nearly killed you."

Careen watched him in horrified fascination. The realisation that it was Jonathan who had been firing the shots slowly dawned on her. She sank back on to the sofa. "How did I get back here?" she asked in a flat voice.

"I saw you lying in the grass and carried you back," he said. "I thought you'd just felt ill; I had no idea I'd. . . ." His voice tailed away again.

"We all need some tea, I think," Louise said in a

matter of fact way. "Hetty, go and ask Cook to send some up."

Hetty scuttled away, but not before she shot Jonathan a questioning look.

"How could you be so careless?" his mother scolded. "Don't you realise what could have happened this morning?"

He sprang to his feet. "Don't remind me, please! But I've learned my lesson and I'll not forget it. Next time I go shooting I'll shout it out, loud and clear."

"But it's so unlike you, Jonathan," Louise said in a more gentle tone. "You're usually such a good shot. Why were you aiming so wide?"

He looked across at his wife and then quickly away again, but not before she saw the misery in his eyes. "I had something on my mind," he said quietly.

Careen could not drag her eyes away from him. Was it Julia he had been thinking of? she wondered.

After the incident was over and forgotten by the others, this question kept torturing her together with Louise's voice saying, "You're usually such a good shot, Jonathan." It kept turning in her mind until she thought she must be going mad. Slowly the shadowy question which had been at the back of her mind since the incident had happened began to materialise; had Jonathan tried to kill her? She knew she was wrong to even consider it. It couldn't possibly be true. Not Jonathan. Not the man she loved so much.

But she could not rid herself of the tormenting thought. Of course it wasn't planned—Jonathan would not do that—he had not known she would be out at the very time he had a loaded rifle in his possession. But what if he had been thinking of Julia and he still loved her? Out there in the loneliness of the early morning. It was all too easy. What if he saw her approaching, alone and unaware of his presence? It would be the easiest thing in the world—just one bullet and it would be all over. He would be free to marry Julia and, as Rodney had no chance of getting enough money to satisfy Colonel Cresswell, Julia might well agree to marry the grieving widower.

Yes, it would be so easy. There would be no witnesses and who would think of doubting Jonathan Steele's word? And who would imagine he would want to kill his bride of only a few months? Careen put her hands over her ears in an effort to stop these insidious seeds taking root in her mind, but she knew it was all too possible that she was in love with a man who had almost succeeded in murdering her.

She tried—oh, how she tried—to convince herself it was fantasy, but to no avail. Once the idea was firmly implanted in her mind she could not rid herself of it. There were times when he caught her staring at him and she had to look away quickly, afraid that her face would betray her thoughts. There was hardly a time when they were together that she did not speculate on whether he had deliberately aimed in her direction and squeezed the trigger; even when she lay in his arms at night she was not free of doubt. Even to know that he had actually done it would be a relief from this nagging worry which was eating away at her and was beginning to affect her nerves.

They were all on edge. Rodney too became more morose. He began to paint weird canvasses with a desperate fury, and even Louise was bad tempered and tended to snap at the servants. Even when Careen received Aunt Rose's joyful letter giving the news that Joyce had a son, she could feel nothing but a mechanical and momentary pleasure. A few weeks before she would have rushed to give Jonathan the news; now she simply scribbled a short note of congratulations and never mentioned it to him.

Hetty still crept around in her soft-footed way, and whenever Careen was on the stairs gazing at Mad

Rupert's brother she materialised from nowhere. "His name was Jonathan, too, you know," she said one day, and Careen fled back to her room, her head in her hands.

Jonathan became more withdrawn and in spite of the closeness of those first few weeks of marriage, they were drifting further apart than ever.

It was as if the whole household was in the grip of the uneasy calm that comes before the storm. And then one night a few weeks after the shooting incident the storm finally broke.

Careen awoke to hear the whining of the wind in the trees outside. For a moment or two she lay there wondering what could have woken her so suddenly and then she knew—there was someone in the room with her. Automatically she put one hand out to feel Jonathan's comforting presence, but her fingers gripped only the cool cotton sheet.

Fear constricted her heart. She opened her mouth to scream but no sound came.

Suddenly she was roughly pinned to the bed and a pillow was pressed down over her face. Her heart began to beat faster; the blood rushed to her head and her limbs kicked out spasmodically as she tried to free herself from her attacker, but he was too strong for her. She was suffocating and there was nothing she could do but die! It was better she should die—better for Jonathan; he would be free and happy without her. She did not want to live knowing he hated her enough to want her dead.

She was still breathing and she realised the pillow was no longer pressed against her face. Still trembling, she sat up and it slid away on the bed beside her. There was no one else in the room—she was still alive!

She took in deep, gasping gulps of air and then, with the realisation of how close she had been to death for yet the second time, she threw herself face down on to the pillow and began to sob hysterically. Tearless sobs racked her as she pounded out her love and fear on the pillow, so loud was her sobbing that she did not hear the bedroom door open.

"Careen! What is it?"

Jonathan rushed over to her, but as he tried to take her in his arms she began to struggle and scream.

"Don't touch me! Don't touch me!"

They struggled for a minute or two until finally, frightened and white-faced, he ran back into the corridor shouting, "Mother! Mother come quickly!"

Almost immediately Louise appeared wearing a long woollen dressing-gown and her beautiful hair done up in braids. She looked at her son's white face. "What is it, Jonathan?" she asked fearfully.

"I don't know. It's Careen, she's hysterical and she won't let me near her."

Louise brushed him aside and went into the room. Jonathan, hovering uncertainly in the doorway, was joined by Hetty, while Louise gripped Careen's shoulders firmly and pulled her towards her.

"What is it, dear?" she asked gently.

Careen clung to her fiercely. "Jonathan!" she whispered, "he tried to kill me!"

Louise stiffened but held on to the girl, rocking her gently in her arms. "Hush, child. You've had a bad dream, that's all."

"It wasn't. It wasn't," she sobbed. "I was wide awake! I put my hand out and he wasn't there and . . . and then he put a pillow over my face. I couldn't breathe!"

"Oh, you poor child. Hush now."

Jonathan came slowly into the room and sank down on the end of the bed. He put a hand out to touch his wife but withdrew it quickly when Louise shook her head at him.

"Don't let him come near me," Careen begged.

"It's all right now, dear; you're awake and quite safe," Louise crooned.

"Careen," Jonathan pleaded, "I didn't . . . I mean I couldn't. . . ." She didn't appear to hear him so he gave up trying.

"I think," Louise said to him in a soft voice, "you'd better call Dr Mandley and then bring up some brandy."

He nodded, scrambling hastily to his feet.

"And," she added, "you'd better move some of your things into the guest-room for tonight."

*   *   *

Dr Mandley closed his bag with a sharp click. "I'd like to talk to her alone for a few minutes," he told Louise, who was standing silently at the other side of the bed. "I shall be down presently."

He smiled at Careen benevolently when they were alone. In the past that smile had always reassured her; it had always epitomised his perfect bed-side manner. Tonight it did not reassure her; it filled her with despair.

"Well, you've given everyone a real shock, young lady."

Careen stared unseeingly at the ceiling. "What is your verdict, Doctor?" she asked in a flat voice.

Dr Mandley perched at the edge of the bed. "There's nothing wrong with you. You're a normal, healthy young woman."

A smile curved her lips. "I could have told you that."

"You know, young lady, you've given your poor husband a nasty fright. You should be ashamed of yourself."

"He tried to kill me."

He patted her hand. "Now, now, you mustn't say that. You're really going to make yourself ill if you persist in upsetting yourself. Why should he want to kill you? You've been married less than six months."

"I don't expect anyone to believe me."

"Please believe *me*, Careen," he said in a serious voice, "I've seen many people who have dreams and nightmares which are very real. It's a good thing in a way—it's a safety valve for our fears. You've had more than your fair share of emotional experiences in a very short time—and this is the reaction."

"You're quite right, Doctor," she said wearily.

"That's a good girl. Do try to be sensible now. If you have any more of these dreams let me know and I'll arrange for you to see a specialist."

"Yes, Doctor."

"I'm going to give you a sedative and you'll have a good long sleep. Your mother-in-law will stay with you for the rest of the night."

The door closed quietly behind Dr Mandley and Careen let out a long sigh. She might have known no one would believe her. Why should they? It did sound ridiculous. But at last she knew what Jonathan was up to. He didn't want to kill her—a few seconds longer with the pillow and it would have been done. The answer was simple enough; he wanted to drive her insane. Once she was in an institution no judge in the world would uphold the conditions of the will. Jonathan would have it all; the house, the money and his freedom. She had no knowledge of the law, but common sense told her this was so.

The tears she had been unable to shed before now began to roll silently down her cheeks; the truth was that, despite her terror, she loved him more than ever. When she looked at him the flames of longing and desire threatened to consume her, and when he smiled at her she could not believe in his guilt although reason told her it must be.

Something like panic possessed her at the realisation that there was no one in whom she could confide; no one who would believe her for one minute. They were all so convinced that she was having bad dreams.

If only Uncle Joseph had not made that wretched will, she could offer him his freedom. But that was stupid, she thought drowsily, if it wasn't for the will Jonathan would not have married her anyway. She could have gone back home to Yorkshire and never known this love which had soared her heart to the heights of happiness and then plunged it down to the depths of despair.

*   *   *

Jonathan sprang to his feet as Dr Mandley came into the sitting-room. "How is she, Doctor?"

Dr Mandley placed his bag thoughtfully on the table. "Healthy enough—physically."

"And. . .?"

"I don't know. She really believes this dream. She'll have to pull herself together pretty sharply or she's going to have a nervous collapse."

Louise's fingers tightened around her cup as she exchanged a glance with her son.

"Perhaps I should tell you something," Jonathan offered slowly. "A few weeks ago I nearly killed my wife. It was absolutely accidental—I was out shooting rabbits and she was walking nearby." He sighed deeply. "Since then she's changed. She's afraid of me—I can tell."

"That explains quite a lot, but not everything. This accident happened at an opportune time. If it hadn't her fixation would have taken another form. She's been under a great deal of emotional strain lately. I believe her mother died not long ago after a long illness?"

Jonathan nodded. "Careen nursed her for four years."

"Her death, as expected as it was, must have been a shock and left a great void in her life. Then there was your marriage which followed before she had chance to get adjusted. There's been a great deal of socialising since then—people she's had to meet—it can be quite an ordeal for one who isn't used to it. There must be a dozen things which have contributed to tonight's climax.

"I'll leave a prescription for some tranquillisers and just be patient with her." He buttoned up his overcoat. "Oh, and I told her, Louise, that you would stay with her for the rest of the night, but there's no rush, she'll be asleep by now."

"I'll go up very shortly," she replied.

Dr Mandley took up his bag and said as mother and son walked him to the door, "The sedative I gave her was very strong, so she should sleep for a long time. I'll pop along to see her tomorrow afternoon."

"Thank you, Doctor," Jonathan said in a thick voice.

After he had gone Louise smiled at her son. "You need some sleep, too, Jonathan. Go along up and I'll stay with Careen."

He looked at her grimly. "I want to talk to you first. Let's go back into the sitting-room."

Louise poured out fresh cups of tea while Jonathan poked the dying embers of the fire. "Were you out of the room?" she asked.

"I couldn't sleep so I went to the study to read for a while—I didn't want to disturb Careen. When I came back I found her like that."

"What has happened to make her like this?"

Jonathan brushed his hand through his hair. "There's probably a lot in what Dr Manley says and he's not even aware of the most important point—Careen never wanted to marry me."

"Nonsense. No one put a gun to her head. It was a heaven-sent opportunity for her to have an important position here and to live in luxury for the rest of her life."

"I'm surprised at you, Mother; you know now she

didn't have any such desire. Because of her kind nature she wouldn't allow me to lose Pierce End. She blamed herself for Uncle Joseph's will and because I was selfish I let her sacrifice her happiness and perhaps even her peace of mind. And for what? This house? In a hundred years' time who will care anyway?" He sighed. "But, I admit I thought it could work out so well. I thought because I . . . oh, what does it matter now?"

He sank wearily on to the sofa and stared into the fire. "I should never have let her do it. I gave in too easily—because I wanted to. If he'd seen I was determined not to be blackmailed he might have given in. And if he hadn't, it would have been better to lose the house than to endure this misery. Anyway, the house doesn't matter any more."

His mother stared at him with growing dismay. "You really love her!"

"Yes, I do, but there's nothing I can do about it now. She hates me so much she really believes this dream."

Louise sat down beside him and gripped his hand. "Oh, my darling, I should have guessed. And I didn't help very much, did I?"

He gave her a weak smile. "I think you did very well, Mother. In the bedroom she wanted you, remember, not me—she wouldn't even let me touch her."

"She'll feel better in the morning. Nightmares always seem unimportant in the light of day, you'll see."

"No, she doesn't think it is a nightmare. I've seen her looking at me since that gun business, wondering if I could have done it."

"But why should she think you'd want to kill her?" Louise asked gently.

"Because of Uncle Joseph's will. Don't you see? The only way I can be free and keep Pierce End is if she's dead. It's not hard to guess what is going on in her mind."

"I'll have a talk with her in the morning."

"It wouldn't do any good. You're my mother and you couldn't be expected to believe in my guilt, and in her frame of mind she probably thinks you're in league with me.

"One thing is certain, I can't go on like this. At first it didn't matter, I was sure I could make her fall in love with me and at one point I thought she was beginning to respond. But after the accident with the gun she withdrew into herself. I can't stand this mistrust.

"What will you do?"

"I've been studying the will and I've come up with an answer. The will stipulates that we cannot dissolve our marriage or be divorced, but there's nothing in it to say we cannot live apart. I'm going up to town tomorrow to check with Baldwin."

Louise drew herself up. "I hope you're doing the right thing, Jonathan.

"I may be sorry, but I'm sure Careen won't." His lips were compressed into a grim line.

"I know what you're going through, darling, and I won't pretend I wanted this marriage, but once it was done I did come to like and admire Careen very much. And if you love her like you say you do, I wish with all my heart it would work out, but in view of what you've told me I think it's best for you to part if you can—I don't like all this bad feeling; it's affecting us all." She looked down at her hands clasped in her lap. "I know what it is to love, Jonathan," she said in a soft voice, "and I know what heaven it is to be loved in return." She raised her head to meet his eyes. "If he hadn't, nothing in the world would have induced me to marry him. I was married to your father for only eight years, and much of that time he was away, but I wouldn't exchange those few short years with him for a lifetime with another man."

She stood up and smiled tremulously. "I'll go up and see if she's sleeping."

CHAPTER NINE

It was late on the following afternoon when Jonathan arrived back. He saw Dr Mandley's car parked in front of the house and almost leaped up the steps, only just stopping himself from cannoning into the doctor and Louise as they came to the door.

"Excuse me, Dr Mandley, but I must see Cook," she said, flashing an encouraging smile at her son.

"Of course, dear lady, run along."

"I'm sorry, Dr Mandley, I had hoped to be back before you arrived," he apologised breathlessly. "How is she?"

"Much better today, I'm happy to report. Your mother, very sensibly, insisted that she stay in bed today, but tomorrow she can get up." Dr Mandley placed his hat upon his head. "I won't call again—unless I'm needed."

After he had gone Jonathan hesitated for a few moments at the bottom of the stairs and then, decisively, took them two at a time. He knocked gingerly at the door and walked in. For a moment he was taken aback by the change in Careen; her face was radiantly peaceful as she listened with an amused smile to Julia's inane chatter and his spirits soared hopefully. It was like a physical blow when the strained, uneasy look returned to her face when she saw him. Because of that he knew he was right in what he was about to do, despite the coward in him who begged him to put off the unpleasant task.

Julia stood up the minute he entered. "I must fly if I'm to be ready when Rodney calls for me. How was your day in the big bad city, Jon?"

"Fine," he replied non-committally, but his eyes never left Careen's face.

Julia leaned over and kissed her cheek. "I'll pop round tomorrow to see how you are. Take care of yourself."

As she went out Careen almost called out for her to stop, but she knew she was being silly—Jonathan would not hurt her now. He came over and kissed her cheek and then after almost perching on the edge of the bed he changed his mind and sat down in the chair recently vacated by Julia.

"How are you today?" he asked politely, silently musing how lovely she looked, with her glorious copper hair fanning out on the white pillow.

"Much better," she answered with a forced laugh. "I wanted to get up, but Louise wouldn't let me. I haven't been lonely though—everyone has taken it in turn to sit with me, even Rodney. What did you do today?"

She had tossed the ball right into his court and now there was no delaying the inevitable. His face took on a stony look. "That's what I've come to talk about." His deep, fathomless eyes bored into her and her heart began to beat faster. She had a premonition; he was going to say something she did not want to hear. Was it a confession? Was he going to admit his love for Julia?

"Yes?" Her mouth was dry.

He stared down at a piece of paper he had taken from his pocket. There was no need to read it; he knew what was printed on it by heart. "I know how unhappy you are, Careen, and I don't blame you—no one could blame you. For the sake of both our happiness we can't go on like this."

He glanced up but she was playing with a piece of ribbon from her bed-jacket. She could not speak for the lump in her throat; she could not even trust herself to look at him. His voice was unnaturally flat and he sounded as if he were giving a carefully worded and well-rehearsed speech. The end was coming, she realised;

her world as she knew it was disintegrating about her and after today she would never live again.

"Are you listening, Careen?"

"Yes," she whispered, almost inaudibly.

"I went to see Baldwin today—you remember? My uncle's solicitors. There's a loophole in the will. . . ."

She looked up at him then. "We can be divorced?"

He forced a smile on to his lips. "I'm afraid not, but there's no reason why we can't live entirely separately. We need never see each other again." He watched her carefully.

"I see," she whispered softly, so softly that he could hardly hear.

"I realise now it was very unfair of me to expect you to give up everything a young woman has the right to expect—dances, friends . . . love. The least I can do is try to make up for it—in part at least."

Careen nodded her understanding, not trusting herself to speak. She was thinking about all the women who would gladly give up dancing, friends—everything—for marriage. How many of them, she wondered, ever regretted the sacrifice? She fought the tears which began to invade her eyes. She couldn't let him see her cry. She just couldn't!

He was trying to make it sound as if she wanted to go, and it was so unfair. Perhaps, she realised, it was a salve to his conscience. He didn't have to put it this way; he had only to ask and she would go to the ends of the earth if he so wished. The most hurtful part was the way he had frightened her into believing he wanted her dead or mad when he had only wanted to frighten her enough for her to be willing to go.

She appreciated now that he no longer needed his freedom; Julia was in love with Rodney and even if Jonathan were free again she would not marry him now. How he must hate her for that!

Well, she would go and never see him again, if that

was what he wanted. How that thought seared into her like a red-hot knife cutting out her heart. Jonathan would be master of Pierce End and his mother would, at long last, be its mistress.

For the first time Careen wondered what Louise's part in this had been. She must know of his plan or if not she must suspect. But Louise would not try to stop him; she had never wanted them to marry. In those first halcyon months of their marriage it had been easy to imagine a softening in her attitude towards Careen. Now, bitterly she acknowledged that any kindness Louise had shown her was purely mechanical, to protect her son's investment. Now she could have both Jonathan and the house.

Careen brought her head up and met his eyes. They did not look triumphant, as she expected, or even pleased; more regretful. Perhaps he was an accomplished actor, too.

"When should I go?" Her eyes glittered angrily. She would not weaken—she must be strong.

"Where do you *want* to go? Back to your aunt in Yorkshire?"

Of course, back to Aunt Rose. Where else? But not yet. Not so soon.

"No."

"Where then, Careen? Where will you go? Perhaps you should take your time to decide; there's no rush."

Hysterical laughter welled up in her throat. He even sounded concerned! She put two hands up to her head in an effort to stifle it. Well, where can I go? she thought. Somewhere I can be alone to sort out my feelings without being smothered by kindness, or pity.

"London. Yes, I'll go to London."

"Do you know anyone there?"

"No, but I soon will. I can get a job."

The stern lines on his face relaxed a little. "You won't need a job, Careen," he said softly. "I'm going to make you an allowance and you'll be able to live quite comfortably without working."

He was buying her off. Another salve to his conscience. Well, he called her a fortune hunter on that first day and she was a fool ever to believe he'd changed his mind. This way, no doubt, he considered he was giving her what she wanted. "Thank you," she said aloud.

He stood up, but she did not look at him. "Don't thank me," he said angrily, "I've messed up your life."

It was not until the door slammed shut that she realised he had gone; the tension left her body and she went limp on the pillow. There were no tears; she was too numb for that, but they would come, later. At least now she knew where she stood—in a way it was a relief.

*   *   *

"It's very nice, Jonathan," Careen said in a dead voice as she turned slowly round in the middle of the room.

"When you've seen the others you can decide which one you want."

She shrugged to herself. What did it matter where she lived? A palace or a hovel—it was all the same without Jonathan.

"I don't need such a large flat; one much smaller will do."

"You're going to have a decent place to live, Careen, not one of those boxes they build nowadays."

She gave him a wan little smile. "In that case let's not tire ourselves by trailing round any more. This one will do."

"Well, it is near the shops and handy for the West End. . . ."

"It's just fine. When did the agent say I can have it?"

"As soon as you want it."

"Can I stay now?"

He looked at her in surprise and then he realised she was quite composed and serious. "I expect so, but what about food and bed linen?"

Careen pulled her gloves off briskly and laid them on the slightly dusty table. "As you said, Jonathan, the flat is very handy for the West End; I'm sure it won't take long for me to buy some."

Jonathan gave a resigned sigh and dropped the door key on to the table. He supposed she was right; it was better to have a clean break than prolong the agony any further. "Very well. You'll have to come back to pack your clothes though."

Careen stared him straight in the face. "Have them packed and sent on to me, Jonathan."

He straightened his drooping shoulders. "I shall go back and sign the lease and I'll open a bank account for you. Meanwhile, you have enough money. . . ."

"Thank you, Jonathan." She held out one steady hand and after a moment's hesitation he gripped it.

"I don't know what to say, Careen. It's rather an unconventional occasion."

"There is nothing to say," she replied with a tight-lipped smile.

"I suppose not. Goodbye, Careen. If you need anything let me know."

She stood erect in the centre of the room until the door closed behind him. The silence in her new home was overpowering and she felt more alone than she had ever been in her life before. For a full minute she stared at the closed door and then she buried her head in her hands and began to sob.

*   *   *

For the first few days Careen's every waking moment was occupied, as she had planned, by cleaning the flat until it sparkled. There were a million and one things she needed to turn the flat into a habitable home and Careen, instead of shopping nearby, deliberately went into the West End, which wasted some more time.

She knew the only hope there was for her to salvage a little happiness was to keep busy—there must be no free time for her mind to dwell on Jonathan and what she might have had if he'd conquered his love for Julia. When she had turned the flat into a show place she decided to implement the second part of her plan—her days would be filled with sight-seeing and her evenings would be filled by visits to the cinema or seeing the latest play. All this she had always longed to do and now she had the time and the money.

Her nearest neighbours in the small but luxurious block of flats were a jolly couple, married for nearly twenty-five years, who had recently retired from a successful business. Careen had become quite friendly with the wife, Mrs McGrath, who was a buxom Scotswoman. At first they had simply exchanged formal greetings when they met accidentally in the hall, then they lingered a little longer over pleasantries and gradually they slipped into the habit of having a cup of afternoon tea together when they were both at home.

"Don't think I'm prying, dear," Mrs McGrath said one day, "and feel quite free to tell me to mind my own business, but it's very unusual for a pretty young girlie like you not to have any friends call."

Careen bit her lip and suddenly as she looked into that kindly and concerned face she found herself telling her the whole story, beginning with the letter from Hart and Hart and ending with her coming to the flat. All the heartbreak that had been bottled up for weeks came pouring out in one flood of words, and when she finished it was a relief to have been able to tell someone who was as detached from it as Mrs McGrath. The only point she missed out was her suspicion that Jonathan had attempted to kill her. Now, completely detached from

him and Pierce End, it was becoming harder to believe
he could have done it, but even allowing for the shooting
incident to be an accident, the attempt to suffocate her
certainly was not.

"You poor wee girlie," she said, pouring out another
cup of tea and passing it over to Careen, who was dab-
bing her eyes. "What kind of man is it who would
marry a pretty girl like you and then abandon her when
she's served her purpose? If you ask my opinion, you're
well rid of him."

Mrs McGrath's plainly spoken words stabbed at her;
she could not deny the truth in them, but she felt bound
to defend Jonathan. "He's not as heartless as that, Mrs
McGrath. He's very kind and considerate, but he can't
help loving Julia no more than I can help loving him;
he just couldn't live a lie any longer. And he didn't
abandon me. He's made me a very generous allowance
and I'm sensitive enough not to want to live with a man
who does not love me. Given time, life would be unbearable for us both."

"You're only a girl yet, you should be looking forward
to a home and family, not looking back as if it's all past.
Think of yourself, girlie—divorce him. What does a
house matter against a lifetime of unhappiness?"

"I couldn't, Mrs McGrath."

"Well, I'm telling you, there's more to life than visit-
ing galleries and museums." Her voice softened a little.
"You must have memorised every picture in the National
Gallery by now and I know you've visited Westminster
Abbey three times at least!"

Careen smiled through her tears. "I don't need to
work—Jonathan has seen to that—so I'm planning to
enrol for a course in shorthand and typing after Christmas; there must be dozens of charitable organisations
who desperately need people to help."

Mrs McGrath shook her head sadly. "Ach, charity

work. That's for old ladies like me. And what about the evenings?"

"Oh, I shall read all the books I've intended to read for years and never got around to and there are always new plays and films to be seen. I shall keep myself occupied, never you fear."

"You're going to spend Christmas with us anyway."

"No, Mrs McGrath. You'll have your family at Christmas and I'll only be in the way."

"We'll be on our own this year," she insisted. "We usually go to our nephew, but he and his family emigrated to Canada in the summer. We'll enjoy your company, dear. Do say you'll come."

"You're a read angel, Mrs McGrath. I'd love to come."

It was a relief to Careen to have somewhere to go at Christmas; it was the one time she had been dreading being alone. Mrs McGrath was right, of course, she could not go on much longer like this. As the days crawled by she found herself brooding more and more and missing the easygoing routine of Pierce End—and particularly Jonathan. When she broke down and told Mrs McGrath the sad tale she had also opened her heart to herself and she knew she had only been fooling herself into believing she could put it all behind her. Now she appreciated that she could not; Jonathan was her life and now he was gone she only existed.

She did not like London; she found its tall black buildings ugly, its never-ending noise deafening, and the ceaseless flow of uncaring humanity frightening. After the peace and spaciousness of Pierce End no other place on earth could compare favourably. The answer, she recognised, was to go back to Witterton, back to Aunt Rose and Uncle Harry, whose affection would blanket her heartbreak; but almost as soon as she thought of it she disregarded that idea. Everyone in Witterton would know she had married the rich owner of Pierce End and how they would pity her when she returned, humbly, in

the role of cast-off wife. If her sorrow was almost unbearable, then pity must certainly be so. One day she
would return to Witterton, but not for a long time; not
until the sadness had subsided a little, as she knew it
must.

On her arrival in London she had informed Aunt
Rose of her new address, but she had carefully omitted
to mention that Jonathan was not with her; they would
naturally assume he was.

Careen enrolled for her secretarial course which was
to begin in January, at the same time deciding to spend
some of her allowance, most of which lay unspent in the
bank, on a holiday abroad in the spring. She brought
the brochures home with her to study and there were
so many places to see. She tackled the problem of choos-
ing the place with gleeful enthusiasm until she came
upon the brochure advertising the delights of Venice—
the place where she had spent those idyllic three weeks
with Jonathan. Was it in historic St Mark's Square that
her love began to grow, or perhaps under the moonlight
in the gondola? Wherever it was, it had happened and
she knew that if she travelled for ever she could never
escape from him.

She saw every new play in London, but very often
when she came out of the theatre she could not remember
what it had been about. Christmas was fast approaching; the shops filled with a million and one delights only
chilled Careen's heart. Christmas was a time for the
family, bound together by love, she thought, not for
those alone in a ceaseless limbo. Walking quickly past the
brightly decorated shop windows, she averted her eyes
from the displays of gifts and the nativity scenes epito-
mising the Christmas spirit of togetherness. With a
leaden heart she chose presents to send back to Witterton
and for the McGraths. Then she forced her heavy limbs
to take her to the toy department to choose a toy for
Joyce's new baby.

Everywhere there were people who belonged. Standing near to her in the toy department was a young woman. Her husband stood by her side with one arm slung protectively round her shoulders and a young child cradled in the crook of his other arm. Swallowing a lump in her throat, she hurried from the store into the biting cold outside.

Careen was finding sleep difficult to come by and when she finally fell into a deep slumber she often awoke feeling nauseous and ill. It was becoming increasingly hard to find a reason for even getting out of bed in the morning.

One morning she was awakened by the doorbell ringing insistently. Pulling on her dressing-gown as she went through the living-room, she noticed it was after eleven o'clock. She opened the door expecting to see Mrs McGrath, but instead she gave a gasp of surprise when she saw who was standing there.

"Rodney! What a marvellous surprise! Come in."

"I wouldn't have come if I'd known you were in bed." He came hesitantly into the room and glanced around as Careen hurriedly drew back the curtains and switched on the electric fire.

"I'm so glad you did," she said with feeling.

"This is a nice flat," he commented as he took off his overcoat and sat down in front of the fire. "How are you, Careen?" he said softly as she sat down beside him.

"I'm fine, and you? What are you doing in London and looking so smart?"

His eyes sparkled. "Wonderful news, Careen—I have an exhibition at Nielsons in Bond Street. My paintings are selling like mad at ridiculous prices and they're clamouring for more!"

She grasped his hands. "I'm so pleased, Rodney; I always knew you were good. I'll go along and have a look. I was only thinking the other day, I need a painting to take the plainness from that wall."

"I really can't believe it's happening, especially the best part—Colonel Cresswell has agreed to allow us to be engaged, and if my success continues we can marry in the spring!"

"That is the best news yet. I'm so happy for you. Where will you live?"

"With the Cresswells I expect," he answered without enthusiasm. "That part of the country has been good for my painting; there's no point in moving into town. Eventually we'll look for a house near Stokeley, but only when I can afford it myself." He broke off suddenly and studied her carefully for a moment. "Will you come to the wedding, Careen?"

She shook her head. "No, Rodney—it wouldn't be right; everyone would feel uncomfortable, especially me." She gave a shaky little laugh before asking softly, "How is Jonathan?"

Rodney looked down at the rug. "I don't see much of him; he seems to have thrown himself into his work. No one gets a smile from him these days."

I'm not surprised, Careen thought, he must be feeling very bitter at the prospect of Julia's engagement.

"I miss you," Rodney said with feeling. "The house seems empty without you."

Careen smiled and patted his hand. "You're sweet."

He did not smile. "I'm not flattering you; I mean it. Everyone seems to wear a long face these days—even Mrs Gilshaw. I don't know what really went on between you and Jonathan those last weeks, but isn't there some way you could iron out your differences?"

Careen shook her head sadly. "I only wish there were."

Rodney clenched and unclenched his fists. "I've known Jon ever since we were small boys and never before would I have called him a fool, but that's just what he is."

"Don't blame him, Rodney," she said gently. "I went

into this marriage with my eyes wide open. You must give Jonathan credit for trying to dissuade me because he did, you know. I've no doubt he's wishing very hard right this minute that he could love to order. Uncle Joseph found a way of making us marry but he didn't come up with a way of making Jonathan fall in love with me." She sighed deeply. "But that's all finished now, there's no point in crying over what can't be undone."

He gazed at her compassionately. "Will you be spending Christmas in Yorkshire this year?"

"No, I'm staying here and spending Christmas with some friends."

"I'm glad you won't be alone. Have you made any arrangements for lunch today?"

She ran her fingers through her unruly hair. "I was just going to have a chop and a salad. Would you like to stay?"

"Good heavens, no. I want you to come out with me for lunch; I can afford to take you now."

"Oh, no, I couldn't. You must be very busy, Rodney."

"Not so busy that I can't take my gorgeous cousin-in-law to lunch! Come on, get your nose powdered and we'll go out on the town."

Her eyes shone brightly. "Give me ten minutes and I'll be ready."

CHAPTER TEN

Time ground on and the eventful year would soon be ended; before Careen realised it Christmas Eve had arrived and instead of feeling better she found herself becoming more and more depressed. She missed Jonathan more than ever and she was feeling more ill all the time; it was nothing she could definitely put her finger on, she was just finding it harder to drag herself out of bed each day.

Since Rodney's visit she found she was thinking about Jonathan even more. No longer did she try to pretend she could put her marriage behind her and forget all about it. There were many hours when she stood in front of the window, just staring down at the never-ending flow of traffic snaking its way through the city. Several times her heart had almost leaped into her mouth when she saw a man who looked like Jonathan outside the newsagents across the street, only to have it subside again and land like lead in her stomach as he turned away.

For a moment she imagined he was there again, but as she watched him turn the corner and disappear from sight the familiar feeling of hopelessness and desolation burned away inside her. Oh, my love, how am I going to live without you! How long before hope dies and I no longer see you on every street?

The print of the newspaper she held in her hand blurred before her eyes. Christmas Eve and Rodney's engagement to Julia had been announced. How she envied their happiness—the precious gift of a lifetime together.

Her eyes caught sight of the bottle of sleeping pills the doctor had recently prescribed. She stared at them, unable to tear her eyes away. Was this the way out of her misery? A way out for her and, more important, for Jonathan. No! She wanted to live—or at least to exist. And what happiness would the proud Jonathan have if his wife was labelled a suicide? This was no answer; she would have to find the courage to continue in this dead-end life she was living.

She closed her eyes and leaned wearily against the wall. She had never seen Pierce End at Christmas. The flowers that had grown so profusely in the garden and filled every vase in the house would be dead now and everything prepared for the winter. Already Sam would have been out to choose a fine tree for the sitting-room—a tree under which the family would put their presents. She could picture the scene; there would be the tree, of course, and the hall, sitting-room and dining-room would be gaily decorated. Had she been there Careen would have fervently thrown herself into the job of putting them up. Tomorrow morning the entire household will attend church and the Cresswells will return with them for lunch and stay for the rest of the day. She imagined the exclamations of pleasure as the presents were distributed and opened and wondered in her misery if any one of them would spare her an instant's thought; perhaps Rodney and Julia, that's all.

Her name was Steele and as Jonathan's wife she was a part of the family, but she would for ever be on the outside—she had never belonged.

The doorbell rang and without enthusiasm she made her way to the door. She blinked stupidly at Hector McGrath.

"Alice wanted me to remind you to come for dinner," he said in his shy way.

"I didn't know she meant this evening. . . ."

"Alice said I was to be sure to bring you."

"Thank you, Mr McGrath, I'll be along in a few minutes."

*　　*　　*

"Why didn't you ask Jonathan to bring those things down for you, Hetty? Or Sam, when he was here before?" Louise scolded as the old woman staggered through the hall carrying a large box of decorations.

"I've been doing this job for almost thirty-four years, why shouldn't I do it now?" Hetty complained in her high-pitched whine.

"I didn't say you shouldn't do it, Hetty, just don't carry too much at once."

The two women went into the sitting-room and stared at the bare branches of the tree.

"Are you really sure you don't want help?" Louise asked in a plaintive voice and frowned worriedly at Hetty, who was already pulling out the tinsel and crepe paper from the box.

"Mrs Louise, I can manage quite well. I shall finish this room this afternoon, although I don't know what kind of Christmas it will be; what with Jonathan sulking like a schoolboy and everyone on edge. Didn't you say you wanted to see Mrs Gilshaw about the holiday arrangements?"

Louise sighed resignedly. "Well, don't overload that tree and do be careful when you get on to that stool—I'm not convinced it's all that steady."

"I think this star will do for the top, don't you?"

Louise shook her head and went out closing the door sharply behind her. She too doubted that it would be a very happy Christmas; there was no doubt that no one had been happy since Careen had left. Drat that girl, she thought irritably, why couldn't she have tried to make Jonathan happy? They'd all tried their best to make her at home, hadn't they? Well, perhaps, she conceded, that first day had been rather off-putting for such a sensitive girl. She couldn't really blame her for wanting to go away. All the same, she wished Jonathan would forget his pride and go and see her, perhaps she might be willing to give it a try again. But it was no use trying to talk to Jonathan about it, he just would not listen.

Louise sighed again and purposefully made her way across the hall. She was halfway across when she heard the crash. Her hands flew to her mouth. "Hetty!" she shrieked, before she turned and ran back into the sitting-room.

* * *

Breathlessly Julia pulled away from a particularly passionate embrace. She put her left hand up and admired the diamond ring on her third finger, turning it this way and that to make it sparkle in the light.

"This is going to be the most perfect Christmas ever," she sighed.

Rodney took hold of her hand and kissed it tenderly. "It's just the *first* perfect Christmas. The ones to come will be even better."

"You can't improve on perfection, darling."

"We can, you'll see."

She gazed at him, her eyes shining brightly. "I can't help feeling a little guilty though; it's not going to be much of a Christmas for Jonathan."

Rodney stared out of the windscreen at the flurries of snow floating past. "It's his own fault."

Julia withdrew her hand. "What a silly thing to say. It's not his fault at all. Careen wanted to leave. She had everything to stay for—a wonderful home, a husband who loves her—what more could any woman want?"

He took her hand in his once more and gazed at her fondly. "Now it's your turn to talk silly; the reason she left was because she loved him and she couldn't bear to have him not love her. I know there must be other things too, but that's the essence of it."

Julia was looking at him in dismay, and then she laughed. "You have got your facts mixed up, haven't you? Jonathan does love her, very much; he told me so —at least, he said . . . now let me see . . . yes, I know." She shuffled round in her seat to face him. "When I said she was a wonderful wife and I didn't blame him for falling in love with her, he said, 'Careen is rather marvellous'. Those were his exact words and even if I didn't know him so well I couldn't have mistaken that look on his face when he said it."

Rodney let out a long low whistle. "Well, it looks as though they are a pair of prize idiots."

Julia leaned forward eagerly. "Do you mean to tell me she does. . . ." She collapsed back in the seat laughing convulsively.

"It would be amusing if they weren't both eating their hearts out over the other and I've done enough of that to be able to sympathise."

She stopped laughing abruptly. "Oh, lord, you're right. We must *do* something, Rod."

"I'm going to have a straight talk with my cousin," he said grimly, "and I should have done it weeks ago. Pride is one thing, but this is plainly ridiculous!"

He turned to her with a smile and, cupping his hands under her chin, he drew her face close. Kissing her, he said, "I love you."

"I love you too, darling."

He leaned over and opened the door for her. "I'll see you in church in the morning. I'm going to see Jon now."

Daintily she stepped out of the car and popped her head back to blow him a kiss. "Good luck, darling."

She slammed the door of the little sports car and watched it, dreamy eyed, as it roared away and out of sight.

Five minutes later the car screeched to a halt behind Jonathan's. Rodney jumped out and with a jolt realised that his cousin was still sitting quite motionless behind the steering wheel. He went round to the other side and, opening the door, he slid into the passenger seat.

Jonathan turned in surprise when he heard him. "Hello, Rodney." He gave him a questioning look.

"I've just left Julia. . . ."

"Is she well?"

"Yes," Rodney replied impatiently. "We were talking about you and Careen . . ." he said abruptly, and then broke off when he saw his cousin's frozen expression.

Jonathan turned to look at him again. "Oh, yes," he said without interest.

"Look, Jon—you should know this, you two made a terrible mistake."

Jonathan's lips curled into a bitter smile.

"No, I meant it. The thing is, Julia believes you're in love with Careen. . . ."

"I am."

"Well, don't you see?" he pressed on excitedly, "there's no problem. She loves you, too. She told me so."

Jonathan looked at him, hope surging through his whole body. "When?"

"Not long after you were married. I was unhappy and uncertain about Julia; I confided in Careen and, as it turned out, she was in a position to sympathise. She admitted she was in love with you." He looked at his cousin, eager for his reaction.

The initial glimmer of hope died in his eyes and his shoulders drooped again. "Perhaps she was beginning to . . . but it all ended when she began to imagine I'd tried to kill her."

Rodney swallowed. "No, Jon, it didn't. She. . . ."

The front door flew open and Louise came running down the steps towards them. She wrenched the car door open as Jonathan began to show signs of animation.

"What is it, Mother?"

"Hetty!" she gasped. "Hetty's fallen from the stool."

Both Jonathan and Rodney got out of the car and Rodney took hold of her arm as they hurried into the house.

"I didn't know what to do. I thought she was dead."

"Have you telephoned for the doctor?" Jonathan demanded, once more in command of the situation.

"Of course. Dr Mandley's been, but I've been waiting for you to come back. She's shouting for you, Jonathan. She insists on seeing you and she won't tell anyone why."

"What was Dr Mandley's verdict?"

"Only bruises and shock, but she'll have to spend Christmas in bed. I warned her about that stool but she wouldn't listen." Louise stopped as they came into the house and laid a hand on her son's arm. "Jonathan, she thinks she's dying."

His mother's expression was so comical that he began to laugh and it broke the tension. Rodney joined in and then Louise out of relief, until they heard a loud commotion from above.

"You'd better go up and see the old girl, Jon," his cousin urged.

Rodney and Louise were still in the hall when her son came running down the stairs five minutes later. His face, miraculously, bore no sign of the strain of the past two months; he looked almost carefree.

"What is it, Jonathan? What did she say?"

"I haven't time to explain now," he said breathlessly as he gripped her hands tightly, "but I'm going for Careen."

*   *   *

Careen sat and smiled shyly across the table, not knowing what to say. Overshadowed by his wife's garrulity, Hector McGrath was no conversationalist. His wife after a moment bustled in and laid a large dish on the table.

"There we are," she beamed, "a lovely leg of pork. Hector, you carve."

Hector pushed his chair back and, picking up the carving knife, began to cut into the flesh. Careen watched him in horrified silence as the colour slowly drained from her face.

"This is for you, dear," she heard Alice McGrath's voice from a long way away. The room went dark just before she tilted sideways and the McGraths' wine-red carpet came up to meet her.

They were such strange flowers—she'd never seen any like them before. They weren't flowers! It was the wall-paper.

"Drink this, dear, it will make you feel better."

Careen's eyes fluttered open. Mrs McGrath's familiar face came floating over her. Why am I lying on this bed? she thought.

She tried to struggle into a sitting position, but a firm arm supported her back and a cup was forced between her lips. She drank the hot liquid greedily and sank back on to the pillow.

"What happened?" she asked dazedly.

"Nothing to worry about, dear—you just fainted."

Of course, now she remembered. She'd been walking across the fields. A cold hand closed over her heart. "He tried to shoot me!"

"No, dear, you just fainted when I served the pork."

The pork! A tide of revulsion washed over her. She swung her legs over the side of the bed and roughly pushing a surprised Mrs McGrath to one side, Careen half ran and half stumbled into the bathroom.

Alice McGrath was waiting by the door when she

came out. "Come and lay down again; you look all in."

Careen gratefully allowed her to help her back into the bedroom and on to the bed. Mrs McGrath pulled the eiderdown over her and sat on the edge of the bed.

"Now, dear, how long have you been away from that husband of yours?"

"Two months."

"Well, dear, I may not have had any young 'uns of my own, but I can see the signs when someone else is. My sister was just the same when she was carrying Andy; couldn't face chicken at all."

Careen turned her face to the wall, despair and misery filling her heart once again. There was no hiding the facts now—the very possibility she had dreaded was happening despite her attempt over the past few weeks to pretend nothing was wrong.

"What am I going to do?" she asked in a pain-filled voice.

"There's only one thing you can do—tell him. He'll have to take you back. It's his duty to take care of you now."

Careen buried her face in the pillow. Oh, yes, he would certainly take her back and gladly. But I want him to take me back for my own sake, she cried inwardly, not because I'm having his child. There must be more to life than being a human incubator, because that's all I would be, of that I'm certain. Once the baby was born a nanny would take complete charge, or worse still, Hetty, and I would be a stranger to my own child.

"I can't go back," she said, her voice muffled by the pillow.

"He has a right to know. A child has a peculiar way of loving both its parents even if they hate the sight of each other. Do you have the right to withhold that from your child?"

Careen sat up and flung herself into Mrs McGrath's arms. "You're so sensible, but I must have time to think.

I won't have to tell him for a while anyway, and if I have a girl I might never tell him."

"A girl has a right to have a dad, too, and besides, why shouldn't she inherit whatever she's entitled to? That sounds like the doorbell; it's probably the milkman calling for his Christmas present. He might forget to leave me that extra pint, but forget his Christmas present? Never!"

Careen laughed as she sank back on the pillow, realising at last how ill she really did feel.

"I'll be back in a couple of ticks. You just lay there and relax."

Careen let out a long sigh as Mrs McGrath went out of the bedroom. Perhaps I won't have to tell Jonathan after all, she mused, and the thought cheered her. I could go back to Witterton and have my baby there. She smiled to herself. Aunt Rose would be delighted to have me, she decided. My baby can grow up along with Joyce's. I'll be among friends—people who have known me all my life. I'll have my own child; no one will pity me then.

For the first time she thought about this baby as a person. My own son, or daughter; someone to live for! To love and love me. No more loneliness from now on and definitely no more despair. I have more than myself to consider from now on.

She heard Mrs McGrath's raised voice in the hall and she smiled to think of kindly Mrs McGrath in true Scots tradition admonishing the milkman before she gave him his present. She heard another voice over Mrs McGrath's. She sat up. Jonathan's voice! No, it couldn't be. But it was unmistakable. She swung her feet to the floor fighting the panic which seized her. Why was he here? Did estranged wives warrant a special Christmas visit? Her first instinct was to hide. She had made her decision to go back to Witterton and she didn't want to be swayed by seeing Jonathan.

Fearfully she stared at the door just before it flew open. What a mess I must look, the foolish thought popped into her head.

His bulk almost filled the open doorway. There was an uncharacteristic wild and unkempt look about him. She wanted to cry out and have Mrs McGrath stay by her. He stepped into the room. He looks so drawn, she thought, and his eyes are so sad.

"You're ill, you've gone so thin," he said, those dark eyes burning into her.

"It's nothing," she answered automatically in a dull flat voice.

Mrs McGrath hovered worriedly behind him. "If you don't want to see him, dear, I'll find someone who'll throw him out."

Careen smiled reassuringly. "It's quite all right, Mrs McGrath."

Jonathan turned and closed the door sharply in her surprised face.

"You shouldn't have done that, Jonathan. It is her flat."

"I don't care, I've come to see you."

She stared across the room. "It can't be so urgent—after two months."

"Don't remind me. They've been the worst two months of my life." He sat down beside her and roughly pulled her round to face him. "I love you, Careen, and I want you back."

She stared at him incredulously for a long minute. She looked into his face, trying to see what he really meant, but there was only anxiety in his eyes; there was no mistaking his expression now. She did not even attempt to question him; for the moment it was enough for him to say "I love you". As she threw herself into his arms his lips came down on hers; all the unhappiness they had experienced over two sad and lonely months was relieved by one long and passionate kiss. For a while she lay there, just enjoying the sensation of having him hold her close.

"I don't pretend to understand this miracle," she said at last, sighing contentedly. "I've lived for so long with the thought that you hated me."

He lifted her chin with one hand and looked into her wide green eyes, now brimming with tears. "I never hated you. I loved you from the moment I saw you dwarfed by that ridiculous chair you were sitting in at the Regina. You looked so defenceless, sitting there not knowing who or what to expect. That was why I resented you so much, not because I really thought you were after Uncle Joseph's fortune. All my carefully controlled sentiments went completely overboard that afternoon and I didn't know how to deal with the situation. If you'd known me a little better you would have realised I would never have agreed to Uncle Joseph's monstrous proposal if I'd not wanted to marry you—the old people could have had the house and welcome to it."

Careen put her head back on his shoulder. "We've caused each other such a great deal of unnecessary suffering."

"It was all my fault—my pride wouldn't let me admit my true feelings and risk a rebuff. It was all very stupid as I've learned. I had so much to gain by admitting my love and all I had to lose was my pride.

"But I've suffered since you left. God, how I've suffered! I moved into the guest-room because I couldn't bear being in our room without you, everything in it reminds me of you. And I used to come and stand outside these flats and look up at your window, trying to pluck up enough courage to come in, but I never did."

"I wish you had, Jonathan," she said softly, remembering the times she had thought she'd seen him.

"Well, that's the kind of man you married. A coward."

"You're not, no more than I am. Just too proud."

He stroked her hair. "Today I'd almost decided to come for you—I couldn't face Christmas without you, even if you did hate me."

"As if I could hate you."

"You had every right to, Careen." He pulled away from her and she looked at him questioningly, waiting with dread for him to confess he had tried to frighten her away. It did not matter now, she would tell him that; she had forgiven him a long time ago.

"I must tell you this," he said softly, as he stared down at his clasped hands which were so strong, yet could be so gentle.

She put her hand over his. "Go on, Jonathan, tell me."

"When I arrived back home this afternoon Hetty had fallen from the stool while she was decorating the tree. . . ."

"Poor Hetty. Is she hurt?"

"No," he said quickly, "at least not badly, but she saw it as some divine retribution for her wickedness." He lifted his head and looked directly at her. "She admitted she put that pillow over your face."

Careen's face grew pale and her hand flew to her mouth. "But why?"

He shrugged. "She's always looked upon me as her own son, which isn't surprising considering she practically brought me up. Anyway, she was unhappy because Uncle Joseph made me marry you against my will, or so she thought. The accident with the rifle put the idea into her head that she could frighten you away. A plan which succeeded all too well."

"Poor Hetty. I'm glad she told you though."

He put his arms around her and pulled her close again. "So am I," he said with feeling. "Even if she hadn't I would have come for you, but the suspicion would still have hung over us like a shadow. She'd have told me earlier, but she was afraid I'd be angry.

Careen looked up at him worriedly. "Will Louise forgive me for marrying you, Jonathan?"

He laughed. "She forgave you months ago; she misses you almost as much as I do. Rodney and Julia's engagement party is next week—now we can have a real celebration."

Careen ran a nervous hand through her hair. Everything had happened so quickly—half an hour ago she had been desperately unhappy and now Jonathan was here and had spoken the words she'd dreamed of hearing for so long.

"I can't come now, Jonathan, not until after Christmas."

"You must, why can't you?"

"I haven't bought any presents."

He laughed again and gripped her hand. "Taking you back is the best present for us all."

Careen gave him a dazzling smile. Of course she had a gift for him—for them all—but she wouldn't tell him yet. No, she would hug the knowledge to herself for a little while yet; all this happiness might be too much to take all at once.

"Uncle Joseph was right all the time. He knew better than both of us."

"He did, didn't he?"

"He told me—on the day we came back from Venice —that I'd thank him for what he had done. Thank you, Uncle Joseph."

Jonathan stood up and looked down at her. For a second she was reminded of their first meeting, only this time the expression on his face could not be mistaken— it was full of love.

He held out his hand to her. "Come along. I'm taking you home."

Run Away from Love

GRACE RICHMOND

CHAPTER ONE

I HEARD the horse's frightened whinney as I came down the lane by Beck's Farm.

Jumping down from Bessy's broad back I ran to the gate which led into the big field.

A man was tugging at the bridle of a horse which had dug its forefeet in and was almost squatting on its haunches in a determined effort to resist any attempt to move it.

"Come on, you brute!" The man brought his free hand round and the leather thong he carried caught the frantic animal a savage blow.

"Stop!"

Almost beside myself I opened the gate and ran into the field.

The man turned to glare at me. He was thick-set, middle-aged, with thinning grey hair. He had steely eyes and a tight mouth above a rock-hard chin.

I knew who he was. Everybody in Mardon knew Silas Oldfield of Beck's Farm.

The horse, realising that I had distracted the man's attention, threw back its head, jerked the bridle out of its tormentor's grasp and set off across the field at a gallop.

" See what you've done!" Mr. Oldfield shouted. " Now I'll never catch him!"

" Leave him to me," I said, but already I was suspecting I had probably bitten off more than I could chew.

If I could not recapture the horse, this man would be quite within his rights in ticking me off.

I avoided looking into his scowling face again and started after the horse, which was now cropping contentedly a couple of hundred yards away.

" Interfering little hussy!" I heard from behind.

I strode on. In a way I sympathised with the man. To have his field invaded by a bossy young woman was bad enough, but to have his own incompetence exposed was the final straw.

But I had to go through with it now I had started, I told myself stubbornly, and approached the horse cautiously aware that it had now lifted its head and was watching me suspiciously.

" Come on, then! It's all right," I said soothingly.

Suddenly I remembered a lump of sugar in the pocket of my jacket. Feeling for it I held it out on the palm of my hand.

The horse watched, then, as I came within a few feet of him, drew back.

" Come on, old fellow!" I said. " It's all right."

His eyes were on the sugar lump. Evidently he knew very well what it was. He had seen sugar lumps before.

I moved towards him, inch by inch, hand held out.

The temptation of the sugar was too much for him. The soft velvet of his muzzle touched my palm and I felt his warm breath as he took the sugar.

I reached for the bridle and he did not resist when, very gently, I led him across the field towards the farm buildings a couple of hundred yards away.

When I reached the gate leading into the farmyard Mr. Oldfield came up behind me.

" I'll open the gate," he muttered, " and then he can be shut away in his box till I decide what to do with him. Ugly, bad-tempered brute," he added with an angry glare at the now docile horse.

Without saying anything I led the horse to the stable at the far side of the yard. It had a neglected look about it, as if it had not been used as a stable for a long time.

" Have you any other horses, Mr. Oldfield?" I asked, though I was sure he couldn't have.

He couldn't even look after the horse he had got—a chestnut, by the way—which badly needed grooming.

He looked at me sharply.

" So you know who I am, eh?"

I nodded. " Someone pointed you out to me in the village one day."

" To answer your question. young lady, I do not have other horses, and I'm not like to have another after my experience with this brute!" He jerked open the half-door and I led the horse into the darkness of the stable. " I bought him in a sale over at Market Tetford last week mainly to please the wife. She seemed to think I might ride to the Hunt. I've changed my mind now. I don't fancy being made to look a fool riding to hounds on *his* back, I can tell you. Never know what caper he might get up to."

I hid a smile. Somehow I couldn't see Mr. Oldfield as a follower of the rather snooty Borford Hunt. I had met quite a few of the men and women when I'd been out showing off horses from Staveleys, where I worked, and I knew that most of the people who followed the hounds would look down their noses at this uncouth bad-tempered farmer who had few social graces.

"What will you do with the horse if you're not going to hunt, Mr. Oldfield?" I asked.

He scowled at the animal which was now reaching up for a mouthful of hay from the rack above his box while keeping a wary eye on his master for any hostile move from that quarter.

"I shall sell him, of course," he growled. "I'm not going to have him eating me out of house and home. I've no use for him about the farm. Even if I kept a cart, which I don't, I doubt if I'd ever be able to get him between the shafts. The farm's all mechanised now," he added proudly.

"How much would you take for him?" I asked and held my breath.

He looked at me, a little taken aback by the question.

"Why do you want to know, miss?" he demanded. "Don't tell me you might buy him!"

"I might find a customer for him," I replied. "I work for Mr. Taylor at Staveleys, the stables in the village. He'd probably buy him off you."

"I'll think it over. I gave over two hundred pounds for him. I refused to give more when I found out he'd a nasty disposition. And I won't take less, my girl," he grunted, looking at me fiercely.

" What's his name?" I asked, patting the chestnut's sleek neck.

" Bright Hope! Dead Loss would be a better name," he said in disgust.

I decided it was time to leave. Besides I'd left Bessy untethered in the lane and though she was a docile old mare, she had a habit of feeding on hedges and I didn't want any more trouble with Mr. Oldfield.

" I'll ask Mr. Taylor if he'd consider buying Bright Hope, Mr. Oldfield," I said. " I'll let you know what he says later."

He did not speak but continued to eye his horse with a scowl. I slipped out of the stable and reached the lane just in time to stop Bessy reaching up for a particularly luscious piece of hawthorn.

I had come to the Staveleys Riding Stables a year before when my mother died and there was no more reason for me to go on living in London. My father had died when I was a child and I had no brothers or sisters.

I had always wanted to work with horses, and even when I was holding down a job in a West End office, I had contrived to hire a mount and go riding on one of the many open spaces around London at the weekends.

When Mother died I had answered a few advertisements but had had no luck until I saw Mark Taylor's ad in *Horse and Hound*. It sounded just the thing and when he invited me to go to Mardon for an interview I lost no time in setting out.

I had got the job. The pay was about half what I was

getting in London, but I didn't mind that. I was to work with horses. That was all that mattered to me.

Mark Taylor employed a head stableman—Paddy Lesley —two stablelads and another girl, Maggie Simms, a pretty red-head, a year younger than me.

There was a flat over the stable which Maggie and I shared. The three stablemen lived in a cottage at the end of the yard looked after by an old woman called Beth Gledhill. Mr. and Mrs. Taylor and their two children lived in " Staveleys ", the lovely old house at the far side of the paddock.

The work consisted in looking after the nine hunters which were hired out during the season to people wanting to follow the hounds but who didn't own horses of their own.

Horses were constantly coming and going at Staveleys, for the most profitable part of Mr. Taylor's business was buying horses and selling them at a profit.

This is where Maggie and I came in. We would ride the horses to hounds, and when anyone admired them— as they often did—Mr. Taylor would take over and quite often effect a sale.

He was generous enough to give Maggie and me a tiny commission when this happened, which naturally made us both all the keener to make a sale.

As I rode home after my brush with Silas Oldfield I thought how wonderful it would be to own Bright Hope myself.

I was no expert but there was something about his build—his powerful hind quarters, the proud way he held his head—that spoke of a jumper, a wonderful horse for the hunting field.

As I rode home in the last of the short winter afternoon a mad idea came to me. When my mother had died she had left me a few hundred pounds.

Why, I thought, shouldn't I buy Bright Hope? I was almost sure I could get him for the two hundred pounds Mr. Oldfield had paid.

Of course, that wouldn't be all I'd have to pay. Not by a long chalk.

Even if I persuaded my boss to let me keep him at Staveleys, I would have to pay for his stabling and feed. That might be more than I could afford, though I would be willing to sacrifice quite a bit to save the horse from going to another owner who might treat him even worse than Mr. Oldfield.

Bessy trotted sedately through the village and soon we came in sight of Staveleys. I had taken the old horse over to Steeple Thatchley to show her off to two spinster ladies who had an empty stable attached to their old house and fancied keeping a horse for occasional rides about the countryside. It would be an excellent place for old Bessy to spend her retirement and I was delighted that the old ladies were seriously considering buying her.

The first person I saw when I trotted into the big cobbled yard at Staveleys was my employer, Mark Taylor. He waited as I approached and looked up at me, a question in his brown eyes.

" Well, Ann, what was the verdict?" he asked.

" They'd like to buy Bessy," I replied, slipping from the saddle and throwing the reins to Bob, one of the stablelads, who had run from one of the loose boxes when he heard Bessy's hoofs on the cobbles.

"Good!" Mr. Taylor said. "You're a good sales girl, Ann!"

He was a middle-aged man with dark hair and a heavy moustache. Maggie, my flat mate, said the latter sent cold shivers down her spine, whatever that might mean.

I found Mr. Taylor a kind, good-natured employer and I was sure he was utterly devoted to his wife Isabel, and his two children, Robin and Pam. In any case, Maggie was in love with Paddy, the head stableman, so her interest in Mr. Taylor's moustache was only a passing fancy.

He was about to turn away when I remembered Bright Hope.

"Mr. Taylor," I began. "I—"

Then I dried up.

He frowned and waited.

"Yes, what is it?" he asked a little impatiently when I fumbled for the right words.

"It's—I went past Mr. Oldfield's farm when—when I came back from Steeple Thatchley," I stammered.

"Silas Oldfield? Well, what about it?"

"He—he's bought a horse. He thought he'd go out hunting—"

"With the Borford?" he chuckled. "I don't believe it."

"He decided not to. The horse is difficult and seems to have taken against him—"

"I don't wonder. Not a chap to endear himself to such a sensitive animal as a horse, I imagine."

I plunged. "He wants to sell the horse for he has no use for it on the farm."

He frowned.

" And you thought I might buy it, eh?"

I shook my head.

" No, Mr. Taylor, I thought—I might buy him." Before he could say anything I went on, a little breathlessly: " I have a little money my mother left me. I've always wanted to have a horse of my own. I thought—"

" You thought you might keep him here, eh?" He shook his head firmly. " You know, Ann, buying horses is a chancy business. How can you be sure this animal of Oldfield's hasn't something wrong with it? I don't suppose you did more than look at it?"

" I just know Bright Hope is all right, Mr. Taylor," I said earnestly. " I—I—"

" You fell in love with the brute at first sight, eh? I suppose that fellow Oldfield was ill-treating it in some way and you went to the rescue."

" Well, yes, something like that," I agreed. " I—I hoped if I bought him you'd stable him here at Staveleys. I can afford to pay—"

He shook his head.

" You're too late, Ann love," he said. " In other circumstances I might have helped you but I've just come back from Melton. I bought two hunters this morning and they'll fill the only empty space we have in the stables when they arrive this evening. I'm sorry but there it is!"

My heart sank. It had been a wonderful dream while it lasted. Well, it hadn't lasted and now Bright Hope would be sold by Mr. Oldfield and I would never find out whether he was a good jumper or not.

CHAPTER TWO

The following morning Maggie and I were early astir.

The Borford Hunt was meeting at Apperley, a little village about four miles from Mardon, and Maggie and I were to take two of the Staveley hunters and show them off to the followers of the hunt.

We knew many members of the hunt, and though most of them knew why we were there none seemed to resent our presence. True, an occasional spiteful remark was passed when we appeared. " Here come the sales girls."

The Meet was at eleven o'clock and at half-past ten Maggie and I took to the saddle and rode the two mares—Roberta and Sally Flynn—out of the stable yard and took the country road to Apperley.

The usual bustle of the Meet greeted us as we rode up to the crowd of horses, hounds and people on the village green. More than one person smiled or waved to us, and the Master—a resplendent figure in scarlet coat astride a magnificent brown horse—actually smiled at us and touched the brim of his hat with his whip.

I looked round to see if there were any followers I had

not seen before. Most of the regular hunt members would not be interested in our mounts. Either they would be riding their own horses or ones hired from stables like Staveleys in the district around.

There were three likely customers. A stout man on an old grey cob, a peroxide blonde in her forties mounted on a horse I recognised as belonging to a rival establishment, and a young man on a nondescript animal which seemed quite out of place alongside the splendid hunters ridden by those present.

More than one pitying glance was thrown in the young man's direction, but he did not seem at all disconcerted. He patted the horse's neck and murmured to it as he looked round and said a word or two to those nearest. I felt sorry for him. Evidently he had borrowed the old horse, probably from a friend, and was intent at least in having a day out on its back, even though he would hardly be able to keep up with the hunt.

He caught my eye and smiled. I smiled back. Not only might he be a prospective customer but I liked the look of him.

He was wearing a hacking jacket and breeches. He had a square pleasant face, a shock of brown hair and very bright brown eyes. His big capable hands looked as if they were used to rough work. I found myself wondering what he did for a living.

As the hounds disappeared into the trees with the whips at each corner of the plantation alert for a view, and the huntsman and his yelping hounds plunging through the undergrowth, the rest of the hunt waited for the first sight of a fox.

They did not have to wait long. A distant toot-toot on the huntsman's horn, a " View Hulloo!" from one of the whips, then the Master, cramming his hat firmer on his head, pushed through an opening in the hedge and, followed by the rest of the hunt, started at a gallop across a big meadow as the hounds streamed out of the covert after the fox.

With Maggie on my heels I urged Roberta on. She was a fine mare and, at the far side of the field, took the first low fence in her stride.

The stout man on the old grey and the peroxide blonde had already fallen behind, so I checked Roberta's pace. It was no use losing my head in the excitement of the chase and drawing away from my prospective customers.

Maggie was somewhere away to the left and I wondered if she had decided to keep near the young man on the unsuitable horse. I found myself wishing our roles were reversed. I felt I could have interested him in Roberta easier than Maggie would be able to do with Sally Flynn.

The stout man on the grey caught up to me. I smiled to myself while feeling sorry to hear the old cob's heavy breathing. Evidently the slope was proving too much for her.

" I hope there's a check pretty soon," the mare's rider declared, riding alongside Roberta, " then maybe I'll catch up."

He dug his heels into the old horse's flanks.

" Not up to it, the old girl," he said. " Have to retire her at the end of the season, I suppose."

" Have you another horse?" I asked.

" I don't take hunting all that seriously," he said. " My wife and I bought a house just outside Apperley six months ago. I've worked in the City up to my retirement. I wanted some exercise so I thought I'd take up hunting. But I don't know if I was wise."

"I'm sure you were!" I exclaimed. "The finest exercise in the world. None better."

He laughed. "You sound a lively young lady. How long have you been hunting?"

"About a year." We rode along in a companionable silence for a while, then he said:

"That's a fine horse you're riding, Miss ——"

"Ann Mawsley," I smiled. "As a matter of fact, she's not mine. She belongs to the Staveley Stables at Mardon. I believe she's for sale."

"Indeed!" He examined Roberta more closely. "I suppose you've no idea how much they're asking?"

"Two hundred and fifty, I believe," I said. "She's worth every penny of it."

"I'm sure she is," he said with another glance, then as we had reached the brow of the hill and could see the hounds and the rest of the hunt streaming away across country below, he touched his hat and urged the old grey into a gallop once more.

Now that I had made contact with my prospective customer I felt I had done my duty for the time being and might as well enjoy the rest of the day.

I knew that if I did not catch the hunt up fairly soon it would run away from me.

From the top of the hill I weighed my prospects. The hounds were running away to the left alongside a wood. It seemed to me that the fox might seek shelter in these trees and that if I made my way directly through the wood to the far side, I would stand a good chance of re-joining the hunt.

He said all this in an assured way that brooked no argument.

I looked at him more closely. He was quite good-looking, I decided, with very fair hair which curled in the nape of his neck, blue eyes and a rather wilful mouth. He was about 28.

A sudden baying from the hounds reached us and I saw both young men look in the direction of the sound. The fair-haired one looked at me a trifle impatiently.

" Let's help him up," he said. " If they find within the next couple of minutes the hunt will be off and Doc Fawcett will be out of reach. He's a real devil for being up with the hounds."

I smiled at the other young man.

" Well, what about it?" I asked.

He shook his head though he frowned as if the sudden movement was painful.

" I can manage quite well," he said. " I don't want you to miss the rest of the run on my account."

" Don't be a fool, man!" the other snapped. " See! Put your foot in the stirrup and I'll give you a shove up."

As if he felt too tired to argue the young man did as he was told. A few minutes later he was established in the saddle on the back of the white horse.

" Will you bring Primrose along?" he asked me and I smiled up at him.

" Of course I will," I said and went to take the reins of the pitiful creature he had ridden to the hunt.

Leading his own horse the fair-haired young man set off along the ride. Following I looked up anxiously at the man I had found lying unconscious such a short time ago.

To my alarm I saw that his eyes were closed. His face was pale and drawn.

" Are you all right?" I demanded and the other man looked round at the urgency in my voice.

We both moved quickly forward as our charge began to slip slowly from the saddle. We were just in time to ease him to the ground.

" Now what?" I asked, looking into my companion's face.

He scowled at me. Somehow I had a feeling that he was not too pleased at the way things were going.

" My uncle's house is reasonably near here," he said. " If you'll stay with our invalid I'll ride over and get my car. It shouldn't take me more than a quarter of an hour. O.K.?"

I nodded. That was the least I could do.

He prepared to mount the magnificent white hunter.

" By the way," he said, looking back at me, " my name's Simon Blake. What's yours?"

" Ann Mawsley," I replied, then he was in the saddle and making for the gate while I looked down into the still face of the man lying at my feet.

CHAPTER THREE

As I waited with my unconscious charge I thought about Simon Blake.

I had not seen him out with the hunt before and I wondered if he was new to the district. I wondered too who his uncle was. He must live in the neighbourhood. Evidently his nephew was staying with him, perhaps for the hunting.

I had taken my jacket off and put it under the young man's head. A cold wind was blowing through the trees and I began to shiver. I wished Simon Blake would come.

I stood up and walked to the gate. The narrow lane was empty. I began to feel very much alone.

Suppose Simon Blake didn't come back! What would I do in the lonely wood with a sick man on my hands?

" Put your jacket on! You'll catch your death of cold."

It was the young man. He was sitting up and looking across at me.

" How do you feel now?" I asked, very relieved to see that he had regained consciousness once more.

" I'm all right," he said. " I suppose it was being jogged

about on that horse made me feel dizzy. I feel an awful fool letting you in for this."

" That's all right," I smiled. " Accidents will happen."

He smiled. " By the way, my name's Barry Hastings. I have a farm at Apperley."

I told him my own name and, as he was holding out my jacket, I took it and slipped it over my shoulders.

" Where's the other chap—the one with the white horse ?" he asked.

" He's gone to get a car so he can take you to his uncle's house," I replied. " His name's Simon Blake."

He frowned as if trying to place the name; then he nodded.

" He must be Matthew Blake's nephew," he said. " Mr. Blake owns Consett Hall. I know his farm bailiff. He told me his boss's nephew was coming to stay until the end of the hunting season."

I heard a car engine in the lane. A minute later Simon Blake came through the gate and made towards us.

" So you've come to, have you ?" he declared, looking down at Barry.

" Yes ! I feel O.K. now. It was good of you to go to so much trouble, Mr. Blake, but I can manage quite well. I'll get off home—"

" You'll do nothing of the sort! You're going to the Hall now I've fetched the car. I rang my uncle's doctor and he should be there when we get to the house."

" You shouldn't have gone to all that trouble—"

" Nonsense !" He glanced at me. " Let's help him up then take him to the car."

But Barry was already struggling to his feet. While Simon took a firm grip on his right arm and I walked on his left. Slowly we made our way to the gate and out into the lane where a big car was waiting. It was a grey Mercedes and was obviously the car of a man with a great deal of money.

" I borrowed one of my uncle's cars," Simon said. " Get into the passenger seat, old man."

He looked at me. " I'll drive slowly if you bring up the rear with the two horses," he said.

" But don't you think ?—"

He shook his head with a frown.

" You must come up to the Hall, too," he said sharply. " You look frozen. I'd never forgive myself if you went off without a hot drink of some sort."

I'd decided that I could take Barry's horse back to Apperley if he gave me the name of his farm, then ride home on Roberta.

But Simon Blake was not a man to cross. He had decided what I was to do. I hid a smile. Except for my employer, I wasn't used to having men give me orders. Somehow obeying Simon Blake seemed a natural thing to do.

Simon turned the car and I mounted Roberta and followed, leading Primrose, Barry's horse.

Presently we came out on to the main road. After proceeding along this for half a mile the Mercedes slowed then turned in between two white gateposts.

I followed up the long drive towards the old house standing on a wooded slope overlooking the parkland below. Over to my right was a lake on which swans glimmered white and mysterious. It made me think of a fairy tale book I had had as a child. There had been an illustration of an ancient house almost overgrown with ivy which had twisted chimneys and crooked gables and funny little turrets at each corner.

Not that Consett Hall had twisted chimneys and crooked gables. Far from it. It had a half-timbered front with mullioned windows and looked, in the half-light, very beautiful indeed.

It was just an impression I got: that behind those half-timbered walls was something I did not as yet understand. Whether it was happiness or unhappiness I had no means of knowing. But the feeling persisted as Simon brought the big car to a halt outside the front door and I clattered up with the two horses.

At the sound of our arrival the front door had opened and a thickset man in alpacca jacket and dark trousers had appeared.

" Has the doctor arrived, Briggs?" Simon Blake asked.

" Not yet, sir, but he should be here at any moment," the servant replied.

" We'd better get you into the house," Simon said looking at Barry. " Let me help you!"

" I can manage quite well," Barry said quickly and slipped from the passenger seat.

While the servant took charge of the horses Simon and I walked at each side of Barry as the three of us went into the house.

A huge fire was burning in an open fireplace in the oak-panelled hall. A wide staircase rose to a galleried landing above. On the walls hung several portraits in oils.

But the feature that caught the eye above all else was the enormous flower arrangement which stood on a table in the middle of the hall. An expert had arranged the carnations, the roses, the other colourful blooms, most of which I did not recognise, in a glorious tableau of colour.

The flowers were as welcoming as the big log fire in the inglenook fireplace.

" In here," Simon said, crossing the thick carpet and opening a door to the right of the stairs.

Another big fire was burning in the comfortable room we entered. This room was filled with massive but comfortable furniture. Wall lights burned in sconces against the panelling even though it was just past mid-day. It was a man's room with a fox's mask grinning above the fireplace and sporting prints on the walls.

Simon pressed a bell push and, almost as if she had been waiting for the summons, a middle-aged woman in a flowered overall appeared.

" Coffee, Martha!" Simon said. " And some of that special cake of yours, if you can manage it."

" I'll bring it immediately, Mr. Simon," the woman said, with an indulgent smile. It was obvious that she was completely under the spell of this good-looking young man's charm.

" Sit down, Mr. ? ——" Simon said, looking at Barry.

" I'm Barry Hastings," Barry said, and with a glance at me : " This is—"

" Ann Mawsley," Simon finished for him. " She told me who she was in the wood."

There came the sound of a car in the drive.

" That's Dr. Elliott," Simon said and went from the room to greet the newcomer.

Barry frowned. " A lot of nonsense! What do I want a doctor for? I just took a toss, no more."

" Better be sure than sorry," I smiled.

Dr. Elliott was a tall bustling individual who listened a little impatiently to Simon's explanation of what had happened in the wood.

" Sit there, Mr.—er—Hastings," he said, indicating a chair by the fire.

He ran skilful hands over his patient's head and neck then had him flex his arms and legs.

" Seems to be nothing much wrong with you," he declared. " You just knocked yourself out. It happens every day in the hunting field. Of course, you've been lucky. You could have broken your neck, I suppose."

When the examination was over Simon asked the doctor if he would like some coffee."

Dr. Elliott shook his head. " No, thanks. Never touch the stuff. Besides "—with a glance at his watch—" I must be on my way. Lot of flu about just now. Still got a lot of people to see. I'll let myself out."

He smiled round, shook hands with Simon then left the room. A moment later Martha brought in a large silver tray on which stood a coffee pot and cups which she put down on the round table before the fire.

" All right, Martha, we'll let Miss Mawsley pour," Simon said and the servant, rather reluctantly, I thought, went from the room.

" Well, tell me about yourselves," Simon said, looking first in my direction then in Barry's.

I busied myself pouring the coffee into the egg-shell thin cups. Barry, after a moment's hesitation, said :

" There's not much to tell about me. I own a hundred acre farm outside Apperley. I keep a few Friesians, some Southdowns and a couple of dozen pigs. I also have a horse. She's outside now ! "

Simon laughed. " If you're going to hunt again you'll have to sacrifice a few cows and buy yourself a decent nag. The one you've got looks ready for the knacker's yard to me! "

I saw Barry's face darken for a moment, then he laughed shortly.

" I suppose you're right, Mr. Blake," he said. " I ought never to have ridden Primrose today. It was just that I've always been mad keen on hunting and as I'd nothing else to ride I had to go out on Primrose—or stay at home."

" Now that we know each other I'll always be able to lend you a horse—at least, my uncle will," Simon declared. then added: " And please don't call me ' Mr. Blake '. Simon's the name. I hope we're going to be friends, Barry."

Barry flushed with pleasure.

" That's nice of you, Simon," he said. Then glancing at me: " But enough of me. I'm sure you're as interested to hear about Miss Mawsley as I am."

" Ann, please," I smiled. " I'm not at all interesting. Quite unashamedly I was out today because I was riding one of my employer's horses and hoped to sell her. I work for Mr. Mark Taylor at the Staveleys Stables."

" Good for you! " Simon cried, taking a piece of cake from the tray. " I met Mark at a party once when I was visiting my uncle before. He had his wife with him. A very pleasant woman."

He looked at Barry who was sipping his coffee.

" Now's your chance, Barry," he said. " Why don't you buy Roberta? She seems a splendid horse to me and would carry you well if you mean to hunt regularly."

Barry frowned. " I'm afraid there's no chance of that. Farming today's a matter of survival. It doesn't run to expensive hunters." There was a hint of bitterness in his voice.

There was an awkward little pause. I found myself comparing the two men: one attractive, assured, dressed in expensively cut clothes; the other pleasant-looking rather than handsome in shabby jacket and breeches whose appearance had not been improved by the fall in the wood.

It was obvious that a yawning chasm lay between the two young men socially. I felt suddenly very sorry for Barry and found myself wondering why.

He looked proud and able enough to stand on his own two feet without any pity from me.

" I'd better be going," he said, putting his cup down and getting to his feet.

" Not yet, surely," Simon cried. " I was hoping you'd stay for lunch. In any case, you should rest a little longer after your fall."

Barry shook his head.

" I'd rather get home," he said. " I only meant to stay out for an hour or two with the Hunt. There's so much to do on a farm. But it was kind of you to bring me here and send for the doctor."

" If you insist I'll run you home," Simon said, but Barry frowned.

" I'd rather ride Primrose," he said. " After all, I can hardly leave her here with you."

" But—"

I broke in with: " I'll ride with you, Barry. Your farm can't be very far if we keep to the road."

" About two miles," he said and Simon, after looking at the two of us, shrugged helplessly.

" I can see you mean to do your own thing," he laughed. " I'd better go and tell them to bring your horses round to the front of the house."

Five minutes later we were mounted. Simon raised his hand in salute.

" I hope it won't be long before I see you both again," he said and I was conscious that his eyes were on me. I felt the colour rise into my cheeks.

As we prepared to leave a car came up the drive. A chauffeur was at the wheel and as Barry and I hesitated, not knowing whether to stay or leave, the man jumped from the car and opened the rear door.

A burly middle-aged man got out of the car. He was wearing a thick overcoat and bowler hat. He looked first at Barry then at me then turned to Simon.

" Your friends just going, Simon?" he asked.

" Let me introduce you, Uncle," Simon said. " Ann Mawsley and Barry Hastings. We met at the hunt today." Looking up at us he added: " This is Mr. Matthew Blake, my uncle."

" Ask them to come in and have a drink," the older man said.

Barry shook his head and said quickly:

" It's very good of you, sir, but I must go. I—"

" Barry has a farm. He's a busy man," Simon interrupted.

" I understand," Mr. Blake said. He frowned. " Your name is Hastings, I think Simon said. I used to know a Tom Hastings of Moss Hill Farm. Any relation?"

" He was my father, sir. He died last year."

" I was sorry to hear it. My farm bailiff often spoke of him."

He smiled. " Well, if you won't come in for a drink I won't detain you. Goodbye."

As Barry and I walked our horses down the drive I heard Mr. Blake say to Simon:

" Who's that pretty girl, Simon? You don't often see good-lookers like that around these days. A big improvement on some of the specimens you've brought with you from London."

I didn't hear Simon's reply. We were too far away by that time, but as we made for the road I felt suddenly curious. If Simon's uncle thought I was as pretty as all that what did his nephew think?

CHAPTER FOUR

" IF YOU were hoping to sell that horse at the hunt today I'm afraid I put paid to your chances," Barry said as we rode side by side on the busy road's grass verge.

" Don't worry about that," I reassured him. " I made the only contact possible, a stout little man riding a grey cob. He seemed interested in Roberta."

We rode along without speaking after that. Presently, after a mile, we left the road and turned down a muddy lane. At the far end was a white gate and beyond this an old stone farmhouse with a big barn on one side and a row of outbuildings set at right angles to the house at the other.

" Moss Hill Farm," Barry said and something in his voice made me glance at him curiously.

He sounded depressed as if there was nothing in the sight of his home to cheer him. I followed the direction of his gaze.

The ivy-covered farmhouse facing out across the cobbled farmyard looked charming enough to me with its tiny-paned windows and with smoke rising from its squat chimneys.

And the rest of the buildings, which had evidently been painted recently, looked spick and span.

" It's a lovely farm, Barry," I cried.

He cheered up a little at my praise.

" Do you think so? I was just comparing it with Consett Hall. I suppose I was being unfair."

" You certainly were! Consett Hall and Moss Hill Farm are two very different properties. One's just a house. This farm is where things—real things—happen!"

His eyes shone. His pleasant face glowed with pleasure.

" You really think so?"

" Of course I do! Anyone who runs a farm is doing a really worthwhile job, Barry."

He reached down and opened the gate.

" You must come in and meet my mother," he said. " I think you'll like her. The horse will be all right for a minute or two."

We crossed the cobbles towards the stone porch. The door stood open and Barry went ahead of me along the stone-flagged passage.

" Mother! Where are you? I've a visitor!" he called.

There were closed doors on each side of the passage but ahead I could see the cheerful glow of a fire. A tall woman came through the open doorway of the kitchen and hurried forward.

Mrs. Hastings had dark hair streaked with grey and the same kindly brown eyes as her son. In fact, she was very like Barry as she stood there, an enquiring smile on her homely face.

" This is Ann," Barry said. " She helped me when Primrose and I parted company in Patchett's Plantation."

Mrs. Hastings looked concerned.

" Are you all right, Barry?" she demanded. "Now I look at you your face is quite pale."

" Oh, I'm fine!" he laughed. "As a matter of fact, Matthew Blake's nephew took me back to Consett Hall in his car. He gave us coffee."

" I don't think you need worry, Mrs. Hastings," I put in. " Mr. Blake sent for the doctor who said your son had come to no harm."

Mrs. Hastings shook her head.

" I told him Primrose wasn't a hunter," she said. " But there! he never listens to me."

Barry put his arm about her still slim waist and dropped a kiss on her dark hair.

" I couldn't resist having a run with the hounds today," he said. " And as Primrose was the only possible means of getting to the hunt I had to ride her."

" I don't know what your father would have said if he'd been alive!"

" My father kept a couple of real horses," he said, with a hint of bitterness in his voice. " They had to be sold, Ann, when he died to help keep Moss Hill Farm afloat."

Mrs. Hastings bit her lip. Evidently this was a sore point between mother and son. I stepped into the gap.

" I think your farm is lovely, Mrs. Hastings," I said, enthusiastically.

She smiled suddenly. " What am I thinking about, keeping you talking out here in the cold passage! Come into the kitchen, both of you!"

She went before us into the big kitchen with its large scrubbed table and brass pans twinkling in the firelight and a big Welsh dresser taking up almost one wall of the room.

" It's one o'clock," Mrs. Hastings declared. " You must both be ravenous. I've some hot soup ready and—"

" I really must be going, Mrs. Hastings," I said, but she wouldn't hear of it.

" You helped Barry," she cried. " That was very kind of you. I'd never forgive myself if I let you go away a couple of minutes after meeting you."

Barry caught my eye and winked.

" You might just as well give in," he said. " Besides, she's not a bad cook, are you, old girl?"

He gave his mother another hug and she pushed him away.

" Get on with you, Barry!" she cried, though there was a fond look on her face. " Why not show Miss Mawsley round while I'm dishing up? I'll give you a quarter of an hour."

" Are you interested?" he asked, turning to me. " There's not much to see."

" I'd love to see the farm," I said and something in my voice must have convinced him that I was not being merely polite for he took my arm and we went out into the farmyard again.

" I'd better put the horses in the stable while we're having lunch," he said.

There was more stable accommodation than Primrose merited. As I watched Barry giving the horses a generous helping of hay I looked round the building with interest. Much of the space had been given up to storing feed, farm implements, even a small tractor. A door had been enlarged at the far end to garage a small sports car.

Barry met my eyes and gave me a rueful smile.

" I suppose you're thinking what a pity it is that

stabling like this should be used as a sort of general store-house," he exclaimed.

" I suppose when your father was alive more space would be given up to the horses?"

" Most of it! Dad was mad keen on hunting. At one time he had four horses, though he did use two of them in the fields. When he died he was down to two hunters and he couldn't afford even those."

He gave a short laugh. " I'm afraid Dad was not quite as careful with money as he might have been. It's proving quite a hard pull to put the farm back on a paying basis again."

I felt suddenly sorry for this young man, still in his twenties, who had obviously been left a load of debts by his father and who had set himself to clear them and make a go of Moss Hill Farm.

Most young men in his position would have sold up and tried something else? There were plenty of opportunities for able young men in the world today.

Or perhaps the farm belonged to Mrs. Hastings and not to Barry. In which case wouldn't he, being so fond of his mother, have felt an obligation to stay with her and carry on for her sake?

" We'd better get on if we're to look over the rest of the farm before lunch," Barry said and we went out of the stable, examined the byre where the cows were milked night and morning, and stood for a few moments in the big barn just now stacked to the roof with sweet-smelling hay and bales of straw. At one end were huge bins for the grain that would be harvested at the end of each summer.

As we walked round an idea came into my head. At

first I told myself I was a fool ever to imagine that Barry might be interested in it.

But as we made for the house again I found myself telling him about Bright Hope, Silas Oldfield's horse, and how I had hoped I might buy him and stable him at Staveleys.

" And Mr. Taylor hadn't room?" Barry asked.

" No! He's just bought a couple of hunters and he needs the space." I looked up at him. " Barry, would— would you consider having Bright Hope here if I bought him? I'd pay for his keep, of course."

He frowned. " You're quite certain he's as good a horse as you think, Ann? From what you say, you haven't done more than round him up and lead him back to Oldfield's stable."

I bit my lip. " I know it must seem strange to you, Barry, but I'm confident Bright Hope's as good as I think him. Sometimes one goes by instinct and in Bright Hope's case I'm sure I'm right."

" And what would you do with him if you brought him?" he asked. " Ride him to hounds?"

I hadn't really thought as far as this. All I'd been concerned with was to rescue Bright Hope from Silas Oldfield—or the kind of unsuitable person Mr. Oldfield might sell him to. Beyond that I hadn't gone.

I must have looked a little downcast for Barry took my hand and gave it a kindly squeeze.

" Don't mind my questions, Ann," he said. " I just want to know more. Would you like me to go with you to see your horse once again before you make up your mind finally?"

" I've made my mind up," I said. " All I'm concerned

about is having somewhere to stable Bright Hope if I buy him."

He stopped and looked down at me. His nice eyes were shining. I could see he was excited about something.

"I'll tell you what I'll do, Ann," he said. "If you buy Bright Hope I'll stable him here at Moss Hill Farm free, gratis and for nothing on one condition."

"What's that?" I asked, my heart quickening.

"That I ride him to hounds during the rest of the season? I'll solve your problem—you'll solve mine!"

"But I couldn't let you in for the expense of feeding Bright Hope," I began, but he shook his head.

"The cost wouldn't be much. Just for his food. After all, the stabling is here whether or not he occupies part of it. Besides," he smiled, "Bright Hope would be company for Primrose."

I laughed at this and he, linking his arm through mine, drew me towards the farmhouse. I have rarely felt happier in all my life.

During lunch we told Mrs. Hardings about Bright Hope. She frowned as she listened.

"Are you sure you can afford to buy him?" she asked, looking across the table at me.

"My mother left me some money," I replied. "I'm sure Bright Hope will be a good investment. Barry will find out how good when he rides him with the Borford in the last weeks of this season."

"I hope you'll be able to find time for all this hunting," Mrs. Hastings said, glancing at her son. "I don't suppose Walter will welcome any extra work."

He grinned. "I shan't let it interfere with the work of the farm, you can be sure. You haven't met Walter yet, Ann. He's been at Moss Hill Farm since the year dot. He's always sighing for the good old days when Dad used to hunt three times a week. Now he'll be able to see the young master riding off to hounds. It should please him!''

The lunch Mrs. Hastings gave us—thick vegetable soup, home-baked ham with pineapple, apple tart with thick cream—was the nicest meal I had had for a very long time. The meals Maggie and I had were usually rushed affairs prepared by whoever happened to be on hand in the flat at the time, usually me!

After lunch I met Walter and a sixteen-year-old boy who comprised the work force at Moss Hill Farm.

Walter was a lugubrious individual with one eye and of uncertain age. Jim, the boy, was a bright youngster who had left school six months before. He was, according to Barry, mad keen on animals and preferred to work on a farm rather than go into a bank in Melton.

Later, after I had thanked Mrs. Hastings for lunch and said goodbye, I went with Barry to collect Roberta from the stable.

" When will you bring Bright Hope to the farm?" he asked me.

" I'll call and see Mr. Oldfield this evening," I said. " If he'll let me have the horse at my price I'll ride him over some time tomorrow."

" I shall look forward to your coming," he said, then as I prepared to mount Roberta: " Ann, thank you for all you did this morning. I feel it was really worth taking that toss for it's brought you into my life."

I smiled up at him. I did not let him see that his words had vaguely disturbed me.

" You may regret meeting me," I declared. " By taking Bright Hope on you may be letting yourself in for more than you bargain for."

" I'm sure I shan't. Somehow I have a feeling that today's going to prove a Red Letter Day in my life."

I said nothing to this but occupied myself climbing into the saddle. Roberta, eager to be off, danced about impatiently.

" I'll see you later," I called to Barry and headed for the gate which Jim was holding open.

As I passed out into the lane I looked back. Barry was still staring after me. Seeing me glance round he raised his hand and waved, then almost abruptly turned and made for the house.

CHAPTER FIVE

I ARRIVED back at Staveleys to be met by Mr. Taylor as I rode into the stable yard.

"Well done, Ann!" he cried, and as I slipped from the saddle and turned to him enquiringly he went on: "I've just had a phone call from an old buffer called Cartwright. He says he saw you out on Roberta this morning and thought he might be interested in buying her."

I was delighted. What a wonderful day this was!

"He's coming over to Mardon tomorrow morning," Mr. Taylor went on. "You'd better be on hand with Paddy to show him Roberta's finer points. Did you give him any indication of price?"

"I said I thought about two fifty."

"Good girl! There'll be a nice bit of commission for you if the sale comes off."

He went off whistling to himself and I led Roberta to her quarters, rubbed her down, saw that she had hay and water in reach, then went to the flat.

I wondered how Maggie was going on. She was mad keen on hunting and would certainly stay out as long as the hounds were running.

If she succeeded in interesting someone in Sally Flynn it would have been a good day for the Staveley Stables.

It occurred to me that if this Mr. Cartwright bought Roberta there would be an empty box in the stables below. Perhaps Mr. Taylor would, after all, have let me keep Bright Hope there if I succeeded in buying her later in the day.

" But it would only have been a temporary measure," I thought. " Sooner or later another hunter would have been bought then Bright Hope would have had to go. No! she'll be much better at Moss Hill Farm."

In my heart I knew there was another reason why I preferred to have the horse at the farm. With Bright Hope to visit I would have a good chance of strengthening my friendship with Barry Hastings.

I frowned at my reflection in the dressing table mirror as I sat before it repairing my make-up. Surely I wasn't getting interested in Barry Hastings. I'd only seen him for the first time today.

I had always had lots of boy friends, but none of them serious. Just because Barry was as interested in horses as I was didn't put him in a special class of his own.

I leaned forward and looked into the glass. I was remembering the words of Simon Blake's father as Barry and I rode away from Consett Hall.

" Who's that pretty girl, Simon? You don't often see good-lookers like that around these days . . ."

I saw a serious little face staring back at me from the mirror with dark curly hair and hazel eyes. A short straight nose, a rather big mouth and a firm and—I hoped—determined chin made up the sum total of my looks.

" A big improvement on some of the specimens you've brought with you from London," Mr. Blake had added and I wondered just how many girl friends Simon had had in his time.

That evening I made my way to Beck's Farm. I had thought of asking Maggie to go along with me for company, then had decided to go alone. Maggie was a bit of a gossip and if she heard about Bright Hope the story would be all over Staveleys within a matter of minutes.

It was a lovely evening. The moon was rising as I walked through the village. There was plenty of light for me to see where I was going as I left the last of the cottages behind and went along the lane which led to Silas Oldfield's farm.

The farmhouse was set well back from the lane and I had to negotiate a muddy track before I reached the big stackyard.

Lights were burning in two downstairs windows and as I made for the door it opened and a man came out of the house.

It was Silas Oldfield. I recognised his thickset figure. He looked across at me as I approached as if surprised that anyone should be calling on him at that time.

I saw the glitter in his hard grey eyes as I drew near.

" So it's you!" he said, and added grumpily: " What do you want?"

" I came about Bright Hope," I said, with a smile. " I'd like to buy him."

" Oh, you would, would you?" he said, rubbing his big hand across his chin with a rasping sound. " And suppose I don't want to sell him."

" But you said!—" I exclaimed.

" I know what I said," he interrupted. " Perhaps I've changed my mind."

" You mean you're going to keep him?"

" I might!" He looked at my slyly. " It depends how much I was offered for him."

Into my mind came some words I had once heard Mr. Taylor say when he was discussing the sale of horses with Maggie and me.

" If you're selling something always ask for much more than you're prepared to accept," he had said. " When you're buying offer a great deal less. The starting price means very little in either case."

" I've been thinking things over, Mr. Oldfield," I said. " I like Bright Hope and I'd be prepared to give you one hundred and fifty pounds for him."

" One hundred and fifty!" he was plainly taken aback by this. He had been so sure I would be glad to pay what he had given for the horse: two hundred pounds. " See here, young lady, if you've come here to waste my time!—"

" Waste your time, Mr. Oldfield," I protested. " Why-ever would I do that?"

" That horse is worth more than that! Why, I wouldn't part with him for—for two hundred and ten pounds."

I turned away.

" Then I'm wasting *my* time," I said sadly. " I might have gone a little higher than one hundred and fifty but—well, two hundred and ten is ridiculous."

I started to walk towards the gate. He hesitated then followed me.

" You seemed to like the horse well enough yesterday,"

he said. " If you were so keen on him then why don't you think he's worth more than one-fifty quid now?"

I swung round to face him.

" I do think he's worth more than one-fifty," I said, " but certainly not two hundred and ten."

" Well, perhaps I might come down a bit," he muttered. " I don't really want to keep him, though I don't doubt I should have any difficulty in selling him. How about two hundred and five pounds?"

I frowned. " I was going to offer one-sixty, but I'll tell you what I'll do, Mr. Oldfield. I'll go as far as one-ninety. Take it or leave it! There are two horses at the Staveley Stables at this very moment I could buy for that, though there was something about Bright Hope that took my fancy."

" When would you take the horse away—if we agreed a price?" he demanded.

" Tomorrow!" I replied.

He hesitated. I made another move towards the gate. He shook his head.

" I mentioned two hundred the horse cost me when I saw you yesterday. I don't want to lose on the deal so—"

" You mean you'll let me have him for two hundred?"

He nodded. " Yes! I wanted the extra for the cost of feeding the brute over the last fortnight, but—well, if it'll help the deal I'll forget what I've laid out on his keep."

I pretended to hesitate and I knew he was watching me anxiously. He was as keen to sell the horse for two hundred pounds as I was to buy him.

At last I smiled and held out my hand.

" Very well, I'll pay the two hundred though I feel I'm paying more than I should. I don't know what Mr. Taylor will say when I tell him."

His expression told me he couldn't care less what my employer, or anyone else for that matter, might think.

" And you'll take the horse away tomorrow?" he asked as we shook hands.

" Yes, if that's convenient," I replied. " I'll bring the money with me when I collect him."

An unwilling glint of admiration came into his cold eyes. He even managed a faint grin.

" You've certainly got your head screwed on the right way for a young lass," he said, then turning abruptly he hurried away across the stackyard to one of the farm buildings at the far side.

I returned to Staveleys cock-a-hoop. Bright Hope was mine. Tomorrow I would ride him over to Apperley and see him settled in at Moss Hill Farm.

Maggie was sitting in the flat, a cup of coffee beside her, staring at the TV set Mr. Taylor had hired for us from a local dealer. She looked round as I came into the room.

" And where have you been on this cold dark night?" she asked. " Got a boy friend you haven't told me about?"

I laughed. " I went for a walk. Any objection?"

I went into the the little kitchenette and poured hot water from the kettle into a cup of instant coffee. When I went back into the living-room Maggie had switched the set off.

" I hear some bloke might buy Roberta!" When I nodded she went on: " You're lucky! Nobody wanted to know about Sally Flynn. I thought that young chap riding that old screw might have been interested. But he sheered off when I tried to interest him and I never saw him again all day. I suppose that peculiar animal he was on didn't last out more than an hour or so."

" As a matter of fact he came a cropper in Patchett's Plantation. His horse put its foot in a rabbit hole and threw him. I was taking a short cut through the plantation and found him."

" Some people have all the luck," Maggie grumbled. " Things like that never happen to me. He was rather nice looking, I thought. Who was he?"

" His name's Barry Hastings. I stayed with him until help came."

" Who found you in an out-of-the-way place like Patchett's Plantation?"

" A man on a white horse," I smiled.

She groaned. " Not that very good-looking type with fair hair and bright blue eyes and wearing super clothes? I spotted him fairly early but he got away while I was trying to interest the peroxide blonde in Sally Flynn. Who was he, Ann?"

" Simon Blake. He's staying with his uncle at Consett Hall."

" So he's rich as well as dishy?" She looked at me critically. " I don't know how you do it, Ann. Here am I going about with my eyes wide open for any presentable man to come along and you, without even trying, have them coming round you in swarms."

" Hardly swarms!" I protested. " In any case, what about Paddy? I thought he was the man in your life."

She frowned. " Oh, Paddy! He's all right, I suppose,

but he's hardly the answer to a maiden's prayer financially, is he? A girl must do the best she can these difficult days."

I went to bed early and lay thinking about Bright Hope and Barry Hastings; but strangely enough my last thought before I fell asleep was of Simon Blake and my first glimpse of Consett Hall and of the eerie feeling I had had when first I had looked across at the old house ...

Mr. Taylor gave me time off on the following afternoon to pay Mr. Oldfield for Bright Hope and ride him over to Moss Hill Farm to his new quarters.

I drew the money out of the bank as I went through the village and reached Beck's Farm about half-past two.

I found Mr. Oldfield waiting in the stackyard. He seemed relieved to see me. I wondered if he had been afraid I might change my mind overnight.

" Where's the horse?" I asked.

" In the stable. I see you've brought your saddle with you?"

I certainly had. Carrying it all the way from Staveleys had tired my arms. I had borrowed it from Paddy who had told me to return it when it was convenient. If he had been curious as to what I wanted it for he did not show it. As for me I intended to tell everybody at Staveleys about Bright Hope when I had delivered him safely to his new home.

Mr. Oldfield led the way to the stable. Bright Hope looked round expectantly as if he believed there was a chance of being released from his dark stuffy prison and turned out into an open field for a while.

" Hullo, old boy!" I said softly and went forward to stroke his long neck.

His eyes regarded me speculatively. Was I going to release him—or was I going to leave him shut away from the sun and the open sky for another long weary period?

I had brought some sugar lumps with me and I held these out to him on the palm of my hand. He took them gratefully and looked for more.

" Only when I've put your saddle on," I whispered, and threw it over his back.

I sighed with relief when he did not resent having the girth tightened under his belly or the reins slipped over his head.

He was evidently used to being ridden and seemed more interested in my producing more sugar lumps than anything else.

He got his sugar and I then led him out into the pale autumn sunshine. He was docile enough as I handed the money over to Mr. Oldfield who gave me a receipt which he had prepared earlier.

" I hope you do better with him than me," he said as I swung myself up into the saddle. " Nasty, bad-tempered brute!"

We reached the road and Bright Hope trotted along as if he was thoroughly enjoying the outing. Only once did his ears go up as the driver of a car gave a loud beep-beep on his horn as he pulled out to pass a lorry.

" You're nearly home now, old chap!" I said, leaning forward in the saddle and giving one of his ears a little tug.

We rode up to the gate and my heart rose as I saw Barry waiting for us, a wide welcoming smile on his nice face.

CHAPTER SIX

" HE'S BEAUTIFUL!" Barry cried enthusiastically as I rode Bright Hope up and down the farmyard.

" I'm glad you think so," I said, for truth to tell I was relieved that my instinct had served me so well.

When I had first seen Bright Hope it had been love at first sight. I hadn't even given him a try-out over a few fences or examined him carefully to ensure that he was sound in wind and limb.

But I had no doubt now. Bright Hope was right. I was sure of it!

" How about taking him into my three acre field and giving him a run?" Barry suggested, and when I nodded my agreement, he crossed to a gate alongside the barn and opened it.

Half a dozen black and white cows were grazing in the far corner of the field. They looked up for a moment as we appeared then bent their heads again to cross the grass.

" Off you go!" Barry cried and I urged Bright Hope into a canter. He moved beautifully and I was suddenly filled with an urgent desire to see how he jumped.

There was a gate at the far side of the field and, with a glance at Barry, I turned Bright Hope towards it.

I heard Barry shout something about being careful, then Bright Hope's canter turned into a gallop and we were heading straight for the gate.

My heart thundered. I was filled with a wild exhilaration. I might be about to break my neck but I did not care. All I wanted was for Bright Hope to prove himself.

"Steady!" I said as the horse checked for a moment as he saw the gate.

Picking my moment, I dug my heels into his sides and, striding forward, he rose like a bird and cleared the gate by six inches.

We landed on soft ground in another field. Some sheep looked up in astonishment at our sudden arrival.

"Well done!" Barry was looking over the gate. "But—oh, gosh, you gave me a fright for a moment."

I grinned. My heart was still thundering but I did not want Barry to guess that.

"How about having a ride yourself?" I asked.

He opened the gate and I rode back into the three acre. I threw him the reins and he prepared to mount.

Without warning Bright Hope backed away.

"Hey, stand still!" Barry cried but once again, as he felt for a stirrup, Bright Hope twisted away. There was an ugly look in his eyes.

"I don't think he likes me," Barry said. "Do you think he's got it in for men?"

"You mean because of Silas Oldfield?"

"He may have been ill-used by other men before Silas Oldfield."

I went to Bright Hope and talked to him. He let me run

my fingers through his silky mane. Putting his head down he nuzzled at my pocket.

As I produced a sugar lump I looked at Barry again.

"He'll have to get used to you if he's to live here at Moss Hill Farm," I said.

He forced a smile.

"Let's give him a day or two to settle down. At first I'll turn him out into the field and let him get used to his new home. Later, when he's used to me I'll try to ride him again."

"You're very understanding," I said slowly. "A lot of men in your position would tell me to take him away and find somewhere else to stable him."

He smiled. "I have a feeling Bright Hope and I are going to be good friends yet. Besides, I made a bargain with you and I mean to carry it out."

"But you've probably let yourself in for feeding a horse that very likely won't let you ride him. Won't you at least let me pay something towards his keep?"

As we walked back across the field towards the farm Barry said:

"There's one very good reason why I won't alter our arrangement in any way. I suppose you can guess what that is?"

I frowned. What did he mean? Then, seeing the look in his nice brown eyes, I knew; and I felt the colour come into my cheeks.

"If you don't keep Bright Hope at the farm," he said quietly, "you mightn't ever come again. Bright Hope's my insurance for the future."

I was spared having to make a reply to this when a shout came from the gate into the farmyard. I looked across the field and recognised the tall figure leaning on the gate.

It was Simon Blake.

I glanced at Barry. There was a frown on his face as if the sight of the newcomer was not a welcome one.

We said nothing more as we covered the distance that still divided us from the visitor. Simon, however, addressed us as we approached.

" I came to see how you were, Barry," he called. " You seem to have got over your fall fairly well."

" It was nothing," Barry said.

Simon held open the gate and, leading Bright Hope, I went past him into the farmyard.

" A nice looking horse," he said, and glancing at Barry : " Is he yours?"

Barry shook his head.

" No, he's Ann's. She's just bought him."

Simon looked curiously at me.

" But I thought—"

I frowned. " I suppose you thought, as I worked at Staveleys, that I wouldn't want a horse of my own."

I spoke sharply and instantly wished I hadn't. Simon's reaction was a natural one. It was no excuse for rudeness on my part.

" He didn't seem to want you to ride him," Simon said now. " I was watching as you tried to get into the saddle, Barry."

" He'll get used to me in time," Barry said, then glancing at me : " You'd better introduce him to his new quarters."

I led Bright Hope across the yard and into the stable

where Primrose turned an enquiring glance at the new-comer.

I removed the saddle and reins, made him comfortable, gave both horses a lump of sugar then re-joined the two young men in the farmyard.

Simon glanced at the saddle I was carrying.

" How are you getting back to Staveleys?" he asked.

Before I could speak Barry cut in with:

" I shall be running her back in my car."

" I can save you the trouble," Simon said quickly. " My car's outside the gate. I'll be going through Mardon so I can drop you off at Staveleys, Ann."

" It's no trouble to me," Barry put in sharply. " In any case, Ann's not ready to leave yet. She's staying for tea before she goes home."

Simon, I could see, was a little taken aback at this; but he was not beaten.

" I'll wait in the car. I've time on my hands so you needn't hurry," he said with a smile at me.

I stole a glance at Barry's face. His eyes were angry, his lips compressed. I waited for the outburst, but it did not come. Instead Barry suddenly burst out laughing.

" I don't blame you, Simon," he cried. " She's worth waiting for. I hope you'll have tea with us. I know my mother will be delighted to meet you."

" Thanks!" Simon said, and his blue eyes were twinkling as, for a moment, they met mine.

As we walked towards the farmhouse Simon said:

" I'm hoping we're going to be friends, Barry."

Barry hesitated only for a moment then he smiled.

" It suits me, Simon," he said and, on impulse, held out his hand which the other grasped warmly.

Mrs. Hastings seemed delighted to meet Simon; and he, giving her one of his charming smiles, won her over completely.

" My husband often spoke of your uncle, Mr. Blake," she said. " A very nice gentleman, he used to say Mr. Blake was."

" You're confusing me, Mrs. Hastings," Simon laughed. " Why not call me Simon then we'll know whether you're talking about me or my uncle!"

We had tea in the sitting-room. I had a feeling it was not used very much. A bright fire burned in the grate, but there was a cold feel to the room, for all that, a stiff look about the dark furniture and the coloured prints against the flowered wallpaper. I would have preferred to have tea in the warm cosy kitchen.

" And what's the verdict about the new horse?" Mrs. Hastings asked.

" He's a good jumper," Barry said. " Unfortunately he doesn't like me. Wouldn't let me get on his back."

" He'll soon get over that," Simon said. " Horses are very temperamental creatures. Tomorrow he'll probably be all over you."

" I wouldn't be too sure of that," Barry muttered.

" I hope he does take to you," I put in. " After all, you're giving him a home and feeding him. The least he can do is let you ride him when you feel so inclined."

" Why aren't you keeping him at Staveleys?" Simon wanted to know.

" There isn't room," I replied. " Besides, I'd rather he was here with Barry. I wouldn't want to have to feel grateful to my boss all the time for giving the horse house room."

Simon was dressed in a beautifully-cut sports coat and tan slacks. There was a yellow silk scarf at the throat of his open shirt. He looked very handsome with his fair hair and bright blue eyes and I couldn't help but compare him with Barry's rather untidy appearance: rough brown hair, honest open countenance, and rather baggy sports coat and flannels and heavy shoes.

" What plans have you for—what's his name—Bright Hope?" Simon asked.

I looked at Barry before I replied. We hadn't really discussed what we meant to do with the horse except hunt him during the rest of the season. Yet if Bright Hope wouldn't let Barry ride him!—

" I'm hoping Barry will be able to hunt him," I said. " When I'm not riding the Staveleys' horses I shall ride him as well."

" He seems to be a good jumper judging from what I saw when he went over that gate this morning."

" I have a feeling he's done a great deal of jumping in the past," I said. " No one seems to know anything about his early history before he came into Mr. Silas Oldfield's hands but I wouldn't be surprised if he knew a bit about show jumping."

" The Point-to-Points will be coming along in April," Simon said. " Why don't you enter him for the Heavy-weights?"

" Isn't that being rather ambitious?" Barry asked, with a frown.

I could see that he did not altogether like the idea, perhaps because it was Simon's. Rather perversely I said:

" It's an idea. What fun it would be if he won the cup."

"You'd get quite a big figure for him if you ever decided to sell him."

"Why should she sell him?" Barry demanded. "She hasn't bought him simply to make a profit."

Simon shrugged. "Sorry! It was just a thought."

He got up and smiled down at his hostess.

"I'm sure you'll excuse me if I go now, Mrs. Hastings," he said. "Thank you for asking me to tea. It was most kind of you."

"Please come again, Mr. Blake!" she cried, a little flustered as he held her hand. "I—we don't have many visitors, do we, Barry?"

But Barry did not reply to this, but looked instead at me.

"I'll run you back to Staveleys," he said.

But I shook my head.

"I wouldn't dream of troubling you," I said. "If Simon's going through Mardon he can drop me off at the stables."

"But I—" he began to protest, but I turned to his mother and said goodbye.

He went to the gate with us, Simon carrying my saddle. Outside in the lane stood a big Triumph sports car. Simon opened the door on the passenger side and I slid into the comfortable seat.

"Goodbye, Barry," I said, looking up at him as he stood by the gate.

He smiled back at me but said nothing. Simon got behind the wheel and pressed the starter.

As we drove away I looked back. But already Barry had turned away. I felt a little annoyed. Was he sulking because I hadn't let him take me back to Mardon, or was he going to join his mother convinced that I had let Simon's well-cut clothes and sophisticated manner steal my senses away?

I heard a soft laugh by my side and turned to look into Simon's smiling face.

" I do believe our friend Barry is jealous of me," he declared and there was something in his voice, and in his twinkling eyes, that brought the colour into my cheeks.

" Why on earth should he be jealous?" I cried.

He did not say anything for a few seconds; but as he changed gear and sent the car rocketing up the lane, he murmured:

" You're a very, very pretty girl, my dear. I don't blame Barry for hating me for taking you away from him when he'd hoped to spend the rest of the afternoon, perhaps the evening, with you!"

CHAPTER SEVEN

WE SAID little on the way back to Mardon. Simon asked me if I would be out hunting on the following day and I said I wouldn't. He also mentioned the Hunt Ball which, as I knew already, was to be held at Consett Hall in ten days' time. He hoped I'd be there.

I said my employer and his wife had promised to take me, which seemed to please him. That was about the sum total of our small talk before we reached the outskirts of the village.

As we drove along the rather straggling street Simon looked at me a little uncertainly.

"I came over to Mardon to see my old nanny," he said. "I always look in on her when I'm staying with my uncle."

As Staveleys was at the far end of the village, I said I would get out and walk the rest of the way if it would help him.

He frowned and shook his head.

"I didn't tell you about Nanny to save me having to take you a few hundred yards further," he said. "I—oh, look here, Ann, will you come and meet her? She's a dear old thing and I'm very fond of her. I—I know she'd like you."

I was rather taken aback by this. Simon wanted me to meet the woman who had had charge of him when he was little! It seemed a strange thing to ask of me, a comparative stranger.

He must have noticed my hesitation for he went on :

" She's a cripple. She doesn't get out at all now. I thought—well, a new face, someone different to talk to—"

I smiled. This was a very different Simon from the one I had so far known.

" Of course I'd like to meet her, Simon," I said. " Which is her cottage ?"

At the other side of the village green," he said. " Let's go !"

There was a row of pretty thatched cottages at the far side of the green and I had often admired them as I had gone through the village since I came to Mardon. It was in one of these that old Nanny Porter lived.

Simon brought the sports car to a standstill at the door and jumped out.

" Wait there !" he told me. " I'll just go in and tell her she has a visitor."

He knocked on the door, turned the handle and disappeared. I sat there waiting for him to return and thinking what a complex character he was. Playboy, hunting man, he could yet find time to visit a crippled old woman who had known him as a child.

Presently he came from the cottage and to my side.

" She's terribly pleased I've brought someone to see

her," he said. " I think you'll like her," he added as I
got from the car.

A big fire was blazing in the old-fashioned grate as we
went into the rather stuffy little room which, in the
firelight, seemed to be full of heavy furniture.

"This is Ann Mawsley, Nanny," Simon said, turning
to me: " This is the wonderfully patient old lady who
turned me from a horrible little boy into the fine specimen
of manhood you now see before you!"

"For shame on you, Master Simon!" the old woman
cried, and looking at me from a pair of faded blue
eyes in a thin face that had known much pain: " Take
no notice of him, miss. He was a good boy as little boys
go; though I wouldn't say the same for him today!"

"Now, now, Nanny, don't start giving any of my
secrets away!" Simon said, a trifle uncomfortably, I
thought.

"Come closer, miss, and sit here," the old woman
said, and I went to a seat in front of the fire. " Master
Simon tells me he met you when you were both out
hunting."

"Yes! We were able to help a rider who had been
thrown from his horse."

" I suppose Master Simon's told you all about how I
came to be in charge of him when he was little more
than a baby?"

I saw Simon frown. " I don't think she'll want to know
anything about that, Nanny," he said; but the old woman
shook her head.

" I'm sure she will," she said sharply, and folding her
thin hands—twisted with arthritis—on her knee, she
went on: " Mr. Blake—Master Simon's uncle—brought

his bride to Consett Hall. Mrs. Blake unhappily died a few weeks after her only child, a little girl, was born. I was engaged to care for little Moira. At that time this young man's father and mother went abroad leaving little Simon with his uncle and in my care. Tragically the aeroplane in which they were flying crashed and they were both killed. As Master Simon's father and my employer were brothers it was natural that the poor little orphan should be brought up with his cousin at Consett Hall."

As the old voice died away Simon said, " Amen !" and smiled across at me.

" Nanny's a sentimental old girl," he laughed. " You must forgive her making the most of very little, Ann."

" But I don't think it is very little!" I cried indignantly, and looking into the faded old eyes: " Thank you for explaining, Mrs. ——"

I broke off a little confused because I did not know her name. She leaned over and patted my hand.

" The naughty boy never introduced us, did he !" she said. " It's Miss Porter. I was never married. I never seemed to have time."

" You know jolly well no self-respecting man would have put up with you !" Simon cried, winking at me.

She shook a pitifully twisted little fist at him in mock anger.

" You're a naughty boy saying things like that, Master Simon," she declared.

He went quickly across to her and dropped a kiss on her snow-white hair.

" Oh, Miss Porter, what can I do, I wanted to go to Birmingham and they've brought me on to Crewe," he sang. " Do you remember who used to sing that, Nanny?"

" Your cousin Moira," she said. " Have you heard anything of her lately, Master Simon?"

He shook his head.

" The last I heard she was somewhere on the Riviera having a gay old time. I suppose she'll be turning up like a bad penny one of these days."

The old woman frowned at this. I wondered if there mightn't be a great deal more behind Simon's words than appeared on the surface.

I wondered what this cousin looked like. Was she beautiful, vivacious, dull, ugly? Something in Simon's face made me wonder if, perhaps, he might be in love with this girl who must have been his constant companion until they were old enough to go their separate ways.

But perhaps it was no more than the flickering shadows thrown by the fire which, for a few seconds, gave his good-looking face an unhappy, even a bitter, look.

" I'm going to ask you to put the kettle on, my dear," Miss Porter said. " We'll have a cup of tea together. I think there's a little piece of cake in the tin on the shelf, Master Simon—"

But he shook his head.

" We won't stay for any tea, Nanny," he said. " We've just come from Moss Hill Farm where we had scones and cakes and made proper pigs of ourselves."

" Perhaps you'd like me to make you a cup of tea?" I offered but the old woman shook her head.

" That won't be necessary, miss," she smiled. " My next door neighbour—who's very good to me—will be looking in later to give me something to eat. I'm very lucky with so many people around me. They all look in from time to time. I'm never lonely."

We talked a little longer then Simon said we must be going. He kissed his old nurse fondly and she put up her hand and patted his cheek. There were tears in her eyes.

As he turned away she smiled up at me.

" It was good of you to call on a crippled old woman," she said. " If you ever feel inclined to look in on me when you're passing I'll always be glad to see you. The door's never locked. Just open it and come in."

I promised I would, then as Simon opened the door and went out to the car, she put her hand on my arm for a moment.

" He's a wild young man, miss," she said quietly, " but he's good and kind at heart. I'd like to see him married to the right young lady before I die. Maybe I shall, maybe I shall."

She let me go then and I went out to join Simon, a prey to very mixed feelings. Had the old woman been hinting that perhaps I might be the girl for her old charge? Or was she just bemoaning the fact that so far Simon had not shown any desire to marry and settle down?

" I'll run you along to Staveleys," Simon said as I joined him in the car, then as he drove round the green : " What do you think of my old nanny?"

" She's a nice old woman," I murmured.

" I hardly knew my mother. Nanny took her place when she was killed. I'm very fond of her."

" And she's very fond of you!"

He glanced at me for a moment.

" It's her greatest ambition to see me a staid family man." He laughed. " Can you see me in that role, Ann?"

For some reason I felt suddenly angry. I felt I had been manoeuvred into a position that was not of my seeking. On one side was Nanny Porter telling me that Simon ought to marry and settle down, and on the other was Simon laughing at the idea.

It was no business of mine in any case so why should they involve me in something that didn't concern me?

" I haven't really thought of you in any role," I said rather coldly, and he, after a glance at my expressionless face, said no more but drew up at Staveleys to allow me to alight.

But as I turned to go in through the stable entrance he said:

" When will I be seeing you again, Ann?"

I looked back.

" Do you want to?" I asked.

He frowned. " Of course I do! Very much."

" Perhaps we'll meet out with the hounds," I said and before he could say any more I disappeared into the darkening stable yard.

CHAPTER EIGHT

I WAS kept very busy in the days that followed. One of the stable lads was taken ill and had to be rushed into hospital for an operation. That threw more of the stable work on to Maggie and me. There was also the string of horses to exercise, and often as day was breaking Maggie and I would be out on the Downs behind the village galloping and jumping our mounts to keep them up to scratch for the people who hired them during the hunting season.

Then there were the people who came for riding lessons, as well as the groups of riders who had to be taken in convoy by Maggie or me for rides round the winter countryside.

The days were rarely long enough for us to crowd into them all that had to be done. It was interesting work and I loved every minute of it, but it was exhausting as well and I was usually so tired when darkness fell that all I wanted to do was have a meal, watch TV for a while then fall into bed about nine o'clock. It didn't give much scope for a social life!

Then one morning four days after I had got out of

Simon Blake's car outside Staveleys, Mr. Taylor asked me to take one of the new horses to the Meet.

" A friend tipped me off that a married couple will be out with the hunt," he said. " The Norths are business people who work in London. They've borrowed a couple of horses from a friend, but from what I hear, the man's about to retire and come to live in these parts. I shouldn't be surprised if he doesn't decide to look round for a suitable mount if he enjoys his day with the Borford."

" And his wife?"

" Oh, that would come later. The thing is to interest him in Gay Boy. If he comes to Staveleys he'd almost certainly look round to see what else we have for sale."

He winked at me and went off, whistling. I hurried up to the flat to get into my riding habit.

I told myself I was a fool to feel so excited. This was just another job: interesting a prospective customer in a horse. But in my heart I knew that I was thinking more of the possibility of my meeting either Barry or Simon, or both, than the Norths.

I had been in touch with Barry only once since I had driven away from Moss Hill Farm in Simon's car. I had telephoned two evenings before to ask how Bright Hope was.

" He's settling down well," Barry had replied. " I've turned him out twice into the three acre and he's seemed to enjoy running round it on his own."

" You haven't ridden him? I rather thought—"

" I want him to get used to me, Ann. My feeling is that he's been badly treated in the past and he's suspicious of strangers. Once he comes to trust me I think I might make another attempt to get on his back."

I had put the receiver down feeling vaguely unhappy. Somehow I felt Barry was getting very little out of our arrangement. Though the horse was mine to ride whenever I wished, Barry was landed with the job of housing and feeding him with only a toss up of a chance of ever hunting on him.

As later I rode to the Meet at Steeple Thatchley I wondered if Simon would be there. It was very likely, I knew, and I wondered if I would be glad to see him or not.

I realised I would have been much better pleased to see Barry ride up on Bright Hope. That would really have made my day!

The Meet was outside Steeple Thatchley's charming old church. The usual crowd of villagers, foot followers and children were admiring the hounds and the score or so riders who were clustered about the Master ready to move off when he gave the word.

I saw the two Miss Joblings by the lych gate. One of the old ladies was in the saddle of old Bessy, the other standing by her side. They waved to me and I went up to them.

"How do you like Bessy?" I asked.

Miss Julie patted the old mare's neck. "She's exactly what we wanted," she said. "Isn't she, Ruth?"

"She certainly is!" her sister exclaimed. "We take it in turns to ride her, though of course we do not go far."

"You're not following the hounds today, then?" I asked.

They both laughed. "I'm afraid our hunting days are over," Miss Julie laughed. "I shall follow the hunt as long as they keep to the road then I shall come back and it will be Ruth's turn for a ride."

I said goodbye to them and went to join the riders waiting for the Master to blow his horn to signal a move off to the first covert half a mile up the road.

It did not take me long to place the Norths. The man was rather stout, the woman slight and a little scared-looking. They were mounted on two quite nice hunters which were pawing restlessly at the ground as if eager to be off.

I had seen lots of couples like them when I had gone out riding around London. Beautifully dressed in exactly the right clothes yet they looked out of place on horseback.

I could picture the man at the seat of an expensive car, the woman shopping in Harrods. Somehow a crisp hunting morning in a remote little village in the Shires did not seem their cup of tea, as the saying goes.

They looked sideways at me as I brought Gay Boy to a halt a few feet away. I smiled.

" Isn't it a lovely morning?" I said. " Just the day for a long run without any checks."

The man with a glance at his wife smiled faintly. I wondered if she was the jealous type.

" Is it difficult country?" he asked. " My wife and I have not been out with the Borford before."

" It has its problems, I suppose," I replied.

I saw his wife gulp as if this was what she'd been afraid of.

" Don't you live in the district?" I asked, pretending to be surprised.

" No, we live in London," he replied.

His wife broke in: " My husband will be retiring soon. We're hoping to buy a house near Apperley."

ahead of me as I took a short cut across a ploughed field to come up with the hunt which had taken a longer route round the shoulder of a hill.

Simon Blake.

Riding beside him was a girl, a girl who rode her black hunter superbly with a straight back and a proudly held head.

Simon looked over his shoulder and, seeing me, slowed. He grinned at me.

" So there you are, Ann! I hoped you'd be out today," he said.

" I've been out all day," I replied. " I haven't seen you before."

" We joined the hunt late. Moira's rather a slow starter. I had to wait till she was ready."

The hunt had run into boggy ground and the hounds were spreading themselves out, noses down, sterns erect, as the huntsman cast around for the scent. What remained of the field sat their horses and watched. Many of them looked as if they were glad of the respite. It had been a long day and this was likely to be the last run before the close of the short February afternoon.

Simon looked at the girl on his right.

" Moira, this is Ann Mawsley," he said. " She works for Mark Taylor at the riding stables at Mardon."

" Does she?" The girl looked at me with a faint smile, then added: " How do you do?" and seemed to lose interest in me immediately.

" Moira's my cousin," Simon said. " We were brought up together."

So this was the girl Nanny Porter had talked about when Simon and I had visited her.

She was very beautiful, I decided, in a dark passionate sort of way. She had a perfect complexion, very dark eyes, and a rather sulky mouth which was pouting impatiently as she looked across at the baffled hounds. These were roaming disconsolately around, egged on by the huntsman as he tried to set them on a new line.

"Oh, come on, come on," she muttered. "It'll be dark before they find and then we'll not have caught a glimpse of a fox all day."

"If you'd got up a bit earlier you might have had more luck," Simon exclaimed. "How did the morning run go, Ann?"

"We had a glorious run though the fox went to ground in Byram's Wood," I said. "There hasn't been much since then but a couple of short runs with nothing at the end of them."

"What did I tell you, Moira!" Simon cried. "You'll have to get up a bit earlier when you know you're going hunting."

She frowned. "Don't forget, I didn't get home until eleven o'clock last night. I'd been travelling all day. I was fagged out."

Bellman, one of the oldest and trustiest hounds in the pack, now gave tongue and a few seconds later huntsman and field were turning to follow the hounds as they streamed away into the twilight.

Simon and Moira went ahead of me. For the first time I was able to have another good look at Simon's cousin if only from behind. She was, I supposed, about twenty-four and was dressed in a beautifully cut dark habit. A close-fitting cap held her black hair in place. From where

I was she could easily have been taken for a slim good-looking boy.

In the failing light the hounds went streaming across country with most of the flagging field dropping further and further behind. All but Simon and Moira with me bringing up the rear.

I was very tired but I refused to give in. I couldn't bear to think that when I was not in at the kill Moira might turn to Simon and say: "Where's that little friend of yours—the one who works at the stables? Gone home, perhaps. Didn't look as if she could stand the pace!"

But there was no kill. We came up with the Master and the hunt servants alongside a thick wood. The hounds were grouped around, many of them lying down, the others sitting on their haunches staring about them.

"He's well hidden in the wood," I heard the Master say. "Far too dark to find him now. Better go home!"

So the few of us who remained made for the nearest road with darkness falling fast and the twinkling lights of a nearby village shining out of the murk.

Simon rode up to me.

"Enjoy your day?" he asked.

"Very much!" I replied.

I noticed that his cousin was riding with the Master who seemed to know her well for he was laughing at something she had just said.

"Has your cousin come to stay at Consett Hall for a holiday?" I asked.

He nodded. "Yes, she's come back for the Hunt Ball. I daresay she'll stay for the Point-to-Point next month."

" Is she married?" I asked, for I thought I had caught a glimpse of a ring on the other girl's left hand.

He frowned as if the question was rather distasteful. I wished I hadn't asked it. At last he said:

" She was. She's divorced now. In fact, the divorce went through only a few days ago."

I wondered if Simon's cousin had come home to lick her wounds. Consett Hall would be a good refuge when the outside world was proving a bleak friendless place.

I caught Simon's eye. He was grinning.

" You're consumed with curiosity, aren't you, Ann?" he laughed. " The story's quite simple. Moira married a man who was wildly unsuitable for her. A pop singer with a group of his own. Everybody knew it wouldn't last. It didn't—hence the divorce."

" I'm sorry," I murmured for there seemed nothing else to say.

He scowled. " Why are you sorry? It was the best thing that could have happened to her. Personally, I'm glad she's come to her senses."

I said nothing else. Suddenly I began to wonder if Simon was in love with his lovely wayward cousin. Perhaps he was pleased that Moira's marriage had ended as it had for that would give him the chance he needed to win her for himself.

As we reached the road Moira joined us. The Master and the hunt went off to the right to the kennels. Simon and his cousin rode with me along the grass verge in the gathering darkness lit up every few seconds by the headlights of passing cars.

When we reached a side road which led to Consett Hall Simon said:

" Come back with us for a meal, Ann. You can leave your horse over-night and I'll run you back to Staveleys in my car later."

I felt rather than saw Moira stiffen. I could almost feel her willing me to say No.

I decided to oblige her. Suddenly I wanted to be alone. I was tired out. I did not feel up to bright conversation with someone looking on who plainly had taken a dislike to me at first sight.

" Thanks, Simon," I said. " But I'd better get back. Mr. Taylor will be wondering what's happened to me. I don't want him to send a search party out!"

" I could telephone from the Hall!"

But I shook my head.

" Goodbye!" I said; and looking at the girl: " It was nice to meet you. I—"

But giving me a frosty stare she turned away without speaking and Simon, after hesitating a moment longer, smiled a little self-consciously, said goodbye and followed his cousin up the lane.

I went on my lonely way feeling thoroughly miserable.

CHAPTER NINE

THE NEXT day I was working in the stables when Paddy, the Head Stableman, came to tell me I was wanted on the telephone.

"Me!" I exclaimed, wondering who on earth could be ringing me up.

Paddy grinned. His merry eyes under the peak of his cloth cap twinkled. "It's a man," he declared. "I didn't know you had a boy friend, Ann."

"I haven't!" I said crossly and, pushing past him, I went out into the stableyard and made for the door of the little office by the gate.

"Hullo!" I said, picking up the receiver. "This is Ann Mawsley speaking."

"Ann!" It was Barry's voice. "I'm afraid I have some bad news."

He sounded upset. I frowned.

"But what's happened, Barry?" I demanded. "Is it—Bright Hope?"

"Yes! He's vanished!"

"Vanished!" I gasped. "But how on earth—?"

"I feel awful about this, Ann. I—"

" But how did it happen? Horses don't just—disappear!"

" You know Bright Hope wouldn't let me get on his back. The only way I could see he had exercise was to turn him out into the three acre. He liked that. He used to run round, though most of the time he was quite content to feed. The grass is fairly good in the field even for March."

" Then—then what happened?"

" This morning I turned him out as usual. He seemed as quiet as he generally did. I went about my work and didn't go to look at him for a couple of hours. It's turned cold and I had decided to bring him in." He gulped. " When I went into the field he—wasn't there!"

" But have you looked for him?"

" I've looked in the fields and woods around the farm but there's no sign of him. I decided to phone you as you're the horse's owner.

" Do you think he's been stolen, Barry?"

" I doubt it. I think he jumped the hedge—there's a fairish gap in one corner. He's probably a few miles away by this time."

I decided there was only one thing to do. I must go to Moss Hill Farm and help Barry look for Bright Hope.

" I'll be with you in half an hour," I said and slammed the receiver down.

I knew that my employer had gone over to Melton Mowbray to look at a couple of hunters he was thinking of buying. I sought out Paddy.

" I'll have to take some time off, Paddy," I said, and at his puzzled frown: " It's a personal matter. I'll try not to be too long."

" But we're so shorthanded with Joe being in hospital," he began, but already I was hurrying away.

It was out of the question to borrow a horse, and there was no bus at that time going in the direction of Moss Hill Farm.

So I sought out Bob, the other stablelad, and asked if I could borrow his bike, an old boneshaker he used for visiting his girl friend in a neighbouring village.

He hesitated when I asked him, but when I said I'd pay him well for the loan, he agreed at once. Rather unsteadily I rode out of the stableyard five minutes later watched by Paddy, Bob and a puzzled Maggie, who had been working in a stable at the other end of the yard.

I pedalled hard through the village and along the Apperley road.

My thoughts were in a turmoil. I didn't blame Barry for Bright Hope's disappearance. The horse had to have exercise and as he wouldn't let Barry ride him there had been no alternative but to turn him out into the field during the day.

I wondered where the horse would be. There were so many dangers for a wandering animal, not least the traffic which flowed in both directions along the road near Moss Hill Farm.

A frightened horse could easily run on to the road in front of a fast car or a lorry. It had happened many times in the past. Invariably the animal had had to be destroyed.

I found myself praying for Bright Hope.

" Keep him safe, please, God," I said to myself over and over again.

Barry, an anxious look on his face, was waiting for

me at the farmyard gate. His expression told me that he had no news of the missing horse.

" I'm terribly sorry, Ann," he said. I shook my head.

" Don't apologise, Barry," I said. " It's not your fault. He had to have exercise. He's got away. There's no more to it than that. The point is—where is he now?"

He was silent for a few seconds then he said slowly :

" It may be a mad idea, Ann, but—well, we know he hasn't much use for men and—and he did let you ride him."

I frowned. What was Barry getting at? Then I thought I knew.

" You mean he—he may have gone off to try and find me?"

" It's a silly notion, perhaps, and there is probably nothing in it, but—well, stranger things have happened. Bright Hope is an intelligent animal and—"

" But how would he know which way to take? He's never been to Staveleys."

Barry shrugged. " If I'm right—and I don't say I am, mind you—he probably would never get round to thinking which direction he should take. He'd just make off—and hope for the best. After all, cats and dogs have been known to walk hundreds of miles and find their way to their destination. I don't say it's the same with horses but—"

I smiled up into his kind concerned face and put my hand on his arm.

" Hadn't we better start looking instead of theorising, Barry?" I asked and he nodded.

" Of course! We're wasting time. I see that!" He pushed open the gate and joined me in the lane. " Perhaps you'd better take one way and I'll head in the other direction. If we don't have any luck let's join up again and try something else."

" I saw no sign of Bright Hope on the road between here and Mardon so he probably hasn't gone that way," I said.

" That's helpful!" he said. " I'll go along here "—he nodded to the left—" and you go behind the farm. O.K.?"

As I was about to move off he said:

" By the way, Walter and Jim are out looking as well so there's a good chance of finding him. Good luck!"

I felt much happier as I made off through the farmyard to the fields beyond. What a nice man Barry was! So many young men finding themselves in his position— made responsible for a temperamental creature like Bright Hope—would have shrugged their shoulders and abandoned the horse to its fate.

Not Barry! He had given his word to do his best for Bright Hope and would keep his promise, however much his work and those who worked for him might be disorganised.

As I crossed the first field there was no sign of Bright Hope. Nor was there as I went through a gate into the second.

My heart sank. The horse might be anywhere. He had evidently had at least an hour's start before he was missed.

I thought I heard a distant shout but when it was not repeated I put it down to my imagination.

I plodded on. There had been heavy rain in the night and my feet sank into the wet ground.

I suddenly realised that I was crying. I dashed the tears

angrily away. Why should I cry for Bright Hope? I hardly knew the horse. I had surely not had him long enough to grow fond of him.

Hearing another shout I glanced back. The shout was repeated and I knew it was my name someone was calling.

"Ann! Ann!"

Then I saw Barry coming through the gate I had left a few moments before.

I ran back towards him. His eyes danced with excitement.

"Young Jim's found him!" he cried. "Walter heard him calling and went to see what was happening, then he came back to the farm for me leaving Jim with the horse."

"But where is he, where is Bright Hope?" I cried almost beside myself.

"I don't quite understand everything," he said. "From what Walter tells me he's in Megson's Quarry!"

"Do—do you mean he's—fallen in?" I gasped.

"That's what we must find out." He took my hand and urged me towards the gate. "Walter's a man of few words and I've got little out of him. But if—if Bright Hope had come to any real harm I'm sure he'd have told me so."

We ran through the farmyard to where the farmhand was waiting by the gate.

"Mr. Hastings says you've found my horse!" I panted.

Walter pulled at his wispy moustache.

"Young Jim found 'im," he said. "Way over at Megson's Quarry."

"Is—is he hurt?"

" I don't think so, miss. Young Jim 'e just says, ' Go fetch the mester. The hoss is 'ere!' And I came straight back to th' farm."

" We'd better get moving," Barry said, and, nothing loath, I trotted behind him as he set off up the lane. But something occurred to him before we had gone many yards and he looked back at Walter.

" Get help, then follow us, Walter," he ordered, then without a word to me, set off again.

The quarry was not very far, perhaps half a mile. We went along a narrow lane and presently came to some rough open ground. A derelict crane and a ruined hut had been left by the people who, at one time, had quarried for stone in this out-of-the-way spot. On Barry's heels I followed him to the edge of the fearsome drop to the rocky floor of the quarry far below.

" Jim!" Barry shouted. " Are you there, Jim?"

The boy's voice came up to us:

" Yes, Mr. Hastings. I'm on this ledge. And so is the horse."

Barry frowned as he looked at me.

" How on earth—!" he exclaimed then walked along the edge of the quarry.

I went the other way. A hundred yards brought me to a stunted thorn bush. Beside it was a sloping path which ran down the clifflike face of the rock and disappeared round an overhang.

" Barry!" I cried. " Come here!"

He hurried to my side. He stared at the path in astonishment.

" But whatever would persuade a horse to go down there!" he muttered.

" That's something we'll never know," I said quietly. " Just now the only thing that matters is getting him up again."

" I'll go down and take a look," he said. " The first priority is to get young Jim up. I don't want him falling into the quarry. His mother might object!"

He gave me a faint grin and started down the narrow path. I held my breath. The path was barely two feet wide. One slip—and he would be over. There would be little chance for him if he landed on the rock floor. below.

And then what would I think? That he had lost his life because he had gone to try to save my horse? I would never forgive myself.

He disappeared round the overhang. I thought I heard voices, then when the waiting was becoming unbearable young Jim appeared and scrambled up towards me.

" What's going on down there, Jim?" I demanded, my voice sharp with anxiety.

" The horse is stuck and can't turn round, miss," he said. " Mr. Hastings sent me up. Wouldn't let me stay with him, though I wanted to."

" But doesn't the path go to the bottom of the quarry?"

" No, miss. It goes no further. It's very old and it's broken away. Mr. Hastings has just told me it must have been used by shot firers when they were blasting the rock down."

" How did you find the horse, Jim?" I asked.

" I was crossing the field and I heard him whinnying. At first I couldn't tell where he could be, then when I stood at the edge of the quarry, I heard him again. I think he must have been frightened, miss."

Just as I was frightened now, I thought, for Barry's safety. He must come up! Much as I loved Bright Hope, Barry mustn't be sacrificed for the horse.

I knew what I must do. I must go down the path and tell Barry he must come up.

" Where are you going, miss?" Jim asked in alarm as I started down the steep slope.

But I did not reply. I tried not to look down into the yawning chasm below. I kept my eyes fixed firmly on the rock face at my side as I went forward, step by careful step.

I looked round the overhang. Barry was about ten yards away. He was talking quietly to Bright Hope who was shivering with fear.

" Barry, you must come back!" I whispered hoping he would hear and that my voice would not startle the horse.

He looked round at me with a scowl.

" Go back!" he said. " There's nothing you can do."

" But you can't turn him on that narrow ledge," I said, trying to force back a sob that rose in my throat.

He ignored me and turned back to the horse.

" There, now, old chap, it's going to be all right," he said gently. " Just take it easy. There's nothing to be afraid of."

I watched, paralysed with fear. What had Barry in mind? He could not even reach Bright Hope's head and if he did what help would that be?

" Help!" I suddenly thought of how he had shouted to Walter to get help. Perhaps that was the answer.

" I'll go and see if Walter's come yet," I called but he paid no attention to me as I turned and scrambled back to where Jim was waiting, white and scared, at the top of the path.

" Go and see if Walter's bringing help!" I said, and, as if glad of having something to do, he turned and ran back across the field towards the farm.

The next half hour was the longest I have ever spent or want to spend.

No sound came up to me from below and I did not dare shout to find out if Barry was all right. More than once I started down the path to see what was going on, then I decided that might do more harm than good, so I stayed where I was.

But at last, to my intense relief, I saw a small group of men approaching. Two were policemen, three were probably farm workers Walter had recruited from the farms around. He and Jim brought up the rear. The policemen were carrying a rope.

The police sergeant who led the little procession gave me a curt nod. " Any developments?" he asked.

" No! Mr. Hastings is down there with the horse. He can't turn it."

" Then we'll have to pull it up!" he said in a matter of fact voice. " This isn't the first time this sort of thing has happened hereabouts."

" Last time it were a sheep," the other policeman declared disgustedly. " Silly creatures! What do they want going down a path like that for, sergeant?"

" Perhaps you might know a bit better if you was a sheep or a horse," the sergeant said bitingly. " Go look at that crane, Mollett. See if it's still working."

The constable, rather subdued, walked across to the old crane. Apparently the jib and the wheel at its end were in working order though the engine in the little cabin had been removed.

" Come on some of you chaps," the sergeant cried, looking round. " Help my man to push the crane into position."

Some rusty lines ran along the edge of the quarry. Evidently the crane could be moved from place to place according to need.

Willing hands brought it to a point where the jib could be swung out over the path on which Barry was soothing the frightened horse.

" I'll just go down and have a word with Mr. Hastings," the sergeant said. " You lot get the rope over the wheel and lower it down to the path. Give us your cape, Mollett! It'll act as a sling under the creature's belly!"

The constable handed over his cape and the sergeant disappeared down the path. I longed to follow and watch what happened next. But I had the sense to stay where I was.

Presently the sergeant re-appeared after the rope had been lowered.

" The rope's safely round the animal's belly," he announced. " Now you men, get a good grip on that rope. You've got a good deal of pulling to do. 'Orses are not light creatures!"

" But isn't Mr. Hastings coming up?" I demanded.

He frowned and just for a moment looked uneasy.

" I told him there was no reason why he should stay with the horse, miss," he said. " But he said the creature was frightened and he'd stay there until it was safely brought to the top. I only 'ope it doesn't kick him before we pull it out of reach."

Dear Barry, I thought. It meant more to him to comfort Bright Hope in the last few frightening moments than think of his own safety.

There came a shout from below, the sergeant gave an order, then everybody—Walter and Jim included—pulled on the rope which was slowly gathered in with the horse swinging a yard from the quarry face as it rose slowly upwards.

Three minutes later Bright Hope was standing, trembling but plainly relieved, a few yards from the edge of the quarry.

Barry patted the long sleek neck.

" Good boy ! I told you not to worry. Your troubles are all over now !" he said gently.

Bright Hope turned his head and looked into the face of the man he had earlier mistrusted. A moment later his tongue came out to lick Barry's face.

" Nothing like a horse for knowing who it's friends are," the sergeant cried. " That animal will go through thick and thin for you in future, Mr. Hastings, you mark my words."

Just for a moment Barry met my eyes. I smiled back at him. We both felt too happy for words.

CHAPTER TEN

THE Hunt Ball was the most important social event in the Borford Hunt calendar.

Not only did it signal the approach of the end of the hunting season, but it was an opportunity for those who had come together mainly on the hunting field to meet in gentler and, some thought, more civilised surroundings.

My employers, as supporters of the Hunt, regularly attended the Ball. It was their custom to take along one of the girls who worked at Staveleys. It had been Maggie's turn last year, for I had only joined the stables a couple of weeks before. This year, so Maggie had told me a few days before, I would be invited.

And so it turned out. Mrs. Taylor came looking for me two days after Bright Hope had been lifted unharmed from the quarry. I was distributing feed in the stables and she looked in at me as I worked in the half-light of the long building.

" Ann, have you a moment?" she called and I went across to her.

She was a big blonde woman with a kindly smile and a

diffident manner which took many people in. All the
buyers who came to Staveleys had to deal with her and
most of them must have thought they were on to an
easy thing.

They soon found out they were mistaken. For Isabel
Taylor was the business brain behind the stables. Her
husband might know all there was to know about horses,
but she did the books, paid the wages, kept things running smoothly.

" My husband and I will be going to the Hunt Ball next
Tuesday, Ann," she said now. " We would very much
like you to accompany us."

When I hesitated, not wanting to seem too eager by
accepting the invitation instantly, she went on:

" You do want to go, don't you, Ann?"

I nodded eagerly. " Oh, yes, Mrs. Taylor. I'd love to.
It's just that—"

" You haven't got a dress?"

" Oh, it's not that." As a matter of fact I had two
dresses bought just before I left London. " It's just that—
well, I don't want you to feel you've to ask me because
you took Maggie last year. I—"

She laughed. " You silly girl, we want you to go to
the Ball with us. Neil, my husband's nephew, is coming
over from Birmingham for it. We'll make a nice little
party."

So it was arranged and I went back to my work. I
wondered if I had made a fool of myself. Most girls
would have jumped at the chance of going to the Ball
and would not have shown any reluctance in accepting
the invitation the moment it was issued.

I wondered what Mark Taylor's nephew would be like.

I hoped my dancing wouldn't disappoint him. I'd been keener on horse riding than dancing and had rather neglected my education in that direction.

I began to think of Consett Hall. So once more I would be visiting the old house, once more I would be seeing Simon Blake—and his cousin Moira.

I wondered what Moira would think when she saw me in such a setting. To her I was little more than a stable-hand. I would have to be ready for a freezing glance, perhaps a cutting remark if she spoke to me at all, which was doubtful.

That evening Maggie made me try on my two dresses. She said she preferred the long red silk because it brought out the highlights in my dark hair, which sounded non-sense to me. I let her have her way though I had a sneaking fancy for the pale blue which I felt did something for me, I'm not sure what!

With the extra work in the stables due to the stable-lad being in hospital, I didn't get a chance before the Ball to go over to Moss Hill Farm to see Bright Hope.

But I rang Barry a couple of times. He sounded disappointed that he could not see me but understood my problem when I explained.

He told me that Bright Hope was fine and had come through his ordeal at the quarry unscathed. When I spoke to him the second time he sounded excited about something, but when I questioned him he denied that anything out of the ordinary had happened since he had seen me last.

I mentioned the Hunt Ball and asked if he would be there. He laughed shortly.

" You must be joking!" he said. " Working farmers don't go to those sort of events."

" Well, I've been invited and I'm just a working girl," I said.

" That's different," he declared and I could hear the smile in his voice.

" When will you be out hunting again?" he asked.

" I'm not sure, but probably the day after the Ball," I replied. " Mr. Taylor wants me to show a new horse, and as the Wednesday country is the best of the week with more people about, I'll have to be there."

" I imagine you'll be half asleep if the Ball finishes late," he laughed, then, a few moments later, he rang off.

On the Saturday afternoon I went over to Melton on the bus and bought evening shoes, bag and gloves. I had a black velvet cloak, a relic from my teenage days, and this still fitted beautifully for my size was much the same as it had been seven years before. The village hairdresser put my unruly curls in some sort of order on the Tuesday afternoon, and when I started to dress for the Ball Maggie appeared and offered to help me, then when I was ready insisted on lending me an antique pendant which had been her mother's. It was perfect with the red dress and I gave Maggie a hug.

" I wish you were coming as well," I said but she only smiled rather mysteriously and said she had a date with Paddy. I could see from the stars in her eyes that she would not have changed places with me for all the tea in China.

We went to the Ball in Mark Taylor's Jaguar of which he was very proud. I sat at the back and spent my time wondering what Simon would say when he saw me. I had just decided that he would probably bow politely and pass on when we drew up outside Consette Hall. Every window glowed like a jewel. Outside the entrance cars from all over the county were lined up to discharge their passengers.

Presently we went into the big hall I remembered so well. Here Neil Lester, the Taylor's nephew, was waiting. He was a slim good-looking young man in his early twenties.

He shook hands with us all then Mrs. Taylor and I went up the wide staircase to the big bedroom that had been set aside as the ladies' cloakroom.

Presently we rejoined the men. Music was coming from somewhere at the back of the house and the four of us followed other guests down a passage to a ballroom which, Mark Taylor told me, had been added to the house in Victorian times by a previous owner.

Many of the men were in hunting scarlet and with the women in their gay dresses, the dance floor presented an animated scene.

"May I have this dance?" Neil invited and leaving my employer and his wife chatting to two acquaintances, we joined the throng on the floor.

I found Neil Lester a pleasant enough young man if rather dull. He told me he was an accountant with a firm of engineers in Birmingham. He didn't get any chance to hunt but quite enjoyed riding. He spoke of concerts he had attended lately, films he had seen, girl friends he had taken about in his ancient Alfa Romeo sports car of which he was terribly proud.

He was not especially interested in me, though he did

say once that he supposed I found it a bit boring stuck away in the country all the time.

I denied this sharply and he frowned.

" But are you sure?" he asked. " Getting up at half-past six on a cold winter's morning and cleaning a stable out isn't my idea of fun."

" There's more to it than that," I said but I did not elaborate and we finished the dance in silence.

While we were dancing he had spotted one or two friends, and after he had delivered me back to Mr. and Mrs. Taylor, he went off to dance with someone else. Isabel Taylor smiled at me.

" He'll be back," she said, though something in her eye told me she was not too pleased at her nephew's desertion so early in the evening.

For my part I was glad I was not to be tied to Neil Lester the whole evening. I looked round the big ball-room. There were quite a lot of people there I had met in the hunting field, and one or two of them smiled or waved as they passed.

When the music started again Mr. Taylor asked me to dance after his wife had been swept away by an elderly gentleman my employer told me was the family solicitor.

I enjoyed the quickstep. Mr. Taylor danced well and I followed the rather intricate steps he produced easily enough. As we danced he said:

" I haven't seen any sign of the family yet."

He meant Mr. Blake, his daughter, Moira, and his nephew, Simon, I knew. We had been received at the entrance to the ballroom by the Master of the Hunt and his wife.

Then suddenly I saw Simon. He was standing in a doorway, a frown on his handsome face. He was fingering the red bow tie which he wore with the beautifully cut white dinner jacket. Something had upset him, I was sure, and I wondered if it had anything to do with the non-appearance of his uncle and cousin.

As we danced close to him he saw me and his face lit up. He gave me a gay wave as we passed and Mr. Taylor looked at me in surprise.

" So you know Simon Blake?"

" Yes! I've met him once or twice."

" I hear his cousin's returned from the south of France."

" Yes, I met her out hunting."

He frowned. " From all accounts she's a problem child. Got married to some jazz singer then divorced him. Come back home to lick her wounds, I imagine, though of course—"

He did not finish the sentence and I looked at him with a frown. He laughed.

" Before she ran away with her pop star everyone in the district was quite convinced she was going to marry her cousin," he said. " Well, now she's free again and Simon Blake's on the spot anything might happen."

I said nothing to this. I was quite sure Mark Taylor was wrong. Simon had not seemed to me a man in love with his cousin, indeed with anyone.

The dance ended and we went back to join Isabel Taylor who was talking animatedly to Mr. Chambers, the solicitor. Mr. Taylor had just suggested that we adjourn to the buffet and bar, which were in an adjoining room, when out of the corner of my eye I saw Simon approaching.

He said good evening to Mr. and Mrs. Taylor then smiled at me and asked me for the next dance. The music had just started again and we went straight on to the floor.

" You're looking very charming tonight," he murmured as he swept me into the waltz. The lights had been lowered and his face was in shadow.

I murmured something feeling vaguely uncomfortable. It was obvious to me that he had never expected to see me at the Hunt Ball. I wondered if at heart he thought I was an interloper. After all, I was only a girl who worked in the stables at Staveleys.

" Where's your cousin?" I asked. " I haven't seen her dancing."

He said nothing for a moment then, a little stiffly, he replied :

" I imagine she's still dressing. She's a very unpunctual sort of person."

I did not know what to say to this so said nothing. After a few seconds he went on :

" You must think my family are a poor lot, Ann. My uncle was called up to London on business this morning and hasn't returned. He rang me earlier and asked me to do the honours."

He asked me then about Bright Hope and I told him about the horse's adventure in the quarry and how he had been rescued.

" And how's Barry? Quite got over his fall in the wood, I hope."

" Yes, he's fit enough now."

"I rather thought he might have been here tonight."

I didn't give him the real reason for Barry's absence. I just said that Barry wasn't much of a dancing man and that seemed to satisfy him.

When the dance was over he asked me to go for a drink. We went into the big room which had a long table loaded with food down one side and a bar at the far end.

"What will you have?" he asked and I said tomato juice would be nice.

He got himself a whisky and soda and led me to a small table in the corner.

"Will you be out tomorrow morning?" he asked.

I nodded. "Yes, Mr. Taylor wants me to try a new hunter out. He bought her in the sales last week."

He looked at me over the rim of his glass. There was a twinkle in his blue eyes.

"Taylor's a smart business man," he declared. "I'll agree that the horses he has for sale are worth the money, but I often wonder if he'd do quite as well if he didn't have pretty girls for salesmen!"

I coloured. He was laughing at me, I knew, and after a moment I laughed with him, though rather ruefully.

"I'm sure you're wrong!" I said. "No one's going to spend a hundred pounds or more for an animal that's been ridden by a girl, whether she's pretty or not. It's the horse that counts every time."

"But the girl helps!" he said; then as the music started up again: "Let's dance again."

I hesitated. "But oughtn't you to—well, dance with other girls? After all, in a sense you are the host."

He shook his head.

" This is the Hunt Ball and the Master is host. I'm just a guest like everybody else."

" Still—"

He took my hand and pulled me to my feet. Half a minute later we were on the floor moving round the big room to the music of a slow foxtrot.

Simon danced superbly. I was only average but he actually made me feel I was twice as good as I really was.

He held me very close and more than once as our eyes met I felt my heart quicken. Surely, I thought, I wasn't falling in love with this good-looking man who was perhaps the most eligible bachelor in the neighbourhood.

What a fool I would be if I let him steal my heart. I was a nobody. He was heir to a fortune.

At the end of the dance he delivered me back to the Taylors.

" I'll have to do a duty dance or two," he said, then added in a low voice which only I heard : " I'll hope to dance with you later."

Then he was gone and I found myself going on to the floor with Neil Lester again and trying to show an interest in his tales of life in Birmingham and the host of friends he had made there in the last few years.

More than once I looked round for Moira, Simon's cousin. But when we went into supper she still had not shown up.

I had also missed Simon. After he had had a couple of dances with girls I had seen more than once out hunting he had disappeared. I found myself wondering if he had gone to see where Moira had got to.

But as we came out from the supper room I saw him

crossing the floor. He was making a beeline for me.

"May I have this dance?" he asked, and when I nodded, he led me on to the floor.

"What's the matter, Simon?" I asked. "You seem upset about something."

He laughed. "You're imagining things! What should I be upset about?"

I coloured. "I'm sorry. I just thought—"

"Then think about something else," he said. "A little walk outside, for instance. It's getting hot and stuffy in here."

We were near the corner of the ballroom where I had first seen him standing that evening. Almost before I realised it we were off the floor and through the half-open door.

I found myself in a narrow passage. Simon, holding my hand, drew me along this and to a little room at the far end. This was furnished as a sitting-room and had a bright fire burning in the old-fashioned grate.

"This is Briggs's parlour," Simon said. "But he'll be much too busy to use it tonight."

I stood there, a little self-consciously. Why had Simon brought me here? He had said something about a little walk outside. Briggs's parlour could hardly be called "outside".

He moved closer to me. There was something in his eyes that set my pulse racing.

He drew me to him and looked into my face.

"Ann, you're very lovely!" he breathed, then his lips found mine in a fierce possessive kiss.

CHAPTER ELEVEN

I suppose that I was so taken aback that at first I made no move. I just lay there in Simon's arms as he kissed me.

Then I came to my senses. I put my hands on his chest and tried to push him away.

But he was stronger than I was and held me easily.

"Simon, let me go!" I protested.

He looked down into my eyes. He was smiling gently as if to still my fears.

"But, Ann, I've been wanting to kiss you ever since I first saw you in the wood the day Barry Hastings was thrown," he declared.

When I said nothing he asked suddenly:

"You do like me a little bit, don't you, Ann?"

I nodded. I liked him more than I was prepared to admit. Not yet, at any rate.

He drew me across the room to an old-fashioned settee against one wall. We sat down and he kept his arm about me.

"Ann, I've been wanting this to happen," he murmured. "Just you and I together like this with no one to disturb us." He raised his free hand and turned my head so that I was looking into his face. " Do you love me a little bit, Ann?"

I felt sudden foolish tears start into my eyes. Did I love him? I wondered. Or was I just allowing myself to be swept off my feet by his charm and good looks?

But he did not give me time to speak. As if he could not wait for me to reply he drew me close and kissed me with a mounting passion that set my senses swimming.

I found myself returning his kisses. I felt to have no control over my emotions now. This man loved me. Something that would have looked impossible half an hour before now seemed the most natural thing in the world.

" Oh, Simon," was all I could find to say as, for a moment, he drew away from me.

I looked into his face and saw the expression there. I couldn't understand it. The blue eyes were no longer looking down at me. There was a faint smile on the lips.

Suddenly I realised that the door had opened and that someone was standing looking into the room.

I dragged myself out of Simon's arms and turned to look across the room. Then I gave a little cry of distress.

For Simon's cousin, Moira, was glaring across at us, though as I turned, she swung round and hurried from the room.

I felt Simon's arms tighten about me again.

" I'm sorry, Ann," he said. " I'd no idea we'd be disturbed. The last person I ever thought would come into the room was—Moira."

I believed he was lying. I remembered how he had returned to the ballroom earlier, plainly upset. I guessed what must have happened. He had gone up to Moira's room to see why she had not come down to the dance and she must have annoyed him by telling him she would come downstairs at her own time, not his.

Had he then, I wondered, arranged to meet her in Briggs's little parlour and taken me there knowing full well that Moira would find us in each other's arms? It seemed very much like it!

When he tried to kiss me again I pulled myself free. I was furiously angry. This man had used me to get back at his cousin. He had wanted to make her jealous, and, judging by the expression I had seen on her face as she left the room, he had succeeded only too well.

" Let me go!" I panted. " I—I hate you! You knew that your cousin would find us together. You—you—"

Words failed me. I got to my feet and, without another glance in his direction, made for the door.

" Ann!" he called after me. " Don't go! You've got it all wrong. Moira means nothing to me—"

I did not hear the rest. I was through the door and blundering along the passage back to the ballroom before the sentence was finished.

I paused before joining the dancers. What a mess I must look! I couldn't let Mr. and Mrs. Taylor see me like this. What would they think?

I retraced my steps and found my way upstairs to the empty cloakroom set aside for the use of the lady guests.

How I wished I could leave Consett Hall there and then and return to Staveleys. But I couldn't. I must wait until the Taylors were ready to leave. That meant that I must return to the ballroom or they would start looking for me.

I bathed my flushed face, repaired my make-up then, when a maid looked into the room and asked if she could help me, I forced a smile and said I was just going downstairs again.

To my relief Neil Lester was standing smoking in the doorway watching the dancers as I reached the ballroom again. He smiled and put out his cigarette.

"Oh! There you are," he exclaimed. "I was wondering where you had got to. Shall we dance?"

A moment later we were on the floor. I saw Simon come into the big room and look round; but after that first glance I kept my eyes averted from him. The next time I looked he had disappeared. There was no sign of his cousin, either, and I wondered if he had gone to seek her out.

How I managed to get through the rest of the evening I'll never know; but at last it was time to go home. As Mrs. Taylor and I came downstairs ready to leave I saw Simon standing in the hall.

"Ann!" he said, moving quickly forward.

"Goodnight, Simon!" I said, forcing a smile; then before he could say any more, I hurried ahead of Mr. and Mrs. Taylor out into the cold night.

I slept little that night. Every time I was about to drop off I saw Simon's face as he had looked. His expression had given him away. Moira had snubbed him earlier. This had been his way of paying her back.

About four o'clock I fell asleep and came to with a start when the alarm went off. Already Maggie was moving about the little flat. As I sat up rubbing my eyes she appeared with a cup of tea which she put down by the side of my bed.

" How did you enjoy the Ball?" she asked. " I didn't hear you come in."

I didn't tell her I had crept into the flat as silent as a ghost so she would not wake and start questioning me about the dance.

" It was all right," I replied, and throwing back the blankets: " Gosh, it's seven o'clock. I'm late!"

She frowned. " What's the rush? We're going hunting—or had you forgotten?"

On hunting days we were allowed to get up a little later. I did not reply but went into the tiny bathroom and began to brush my teeth vigorously.

During breakfast Maggie questioned me about the Ball, and I tried to satisfy her curiosity by telling her about Neil Lester, the supper, the members of the hunt who had been present.

" And what about that dishy man on the white hunter?" she asked. " You know who I mean: Simon Blake?"

I frowned as if I was trying to bring him to mind; then I shrugged.

" I believe I saw him there," I said in as off-hand a voice as I could manage.

Fortunately Paddy knocked at the outer door at that moment and Maggie went to see what he wanted. She stuck her head into the little kitchen.

" Paddy wants us to give a hand until we set off for the Meet," she said. " We'd better leave the dishes until later."

I was glad of the interruption. I didn't want to discuss Simon Blake with Maggie or anyone else.

At half-past ten Maggie and I set off for the Meet at Dumbleford which was a five-mile ride. We were riding two horses Mr. Taylor was keen to sell. Sometimes he kept his purchases to hire out during the hunting season, but these two animals—a chestnut and a grey—he wanted to sell as quickly as possible. The stables could only accommodate a certain number of horses and at present every inch of space was taken up. This meant that Mr. Taylor could not pick up a bargain even if he came across one. If he sold either the chestnut or the grey he would turn a nice profit and make room for something else.

The morning was cold and windy with a hint of rain to come. Usually, I enjoyed jogging along the country roads to the Meet but today I would much rather have stayed behind working in the warm stables.

Maggie tried to find out more about the Hunt Ball, but when the only replies she got to her questions were grunts she finally gave up and rode a little ahead of me as if she found me a poor companion.

The usual crowd of horsemen and foot followers awaited us on the green at Dumbleford. The huntsmen and whippers-in were collecting the hounds together as they waited for the Master to give the signal for a move to draw the first covert. To my relief there was no sign of Simon and his cousin.

I usually enjoyed this moment of bustle and anticipation. But today I had little interest in what was going on around me. I couldn't even get up enough enthusiasm to look round and see if there were any prospective purchasers present for the horses Maggie and I were riding.

Maggie had moved away from me and was talking to a young girl riding a pony and an older man, perhaps her father, who was mounted on a placid-looking horse. They seemed to be admiring Maggie's grey so it seemed as if she had interested a prospective purchaser already.

I heard the toot-toot of the Master's horn and as the company moved away I fell in at the rear of the procession.

Somewhere down the road I heard the clatter of hoofs. A late-comer, I thought, and did not look round.

But a few moments later I heard a voice I recognised say my name. I looked round eagerly.

"Barry!" I cried and watched him ride up on Bright Hope, a broad smile lighting up his pleasant face.

So this was why he had sounded excited when I had telephoned him before the Hunt Ball.

Bright Hope and he were friends. The horse had even consented to being ridden by Barry to the Meet.

"I kept it as a surprise," he said now riding alongside. "The day after we hauled him out of the quarry I turned him out into the three acre as usual. I made sure he didn't escape again by standing watching him as he galloped round. Presently he came up to me and started giving me one or two playful pushes. At first I thought he wanted a sugar lump—but I was wrong. He wanted me to get on his back and ride round the field."

"And you've brought him to the Hunt today!" My eyes were shining. I felt happier than I had felt for a very long time. "Oh, Barry, I'm so glad!"

"So am I—for your sake!" he smiled. "I've spent quite a lot of time on his back in the last few days. He's as intelligent as he's strong. He can jump literally anything. You'll love him, Ann, when you ride him."

" I'm sure I will!" I cried.

"Would you like to swop mounts?" he asked. " I'll ride your horse. You ride Bright Hope."

But I shook my head.

" Thanks for the offer, Barry, but I'd better not. I'm supposed to sell this chestnut if I can. But I'll ride with you as far as I'm able. I want to see how Bright Hope jumps."

We had not long to wait at the first covert. The hounds were soon away in full cry.

Barry and I followed the field across some open moorland which is a feature of the Wednesday country of the Borford Hunt. The hounds crossed this without a check then raced away across some fields whose hedges and fences gave the bolder jumpers a field day.

I let Barry on Bright Hope get ahead of me so I could see my horse jump. I thrilled as man and horse sailed over the first obstacle—a five-barred gate—then after crossing a rough meadow I held my breath as they took a thick hedge in their stride.

The hounds ran into a wood and as the huntsman followed them, Barry and I—with the rest of those who were still in the hunt—waited at the edge of the trees.

" Bright Hope's wonderful, Barry!" I cried excitedly. " And you rode him superbly."

He smiled with pleasure at my praise.

" You'll come over to the farm when you're free and ride him yourself, won't you, Ann?" he asked.

" I can hardly wait!" I declared.

He said no more but there was something in his eyes

as he looked at me which made me feel vaguely uncomfortable.

I had lost the cap I wore as we raced across the moorland earlier and my dark curls had been blown all over the place by the stiff breeze. I decided I must look a fright with my red face and my eyes as excited as a schoolgirl's.

I tried to do something with my hair. Barry shook his head.

" It looks wonderful just the way it is," he said quietly.

I was glad that at that moment the hounds streamed out of the wood again. The chestnut responded to the urgent pressure of my knees and set off at a gallop across the field.

The fox finally ran to ground in a small cave at the foot of a wooded hillside. I heard the Master say in disgust that we'd be wasting our time trying to rout him out of such a stronghold and that the sooner we found another fox the better.

But foxes were few and far between that day and the hunt trailed rather disconsolately after the hounds as they went from covert to covert trying to find foxes that were not there.

Later it came on to rain. I looked round for Barry, but he was nowhere in sight. I wondered if he'd taken Bright Hope back to Moss Hill Farm. It rather looked like it.

I felt rather depressed as, hearing the Master say that they might as well take the hounds back to stables, I put the chestnut on his way for Mardon.

Maggie reached me. She was cock-a-hoop. The man and daughter I had seen her talking to earlier were defin-

itely interested in her mount and had promised to visit
Staveleys on the following day to discuss buying the
grey.

" Any luck?" she asked, but I only shook my head.
We rode along in silence for a while.

" I haven't seen anything of your friend on the white
hunter," Maggie said at last.

" Perhaps he was riding a horse of another colour," I
said, with a frown. " He has other mounts, I'm told."

She seemed about to say something else, then hearing
the sound of hoofs behind, she looked over her shoulder
then whispered fiercely:

" Talk of the devil! Here he comes!"

It was Simon all right. He rode alongside me and raised
his whip in salute.

" Good afternoon, ladies," he said. " Rather a disappointing end to a good early start. Or so I hear. I
didn't join the hunt until fairly late."

I introduced him to Maggie who gave him her most
ravishing smile. He looked especially handsome in scarlet
coat, breeches and a hunting cap. He was riding a good-
looking brown hunter.

He kept up a flow of small talk but I could see from
the glances he threw in Maggie's direction from time to
time that he wished she would leave us alone.

Rather perversely I was glad she didn't depart. I had
no wish to be left alone with Simon after what had
happened the night before.

Then unexpectedly the man who was interested in the
horse Maggie was riding came up and began to ask her
one or two further questions about the grey.

Simon drew closer to me. His eyes were uneasy as if

he was not sure how I would take what he was about to say.

"Ann, I'm sorry about last night!" he muttered. "I hope you'll forgive me. I acted very badly."

I bit my lip. What should I reply to such an abject apology? Rather awkwardly, I said:

"It's all right, Simon. Forget it!"

"But I can't. I'm sure you thought it was a put-up job when Moira appeared like that."

And that was exactly what I did think but I didn't say so. We rode along in a rather tense silence for a while then, when the man who had been speaking to Maggie, rode off to join his daughter again, I said:

"This is where we part company, Simon. We'll take the short cut through Barker's Copse, Maggie."

"But, Ann!—" Maggie gasped, but I did not wait for her. A few moments later I was through a gate into the wood and when I looked back the trees hid Simon from me.

CHAPTER TWELVE

MAGGIE AND I were kept very busy during the rest of the week. It was not until the following Saturday that I managed to get over to Moss Hill Farm to see Bright Hope again.

Barry had not hunted my horse again that week. He told me this when I cycled over to the farm on Bob's cycle.

" I've had too much to do on the farm to go hunting," he said, " but I have ridden him occasionally around Apperly. I've also put a few jumps up in the three acre, but of course he thinks nothing of those. Just jumps them as if they're not there!"

He said this proudly, his eyes shining.

" I'd like to ride him, Barry," I said and he laughed, a trifle self-consciously.

" Of course you would!" he cried. " After all, Bright Hope is your horse, not mine. Why don't we go out together? I'll ride Primrose."

And so it was arranged. Twenty minutes later we left the farm and, following a track, came out on to the open downs. It was a sunny day with more than a hint of spring in the air. High overhead a high-flying jet traced a white trail across the blue sky. In sheltered corners snowdrops and crocuses made brave splashes of colour. The turf beneath the horses' hoofs was green and springy.

It was a day for feeling glad to be alive, a day to send the blood coursing through one's veins.

Bright Hope was restive. He made it perfectly clear that the sooner I let him have his head the better.

" Don't wait for old Primrose and me," Barry laughed. " Off you go!"

So for the first time I rode my very own horse at a fast gallop along the ridge of the downs with the breeze playing havoc with my hair and the wild beat of my heart matching the thunder of Bright Hope's hooves on the turf.

I looked round. Far behind I could see Barry making the best pace he was able on old Primrose. He waved to me to go on and once more I set Bright Hope at a gallop.

We found a stone wall barring our path. Bright Hope took the obstacle in his stride. There were fences, a broad stream. Bright Hope leapt them as if they didn't exist.

At last I drew him to a halt and slipped from his back. He turned his splendid head and I could have sworn he smiled at me.

" Well done!" I whispered and pulled a velvet ear.

We waited for Barry. Presently he opened a gate in the wall Bright Hope had jumped effortlessly. As he led Primrose through he grinned at me.

" Now what do you think of him?" he asked.

" He's an even better jumper than I thought," I said, enthusiastically.

" Good enough for the Point-to-Points?"

" I shall certainly enter him."

" Will you ride him?"

" Why not? There's no rule against a girl riding in the Borford Point-to-Points, though some hunts have different rules."

" Good for you! Bright Hope will be up against some of the best horses in the county but—well, I think he'll acquit himself well."

We rode back the way we had come. We talked about the end of the hunting season and how long it would seem before the following October when the next season opened.

Bright Hope carried me quietly along. The brisk gallop along the downs was all he had needed to satisfy him. Now he was evidently prepared to take it easy until the next chance to stretch his legs arrived.

" You'll come back to the farm to see my mother, won't you, Ann?" Barry asked. " She'll want to hear all about Bright Hope's gallop."

I gladly accepted the invitation. It was nice of Barry to ask me. If I went back to Staveleys there would be nothing to do but sit in the flat and watch TV. Maggie, I knew, had gone over to Melton on the bus to have her hair done.

When we had put Bright Hope and Primrose in their stable with hay and water within reach, we went into the house. Mrs. Hastings was delighted to see me.

" I'm so glad Barry brought you back," she cried. " I've got the kettle on so we'll have a cup of tea. It must have been cold out riding in spite of the sun."

I thoroughly enjoyed the " cup of tea " Mrs. Hastings had promised. In fact when she kept piling my plate with all the good things that had appeared like magic on the kitchen table, I protested.

" I just can't eat any more," I cried.

" Nonsense! Just try another of these little sausage rolls," she exclaimed. " Barry loves them."

" Mother, leave her alone!" her son laughed. " Just because you stuff me with more food than is good for me is no reason why you should cram Ann with your baking."

" I'm sorry, love," his mother apologised. " It's just that I like to see that everybody has enough to eat."

Walter and Jim, Barry said, finished work at mid-day on Saturday which left him a fair bit to do himself. When I volunteered to help his mother to wash up, he left us together and went out of the house to bring in the cows for milking.

Mrs. Hastings, as she filled a bowl with hot water, smiled over her shoulder at me.

" Barry's a good boy," she said. " I was afraid at one point—a year or so before his father died—that he would leave farming and get a job in town. But now his whole life is bound up with Moss Hill Farm. I don't think he'd move away if he was offered the best job that was going, away from the countryside."

" What sort of job would have interested him—if he had left farming?" I asked curiously.

" Oh, something to do with machines. He went to engineering college in Birmingham for a couple of years after he left school, then when his father became ill he was wanted at home. But I never expected him to stay permanently."

As she handed me a plate to dry she said:

" Of course, it's time Barry married. But he hasn't shown any interest in that direction yet. Naturally, I shall stay and look after him here at the farm as long as he wants me, but my sister—she lives in Devonshire—has been pressing me for a long time to go and live with her. She's a widow, too. It would allow me to take things easier."

I wondered if she was sounding me out, trying to discover if I was in love with her son. I did not give her any help but put the last plate down on the table beside the sink and asked if there was anything else I could do to help her.

But she shook her head.

" No, love, you've done enough. Go out and see what Barry's up to. He should have got the cows in from the field by now."

So I went out into the cold afternoon. The sun had gone now and a cold breeze was blowing across the farm-yard.

I could see a light shining beyond the open door of the cowshed. Making for it I looked in at Barry who was getting the cows ready for milking.

" Hullo there!" His white teeth flashed from the tanned darkness of his face. " Ever milked a cow?"

I shook my head. He put a stool alongside a Fresian. "Take a seat, lady!" he invited, and, after a moment's hesitation, I sat down.

He put a bucket in position then showed me what to do. I didn't succeed very well at first but after a few minutes, with Barry's hands over mine directing the creamy jet, I told him to leave me to it and got on very well.

"I'm hoping to put in proper milking equipment," he said, watching me, a little frown on his face. "Of course, it costs money but I believe the bank will lend me enough now the farm's paying better than it's paid for some years."

He took a pail and a stool and went to milk a cow further along the line of stalls. It was pleasant working together in the warm silent cowshed, the only sound the squirting of milk into the pails, the stir as the animals moved their feet in the straw.

I proved an apt pupil and later, as we left the cowshed, Barry said I had almost halved his work that afternoon.

"You took to milking like a duck to water," he said.

"Don't you mean like a cow to pasture?" I laughed.

We went across to look at Bright Hope and Primrose who were contentedly eating the hay Barry had earlier left for them.

"I ought to be going," I said.

"I'll run you back to Mardon," he said.

"I've got Bob's bike," I pointed out. "I'll have to take it back. He may want it tonight when he visits his girl friend."

"I'll put it on the back of my car," he said, and when I still hesitated: "Please, Ann!"

"All right," I smiled.

While he was tying the cycle in place I went back into the house to say goodbye to his mother.

She held my hand and looked into my eyes.

"It's been nice having you, Ann," she said earnestly. "Come again soon."

" I suppose I'll be coming quite often now Barry's letting me keep Bright Hope in your stables," I said. " I only hope you don't get tired of me."

" There's no chance of that," she said, and something in her voice brought the colour to my cheeks. I turned quickly away and hurried out to join Barry.

His little sports car made short shrift of the journey back to Mardon. Just outside the village he pulled up. He turned to me and took my hand.

" Ann, you must know that I've fallen in love with you," he said in a low voice.

I bit my lip. What could I reply to this? I liked him, but—he had taken me unawares. I hadn't anything to say.

He smiled gently.

" Don't worry," he said quietly. " I don't expect an answer now. I just wanted you to know how I feel. I realise I've very little to offer you except—my love."

" Oh, Barry, I like you but—well, I've never thought of you like that," I said awkwardly.

He pressed my hand.

" I hope you'll think now," he murmured. " Some things need getting used to—like milking!"

He started the engine and drove through the village. When he drew up outside Staveleys he jumped out of the car and untied the cycle from the back.

I stood watching him in silence. I felt rather unhappy. I wished he hadn't told me he loved me, not just then. I had wanted our friendship to go on as before, me going over to Moss Hill Farm to ride Bright Hope, meeting Barry out hunting, feeling that he would always be there at the farm if ever I needed him.

He wheeled the cycle into the stable yard and I followed. In the cold light of the March afternoon the cobbled yard was quite busy. Riders who had hired horses for the afternoon were returning from their expeditions around the countryside, and Paddy and Bob were taking over their charges and leading them to their stalls in the warm stables. Mark Taylor was laughing and talking with a group of young people who regularly came to Staveleys for a riding lesson every Saturday afternoon under my employer's guidance.

A few curious eyes were turned towards us and Barry frowned.

" I'd better go," he said and I followed him out to the car again after leaning Bob's bike against a wall.

" When shall I see you again?" he asked as he slipped behind the wheel of the little car.

" I'm not sure," I replied. " One of the stableboys is in hospital and there's more work. But I'll be ringing up about Bright Hope."

" Good!" He started the engine, then looked at me with the quiet kindly smile I was getting to know so well. " About the other thing, Ann. Don't let what I said worry you. I oughtn't to have sprung it on you quite like that. But—well, however you feel about me, it won't make any difference to my feeling for you. I'll always love you!"

Then he let in the clutch and moved away. I stood looking after him until the little car disappeared round a bend in the road.

I didn't feel like going into the stable yard again to face those curious eyes. After all, it was my afternoon off. I decided to walk back to the village store to buy a pair of tights. I'd laddered a pair the day before. I badly needed a replacement.

The little store faced the village green. After making my purchase I came out into the road and hesitated. What now? Should I go back to the flat—or go for a walk?

Suddenly I remembered Nanny Porter, Simon's nurse. I had promised to call to see her again the day I had visited her cottage with Simon.

I crossed the green in the failing light. There was a light in the cottage window and as I raised my hand to knock on the door I heard the low murmur of voices.

So Nanny had a visitor, I thought. I hesitated, wondering whether to turn and hurry away or open the door and walk in, as I had been told to do when I was there before.

The decision was taken out of my hands, for suddenly the door was pulled violently open and Moira, Simon's cousin, appeared.

Her eyes were blazing, her red mouth working with fury. She stared at me as if she could hardly believe her eyes, then with an impatient exclamation, she pushed past me and hurried off to the right.

There was a little car parked a few yards away and, getting into this, she started the engine and drove away at a great pace.

" Who's that? Who's standing at the door?" Nanny Porter's voice called, and, because there was nothing else for it, I pushed the door wider and went forward into the stuffy little room.

Nanny Porter was sitting in exactly the same place as when I had visited her before.

" So it's you, Miss Mawsley," she said. " Come over here and sit beside the fire. It's a cold day."

" How are you, Miss Porter?" I enquired, moving forward.

A twinkle came into her faded blue eyes.

" All the better for seeing you, my dear," she replied. " I think you may have seen my last visitor as you went out?"

" Miss Blake?"

She nodded. " Yes, Miss Blake! I don't think she altogether liked what I had to say to her."

I felt uncomfortable. I had no wish to hear what the quarrel between Simon's cousin and nurse had been about. It was one of my business.

" A very headstrong young lady is Miss Moira!" the old voice went on. " She's changed very little since she was a child in my care. She used to run to me when anything upset her or she meant to do something naughty she knew I wouldn't approve of. It was as if she was defying me—defying life, if you like—and she seemed to take a wicked pleasure in seeing the shocked look on my face when she told me her plans. She came to see me the night she ran away with that singer. I begged her not to go—but she went. And see where that ended!"

I wondered, in spite of myself, why Moira had come to see her old nanny today. I was soon to know!

" She came to see me today because she believes Master Simon has fallen in love with someone else, miss," the old voice said and there was something in the faded blue eyes that brought the colour rushing to my cheeks.

" Of course I told her he had a perfect right to fall in love with anyone he liked," Miss Porter went on. " But she was furious at that. She said he was hers—always had been—and she meant to marry him."

I bit my lip. I wished I was several miles away from that dimly-lit, stuffy little room. I longed to turn and hurry out into the cold evening and return to Staveleys. Yet I couldn't just run away like that. I had come to visit this old woman. I must stay at least for a few minutes then retire in good order.

As I struggled to find something to say, something that would lead the conversation away from Simon and Moira, the old woman leaned over and tapped my knee with a bony finger.

" Take care, young lady," she said quietly. " Moira Blake is a dangerous person to cross."

I jumped up at that.

" I don't see what she has to to do with me," I said sharply.

" You will—if you don't watch out," she muttered.

I tried to say something else, found the words stuck in my throat, then as the old woman turned to stare into the fire, I swung round and made for the door.

CHAPTER THIRTEEN

I TRIED to put Nanny Porter's words out of my mind in the days that followed. It all seemed so utterly ridiculous. Even if Simon Blake had shown a certain amount of interest in me it did not mean that he had had any intention of asking me to marry him.

Moira Blake had no reason to be jealous of me. The very thought was ludicrous.

Gradually I forgot the warning the old woman had uttered. I was kept too busy to allow any time for brooding. The stableboy came out of hospital but he was only allowed to do very light duties at first so Maggie and I were kept at full stretch.

Then there were one or two days with the Borford to show off new horses Mark Taylor had bought as well as riding lessons to give and groups of riders to escort around the countryside.

But I managed to get over to Moss Hill Farm a couple of times to ride Bright Hope. Barry and his mother were always delighted to see me and on each visit, after a ride on the downs, I went back to the farm for tea.

Barry was his usual kind easy-going self and never said

any more about having fallen in love with me. I was glad he didn't. I still wasn't sure what I would say if he asked me outright to marry him. I just wanted to stay as I was—at least, for the time being.

Then one bright morning at the end of March Mr. Taylor called Maggie and me into his little office in the stable yard.

" You know that Joe's fit and well again now," he said, " so this seems a good time to thank you for all you've done while he's been out of action. But I feel like doing more than just saying thank-you; so I'm going to give you a day off, tomorrow, if that suits you."

" Super!" Maggie breathed. " Thanks ever so much, Mr. Taylor."

I echoed her words and we went out into the sunshine.

" What'll you do?" Maggie demanded. " How about going up to London for the day? We could catch the early train—"

But I shook my head.

" It's the last day of the season tomorrow," I said. " I'm going hunting!"

" But that won't be any holiday," she cried.

" It will be for me!" I laughed and hurried off to telephone to Moss Hill Farm and tell Barry my news.

He was delighted. " It will be the first time you'll have ridden Bright Hope out hunting," he said. " It'll be good practice for the Point-to-Points!"

" Will you be able to come out?" I asked.

" Afraid not, Ann! Walter's got bronchitis so it's all hands to the pump." He sighed. " If only I could! But there's too much to do here."

" Never mind," I comforted. " There'll be other days!"

The rest of the day seemed to crawl by. All I could think was that the next morning I would be riding my own horse to the last Meet of the season. I had despaired of ever doing so—at least that season—but in a few hours my ambition would be realised.

I was up early next day. There was plenty to do before the Meet. I had to go over to Moss Hill Farm to collect Bright Hope, then I had to ride him to Baynes Green where the Meet was being held.

I borrowed Bob's cycle and set off after breakfast. It was a lovely spring day with the sun pouring down from a clear blue sky. I thoroughly enjoyed the ride on the stableboy's old bike as I passed through narrow lanes where a dusting of tiny green leaves was showing in the hedgerows and the birds were singing their hearts out in the trees overhead.

Barry was waiting for me at the open farm-gate. His eyes were shining as I rode towards him.

" Bright Hope's raring to be off!" he cried. " He seems to know you're coming. Every time I've gone into the stable he's looked round. When he's recognised me he's turned quickly away as if to show he was disappointed I wasn't you."

" Nonsense!" I laughed. " I should think he hardly remembers me. I'm not in and out of his stable all the time as you are, Barry."

We went together to saddle the chestnut. I was borrowing the saddle and bridle from Barry because the ones I had ordered a week before from a saddler in Melton hadn't yet arrived.

Bright Hope turned his lovely head and watched me as I tightened the girths. I went and held out a sugar lump and he gave me a playful push with his head when I failed to produce a second.

Out in the yard Barry gave me a leg up into the saddle.

" Good hunting!" he said.

" I wish you were coming," I said suddenly.

" So do I," he smiled. " But it just can't be done."

He held open the gate and, giving him a last wave, I rode down the lane and set course for Baynes Green.

This was about three miles beyond Consett Hall. As I jogged along I wondered if Simon and his cousin would be out.

Baynes Green was the nearest Meet for them so it was likely, especially as this was the last day's hunting. Simon was the sort of man who would squeeze the last drop out of the season.

I went along a lane which gave me a distant view of Consett Hall. Once again I felt as I had felt once before when I had looked for the first time at the old house. Uneasy, an uncomfortable feeling that this lovely old mansion with its tiny-paned windows and half-timbered front was not for me, that the further I kept away from it the better it would be for my peace of mind.

The Baynes Green Meet was an early one, and with a glance at my watch, I pushed Bright Hope into a trot.

As we went round a bend in the lane I saw two horses ahead. My heart sank as I recognised the riders.

Simon looked back as I rode up. His cousin stared straight before her as if she had not heard the clatter of Bright Hope's hoofs.

" Ann!"

Simon seemed delighted to see me. He drew his horse

alongside mine. As Moira made as if to go ahead he said sharply:

"Moira, look who's here!"

She turned and looked back at me. There was a faint smile on her pale beautiful face.

"Hullo!" she said then rode on ahead of us.

Simon's lips tightened. I saw a cold angry light fill his blue eyes for a moment, then he was smiling again.

"That's the horse you were riding when I called at Moss Hill Farm that day, isn't it?" he asked.

I nodded.

"Yes! It's the first time I've had a chance to bring him to a Meet."

"Looks like a good jumper!"

"He can clear most things," I said proudly, and my words must have reached Moira's ears for just for a moment she glanced round to give Bright Hope a critical stare.

A few minutes later we reached Baynes Green. The hunt was just moving off and we fell in behind the horsemen who were following the hounds to draw the first covert.

Simon was riding a big black horse I had not seen before. Moira was mounted on the magnificent white hunter which Simon had been riding the day he had helped me when Barry had been thrown in the wood.

I drew a little away from Simon and Moira. I preferred to be on my own. I had no time for anything but the business in hand: jumping Bright Hope when the hounds came out of the covert and started to run across the difficult countryside which made up the Tuesday country of the Borford Hunt.

It was noted for high fences and five-barred gates. There was more than one water jump to test the strongest horse. Several limbs had been broken—even a neck some years before—as keen riders crammed their hunters at some of the virtually unjumpable places.

I heard the Master's horn ring out, then, as the hounds streamed from the plantation, I followed the jostling crowd of riders as they pushed through an open gate which led from the lane into the open meadow.

Simon and Moira went out of my head then as I felt Bright Hope's stride lengthen. Soon we were up with the leaders racing for the first obstacle, a thickset hedge. Three riders went over, the fourth refused. Bright Hope did not hesitate.

" Up and over!" I whispered. " Oh, good for you, Bright Hope!"

Then we were off again with the hounds well in sight and less than half the field still in the hunt. Out of my eye corner I caught a glimpse, for a moment, of a white horse. I wondered if Simon was up with the leaders but did not trouble to look over my shoulder to find out.

There was the inevitable check after a fine run of two miles. Bright Hope fidgeted impatiently. The delay was almost more than he could bear.

At last there was a whimper then a baying of excited hounds as the huntsman called the pack to the new line; then they were off with Bright Hope and the rest of the field in close pursuit.

I found Moira riding a few yards behind me.

" Where's Simon?" I asked as, just for a moment, she came alongside as we raced towards a low hedge.

She pursed her lips. " I haven't the faintest," she

drawled then sailed over the hedge just ahead of me.

I forgot her for a while for there were high fences to be jumped, though I was always conscious that she was somewhere near for the white horse was a prominent feature of the landscape.

At last the hounds ran into a wood. Most of the hunt followed but, as I made for the gate, Moira rode alongside.

"They'll take twenty minutes to hunt through the wood," she said. "I've ridden this country since I was a child. I know a way of reaching a place where we can be right up with the hounds as they come out of the trees. Follow me!"

I hesitated. Some instinct warned me to stay with the others in the wood. Then I wondered if, after all, I had misjudged Moira. Why should I assume that she had some ulterior motive in suggesting I follow her across country rather than bury myself in the trees? In any case, what harm could come to me in the open?

So I turned from the wood and went after Moira on her white horse.

For a few hundred yards we went along the side of the wood, then Moira jumped a low gate into a field and set off across it at a fast pace that even Bright Hope found difficult to match.

At the far side was a low bank and at the top of this a fence. Seeing that Moira was making straight for this formidable obstacle I held Bright Hope back.

But before Moira reached it she looked over her shoulder.

"Come on!" she cried. "They'll beat us out of the wood if we don't press on."

I felt that this was a challenge. As Moira set her horse straight at the fence Bright Hope was within feet of the white hunter.

" Steady, old chap!" I whispered, but his blood was up.

He had seen the low bank topped by the fence and his ears were laid flat on his head as he raced towards it.

When Moira was half a dozen yards from the bank she pulled on her horse's rein. The big white animal swerved away to the left and ran parallel with the bank.

I knew then that it had never been her intention to jump this almost impossible fence.

All she had wanted was to lure Bright Hope—and me—to our destruction.

Just before Bright Hope gathered himself together and took off I suddenly knew something crystal clear.

If the members of the hunt who had gone into the wood hadn't known it was the only way, they would have been jumping this fence now.

As Bright Hope rose like a bird at the fence some of Nanny Porter's last words came into my head : " Moira Blake is a dangerous person to cross so—watch out!"

I daresay my game horse would have cleared the bank and fence in spite of their height but for one thing.

Wire !

It caught Bright Hope's forelegs and sent him hurtling forward. I was thrown from the saddle and remember nothing more as I landed with a stunning crash that sent me down, down into a black pit.

CHAPTER FOURTEEN

WHEN I came to something soft was touching my face. I opened my eyes and stared around in bewilderment. What had happened? Where was I?

I was lying on my back staring up at the blue sky. Suddenly I heard a soft whinny close at hand then a rough tongue touched my cheek.

I remembered everything then. I had taken a toss and was lying where I had fallen in the field at the other side of the wired fence.

" Bright Hope!"

Someone said the words in a panic-stricken voice which in a daze I realised must be mine. I struggled up and gave a gasp of agony as pain stabbed at my right shoulder.

Bright Hope was standing over me. As far as I could tell he seemed sound in wind and limb. I had been terribly afraid he might have a broken leg, but—thank God?—he seemed to be all right.

To my relief, after giving me another lick, he moved away and began to crop the long grass which covered the field in which I lay.

I looked round. There was nobody in sight. Moira, I supposed, would be far away by now delighted at the success of her little plot!

Slowly, carefully, I got to my feet. I held my damaged right shoulder with my left hand. I had seen too many broken collar-bones not to know what had happened to me.

I looked round. The fence which had brought Bright Hope down ran from side to side of the field. Away to the left was a stone wall and in this was set a farm gate.

I went across to the horse. He gave me an enquiring look out of his dark intelligent eyes.

" Come on, boy! Follow me!" I said, and, with trailing reins, he kept a few yards behind me as I made across the field.

I had to open the gate and the pain from my right shoulder made my head swim; but as we passed through into the next field, I slipped my left arm through the reins then, left hand supporting the damaged shoulder, led Bright Hope back towards where I had last seen members of the hunt. If I came upon a straggler I would be able to appeal to him for help.

I had another gate to open before I came out on to the track along which I had followed Moira when she had lured me away from the main body of the hunt.

Reaction was setting in now and I felt sick and dizzy. I gritted my teeth. I mustn't faint. Somehow or other I must keep on my feet until I found someone. If I lost consciousness again—and didn't regain it for some time— I could lie in this lonely place for a very long time.

Staggering from side to side like a drunken man I

presently reached the gate into the wood. I looked hopefully along the ride between the trees hoping to see that the fox had evaded the hunt and that the hounds were checked as they tried to hit off a new line.

But there was no one in sight. The wood appeared to be empty though I thought, as I stood there, that I heard a faint Hulloo in the far distance.

There was nothing for it but for me to make for the nearest road. I had not hunted the Tuesday country before and was very hazy as to my whereabouts.

But I did remember the way we had taken to reach the wood, and, still leading Bright Hope, I set off towards a high thickset hedge I had jumped earlier that morning.

Somehow, as I trudged along, jumping that fence seemed hours ago; yet it was probably only twenty minutes before.

I had no idea how long I had been unconscious when I had been flung from Bright Hope's back. A minute, half an hour, an hour? The likeliest guess I could make was that I had been out cold for a few minutes, though it seemed like hours.

On I plodded. My shoulder in spite of the support I was giving it with my left hand, was unbelievably painful. At one point I felt I could go no further and sank down on to a tree stump.

Bright Hope stood patiently beside me and as I looked up at him I wondered if I might be able to scramble back into the saddle.

Then I knew I'd never make it. I would have to use both hands and the resultant agony would not be worth the effort.

As I rose painfully to continue my slow progress

towards the nearest road I heard a shout from behind. I turned and saw to my relief a man on a black horse coming towards me.

Only when he was within a hundred yards did I recognise Simon Blake.

He jumped from the saddle when he came within a few feet then ran to my side.

"My God, what's happened, Ann?" he demanded. "Are you badly hurt?"

"I—I think I've broken my collar-bone," I whispered. "I—took a toss—"

He must have caught me as I fell for when I came to again I was lying on the ground, my head pillowed on his rolled-up jacket.

"You poor kid! You're as white as a sheet," he said. "I looked for you in the wood, then someone said they'd seen you following Moira along the wall. I went that way and caught up with Moira but she said she'd no idea where you were. So—I came back to look for you."

"Thank you," I muttered. "I—I was making for a road, then I was going to find a house with a telephone—"

"As soon as you feel fit enough I'll put you up on your horse," he said. "Then I'll take you back to Consett Hall. It's not far away."

I sat up and, kneeling beside me, he took off the bright yellow scarf he was wearing and folded it into a sling. When he had adjusted this over my left shoulder with the right arm held tightly to my chest he said he thought that would help until he could get a doctor.

He helped me to my feet and said he would put me on Bright Hope's back. I did not protest. My legs felt like jelly. I doubted if I could have walked half a dozen yards.

Bright Hope stood as still as a statue as Simon took me in his arms. Just for a moment his face was very close to mine and my heart missed a beat for I was sure he was about to kiss me.

But he didn't. Instead he set me in the saddle and, rather gruffly, told me to hold on with my left hand.

Then leading the two horses he started off across the big meadow beyond which, he had told me, was a road.

The rest of that journey remains a blur in my mind. I must have kept my seat in the saddle for I have a vague recollection of Bright Hope being led through a gateway and out on to a road, though after that certain details became confused.

Someone lifted me from the horse and someone else laid me on something soft; then there was the sound of an engine and a soothing motion that must have sent me to sleep, for the next thing I remember is being carried into a building and placed before a bright fire.

I heard a voice close at hand.

" Did you get the doctor, Martha ?"

" Yes, Mr. Simon. He's on his way !"

This is where we came in, I thought drowsily. Martha could only be the maid who had brought coffee that morning Simon and I had brought Barry back to Consett Hall for the doctor to examine his possible injuries.

I looked round. I was lying on a divan before the fire. Simon was not in sight but when I raised myself on my sound elbow, I saw him beyond the divan.

" Hullo there !" he smiled. " How's the arm feel now ?"

" Reasonably comfortable," I replied, then with a frown : " Why have you brought me here ? Shouldn't you have got an ambulance and sent me to the hospital?"

He shook his head.

"It would have taken an ambulance a long time to come from Melton, then you'd have had the return journey." He grinned. "I stopped a rather surprised farmer in his car and he ran us both back here."

"And—the horses?"

"Oh, they're all right. I left them with a chap I know who lives by the roadside. He's promised to keep them in his stable until we send for them."

He went past me and held out his hands to the blazing fire. He was dressed in breeches and scarlet coat still. I noticed a black streak on the creased coat and wondered if that was a result of screwing the coat up and putting it under my head as I lay on the muddy ground.

"Why didn't you follow the rest of us into Carling's Wood this morning?" he asked, giving me a curious look over his shoulder.

"I followed your cousin," I replied. "She said she knew the way and that we would get well ahead of the hunt and be up with the leaders when the fox broke from the wood."

"But—how did you come to take a toss?"

It was on the tip of my tongue to explain about his cousin's spiteful trick—but I didn't. Who was I to be a tale-bearer? I knew what Moira Blake was like now. If her cousin was ignorant of her real nature it was not my duty to enlighten him.

"I tried to jump a fence that unfortunately had been plentifully supplied with wire," I said, and shuddered, thinking what might have happened if my luck hadn't held.

Bright Hope might have broken his back. I might have broken my neck.

Instead we had come off comparatively lightly. I was suffering nothing worse than a broken collar-bone and shock. Bright Hope was all in one piece, thank God.

"You ought to have more sense," Simon said, but something in his eyes told me that he didn't altogether believe my story.

The doctor came a few minutes later. After he had set the fracture he looked down at me as I lay on the divan.

"You really ought to stay where you are for a little while, young lady," he said. "The broken collar-bone is nothing; but you've given yourself a nasty shaking up. May be a few days before you're back to normal."

I frowned up at him.

"But I must get back to Staveleys," I cried. "I'm all right. A good night's sleep is all I need."

"And that's exactly what you're going to have—at Consett Hall," Simon put in. "And forget about Staveleys. I telephoned your boss, Mark Taylor, when we arrived at the Hall half an hour ago. I said I intended to keep you overnight and he agreed it would be the best thing."

"But—" I began, but already he had turned away to show the doctor out.

When he returned he crossed to a drinks cabinet at the end of the large room.

"I think a glass of sherry should help to bring the roses back into your cheeks," he said, returning with two glasses. There was a twinkle in his eyes as he handed one to me.

" Cheers!"

" I hate being so much trouble! I'm sure it wouldn't have done me any harm to go back to Staveleys."

" And who would have looked after you?"

" Maggie, my flat mate. She—"

" I hardly think she'd welcome having an invalid thrust on her. She must have lots of things to do without an added burden."

It was no use arguing with him—I could see that.

" I'll tell Martha we'll have some lunch," he said, and, leaving me to finish my sherry, he left the room.

I looked round.

This was the room of a rich man. The furniture, the ornaments, the rich velvet curtains, the pictures on the walls, all spoke of wealth and good taste.

It must be wonderful to live in such luxurious surroundings, I mused, then scowled at the thought. Where were my fancies leading me now?

I did not pursue the idea further for at that moment I heard the sound of hoofs out on the drive beyond the window. This was followed by voices, then the slam of the front door.

" Moira!" I heard Simon exclaim. " You're early, aren't you?"

His cousin's reply came, clear and penetrating:

" I missed you, darling. When I couldn't find you anywhere I decided to come home. I realised you must have got fed up and bored. It wasn't a particularly good hunt I didn't think."

Simon said something in a low voice, perhaps telling his cousin that I was within earshot, then I heard their approaching footsteps.

CHAPTER FIFTEEN

I WISHED, hearing the voices, that I could escape. I had no wish to stay in that house now that the girl who had so obviously shown that she hated me had returned.

But before I could make any move the door, which was ajar, was pushed open and Simon came into the room.

" Well, come on, Moira!" he said, looking impatiently over his shoulder. " She's in here!"

I knew that Moira was afraid I might have told Simon of her treachery in leading me to what might have been my death or at least serious injury. It showed in her face, though she managed to conjure up a smile and an appearance of concern for the sling which hid the bandage binding my broken bones into place.

" Hullo there!" she said. " What's happened to you? The last I saw of you you were heading for that impossible fence. I swerved away from it when I saw what it was like. I called a warning and thought you had followed suit. I didn't look back. I was quite sure you would follow me."

She was lying, of course, and she knew that I knew it.

But she was gaining confidence now. She realised I hadn't given her away, and she knew that every moment that passed would make it more and more difficult for me to open my mouth and lay the blame for my accident on her.

I glanced at Simon. He was watching his cousin with an enigmatic smile. He had lit a cigarette and he narrowed his eyes against the smoke as he drew on it.

" Moira," he said, when she fell silent, " why did you ride on without making sure that Ann was safe? You knew the fence was dangerous, didn't you? She obviously didn't."

The colour came into the pale face, the dark eyes flashed.

" She can surely look after herself," she cried. " I called a warning and she saw me swerve away. Why didn't she follow?"

" I was too near the bank and fence," I couldn't resist saying. " Bright Hope was practically taking off as you swerved."

" She might have been killed," Simon said severely, still looking at his cousin.

Moira's face was a cold mask now. No more excuses from me, her glittering eyes seemed to say.

" I'm sorry about that," she snapped, then, turning on her heel, she hurried from the room.

Simon looked at me with a comical expression of despair, then he threw his half-smoked cigarette into the fire.

" Poor Moira," he said. " She takes things to heart so. She always did."

I said nothing to that. If he couldn't see through his cousin who was I to point out her failings?

"What about the horses?" I asked. "Barry will be anxious if I don't ride Bright Hope into his farmyard at the end of the day's hunting."

"I'll telephone him and tell him what has happened," he promised. "I'll send a man over to collect the horse. He can bring mine back here then ride yours over to Barry's place."

"Thank you," I said, gratefully.

There came a knock at the door and Martha came in carrying a tray.

"Your lunch, miss," she said and set the tray down on a little table beside the divan. "It's a cup of hot soup and some chicken sandwiches. I thought you'd find those easier to handle than having to use a knife and fork."

"Martha thinks of everything!" Simon laughed. "How about bringing me the same? I don't feel like a proper lunch in the dining-room today, Martha."

"Just as you like, sir," the woman smiled. "I just thought that Miss Moira—"

"Miss Moira can eat by herself for once," he said shortly, and, drawing a chair up beside the divan, he took up the cup of soup and a spoon and said he would feed me as my arm was out of action.

It was a merry meal. Simon put himself out to amuse me though more than once I saw him glance towards the door as if half expecting it to open at any moment and his cousin stalk into the room.

But Moira kept well out of the way during the whole of the afternoon that followed. After lunch Martha had shown me up to the bedroom I was to occupy, and she suggested in her kindly way that I might lie down and have a little rest.

" You look pale and drawn to me, miss," she said, and I had to admit that I felt exhausted.

So I took off my riding habit and let Matha cover me with the thick eiderdown. When she had left me, and before I drifted off into a deep sleep, I examined as much of my surroundings as I could see; for Martha had pulled on the thick curtain before she left the room and little daylight got into the room.

It was a big room with massive furniture. The bed was enormous and I felt lost in it. The walls were oak panelled, the ceiling an intricate pattern of plasterwork. The carpet, I had noticed, had a thick pile and I had felt to be sinking into it up to my ankles as I had walked across to the bed.

Somehow the room oppressed me. I wondered when it had been used last and by whom. I wondered if anyone had ever died in it. It was that sort of room!

Then I fell asleep. . . .

A voice wakened me. I lay for a few seconds drowsily wondering where I was. Then I knew. I was in one of the guest rooms at Consett Hall.

" You're not wanted here. Go away!" the voice whispered, and I sat up staring wildly round.

Who was in the room? Had they opened the door and slipped in while I was asleep?

The light which had shown round the edge of the heavy curtains when I had gone to sleep had faded now. The room was in pitch darkness.

" Who is it? Who spoke?" I demanded and was ashamed to hear how shaky my voice sounded.

" Not wanted! Go away!" the ghostly voice breathed.

I had seen a little lamp on a small table by the bedside. I groped with my good hand and found it. A moment later I pulled the little cord and light sprang up though it did not reach the corners of the big room.

I stared fearfully round. But there was nobody there. Unless whoever had spoken was hiding behind a chair or inside the massive wardrobe, the room was empty.

Slipping off the bed I walked round peering into the wardrobe and a tall deep cupboard which was nearly as big as a small room.

But there was no sign of an intruder.

" Go away! Go away!" the voice persisted, and I stood, bewildered, in the middle of the room.

Where was the voice coming from? And whose voice was it?

Of one thing I was certain. I couldn't stay in the room a moment longer.

I reached for the long dressing-gown Martha had left at the end of the bed and somehow huddled myself into it. She had taken my riding clothes away to sponge and press. I must get them back, dress, then—in spite of Simon—set off back to Staveleys.

I had no intention of spending a night in this room.

I opened the door then gave a startled gasp. For Moira was standing outside. She looked at me in surprise.

" I was just coming to see if you were all right," she said. " Martha said she looked in half an hour ago and you were sound asleep."

" I wakened a few minutes ago," I said shortly. " I feel fine now. I don't see any reason why I should stay the night. I feel perfectly fit enough to go home."

She looked at me curiously.

" Has anything upset you?" she asked.

I was on the defensive immediately. I wasn't going to let this girl suspect how I felt.

" Upset me?" I frowned. " I don't quite understand."

She looked uncomfortable.

" It's just that—" She looked past me into the room. " I don't think you ought to have been put in this room. It's silly, I know, but—well, it's supposed to be haunted."

I felt a cold shiver run down my spine. The voice I had heard had certainly sounded ghostly, yet—yet I was a pretty down-to-earth person. Ghosts were not much in my line. Somehow I couldn't believe that the voice I had heard had come from other than human lips.

Yet if there was no one in the room how could anyone have spoken?

" You're trembling," Moira said, her eyes full of concern. " Let's go downstairs. You need a drink and a warm by the fire."

I was quite agreeable to this and accompanied her along the corridor and down the wide staircase. We went back into the big sitting-room where I had had lunch with Simon.

" What shall it be—sherry?" Moira asked.

I went and sat before the fire.

" Thanks! I don't want a drink."

" A cigarette, then?"

I shook my head.

" Would you mind asking Martha if she'll let me have my clothes back? I'd like to dress and get back to Staveleys."

She frowned. " But whatever would Simon say if he came back and found you gone? He'd never forgive me for letting you go."

" Isn't he here?"

" No! He decided to go over to Apperley with your horse. My uncle rang up and Thompson—the chauffeur—who had fetched Simon's horse and yours—to the Hall, had to set off to meet Uncle Matthew off the London train. So Simon decided to deliver Bright Hope to Moss Hill Farm and tell Mr. Hastings what had happened to you."

" I'd like to go back to Staveleys all the same," I said, " so if you wouldn't mind getting my clothes—"

" Well, if you insist!"

" I do! And I'd be very grateful if you'd telephone for a taxi to take me home."

She turned and made for the door. I could not see her face but something about the set of her head and shoulders told me she was delighted at the turn events had taken.

I was to be out of the house before Simon got back. That suited her very well indeed.

Left alone I thought again of the voice I had heard as I lay in bed in the guest room. Where had it come from? Was it really the voice of a ghost.

Then I scowled at the flames. What a fool I was! It had been someone hiding behind the oak panelling of the walls. Consett Hall was an old house. It was probably riddled with secret passages. Perhaps one passed within a few feet of the bed on which I had lain.

But who would play such a trick? Who else but—Moira!

I remembered how, after searching the room, I had opened the door and found her on the threshold. She had had ample time to leave the secret passage and run from the room next to mine and reach my door before I opened it.

Should I challenge her when she came back? Then I decided against it. She would only deny having anything to do with the phantom voice. She would laugh in my face and defy me to prove what I said. No! the best thing was for me to leave Consett Hall and never enter it again.

I heard someone in the hall. Thinking it was Moira bringing my clothes I stood looking expectantly towards the door.

But when the handle turned and the door opened it was Simon, not Moira, who came into the room. He looked angry.

" What's all this I hear?" he demanded. " I've been over to Moss Hill with your horse. I got a lift back. I've just seen Moira and she tells me you're leaving immediately!"

" Yes!" I faced him definatly. " I'm going as soon as I get my things. Moira was to bring them to me—"

He crossed the room in three giant strides. His eyes were blazing. His fists were clenched. I thought he was going to hit me.

" Why are you always running away from me?" he almost shouted. " Don't you realise that I love you? Your place is here with me. I won't let you go!"

" You've no option! I'm not welcome here so—I'm going."

" Not welcome here! What on earth do you mean?"

" Someone played a trick on me." I told him about the ghostly voice in the bedroom. I added a little bitterly: " I suppose you didn't know that the room I had been put in was haunted.

He stared at me as if I had gone off my head, then he gave an exasperated laugh.

" Haunted my foot!" he cried. " Who told you that nonsense?"

" Why—Moira!" I exclaimed, taken aback at this reaction.

His blue eyes looked like chips of ice.

" Moira!" he repeated. " But why should she tell you such a cock and bull story?"

" I suppose she doesn't want me here. In her opinion, I imagine, I'm not the sort of person who's usually entertained at Consett Hall."

" So you think she thought up this haunted room nonsense to get rid of you, eh?" His lip curled. " You'll be telling me next that it was her voice you heard behind the panelling."

I did not say anything to that. Sudden tears had flooded into my eyes and I turned away so he would not see them.

He stared at the back of my head for some time, obviously furiously angry, then suddenly he swung round and made for the door.

" I'll fetch Moira!" he said. " We'll have this out here and now."

He opened the door. Out of my eye corner I saw Martha standing there about to enter the room with my clothes.

" Where's Miss Moira?" he demanded.

The maid shook her head.

" I don't know, Mr. Simon," she said. " I think she may have gone for a walk. I heard the side door close a few minutes ago."

He stood there, a baffled look on his face as if he did not know what to do next, then pushing past Martha he disappeared into the hall.

" Are those my clothes?" I asked and when the woman came forward: " I'd be glad if you'd help me get into them, Martha."

" But whatever for, miss?" she asked.

" I'm not staying; I'm going home," I said shortly.

She took one look at my face and must have decided it was no use arguing with me. She could see I was upset and must have realised that I had quarrelled with Simon and intended to get away from the house without delay.

She helped me into the riding habit which was now clean and carefully pressed. As I sat down, tired after the exertion of struggling into the clothes with a painful arm hindering me, I heard a car come up the drive to the front door.

" That'll be Mr. Blake back from London," Martha said and went from the room to open the door for her master.

But in a few seconds she was back. She looked at me in surprise.

" It's the young man who was here the other day," she said. " He says he's come to see you, miss."

I got to my feet. Relief swept over me. Barry was here. He would take me away from this awful house.

CHAPTER SIXTEEN

BARRY CAME into the room and made straight towards me. His face was full of concern.

" Ann, are you all right?" And before I could speak: " Ought you to be up? Simon told me that—"

" I want to go back to Staveleys, Barry," I said. " Will you take me?"

He frowned. " But is that wise? You look very pale. I expected to find you in bed."

I shook my head a little impatiently.

" I've only broken my collar-bone, Barry! I'm quite well enough to go home."

" Where's Simon?" he asked.

" I don't know," I replied and something in my voice must have told him that all was not well between Simon and me, for he said: " I'll run you back to Staveleys now, if that's what you want."

" It is!" I said, and smiling at the hovering Martha: " Please thank Mr. Simon for all his kindness and say I'm sorry I had to leave so abruptly. I think he'll understand."

" Very well, miss," she said but she was frowning as I

went past her and out into the hall. I suppose she thought I might at least have waited until Simon returned before leaving. She didn't realise that to me this was a heaven-sent opportunity to get out of the house without any more explanations and excuses.

Barry's little sports car was in the drive. I slipped into the passenger seat and he started the engine. As we drove down the drive he said:

" This will put paid to your chances of riding Bright Hope in the Borford Point-to-Points."

I nodded sadly.

". How is Bright Hope? Have you examined him since Simon brought him over to the farm?"

" Yes! He's in first class shape. He doesn't seem to have suffered at all. You were the unlucky one."

He frowned. " How did you come to take a toss like that, Ann? You must have been trying something pretty big."

I longed to pour everything out to him. But I just felt too tired, too discouraged, to start explaining about Moira and how she hated me to the extent of trying to injure me and perhaps kill my horse.

So I just said: " I admit I bit off more than I could chew. I'm only glad my stupidity didn't harm Bright Hope in any way."

He was silent for a while then with a worried frown, as if he was not sure how his words would be received, he said:

" Will you withdraw Bright Hope from the Point-to-Points now you can't ride him?"

I frowned. I hadn't got to thinking as far ahead as this yet.

" I don't know—" I began.

Quickly he said: " How about me riding him, Ann? That is, of course, if you haven't anyone else in mind."

I smiled. " Why, Barry, of course. What a marvellous idea."

" I saw a list of the entries for the Heavyweight Cup and Simon's name is on it, otherwise I might have thought you'd have asked him to take your place."

I shook my head.

" No, I wouldn't have asked him. In any case, why would he want to ride Bright Hope when he has mounts of his own? Which horse has he entered? The white one?"

" Yes! White Emperor, that's the one."

" Are there many entries?"

" About a dozen. I know most of them. None are up to the standard of Bright Hope—or White Emperor."

I drew a deep breath. So the race would be decided by two men who both said they loved me. Who would win: Barry or Simon?

Suddenly I said:

" I'd like to see Bright Hope, Barry. Just to convince myself that he really is all right."

He grinned. " Good! I was hoping you might say that. Anything that takes you to my farm is good news for me."

Presently we left the main road and took the lane which led to Moss Hill Farm. It was dark, of course, and the headlights of the little car lit up the cobbled farm-yard and the low homely farmhouse at the far side.

I remembered suddenly how I had felt when I had first set eyes on Consett Hall. This was very different.

Moss Hill Farm looked welcoming, almost as if I had come—home.

Mrs. Hastings must have heard the car for she came to the door and looked out.

" Is it you, Barry?" she called, peering into the darkness.

" Yes! I've got Ann with me. She's come to look at her horse."

Before we visited the stable we went into the house. Mrs. Hastings shook her head sadly as she looked at my bandaged arm.

" You look very pale, child," she said. " You should be resting, not rushing about in motor-cars. I thought Barry said you were staying the night at Consett Hall—"

" She decided she preferred to go back to Staveleys," Barry put in quickly, probably believing I might be embarrassed by his mother's curiosity.

" Why not stay the night here?" she persisted. " The spare room bed's aired. It would be no trouble."

" I think—" I began, but this time Barry said nothing. Looking at him I could see from his expression that he thought his mother's suggestion was an excellent one and he was hoping I'd fall in with it.

" I suppose they'll expect you're staying at Consett Hall—Mr. and Mrs. Taylor, I mean," Mrs. Hastings went on; and when I nodded: " Well, then, there's no problem."

I could see that both mother and son genuinely wanted me to stay so I said I would, though secretly I would have preferred to go back to Staveleys where I could have been alone except for Maggie, and she didn't matter.

While Mrs. Hastings went into the kitchen to see about something to eat, Barry and I went out to the stables.

Bright Hope looked round from his stall as we entered the warm sweet-smelling place.

" He's glad to see you!" Barry said. " Didn't you see his eyes light up when you walked in?"

I patted Bright Hope's slender neck and pulled his soft velvety ears. Barry had some sugar lumps and he shared them between the two horses, old Primrose licking his hand affectionately even when the sugar was gone.

Later we went back to the house. In the darkness I slipped and would have fallen except for Barry who took my good arm and steadied me. I looked up into his face and saw there an expression that set my heart thundering. There was something in his eyes that told me his feelings for me had in no way changed since he had told me a few days before that he loved me.

Mrs. Hastings had a meal ready. She cut the sizzling slice of tender steak into small pieces so that I could feed myself with one hand. I was surprised to find how hungry I was. We finished with apple pie and thick cream washed down by two cups of tea.

There was a bright fire in the parlour and while Barry went out to feed the cows and his mother washed up, I sat watching the television. This went against the grain but I did not need either Barry or his mother to tell me I was useless as a helper with a broken collar bone.

Later, Barry and I talked about the Point-to-Points the following week.

" You're quite sure you want me to ride Bright Hope?" he asked, his nice face uncertain. " If you feel your horse would do better if ridden by a professional I can mention a few people you could approach."

I shook my head.

"I want *you* to ride him, Barry," I said firmly. "I know you'll do your best."

"He's good enough to win," he said quietly. "If he loses it will be my fault, not his."

I went to bed early. I felt exhausted and my arm was aching. Mrs. Hastings said she would go upstairs with me and help me to undress.

The spare room had a big double bed, a rather rickety wardrobe and dressing table and a faded red carpet and curtains.

"There hasn't been much call for a room for visitors lately," Mrs. Hastings said as she laid a newly aired nightgown on the thick eiderdown. "When my husband was alive his sisters used to visit us pretty regular and my brother would look in from time to time. But in the last year few have come to the farm. Of course, if I'd had other children the room would have had plenty of use. But I only had Barry."

She said this regretfully and I realised that she must have hoped for a daughter but had been disappointed.

She was tenderness itself in helping me to get out of my clothes and into the nightgown which smelled of lavender.

As I got into bed she hung my clothes in the wardobe. As she closed the door and turned towards me I saw that she was frowning.

"Ann, I want to ask you something," she said quietly.

I looked at her, puzzled.

"Yes?" I murmured.

" It's about Barry!" She hesitated, then drew a deep breath and plunged: " You know he's in love with you, don't you?"

My heart gave a lurch. What was I to say to this? I knew that Barry loved me because he had said so. But I didn't feel like discussing anything so intimate with his mother.

She stared down at me. There were tears in her eyes.

" Barry's all I've got," she said slowly. " I couldn't bear to see him hurt."

" I don't want to hurt him, Mrs. Hastings," I exclaimed. " I like him too much to do such a thing."

" Yes, but do you love him?"

I bit my lip. I was tired out. My arm was hurting.

" I don't think you've any right to ask me such a question, Mrs. Hastings," I said sharply.

She said nothing for a few seconds then rather shame-facedly she turned away.

" You're quite right," she said. " I've no right at all to bring this up and Barry would be furious if he knew what I'd just said to you. But—"

She paused and seemed to be searching for words.

" All I beg of you, Ann," she went on in a low voice, " is that if you don't love him, you'll end it now. Don't leave him uncertain as to whether you care for him or you don't. Put him out of his misery right away and then he can get on with living. Just now he's existing on hope."

Abruptly she opened the door and, switching out the light, went from the room leaving me in the darkness, a prey to my unhappy thoughts.

CHAPTER SEVENTEEN

I NEED hardly reveal that I slept little that night. My arm ached intolerably, in spite of the pain-killing tablet the doctor had earlier told me to take on going to bed. In addition I worried terribly over the two men who had come so unexpectedly into my life.

Simon Blake. Barry Hastings.

They both said they loved me. But did I love either of them? They both had so much to recommend them. Simon was gay and dashing, good-looking, rich. Barry was more serious, kindly, gentle, patient.

Towards dawn I fell into a troubled sleep to be wakened, at nine o'clock, by Mrs. Hastings who brought me a cup of tea to bed.

"I must get up!" I cried when I heard how late it was.

"Nonsense! Just stay where you are for a bit." She smiled down at me. "How's the arm?"

"A little better. It's not aching as much as it did."

"Just rest for a while longer. Barry's out in the fields. Later, if you still want to go back to Staveleys, I'm sure he'll take you in his car."

So I lay there staring at the ceiling and thinking how my life had changed since I had gone past Beck's Farm that afternoon and found Silas Oldfield ill-treating Bright Hope.

Was I any happier? I wondered. Certainly I was more bewildered.

It seemed to me that before I met Simon and Barry I had had an uncomplicated life. I had not had to analyse my feelings. I had got up early, worked hard all day then slept the sleep of the just until it all started over again. I may have been bored at times but I had never been unhappy, as I was now.

Later I managed to go along to the bathroom then struggle into my clothes. Mrs. Hastings looked in as I was combing out my tangled curls.

" Why didn't you call me?" she cried. " I could have helped you get dressed."

" I've managed," I said. " I think I'd like to go back to Staveleys now, Mrs. Hastings. But please don't worry Barry if he's busy. Perhaps you'd let me telephone for a taxi."

" Barry's downstairs now," she said. " He usually comes in for a cup of coffee about this time."

" Then I'll come down," I said, and something in my face must have told her that I would not welcome an invitation to stay for lunch for she said no more but went out of the room ahead of me.

Barry jumped up when I went into the kitchen.

" How's the arm?" he asked.

" Much better, thanks," I replied. " I'd like to go back to Staveleys. I told your mother that I could ring for a taxi if you were busy—"

He frowned. " I was rather hoping you'd stay for lunch."

I smiled. " I think Mr. Taylor will expect me to go back. There are quite a lot of odd jobs I can do even with one arm out of action."

He shrugged wide shoulders.

" As you wish," he said. " Do you want to go now?"

" If that's convenient to you."

I thanked Mrs. Hastings for putting me up. She held my hand for a moment before I followed Barry out into the farmyard.

" I hope I didn't upset you last night, Ann," she said in a low voice. " If I did, forgive me. I—"

Impulsively I kissed her.

" You were right to say what you did," I said quietly, then turned and hurried away.

Barry and I went to look at Bright Hope who had been turned out into the three acre earlier that morning.

" He looks happy enough, doesn't he?" Barry said as we watched my horse galloping round the field.

" I'll always be grateful to you for taking him in and caring for him so well, Barry," I murmured.

Just for a moment his eyes met mine.

" I'd do much more for you than that, Ann, and you know it," he said then hurried off to fetch his car from the outbuilding.

We said little on the way back to Staveleys. I wondered what Barry would have said if I had told him of his mother's plea on the previous night.

" If you don't love him . . . end it now," she had said. " Just now he's existing on hope."

More than once on that short journey I opened my

mouth to say something but always I remained silent. It seemed so final to say baldly: " I don't love you, Barry. I never want to see you again."

I did want to see him again. I wanted to see him ride Bright Hope in the Point-to-Points. I wanted him as a friend. I liked him . . .

But did I love him? Ah! that was the trouble. I just didn't know.

" Get better for the Point-to-Points," he said, when he dropped me at Staveleys. " I'll take charge of Bright Hope. All you need worry about is being there on the big day—to see him win!"

Then he drove away and I went into the stable yard and crossed to the door which led up to the little flat I shared with Maggie.

My broken collar-bone knitted with surprising speed. Even the doctor was surprised.

" You see what comes of being young and healthy," he smiled after he had examined my shoulder. " A few days more and you'll be able to take your arm out of its sling."

Mr. Taylor was very understanding during the week after my accident. I was given light duties more to keep me interested than anything else and Maggie surprised me by turning out to be quite a good cook and house-keeper. Previously I had done most of the work in the little flat though the arrangement was that we should share it equally. Housework just wasn't Maggie's scene.

But now she buckled to and proved her worth as cook and housekeeper. More than once she said:

" Your accident's a blessing in disguise, Ann love. I've seen a certain look in Paddy's eye lately that tells me he might be about to pop the question; and what good will I be to him if I can't cook and clean? He's told me several times what a good wife and mother his old Mum has always been! So it's up to me to be at least as good!"

I tried not to smile at this for in spite of Maggie's good intentions many of her efforts were still a bit slap-dash. But she would improve with practice, I told myself, and perhaps Paddy's Mum would make allowances for her daughter-in-law if Maggie really did manage to get her son to the altar.

Simon rang up once to ask how I was. Maggie ran up from the office to say he was on the telephone and I asked her to tell him I was getting on quite nicely.

" But aren't you going to speak to him yourself?" she demanded, wide-eyed with amazement.

I shook my head.

" I'd rather not," I said shortly and she went away shaking her head in puzzlement.

Barry called one afternoon when I was in the stable yard enjoying the spring sunshine.

" How's the arm?" he asked.

" Almost better," I replied. " What's the news about Bright Hope?"

" Jumping everything in sight," he said, brown eyes shining. " It'll be a good horse that beats him in the Point-to-Points. I've taken him over the course and he treated every jump the same—as if they were about six inches off the ground!"

We talked about Bright Hope for a few minutes then he said he'd better be going. As he turned away he said:

" I hear Simon Blake's gone to London."

" Then he's withdrawn from the Point-to-Points?"

He shook his head.

" I don't think so. I imagine he must be coming back in time for the race."

I asked him how his mother was and he told me she was well, then he smiled shyly, said goodbye and went back to his car. I think we were both glad the meeting was over. There was something between us that was a barrier to the firm friendship we had first known.

" Just now he's existing on hope," Mrs. Hastings had said.

I sighed. How much easier life would have been if Barry had not fallen in love with me, I thought as I made my way back to the flat.

As the day for the Point-to-Points came nearer, I began to grow excited—and anxious. For some reason it had become very important to me that Bright Hope did well in the race.

In spite of what Barry had said about there being little opposition except for Simon's horse, I knew, for instance, that my employer had entered Bracken, a big bay gelding which I knew from experience was a good jumper though a bit slow over the ground. Then there were other people in the neighbourhood—all members of the Borford Hunt—who had entered hunters. Some admittedly stood little chance of being in at the finish, but two or three were in with what I considered a good chance.

No! Bright Hope would have plenty of opposition to overcome if he was to win in the Heavyweight Class.

The day of the Point-to-Points dawned clear and bright. I sighed with relief as I looked out of the window and saw the blue sky and the glitter from the rising sun on the stable roof. Paddy was walking across the yard and he glanced up. Seeing me at the window he gave me a cheerful grin and the V sign for victory. I turned away feeling considerably cheered.

I had been allowed to take my arm out of the sling the day before but it still felt stiff and fairly painful; yet I knew I was on the mend and that brightened the day for me.

Barry had said he would ride Bright Hope over from Moss Hill Farm shortly before the Heavyweights race, which was to be the second event of the afternoon's programme.

" I'll see you on the course," he had said on the telephone the night before, and as I replaced the receiver I wished desperately that I could have been with him preparing my precious horse for the most important day of his life.

I tried to possess myself in patience during the morning by helping about the stables; but there were still very few things I could do until my arm was quite better and the time passed slowly.

But at last, after a light lunch, Maggie and I got into the back of Mr. Taylor's car for the drive to the course which was five miles away.

Mr. Taylor was to ride Bracken. He was dressed in scarlet coat and white breeches with a stiff velvet cap on his head to lessen any damage that might come from a fall.

I thought about Barry and wondered what he would wear. He hadn't any proper hunting clothes, I was sure. No doubt he would appear in the hacking jacket and breeches I had seen him wearing when out with the hunt.

Simon, of course, would be impeccably dressed. That went without saying. Mr. Taylor might look smart but Simon would look even smarter. He did not go to one of the best tailors in London for nothing!

A marquee had been erected at one side of the field and part of this was being used by the Clerk of Scales to weigh each competitor before his race.

As we all arrived and piled out of the car in the car park, we could see a stream of young men in scarlet coming from the Weighing-In tent carrying their saddles and weight cloths and making for their horses, whose bridles were held by grooms.

I looked round for Barry and Bright Hope, but they were not in sight.

Mr. Taylor and his wife hurried off to find Bracken, who had been ridden over by Paddy. Maggie, with an apologetic look in my direction, abandoned me and trailed after them. She was more interested in Paddy than the first race which was about to start.

I felt miserable and alone. Where on earth was Barry? Was he going to let me down after all?

" Hullo, Ann!"

I swung round. Simon, as immaculately dressed as I had earlier pictured him, tapping his shining riding boots with his riding whip, was smiling down at me.

" How are you, Ann?" he asked when I did not speak.

I forced a smile.

" Fine!" I said. " You are riding in the race, then? I heard you were in London."

" I'd a little business to attend to," he said. " I came back late last night."

A bell rang and we both looked towards the starting line. The Lightweight Race was in progress.

" Where's your horse?" Simon asked. " I gather Barry Hastings is riding for you?"

" Yes, he's not turned up yet," I said, trying to hide my nervousness at Barry's non-appearance.

" He's cutting it a bit fine," he said. " It's time to weigh in for the Heavyweights so I'd better be going to collect my weight cloth and saddle. Be seeing you!"

He saluted with his whip and walked towards the marquee. Where was Barry? Suppose he and Bright Hope had had an accident on the way to the course!

Then suddenly I saw him. He came riding into the field, a sturdy dependable figure astride Bright Hope. He was in scarlet coat and white breeches and he grinned when he saw my surprised glance.

" I hired them for the day," he said as I ran forward to meet him. " I couldn't let my owner down, now could I?"

" Oh, Barry, I'm so glad to see you!" I cried.

" I told you I shouldn't bring him on to the course until a little before the race," he said. " No use in upsetting him. He's a sensitive creature."

He jumped down and handed Bright Hope's bridle to me.

" Will you look after him until I come back?" he asked; then he laughed: " As if I need to ask you that. You think as much of him as I do."

Then he strode off and I was left, bridle in hand, staring after him until Bright Hope turned his head and nipped playfully at my sleeve.

CHAPTER EIGHTEEN

I HARDLY noticed the end of the Lightweights Race. I stood near the starting post, Bright Hope's bridle in my hand listening to the cheers of the crowd as they urged the winner over the last fence and across the field that divided him from the winning post. He was a hundred yards ahead of anybody else in the race.

Soon enough Simon and Barry would be covering the same course. Which of them would win the race? Or would they both be beaten by another horse, perhaps Bracken which Mr. Taylor was riding?

They came from the Weighing-In tent together. They were talking animatedly and Barry suddenly laughed at something Simon had said.

I felt suddenly out of it, perhaps a little jealous that they were such good friends. Surely a girl had a right to expect two men who had confessed themselves in love with her to be deadly foes!

Then I too laughed. What a fool I was! Simon and Barry were civilised young men. The fact that they both loved me need not make them enemies.

Simon's groom, seeing his master, was now leading his

charge from behind the marquee. I thought what a magnificent animal White Emperor was. He was a heavier, stronger horse than Bright Hope. Surely, I thought, my horse hasn't much chance against such an opponent.

Then I cheered up. Whatever Bright Hope might lack in weight and strength he more than made up for in spirit. Just now he was behaving like a restive racehorse, throwing his head up, flattening his ears and dancing sideways much to the alarm of a number of spectators who were watching the winner of the Lightweight Cup being led in.

" I'll take him!" It was Barry's voice, calm, steady.

He gave me a warming smile as he threw the saddle over Bright Hope's back and adjusted the weight cloth—whose pieces of lead had brought him up to the required weight of fourteen stones—while I tightened the girths.

Simon stood by as his groom prepared White Emperor for the race. In the background could be heard the raucous shouts of bookmakers urging the crowd to back their fancy.

" They've made White Emperor favourite at two to one," Barry said in a low voice. " Bright Hope's five to one, the same as your boss's horse."

So the betting fraternity favoured Simon's mount, did they? I smiled to myself. Well, perhaps there were going to be a number of disappointed gamblers in half an hour or so!

As the bell sounded for the riders to mount Simon looked across at Barry and me.

" May the best man win!" he said and there was something in his eyes that brought a hot flush to my cheeks.

I hid my face against Bright Hope's shining side as Barry swung himself into the saddle.

It was obvious to me, if it wasn't to Barry, that Simon had offered me a chance to choose between them.

If I couldn't make up my own mind, let the horse that won make it up for me.

The riders lined up at the starting post. There were twelve in the race. Barry's number was 4 and Simon's 7. Mr. Taylor on Bracken was at the far end of the straggling line. His number was 12.

I held my breath. In a very short time I would know if Bright Hope was as good as I thought he was.

As the starter's pistol cracked and the horses made for the first fence I looked round. Though most of those present were congregated near the finish others had gone to line a hedge which ran down one side of the first big field. Doubtless many others had taken up vantage places out in the country around the course, but I decided I would join those near the first fence which was also the last.

I would then see at close range the final effort made by the first horses to jump clear and make for the finishing post which would be in about twenty minutes' time.

As I was about to move off I heard a voice I recognised at my back. I looked round. Moira was standing a few feet away, a smile on her beautifully made-up face. She was dressed in a long mink coat with a tiny hat of the same fur on her dark hair. She looked very lovely.

" You seem to have recovered from your fall remarkably quickly," she said, giving my brown wool trouser suit a supercilious glance.

" The doctor says my bones heal quickly," I said.

" I'm so glad!" She took a cigarette case from her smart handbag and lit up. She did not offer me a cigarette.

" I was just going to get a good position near the last fence," I said.

" I'll come with you," she exclaimed.

" The field's pretty wet," I pointed out with a glance at her shoes.

" I don't suppose it's any wetter by the fence than it is here," she said and we started across the field together and took up a position with a little crowd. This was pressing against a white tape which had been put up to keep them off the actual course.

There were a number of excited children with their parents and I smiled listening to some of the eager questions that were being asked.

Moira lit a second cigarette and stared around her as if bored. I wondered if she had come to the Point-to-Point because she had known that I would be there and she didn't mean to leave her cousin unattended.

A man looked over the fence and called to one of the stewards.

" Two of them have fallen at the brook," he said and my heart gave a lurch. Had Simon fallen? Or Barry? Or both?

" But that's unlikely," I told myself, and soon afterwards reassurance came when the man appeared once more to shout the names of the two competitors who had fallen. Both were unknown to me.

" I wish we could see them going round," Moira grumbled. " There must be a better place than this."

A few people had congregated on a slope at the far side of the field.

"I daresay you'd see more from across there," I said. "It's higher ground."

I hoped she would decide to cross the field. I was not as keen on having her company as she was evidently keen to have mine.

"Let's go, then," she said and, ducking under the tape, she set off across the field.

I did not follow and she looked back.

"Come on!" she called and when the people around me turned to look at me in surprise, wondering why I hadn't followed her, I sighed and went under the tape.

The slope was certainly a good vantage point. I could see the fences that the riders had to jump for they were marked by red and white flags.

At the moment there were no horses in sight. They must still be heading for the far side of the course, I supposed. I glanced at Moira. She was shielding her eyes from the sun with her gloved hand. There was a tense look on her face.

I wondered if she was anxious for Simon's safety. Had I misjudged her after all?

"Come on, Simon!" she muttered suddenly, and glancing at me: "I've had a big bet on him to win—and I don't like losing money."

The words tickled me and I laughed out aloud. She scowled.

"What do you think's so funny?" she demanded.

"Nothing!" I chuckled. "I just thought you were anxious—because Simon might have fallen."

She said nothing to that but continued to look towards

the nearer fences impatient for the first horses to appear.

We had not long to wait. Suddenly Moira gave a sudden shout:

" There they are! And it's Simon on White Emperor!"

I felt my heart sink. So Simon was in the lead. Where was Bright Hope? Had he fallen?

Then I drew a sharp breath. For another horse had come into sight. As White Emperor flew effortless over the next fence to the last Bright Hope was barely ten yards behind.

" Come on, Simon! Come on!" Moira cried, eyes blazing.

" Bright Hope! Catch him, Bright Hope!" I muttered as the two horses thundered across the wet pasture towards the last fence.

I could see Barry's face, grim, intent, as he leaned forward in the saddle urging Bright Hope to still greater effort. Simon was using his whip and my practised eye could tell that White Emperor had given of his best and was beginning to flag.

Something took my attention from the two horses racing up to the fence. A scream, a white scrap of something against the dark turf brought my head round.

A small child had escaped from its mother at the far side of the field and, like Moira and I, had slipped under the tape and was heading into the middle of the field.

The two horses took off almost simultaneously. I held my breath. The child was safe. The animals would land at least ten yards from it.

Then I looked back towards the next to the last fence. Three horses had jumped this and were now heading for the final fence before the finish.

It was their riders who would land on the child, for they could not see him and there was no way of warning them.

I started to run down the slope. I had some mad idea that I might be able to reach the child and save him before the three horses took the fence.

Of course, I was too far away; but as I ran forward I saw a sight I shall never forget as long as I live.

Barry on Bright Hope, who was only a few strides from victory, having passed the tiring White Emperor, tore at the reins and, swinging the horse round, raced back the way he had come.

Reaching down, he snatched the child up and urged his mount out of the path of the horses which, jumping the fence, landed on the spot Bright Hope had left only a split second earlier.

It had all happened in a few seconds, though they had seemed like hours to me as I ran down the slope in my hopeless attempt to reach the child.

I went across to the crowd where Barry was handing the child over to his distracted mother.

" Don't scold him!" I heard him say. " He was just excited, like everyone else, weren't you, old man?"

" But you lost the race!" someone in the crowd cried.

Barry said nothing to that but, as he saw me coming towards him, he shook his head sadly.

" I'm sorry, Ann," he said quietly. " I would have won for you if that hadn't happened. Bright Hope is a wonderful horse."

" And so is his rider," I said and suddenly knew that all my doubts had been resolved.

This was the man I loved. I was as sure of that now

as I was sure that the sun would rise on the following day.

We went back to the crowd gathered at the winning post. I led Bright Hope proudly as if he was the winner. Spontaneous applause broke out and I looked up at Barry through a mist of tears which, quite suddenly, had filled my eyes.

Simon was standing beside White Emperor. Moira, a delighted smile on her face, was congratulating him.

He did not seem to hear what she said. He was watching Barry with me.

" Congratulations, Simon!" Barry cried and held out his hand to the winner. " It was a wonderful race."

Simon smiled but it was not the smile of a victor.

" It was your race, Barry," he said. " If you hadn't done what you did you would have beaten White Emperor by twenty yards."

" Perhaps I didn't really lose," Barry said gently and looking down into my face saw there all that he wanted to know.

Simon nodded.

" Before the race I said ' May the best man win!' he said. " He seems to have done that very thing."

He glanced at the girl by his side.

" Come on, Moira, let's go and collect your winnings while the groom looks after White Emperor," he said with forced cheerfulness, and after giving me a last look as if to remember me always, he tossed the white horse's reins to the waiting groom, took his cousin's arm and hurried her away towards the bookies.

Barry jumped down from Bright Hope.

" He needs a brisk rub down and a blanket throwing

over him," he said. " Then shall we take him—home?"

I nodded. I tried to say something but the words would not come. He took my arm and together we led Bright Hope across the field towards the marquee.

Later we would talk about the future. Just now all that mattered was that there were no doubts any more.

Life for us both would now take on a new meaning, a new beginning . . .